## ~ THE TESSERACTS SERIES ~

# SUPERHERO UNIVERSE

## TESSERACTS NINETEEN

SELECTED and EDITED by

# CLAUDE LALUMIÈRE
# &MARK SHAINBLUM

EDGE SCIENCE FICTION AND FANTASY PUBLISHING
AN IMPRINT OF HADES PUBLICATIONS, INC.

CALGARY

Superhero Universe: Tesseracts Nineteen
Copyright © 2016
All individual contributions copyright by their respective authors.

This is a work of fiction. Names, characters, places, and incidents are the products of the author's imagination or are used fictitiously and are not to be construed as real. Any resemblance to actual events, locales, organizations, or persons, living or dead, is entirely coincidental.

Edge Science Fiction and Fantasy Publishing
An Imprint of Hades Publications Inc.
P.O. Box 1714, Calgary, Alberta, T2P 2L7, Canada

Selected and edited by Claude Lalumière and Mark Shainblum

Cover art by Jason Loo

ISBN: 978-1-770530-87-4

EDGE Science Fiction and Fantasy Publishing and Hades Publications, Inc. acknowledges the ongoing support of the Alberta Foundation for the Arts and the Canada Council for the Arts for our publishing programme.

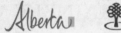 

Canada Council   Conseil des arts
for the Arts      du Canada

Library and Archives Canada Cataloguing in Publication

CIP Data on file with the National Library of Canada

ISBN: 978-1-770530-87-4
(e-Book ISBN: 978-1-770530-88-1)

FIRST EDITION
(E-20151207)
Printed in Canada
www.edgewebsite.com

# CONTENTS

∞   ☼   ∞

# FOREWORD: A NEW UNIVERSE OF CANADIAN SUPERHEROES

*Claude Lalumière*

**I FIRST MET** Mark Shainblum way back in 1989, when he walked into my (now defunct) Montréal bookshop Nebula. We instantly hit it off and have stayed friends ever since, in part because of our profound but complex passions for superhero fiction, comics, SF, and, yes, Montréal (where neither of us live anymore).

By then Mark was already an accomplished writer and publisher, having co-created the iconic superhero comics series *Northguard*, to name his signature work.

Years passed. I said farewell to bookselling and started editing anthologies (and writing for them, too). One of my dream projects was to put together a Tesseracts volume dedicated to the superhero genre. I always knew I wanted Mark, one of Canada's leading experts on this particular theme, as my co-editor, should I ever bring the idea to fruition.

EDGE Science Fiction and Fantasy Publishing — publisher of the Tesseracts anthologies — perhaps tiring of my ceaseless pestering for this volume to happen, finally acquiesced.

Canadian writers sent us 221 submissions, with more good superhero fiction and poetry than any one volume could contain. Mark and I read and debated and reread and debated some more… until we narrowed down our selections to these twenty-five texts.

Within these pages are superheroic scenarios unfolding all over the Canadian landscape— but our authors also let their imaginations roam beyond our borders to tap into whole universes of superhero tropes, subgenres, and archetypes.

—Claude Lalumière
Vancouver, BC
April 2015

∞   ✧   ∞

**CLAUDE LALUMIÈRE** is the author *Objects of Worship*, *The Door to Lost Pages*, and *Nocturnes and Other Nocturnes*.

# DIARY OF A TEENAGE GRIZZLY

*Patrick T. Goddard*

*Dear Claude and Mark,*

*Sorry I couldn't come up with something new for your anthology. But I remembered telling Claude at a party once that I'd been a teen superhero in the 1980s. I dug up my diary from 1983, when I'd just gotten my powers and Calgary was turning into the epicenter of superheroic Canada. The Time Crash of '86 retbombed our powers, but words on paper somehow always manage to survive these crises…*

Saturday, September 10, 1983

Dear Diary,

This summer, I got a chance to start fresh. We got posted from Edmonton to Calgary,* which I was very glad for. Shortly after moving in, we took our holidays in the Rockies. I sort of enjoyed myself, except for having to deal with my brothers. I went for a long walk by myself and got lost. I found a bear cub, and I knew to be careful, except that he looked like he was hurt. I got closer, and that's when I heard a big roar and before I could run away there was a giant grizzly bear in my way. Then I don't remember anything. It was weird that I didn't wake up in the hospital or something, because I guess I got attacked. But I was okay. Except for the fact that I didn't have any clothes, they were all torn up on the ground.

When I got back, there were Mounties all around. I'd been missing for three days! Mom & Dad were really worried, of course. But I didn't want to answer a bunch of questions. I didn't even know what had happened! I was just really, really hungry. I got very upset and then I just stood up and roared! Everyone was scared. I had turned into a grizzly bear! All I wanted to do was eat something. My mom calmed everyone down (she's a nurse, so she's good at that), and then she calmed me down, and then I turned back into Patrick. It was really weird.

School started last Tuesday. The bus dropped me off about ten blocks from my new school, Notre Dame, which is down-town.** It's a Catholic school, so we have Religion for home-room. They gave us a New Testament on the first day. I sing in the church choir on base and I do the Readings sometimes, so I already know a lot of it. I think Jesus would have been a good superhero if he had fought the Romans instead of being crucified.

Mom and Dad don't want me hurting or scaring anyone, so I have to go to this school to learn how to control my powers. My class is 8X. So far school is all right. The only thing that peeves me is that we have to take extra classes because of our powers, so we don't get options, like Music or Drama.

Anyway, remember how I swore I'd never repeat "the Chantal Syndrome"? Well, there's this girl called Michelle. She's fairly short, and has blond hair, and... well, I can't exactly put it on paper. But I saw her on the first day and she had a cold and I wished she was in my class and she was.

* *My father was in the Army, which made me an Army brat. This was my eighth move in thirteen years.*

** *Normally I would have gone to Sir Samuel Steele Junior High, on base, but it didn't have an X program. Besides Notre Dame, only North West Academy offered superneeds classes, but it was private and we couldn't afford it. A couple of my classmates left Notre Dame for North West and joined the T-Force in grade 9. I hated those guys even before I found out they were funded by the Think Tank.*

Monday, September 12, 1983

Today has not been that great. Religion was boring, as usual. We're always talking about Great Responsibility. The teacher is, anyway.* It was in that class that another thing about Michelle came to my attention: her voice. It's so-o-o tiny! I mean, you can barely hear her, except when she's not in class, strangely enough. It's like a version of my particular type of schizophrenia. I'm grim and studious in school, and at home I'm the opposite. Anyway, at lunch, I was in the library sitting by myself and doing my work when those troublemakers, the Sick Six, came in. They annoyed me so much I barely managed to stay in Patrick-form!

*Since homeroom was also our Religion class, every teacher was potentially a Religion teacher. Ours that year was also our French teacher. None of my teachers were nuns or priests, except for Brother Jakob, who was a Jesuit and taught Language Arts. They all must have known that we had superpowers, but not all of them acknowledged it openly. They also had to teach the rest of the school. Some of them made a real point of not giving us special treatment, even while they had to follow the special lesson plan they were given. It was very slapdash and patchwork.*

Tuesday, September 13, 1983

When I got to school this morning, one of the first things I did was get out my drawing equipment. I started drawing and reluctantly attracted a crowd. After having my binder passed around for a while, I got nervous, so I took it back and went to class. Religion period was stupid! We had to find twenty-five good points about one supervillain— in my case, the Black Angel.* How dumb! Then we found out that we had no choice in going to Weapons Shop or Costuming. All the guys had to go to Shop! Talk about reverse chauvinism! Lunch period finally rolled around, and as usual I went to the library to do my work. In Danger Gym that afternoon, I learned — the hard way — that Mr. Bentley really was the Drillmaster!**

*The original Masked Marvel's WWII arch-villainess, a home-grown Nazi who went to prison after the war and disappeared. I wish I could remember what I'd written! I remember mentioning that she had nice hair, like an opera valkyrie.*

*** Some teachers had genuine connections to the super-world. Bentley had the ability to not only imitate the powers he could see but also transmit them through some kind of low-level telepathy. Acrobatess told me he'd tried out for the Action Gang in '76, while he was at university, but they turned him down (even though he was a friend of her brother, Acrobatic Lad). They did keep the Drillmaster on for some of their training sessions, but after Acrobatic Lad was killed in '77, Bentley went back to school and became a Phys. Ed. teacher.*

## Wednesday, September 14, 1983

At school, waiting for first bell, I got out my book and read. After about twenty minutes I left my spot because of the crowd. I can't stand it; I feel crushed by the people around me, but I don't want it to make me transform. At lunch, in the library, I did my Special Studies homework.* Amazingly, five of the girls from my class were there! They're almost never in the library! Even with my resolution not to repeat "the Chantal Syndrome," I find myself daydreaming about Michelle.

*\* Special Studies was where we learned superhero history. But our teacher was incredibly lame and had no idea what he was talking about. In grade 9, he became our French teacher, which he was also terrible at. I think you can understand why a bunch of us might go off on our own to try to get our superheroic education from actual superheroes.*

## Thursday, September 15, 1983

Last night, I once again dreamed of Michelle. God help me. This is exactly what happened with last year's "Chantal Syndrome," but I can't help it. In fact, about the only thing I can do is not tell Michelle how I feel.

Let's skip ahead to lunch hour. I was sitting quietly, doing my English homework, when a horde of guys came in, most prominent among them were Stephen, vice-president candidate, and Jimmy, his campaign manager. They were putting "Vote for Stephen" cards and stickers all over the place! They were annoying me so much, but I didn't want to turn into the Grizzly.*

After the last bell, Michelle asked what the homework assignments were. I listed them off, just like that (sound of snapping fingers)! Michelle retorted with a friendly, "You really *are* a brain, aren't you?" Then she asked me if we had Danger Gym the next day. I didn't know (we did, though). Touché!

    * *They weren't annoying me on purpose. We all knew everyone's powers and weaknesses from Religion class, and on the whole my classmates were fairly sympathetic to my condition.*

Friday, September 16, 1983

Today was a strange day. I ate and went to the library to do my Math homework. But I couldn't because the library was closed. I wouldn't let a little thing like that stop me from doing my homework, so I got my things and went outside. I finished my Math homework and got back to reading *Our Multiverse*.* These two girls came by and started reading over my shoulder. I left immediately and found a nice cool spot to be alone, but the two girls followed me. They said they were in 9X, and that they were, respectively, the smartest girl in the world and the best athlete, and then they left. Thank goodness.** Also today, we had our photos taken. Everyone was really dolled up, but to me it was Michelle who was most beautiful. She has to wear the same bracelets all the time, because they give her her powers and she says they won't come off, but she always makes them look different. Well, last class was English, which was just a reading period. But Brother Jakob gave us detention anyway! On the way out, I remarked to Michelle, "Sometimes I think I'll never get used to you civvies."*** She then said, "I've been a civvy all my life." That ended the conversation.

    * *Our Multiverse was a big color hardcover with painted renditions of the home planets of all the known alien worlds, subatomic realms, weird dimensions, and alternate timelines. I was one of the rare kids in school who checked it out. Most of this material was public knowledge, but we lived in Alberta, where even history teachers could deny the Holocaust. I found out from Tyrannus, who was in high school when I met him during the third Borgni*

*invasion, that Alberta schools taught the Parallel Earth history where the USA won the War of 1812. It just goes to show how people pick and choose the science they "believe in."*

*\*\* This wouldn't be my last encounter with Miss Mind and Maiden Might. There's a stereotype of Bad Catholic School Girls, but they didn't really fit the trope. For one thing, we didn't have uniforms. For another, they weren't really bad girls: they just used me as a foil to play at being supervillains while they were still in junior high (which, in Alberta, goes to grade 9). They ditched their careers right after the Think Tank tried to recruit them. They went off to high school, and I never saw them again. Which I still kind of regret. But being a teenage weregrizzly, and a Catholic one at that, meant reining everything in.*

*\*\*\* The civilian world is called Civvy Street by military folk. As I found out later, certain super-types use the word "civilian" like carnies used the word "rube."*

Monday, September 19, 1983

After lunch today, we had a special "Powers and the Law" class.\* The best part was that we missed Special Studies! Hurray! One of the high points of the day was talking to Michelle. I think we're really opening up a line of communication, which is good. I seem to be able to make her laugh fairly easily. After "Powers and the Law," I again joked with Shel — that's what I call her now — about civvies, at which she and Beth laughed. I really think that Shel and I are gonna be at least good friends.

*\* This was just before Mulroney created his agency to monitor all of the superheroes and split the Action Gang into East and West, basically forcing the team to open a Calgary HQ. We never had anything like the US Mutant Registration Act in Canada, but we didn't need to. The Mounties had files on all of us, using laws that went back to the Communist witch-hunt and World War One, when "aliens" meant Eastern Europeans. The next year, when I got the invitation from the Action Gang join the A. G. West, I never for a second questioned how they got my phone number. I assumed it was either because they were superheroes or because I had a military family, or a little of both.*

Tuesday, September 20, 1983

We held a special Mass to start the year.* Boy, some of these guys are really rude. Nick and Jeff were bugging each other when they were doing the Readings. Talk about idiots! It was even the parable of the sower, where Jesus says, "Whoever has ears to hear ought to hear." All afternoon I was bored, except during Danger Gym, which was fun.

* *Notre Dame Cathedral was just down 18th Avenue SW from us, separating Notre Dame Junior and Senior. Notre Dame Senior High was a completely normal school. The entire "X" class was being phased out: in 1983-84, 7X was gone, and we would be the last special students at Notre Dame. Either they were phasing out the program because the teachers were so awful or they gave us the worst teachers because they were cancelling the program.*

Wednesday, September 21, 1983

In Language Arts class, I noticed Michelle repeatedly staring at me. This continued through to lunchtime. She was staring at me! I don't believe it!

Thursday, September 22, 1983

At lunch, as usual, I went to the library. Michelle was, strangely enough, also in the library. Miracle! Miracle! I couldn't believe it. I was shaken. I was stunned.

For a while I thought she was eyeing Brad, but that was just paranoia. After gym class, Shel talked with Jimmy. But the expression on their faces gave it away. They didn't look so happy-go-lucky, as they usually did. They seemed dead serious, something I'd never seen in either of them. I deduced that Michelle likes Jimmy. What else could it be? It sure makes me feel rotten, especially with the dance next Friday.

Friday, September 23, 1983

We had to change places in Special Studies class. The move put me even further away from Michelle, but I can feel her slipping away anyhow.

Saturday, September 24, 1983

This morning, I took off with my friend Ron for Chinook Mall. Boy, is it ever big! It seems to be even bigger than Northwood back in Edmonchuk! When we were done shopping, we noticed a bus at the stop. We ran to catch it, but it left without us. We were fuming mad! We decided to walk home. On the way, we passed another bus stop. I know the routes, so I coaxed Ron into waiting to grab this bus. It took us up to Eaton's on 8th Ave. My plan was to take my regular bus home from downtown. Ron followed, reluctantly. But we ran into the Grey Goliath!

The Grey Goliath was a bank robber who could become a giant made of stone. There was no way the normal police could capture him! Ron whined and tried to get me to run away and go home, but I had to help the police. So I got him to hold my records and my glasses and I thought hard about how much I hate people who whine and run away, so I turned into the Grizzly!

We had a pretty big fight, but I won. Good thing I remembered some of the moves from Danger Gym! I don't think there was too much damage, and nobody got hurt (except for the bad guy), and the police were really nice to me. I wanted to turn back into Patrick, so I sang to myself. That calmed me down, and I turned back.

The police took me and Ron home. Ron was frazzled by the experience, and I had missed my choir practice. It's a good thing my dad's not the type to ground first and ask questions later.

Monday, September 26, 1983

The jig's up! Someone finally figured out the Michelle connection! What shocks me most is that it was that idiot dumyuk Tony who guessed! The scene: our school library. I walked over to Michelle and asked her to explain why she'd been mocking me by using fancy vocabulary whenever she talked with me. Ol' barnacle-brain there* said to me, "You like Michelle, eh?" I wanted to kill him, but what he said next *really* enraged me. Quote: "Hey, Michelle, Patrick likes you!" I said that was ridiculous. Then, Tuyen started ribbing me, too, but he stopped after I asked him to.** After lunch period, I became very self-conscious: did she really suspect the truth? Does she like me? Did Tony blab to anybody else? Who? What? When? Where? How? Aagghh! I'm going nutso! Now I have to tell her how I really feel, maybe this week.

* This is in reference to Tony's aquatic powers.
** Tuyen, being a telepath, knew everything, but he was a nice guy and very calm and collected for his age. I think his immigrant background helped him: he'd been trying to pass as a normal Canadian kid since he got off the boat from Vietnam when he was five.

Wednesday, November 16, 1983

It's been quite a while since I wrote last, but here's a quick rundown: at the Halloween Dance I very nearly broke down, but Stephen helped me out.

I've been having a hard time controlling my transformations into the Grizzly. It often happens in the mornings, when I'm fighting with my bratty youngest brother to get him out the door. My parents both work, so I'm responsible for the morning routine. I can't talk to my parents about it: they just tell me I have to get my act together, since we can't afford to be constantly buying me new clothes. We talk about our powers in Religion and Special Studies class, but it's usually about not using them or making sure no one knows we have them. Most weeks recently have been the same. On Saturdays, I head to the comics shop in Bridgeland, then go downtown to the library or the 8th Avenue Mall or the Devonian Gardens. On Sundays, it's church, where I sing in the choir, and chores and babysitting.

The rest of the time, there's school. That first dance wasn't bad. Miss Mind and Maiden Might from 9X asked me to dance with them and their friends, and one of the girls in class taught me the Time Warp.

And then there was the Halloween Dance. It had a '50s theme: for example, skirts with construction-paper poodles. I didn't have a costume, but I did have a mission. "The Chantal Syndrome" was all about a girl I liked in grade 7, who was really friendly and sweet with me until I told her my feelings and she turned ice-cold. I didn't want this to happen with Shel. I still hadn't seen her with a boyfriend, and we'd once run into each other downtown as superheroes, chasing a guy called the Green Dragon through Chinatown. Her bracelets gave her power blasts, so she called herself Blast, but I thought Quanta was a better name, and she adopted it. I thought that, if Grizzly and Quanta made a pretty good team, so could Patrick and Michelle. I really built it up in my mind.

Notre Dame has two gyms: Danger Gym is in a separate building across the street, but the normal gym is on the second floor of the school, where we have our assemblies and air bands and dances. I spotted Michelle as soon as I walked in. She was with the other girls from our class; the guys were all clustered together further down, with Miss Mind and the 9X girls across the dance floor on the other side.

I spent quite a while not dancing and chatting with Tuyen and Robert. Rob was starting to find the idea of being a real superhero very cool, mostly because you could beat people up if they were bad guys. I was sort of trying to ignore him and talk to him at the same time, to distract myself while I was doing reconnaissance on Michelle. I had decided that I was going to tell Michelle how I felt. But I had to wait for just the right moment. I had to be sure that she wasn't dancing with anyone else.

Finally, I decided to make my move. To keep myself calm, I hummed under my breath. I went over to where she was sitting, with Beth and the twins. She was gorgeous when she was laughing. I'd never known anyone more beautiful to me. She looked up at me and smiled. And I asked her to dance.

She kind of hiccupped a laugh and shot a wide-eyed look at Beth, who shot back a sideways *You're on your own— I told you this would happen* glance. Then she and the twins gave Michelle some space. Beth was a precog, so I guess she had told Michelle what would happen, because Michelle's reaction looked like she'd been practicing it. She closed her grey eyes and, still smiling, shook her head. "Thanks, but I don't think so," she said politely. Then she turned away.

I walked back to Robert and the guys, like a robot in '50s B-movies. My legs were stiff, my feet were too big. Then I started crying. First, a trickle. Then a torrent. I needed a bigger body just to contain the heartbreak and rage. I began my transformation into the Grizzly.

Even as I was changing, I remember being angry and then feeling guilty for being angry: angry at being so stupid and clearly missing some obvious signal; at setting myself up the way I always did for rejection and pain; at hoping that someone would see past my scrawniness, thick glasses, and crooked teeth and just take me for who I really was; at having so many feelings and not being able to just be normal for once; at scaring all these ordinary kids who just wanted to go to a junior high dance; at not being able to stop at my transitional form the way I've recently figured out; at the knowledge that I was the Grizzly, that the Grizzly was my true, deep-down self— a shaggy mountain beast that was realer than I could ever allow Patrick to be, and the Grizzly roared to life under that mirrorball while Michael Jackson's "Human Nature" faded out.

Michelle didn't even try to hit me with her power bands. Tuyen didn't try to control my mind, Robert didn't use his ultrasonics, Tony didn't use his strength, Jimmy didn't teleport me out of there. They didn't need to. The gym was too small, the music too loud, the lights too bright. I ran for the exit on my own pure instinct. I smashed the doors open, veered left into the hall, crushed lockers with my shoulders like a massive pinball of muscle and claw. I needed more space, and I felt like howling all the way to the stars. I ripped the door at the end of the hallway off its hinges, but I couldn't fit through the frame. I pushed and tore, but the walls were concrete and wouldn't give.

The next voice I heard was Stephen's. I don't know what he said. Sometimes I lose my human language skills. But his tone was cool and jokey and low-key. He could afford to be that way, even in this situation. His agility, strength, and super martial arts gave him even odds in a fight with the Grizzly. He leaned against a wrecked locker, arms folded loosely, making wisecracks about how his father was the head of the Separate School Board and would have to explain this to the parents. They already didn't like the extra fees and insurance they had to pay because of us X-freaks. Stephen said, "But it's not our fault we were freaks. We can't do anything but be who we are, and the bushels around here aren't big enough to hide our light."

I slowly turned back into Patrick. I had lost my glasses and my clothes. Stephen gave me his suit jacket and helped me out the hall door and up the stairs to my locker, where I had my gym clothes. He asked if I wanted to call my parents to come get me. I didn't. But my bus pass was in my wallet. He actually went back to the gym to get it for me. He found my glasses, too. He said he'd straighten everything out with his father. I'd be all right. There'd be other dances.

I said, "Thanks," and went out the back door to go and wait for the bus to take me to my little, normal home. I never want to become the Grizzly again.

∞   ☼   ∞

*A couple of weeks later, I got a call from Stephen— or should I say, Man O'War. He, Rob, Tony, Tuyen, and Jimmy had decided to take on super-identities and see if the Justice Alliance, who were headquartered in downtown Calgary, would train them. But they arrived just as the Myth Masters had beaten the team and taken over the building. So now they were trapped— and Quanta was with them. The Grizzly went charging to the rescue, and it caused enough chaos and confusion to give the Alliance time to come back and send the bad guys running. Acidonna told us to give up superheroing before we got ourselves killed like her Justice Teens. Instead, Man O'War and I started meeting at lunchtime with Flying Fox, Lakyr, Mynde, and Transit to talk about how to become full-fledged superheroes. It didn't last more than a year. Transit quit the first time he got hurt; all Mynde wanted was to get his learner's permit and be a normal Alberta teenager; Lakyr was caught using his powers at a swim competition; Flying Fox's parents grounded him; Man O'War decided that it wasn't good for his long-term political career.*

*But I'd been thinking of Stephen's "light under a bushel" comment. It's from Matthew, the Sermon on the Mount, where Jesus says, "Ye are the light of the world. A city that is set on a hill cannot be hid. Neither do men light a candle, and put it under a bushel, but on a candlestick; and it giveth light unto all that are in the house." What right did we have to hide our powers and abilities?*

*What right did we have to not help people? What right did we have to be so small and selfish?*

*So when everyone else whined or ran away or otherwise hid their lights, I continued to fulfil my Grizzly destiny. At least, until Professor Chronos came along with his own insane prophecies and used poor Quanta to destroy the Time Barrier. But that's a whole other crisis.*

∞   ☼   ∞

**PATRICK T. GODDARD** is a Montréal writer, translator, and performer. His plays include the musical *Johnny Canuck and the Last Burlesque.*

# JESSICA AND THE TRUE NORTH

*Kevin Cockle*

HE WAS TELLING her about how identity was a pattern; how his algorithm detected patterns, and detected patterns implied hidden patterns. She registered the pride in his voice more than the content— pride and delight. The math made him happy in an uncomplicated way, and if he'd just stuck with that — the math he'd formulated, as opposed to what he'd done with it — he'd have seemed almost harmless. But math wasn't harmless, and neither was Rickard Acheson.

A mere lad when they'd apprehended him a dozen or so years ago; an attractive man in his late twenties now. Gone was the casual "start-up guy" style he'd once affected: now he looked as though consultants dressed him for television. Broad shoulders. Shiny black hair. Tailored suit. "Times change, Jess," he said, smiling in triumph.

"People don't," she said, keeping her voice level, giving him nothing to read.

"That's funny, coming from you."

"You know what I mean."

"Yeah, I do," Rickard said. "Chthonic Sun" had been his online alter-ego in his rebellious teens. Now he just went by "Rick." "We stay the same, and the world revolves around us. You guys were the big heroes back in the day, the Seer and the Rock. Now look at you." Acheson gave her a sympathetic, almost parental smile. "There was this profile on one of those online dating sites last year— who the guy was, what he expected. Put his tax return online so people could see what kind of cheques he could write. Had a habit of hitting women, so he just led with that. Didn't lie about it, didn't try to cover it up. Said that being with him would be well-rewarded, and that prospective applicants should expect to get hit from time to time. Guess how many responses he got."

Jessica said nothing, could tell she was being baited.

"Three thousand, Jess," Rickard continued. "3482, to be precise. Dating service didn't take his profile down. Police didn't do shit. People bitched like they do online; other people bitched right back, like they do about free speech. In the end, guy got what he wanted. So did some girl. What we in the math biz call a Pareto optimal solution."

Jessica stared out the window into dark clouds, thirty thousand feet above Lesser Slave Lake, Alberta. "What's your point?"

"That's the world now, Jess. That's why I'm the hero now, and you and the rest of True North are the criminals."

"You're an asshole."

"If by 'asshole' you mean *Wired*'s Man of the Year, then, yeah, I'm an asshole."

Jess looked at her dim reflection in the darkened plexiglass porthole. Haunted, bleak eyes looked back at her from a nervous, patrician face. She'd been gangly-beautiful at eighteen — more willowy than frail — but approaching fifty now, the neurological stress of her Gift had given her a thin, brittle aspect. She looked like a woman made of fine china. Felt like one, too.

There was a gradual change in forward momentum, barely detectable by the plane's occupants. Jessica marveled at the technology: the silence of the thrusters shifting to vertical descent; the businesslike opulence of the passenger cabin— like a well-appointed hotel room in the sky. She guessed that the plane was the civilian version of a military command jet, but it was so hard to parse what was military, what was corporate, what was government these days.

She turned her most arctic gaze upon Rickard, gave him those pale polar blues. Must've been an accusation in her expression, because after a while he said: "Hey, you made the deal, Jess. You came to us. I'm good, but the program never would have found *you*. Your identity isn't well defined— it's as much noise as it is signal."

"Pareto optimal," she breathed. That got a smile out of him.

∞   ☼   ∞

The office was spartan, utilitarian, all hard edges and efficiency. Jessica lay down on the portable military cot and stared at the white ceiling tiles. Somewhere in the distance, she could hear the ventilation system humming, circulating stale air throughout the complex. She guessed that it was an orphaned mine, repurposed. She guessed lend-lease: a special rendition site for uncooperative supers, foreign or domestic. There was a good buck to be made in special facilities management these days.

*Your identity's not well defined.* Bastard said that right to her face. It was true though— she drifted, Jessica Delaqua did. Came with the territory. She didn't read minds exactly; she merged with them, changed them, got changed by them. As much empath as telepath. Life after True North was difficult— trying to find a straight job; trying to keep a job without drawing attention to herself; trying to be somebody in particular long enough to get traction in a world that just wouldn't stand still. Without the team, without her structured role as the Seer... Jess crimped her lips, hardened her heart. She didn't want to get emotional in this place.

"It's going to take a while," Jessica had told Rickard before he'd left.

"Like hours? Or days? Because we'd prefer hours."

"He knows how to shut me out. He's strong."

"You don't have to tell us how strong he is. You're his weakness, though."

It'd been a long flight, it was late, and Jess needed to rest. She doubted she would sleep — she hardly ever did — but she needed to relax, let her body recharge.

Rickard was wrong about her and Josh. It's not that she was Josh's weakness and vice-versa— like some kind of Hallmark Card version of need. It was more biochemical and subatomic than emotional, though there had been plenty of emotion at times. His invulnerability and her openness fit together in some strange, cosmic way. He was so solid, so present, so much one thing; she was all differential, in constant flux, sliding in and out of sight. He was matter; she was energy.

There was no algorithm for what she and Josh were together. They weren't two distinct parts when you put them in a room; they formed a thing that couldn't easily be quantified. Rickard had not been merely wrong: he could never be exactly right.

Jess didn't have line of sight, but she could feel the various entities in the building with her. Muted, shielded the way Rickard had been. Lacking in malevolence. Rickard may have been a supervillain of sorts, but the handful of technicians and guards in the complex weren't what Jess would call "henchmen" or "minions." They were probably civil servants. No more or less evil than that.

Her mind registered a crystalline ping deep below her. Had to be Josh. Cold and hard as a diamond down there, somewhere.

∞   ☼   ∞

"Been a while, Jess," Josh said, his voice amused, his cobalt eyes furious. "Looks like you've been off your meds."

They had him in a full-body metal casing on wheels— like a combination canister/wheelchair. He could move his head: that was it. Jess knew they couldn't hurt him without killing him outright, but Josh needed to eat, needed to breathe, needed to sleep, same as anyone else. They'd been at him, Jess could tell. Softening him up for her.

For all that he looked surprisingly good, and defiant. His silver-grey hair had grown long around his shoulders since she'd last seen him. His lupine face was lined, but still vital; the eyes still piercing. He had lost the friendliness of his youth— that kind of serve-and-protect charisma that had made him their spokesman. He looked angry now, and threatening, despite his captivity.

Jessica stepped to her right along the curved wall of the interrogation chamber. All along the curve, at a height of about ten feet, an unbroken pane of one-way glass encircled the space. Cameras and sensor equipment occupied hubs in the ceiling. A single chair and table occupied the middle of the room; she took off her parka and hung it on the chair back. The room was chilly, but she wore a long cream-colored cable-net sweater, heavy trousers, winter boots. She came round the table and sat against it, facing Josh in his holding can.

"It would be better if you just told them what they want to know."

"Well, it would be smarter," Josh grinned. "I don't know if it'd be better."

She reached out with her mind, probing the weird facets and angles of his. By default, his body possessed some baseline degree of invulnerability, but it was his will that was the source of his real power. When he set his mind just so, bullets would bounce off his skin. When he decided to relax, he could shave. He was all about conscious intent.

She could "hear" him framing his own thoughts in first-person, making himself opaque to her and deflecting her pulses up and out into space. She imagined her mental energy kaleidoscoping out of the room, at wavelengths invisible to the human eye.

Not being able to read him unless he wanted her to... that's what had drawn her to him all those years ago. Having to trust him — to make the choice to trust him, rather than just read him and see — that had been intoxicating once.

"They want to know where everyone is," Jess said quietly. She'd memorized the priority list. It was short.

"I'm sure they do," Josh said.

"Where's Jimmy Santana?" Jess stared as she asked the question, giving him what Josh used to refer to as her "gunslinger" eyes. "Where's Cobain and his dogs? Where's Donna Crow? Why aren't they generating any data? Where did they go, Josh?"

"Where'd Jessica Delaqua go?" Josh countered.

"Where didn't I go?" Jess said. "Montréal. Toronto. Calgary. Victoria. Points in between."

"Was it easier in small towns?"

"Nope."

"I'm sorry about that," Josh said, his voice softening. "Truly."

"What about the water installations? They know you're planning to bomb them, or disrupt some of them, somehow. You wouldn't poison reservoirs just to get at the water companies would you?"

"What do you think?"

"I don't know, Josh." That was honest truth, and she let him hear it.

"Water belongs to every Canadian, Jess. It's not private property. People're suffering."

"They're not interested in why you're doing this. They want to know what you're going to do, and when."

"I know. That's their whole problem when you think about it. Not caring about why we do what we do."

Jess took a deep breath. "Where's Donna Crow?" She said.

∞   ☼   ∞

Two days later, Rickard confronted Jess in her room. Somewhere, she reflected, the man must have a huge closet on base. He wore another sharp-looking Bay Street special— suspenders and all. Great looking shoes with little tassels.

"This isn't working," Rickard said, pacing hands-in-pockets in the cramped space.

"I told you it would take time," Jess said, sitting on her cot, looking at the linoleum floor.

"It occurs to me that we could probably make him talk by torturing you in front of him."

Jessica looked up sharply, giving fear and disgust a tangible, flesh-and-blood expression. Her stomach plunged at the thought of some as yet nameless atrocity, and she made sure Rickard could see her distress — made him feel it — in her eyes, in the set of her lips, in the rising color of her cheeks.

"Jesus— I'm kidding," he stammered. "God's sake, Jess— when're you going to realize that we're the good guys here?"

"I don't have to read your mind to know that you believe that."

"Can you read opinion polls? Every time he blows shit up, investors sue the government— putting taxpayers on the hook. Bond yields jump; the currency tanks. Approval ratings for the True North are at all-time lows. We're talking, it's you guys and Ebola Prime: neck and neck."

"Say the readers of the *Financial Post*."

Rickard pulled up a chair, sitting close enough that his knees almost touched hers. "No, Jessica, that's the thing. People don't want to be saved by Captain Crusty anymore. They don't want to be lectured on right and wrong by some circus freak. Maybe you should tell him that. Maybe you should tell him how much you're getting paid."

"Fuck you."

"Yeah. When it came down to a choice between being homeless and being safe, you took the latter. We all do. Except for him."

"He's getting tired," Jess said quietly. "I'll get what you want."

∞  ✿  ∞

Jessica squeezed the bridge of her nose between her eyes. Eight straight hours today— maybe nine. *Push him hard*, Rickard had said. *You get to rest, he doesn't.*

"You okay?" Josh said.

She chuckled without mirth. "Yeah. I'm fine."

"Is that it then? You done?"

Jess put her hands on her hips, set a nonplussed expression on her face. "I don't know who's a bigger jerk," she said. "You, or him."

"Pretty sure it's him."

Jess smiled at the odd break in tension. "This is serious, you know," she said.

"Yeah," Josh nodded.

Jess stepped closer, eyes staring into Josh's. Summoning her power. She felt his mind rising like a sheer cliff above the crashing waves of a midnight ocean. He kept up the internal babble in first-person, his concentration just as strong now as when they'd started. "Where's Jimmy Santana?" she whispered.

"You tell me," Josh whispered back.

"Where's Cobain?"

"Keep sayin' the names, darlin'."

"I am. I have been. I don't know if I…"

"Listen," Josh hissed.

Jess frowned. Then she heard it.

A dull thump from somewhere above.

Dust spilling down from the ceiling of the interrogation room.

A low-frequency thrumming through the floor.

The pop-pop-pop of semi-automatic weapons. Inside the complex.

Running footsteps outside the room: military boots hard on concrete.

Jess whirled as the door to the interrogation room crashed open. She stood in front of Josh on instinct, as though shielding him would make any difference.

Two men in black combats rushed into the room. Jess reached out with her mind, but the men had the same jamming implants that Rickard was using. She couldn't push through the static.

Shooter One raised his C7, while Shooter Two took up a flank position.

And the room heaved as though it were at sea.

Jess hit the floor as electronics crashed down from the ceiling. A huge crack opened in the far wall; glass shards cascaded to the floor, revealing the observation gallery above.

"Run!" Jess cried to the soldiers as they struggled to regain their feet.

"That would be Donna Crow," Josh gloated. "Welcome to hell, fellas!"

A claxon sounded: the panicked wail of a sinking ship.

Jessica fell again, hurting her wrist. The soldiers reeled out of the room, self-preservation overriding their mission parameters.

Josh's chair tipped over; he hit the floor with a clang. His head was close to Jessica's. He laughed. "You did it! It worked!"

Jessica grinned, though her head felt as though it would split. Bouncing signals off Josh's angled mind always worked eventually, but it had taken so damn long this time, taken so much out of her. She had begun to worry that she'd grown too old, or perhaps become too broken inside to muster the requisite focus.

The True North had been summoned.

∞   ☼   ∞

Fire blazed from the superstructure of the complex and the outbuildings, melting snow, casting long shadows against the distant treeline. The smell alternated with the breeze: now a bonfire at a bush-party; now burning rubber at a landfill. They had Rickard tied up, not that he'd have tried to escape. One of Cobain's hounds stood guard on Acheson, eyes glowing like twin ruby-colored embers, night-black hackles raised. Cobain himself was barely visible in the shifting light— just one more shadow among many. Donna Crow flickered on and off, gradually growing more and more insubstantial, as if drained by the tremendous energy-expense of the eldritch earthquake she'd wrought. Jimmy brought up one of the base's black Silverados, then dematerialized. And Josh was free, dressed in a denim shirt and jeans. He'd made himself impervious to the elements.

Rickard sat on an overturned plastic bucket, teeth chattering. Jess assumed it was mostly nerves: with a debris fire nearby, it wasn't unbearably cold, and there wasn't much of a wind. He looked up at her, miserable and terrified in his ruined suit. *His costume*, Jessica realized.

"They're… the True North's not real?"

"I don't know," Jess shrugged. "They're real-ish, I guess. They're like… figments of my imagination, or parts of my personality, fractured into reality when my mind crashes against Josh's. They talk. They're objective to us, when they're around.

They have life of some kind. We don't really understand the mechanics."

Rickard struggled to comprehend. In the distance, Josh swung easily up into the pickup's cab. "You planned this?" Rickard croaked.

"Contingency. We figured if Josh ever got captured, it'd be a good way of turning the tables. Catching you in the bargain was a bonus. He does that: turns defense into offense. You guys underestimated him."

"We underestimated you."

"Well. That goes without saying."

"He didn't allow himself to be captured on purpose, did he?"

"You'd have to ask him.".

"What are you going to do with me?"

Jess considered the question. "What you do is important," she said at last. "I'm guessing Josh'll put you to work. We don't have the expertise to counteract these search algorithms of yours; you do. Josh'll need money; he'll want to cause mischief— you can help with that. When you think about it, he'll probably want you to be a bit more of the old Chthonic Sun, a bit less of the new Rick Acheson." Jess paused, letting sympathy creep into her tone. "If you don't cooperate," she continued, "he'll probably give you to Cobain. It's your call, but I would avoid that if you can."

The truck pulled around in a wide circle, then stopped. Josh got out, pulled Rickard to his feet, threw him in the back with the practiced ease of a sanitation worker heaving a glad-bag. The fuligin-colored hound leapt into the canopied bed as well, maintaining hideous eye contact as it hunkered down. Josh slammed the gate on Rickard's panicked whimpering, trapping him in the dark with that monster.

"All set?" Josh smiled as he opened the passenger door. Jess stepped around, leaned in to kiss that stubbled cheek.

"I'm not going with you."

"Like hell. I'm not leaving you out here."

"There's a road. It'll be daylight in an hour. I'll get by."

"Don't be an idiot. Why the hell would you leave?"

"Because nothing's changed for me," Jess said, making the kind of eye contact that spoke louder than words. "We're not arresting bad guys and being parade-marshals at the Calgary Stampede anymore. I might not always know precisely who I am, but I'm pretty sure I know who I'm not. And… Rickard's right, Josh. Maybe not about everything, but on a lot of things, he is. Right enough, anyway."

"Bullshit."

"I'm not going to have this argument with you again. I'll survive, Josh. I was surviving. And maybe I'll do some good my way."

"You're spreading yourself way too thin, Jess. Your way is killing you."

"How do you think your way is going to end?"

That caught him up short. They both smiled as they realized it was the first time she'd ever stalemated him like that.

"Go," she said, drawing her piano-player's hand down his chest. "I'll be okay. Don't get captured again."

Josh crimped his lips, unconsciously mimicking Jess with the gesture. Then he addressed a nearby shadow: "Watch out for her."

A piece of darkness nodded; a shaft of moonlight smiled.

Jess stood with arms crossed, feeling Cobain looming beside her as they watched the truck bounce along open ground, then turn onto rough-hewn trunk road.

She was about to tell Cobain that, where Josh was going, he would need Cobain more than she would. That the things Josh would need to do, he wouldn't be able to do by himself. That she knew she looked fragile, but she was stronger than they realized. That in the coming storm it would be Josh who would be broken, not her.

She was about to say those things, when Josh opened his mind to her one last time, and let her in.

∞   ✿   ∞

Born in British Columbia, **KEVIN COCKLE** now lives in Calgary.

# PSSST! HAVE YOU HEARD... THE RUMOR?

*D. K. Latta*

**MY FULL NAME?** Anthony Samuel DeMulder— Tony "Spats" DeMulder to those who know me, on account of my keen dress sense. I haven't actually worn spats in ten years or more — got to keep with the times, eh? — but the nickname stuck.

I'm whatcha might call a businessman who engages in the sort of activities that don't always get reported in their entirety to the Revenue boys up in Ottawa.

The truth is— I'm a racketeer. I don't mind admitting to it. Not now anyway.

And I was pretty good at it, too. I ran most of the east side and parts of the docks. I had a couple of dozen guys directly under me with another hundred or so who, one way or another, were working for me— even if they didn't always know it themselves. I had a girlfriend and two mistresses. Or maybe I had two girlfriends and a mistress. I lived in a penthouse apartment and had another place in Petawawa for my ma.

Yeah, I was on top of the world.

And then it all fell apart— because of him.

*Who him?* you ask. That guy, that actor— Ken Anton. Though I guess his real name was Antonowicz or something. He was a Polack but changed his name when he got into showbiz. Y'know, the radio actor. Some say he was one of the best in the world, if you like that sort of thing. Me, I like that guy with the dummy— what's his name? Well, don't matter. Anyway, Ken Anton— that's when it all started to fall apart.

I know what you're thinking. How could that be? Didn't something happen to Anton? It was in the papers and the papers don't lie— right?

Sure. But they don't always know the whole story, either. Let me tell you how it went down.

The first time I saw Ken Anton was at the Palais Royale down by the harbour. I didn't really understand the music— "jazz" ain't my thing. But for a man of my, y'know, civic standing, you don't go places to see things, you go to be seen. So I used to entertain my cronies — I mean, my business associates — down at the Royale. And Anton was sometimes there. For a radio actor he was a good-looking Joe, with slicked back black hair and a lip mustache— broad at the shoulders, too. Someone told me he used to be an athlete or something. Anyway, there'd usually be a dame or two with him, and other stars dropping by his table. Lorne Greene, John Drainie, the comedian, Johnny Wayne, that coloured musician, Oscar Peterson. I didn't know most of them to look at, but people would point 'em out to me.

Anton kept to his tables and I kept to mine.

Except then one night— he didn't keep to his.

It was a Friday and the Drummy Young Band was on the bill.

I'd seen Anton cut a rug on the dance floor, as they say. He was a decent hoofer, I guess, light on his toes. So I didn't think too much about it when I saw his head appearing and disappearing through the bodies, even as he seemed to be getting closer and closer to my table. I only got suspicious when I noticed he was alone, no dame in his arms. I realized he wasn't dancing, but walking— toward me.

He stopped at my table, a mad glare in his eyes.

One of my boys stood up, to put himself between me and the Fancy Dan. But I waved him down, at that point more amused and curious than anything.

"Are you Anthony DeMulder?" he asked, pronouncing the "th" as a "t" like some boarding-school priss.

I took a long puff on my cigar. "I might be."

"We have a mutual acquaintance in one Marie-Josette Bouchard."

"Who?" I asked, genuinely confused.

Then one of the dames beside me, Bessy, giggled, and leaned toward my ear and whispered, "He means Josie."

"Oh, Josie!" I said. "Yeah, I know Good-Time Josie." Then I frowned and looked around. "Say— where is she? She went to powder her nose a few minutes ago and ain't come back."

"Nor will she, you Neanderthal," fumed Anton.

"What's with you and not pronouncing 'th'?" I asked. "You got a speech impediment, buddy?"

"That's how it's supposed to be pronounced," said The Book idly, seated on the other side of Bessy and sanding his nails with an emery board. The Book looked at the world through wire-rim glasses and was lean and always well-tailored— he made even me look like a slob. He was smart, too. If he said something was so, dollars to donuts it was so. He was good with my ledgers— and even better sliding a stiletto between someone's ribs.

I pushed out my lower lip and nodded. "Okay— I stand corrected. Now apologize for calling me a caveman before you wake up at the bottom of Lake Ontario wearing a new pair of cinderblocks for rubbers."

"I will do no such thing," Anton said. "I found that young woman crying in the hall, with a bruise under her eye that she said you gave her."

I thought for a moment, then snickered. "Say— that's right. I gave her a little love tap in the car on the way here. But I was just making a point. I told her to wear the fur stole tonight, the one I gave her— and she didn't. Said it made her cry to think of the little animals all naked during the winter. So I made her cry. But it's nothing a little face powder won't cover over."

Anton glowered. "Well Mademoiselle Bouchard is gone. I gave her eighty dollars and, with luck, she's halfway to the bus station and on her way back to Trois-Rivières."

I wasn't sure if he was pulling my leg. I glanced at Bessy; she nodded slightly. "Josie has family in Québec," she said, then shrunk back, like she was afraid I might hit her, too.

"You gave money to my girl and sent her out of town?" I growled. I'm not sure what surprised me more: that this prima donna would hand eighty smackers to one of my girls or that he was so suicidal he'd brag about it to my face.

"What's more," Anton continued, "I'm going to keep my eye on you from now on."

"You're— what?" I bellowed, rising from my chair so fast that my single malt spilled all over the white tablecloth. Bessy yelped. The other girls at the table went white. A couple of my guys put their hands in their jackets, in case they needed to draw their heaters. The Book just blew casually at his trimmed fingertips like nothing was happening at all. "You threaten me

— Tony 'Spats' DeMulder — in front of my people, at my table?"

I'll give the actor credit. He didn't flinch. But I think his confidence came more from ignorance than anything. Like he'd acted this scene too many times to know the difference between real life and make-believe.

It was almost funny when he started to peel off his expensive dinner jacket. "I should warn you, Mr. Spats, that I've played both d'Artagnan and Mercutio on stage to rave reviews. And I do my own stunts."

It took me a minute to realize that he thought I was going to fight him. If I hadn't been so mad, I might have laughed. Instead, I sneered: "Boys, plug this—"

"Not exactly a private club, is it, Spats?" said The Book quietly.

Still red-faced with anger I looked around and realized almost every eye in the room was on us. No one was dancing. The band was still playing, of course— they were pros. But even the musicians were watching us over their bobbing instruments. I froze, beating back my anger. It had got me into trouble a time or two before. Then I straightened my tie with a little too much force and deliberately sat back down.

Now it was Anton's turn to look foolish, standing there with his jacket over his arm, looking ready to duke it out, but with no one stepping up. Finally, with a flap of his jacket like it was a bullfighter's cape, he slipped it back on. "I trust I've made myself clear," he said. Then he nodded politely at the dames. "Ladies."

As he turned away, I muttered under my breath: "Enjoy the rest of your evening, punk. Really— enjoy it while you can."

But now? Well, I really wish I'd left well enough alone.

∞   ☼   ∞

Yessir, I was the detective on the Ken Anton case. What's that? Oh, sure: for the record I'm Detective Constable Chet MacDougall. Been in plainclothes all of two years.

The Anton case was kind of a big to-do— what with him being a celebrity and all. I even got quoted in the papers a couple of times. Me! My mom clipped those and put 'em in a scrapbook.

Anton was an actor. Did stage, but was probably most famous nationally as a radio actor, doing stuff on the CBC. Even did some work down in New York, I guess. Folks were naturally kind of interested in a rubbernecker sort of way— it's not like there are too many big-name stars in Canada, are there? And to get himself murdered—

Oops. Guess I shouldn't say things like that, eh? I mean, officially, the case was ruled accidental— but we all knew better.

See, Anton had had a bit of a dustup with this slimy wise-guy, name of Tony "Spats" DeMulder— right in front of a few hundred people in the Palais Royale, of all places. Not exactly low-profile. According to witnesses, Anton all but called Spats out— like Anton thought he was living out some swashbuckler story and he was Ronald Coleman or something. Well, Spats didn't do anything then— but Anton ends up dead a couple of days later.

He was found in his bathtub with a script scattered on the floor. He liked to rehearse his lines in the tub— maybe the echo reminded him of a stage. So there he was, naked as the day, pages on the floor— and a radio that cost more than I make in a month bobbing in the water next to him. Apparently that was something else he liked to do in the bath— listen to the radio. He even had a little wooden table custom-made just for it.

How do I know what he liked to do in the bath? We interviewed some of his lady friends. Let's just say Mr. Anton didn't always bathe alone, if you get my meaning— lucky stiff. Uh, I guess that's a poor choice of words, considering.

Anyway, the radio in the water told us what had happened even before the coroner did. Anton had been electrocuted to death.

An accident— right? I mean, we had Spats in for a few conversations, but that's what we had to conclude in the end. I mean, that's what my superiors told me to conclude. Given the notoriety, they just wanted the case wrapped up. Between you and me, I'm not convinced a few of them weren't above taking a payoff from Spats. Toronto may not be a sin city like Montréal— but Toronto-the-Good ain't as "good" as we like to claim, neither.

But let me ask you: how did the radio get in the bathwater? I mean, the little table was lower than the top of the tub and a couple of feet away.

Yeah, makes you think.

∞   ✿   ∞

I want you to know that I'm only telling this to get it out there that I'm an innocent girl in all this— 'kay? I don't know nothing about— I mean, I do not know anything about any criminal activities on the part of Mr. DeMulder and his colleagues. I'm just a nice girl who ended up with the wrong friends. My agent wants me to make that perfectly clear, eh?

Yeah, my agent. He figures my story might make a good movie. *The Lady and the Mobster* or something. You can't see me over the phone, but people tell me I'm the spitting image of Ella Raines.

So anyways, my name is Elizabeth Schevchenko— Bessy. I moved to Hogtown from Saskatchewan about a year and a half ago, eh? I was sort of a girlfriend of Spats— I mean, Mr. DeMulder. But, really, I was more The Book's girl. No, that makes it sound all wrong. Like I was a tramp.

Let's start again.

I used to step out sometimes with a guy called The Book— he was called that on account of how smart he was. No— I never knew his real name. Funny that, eh? Anyway, The Book, he was kind of Spats's — I mean, Mr. DeMulder's — right hand. He did things for him— sometimes nasty things.

All I know about the actor fellow is that he and Spats — I mean, Mr. DeMulder — had a fight over a girl named Josie, eh? I was there when it happened. Then a couple of nights later The Book dropped by my apartment and his sleeves were wet. I said to him, I said: "Why're your sleeves wet, Bookie?" (I was the only one who ever called him Bookie).

He laughed in that way he did— like he had seen someone laugh in a movie once and was trying it on for size. He laughed and said he had been helping a guy with his bath.

I didn't understand what he meant. I figured it was gang-land lingo for something— uh, I mean, the way people in his profession talked, eh? But then the next day I read how that actor — that Ken Anton — how he was found dead in his bathtub. But that's all I know— cross my heart and hope to die.

Uh, I shouldn't have said that. Not given what happened— later.

∞   ☼   ∞

Sure, me don't-a mind talking about it— not now. All-a the bad men, they gone away, so I'm a-happy to talk.

I run a little grocery store near whatcha call Cabbagetown. I work-a hard for me and my family. But these thugs, they demand money. Say if I don't pay, bad-a things happen. Maybe my store burn down. So what am I to do, huh? I pay up, that's-a what. This goes on for months.

But then there was-a thing happen— an odd-a thing.

Some of the boys come around my shop one night, for the payoff. It was about eight— I remember because I was-a listening to my favorite radio show as I close up. I always listen when I close up. And these-a punks come in. I don't-a know their names, but one of them was that creepy fellow, the one-a with the glasses who always dress like he's-a going out on the fancy date.

The Book? Yeah, yeah I think that's-a what the others called him sometimes.

So this Book, he and the others come to my shop. They want-a their money. But as I getting it for them, suddenly they hear a siren— like the police. They get all scaredy-like. One of them pulls a gun, like he thinks I ratted on them. Then a voice starts shouting at them, telling them the gig she's-a up and the place is surrounded.

Two of the guys, they act-a like they want to shoot it out. But The Book, he says no— that's worse. Just give up and let the lawyers work it out. So they walk outside into the street, arms up, saying don't-a shoot us Mr. Police Officer, we give up.

Only— there's-a no one there.

I watched from the window and there was-a no cop and no cop-a cars. These tough guys are standing in the street, arms over their heads, looking like chumps, and no-a cop. People on the street start-a laughing at them— including other folk from who they normally take-a the money. The Book, he looks around, trying to figure out who-a pulled the prank. Then he and his guys they-a get in their car and drive away. And they forgot all about the money I was supposed to give them.

What's-a that? The actor? Sure, I remember reading about how that nice Mr. Anton died— so sad. He was-a fine actor. I learned the English listening to him on the radio. He could-a gone down to the States and become a big movie star, but he wanted to stay-a here in Canada.

Say— now you say it, I remember. That thing in my store, with the cops that weren't-a there— that was only a few days after he died.

∞   ☼   ∞

They call me a "Lady Reporter"— which pisses me off. 'Scuse my French. But that's my point. I cuss like a French-Canadian sailor. I can write as well as any of the men. I smoke like a chimney. And I can drink most of them under the table. But I'm still the "lady." I've busted my hump at this paper for fifteen years. I've written the advice column for sappy housewives when the only advice they really need is: "Leave the bum." I've covered fashion shows— and I'm bloody color-blind!

If there's any good that came out of the last war it's that a lot of men went overseas and gals like me got a chance to sit in the big boy chairs. Like the crime beat.

Brother, the stories I could tell you.

But the really interesting stories are the ones I can't tell— the ones I know are out there but I just haven't yet managed to pin down enough to go to press.

Like what? Well, you know how there are all these masked mystery men these days— here, and down in the States, and overseas. They're supposed to be mysterious, enigmas— but most of them have names, have costumes, they leave calling cards and don't mind being photographed if it makes 'em look good. So much for mysterious.

But there's this one guy— brother, he's so mysterious he's like a Chinese puzzle box buried at the bottom of Oak Island. He's so mysterious I bet only Ambrose Small has his phone number— if you get the gag.

He's so mysterious most people don't know he exists.

Even those who come in contact with him— well, they more have to infer his existence. That's how mysterious he is.

I call him... The Rumor.

I call him that on account of the fact that you only get hints and whispers about him. That and the only real evidence I've pinned down is his voice. Or, at least— a voice.

The first instance I heard about was from a cop I know who told me about an anonymous tip they got about a jewel robbery. Nothing strange about that. They dispatched a prowl car, they nabbed the crooks. Everyone's happy. Except when the detective who got the tip checked with the switchboard— no one there could remember putting the call through.

Then there was that kidnapping. You know the one— that little Van Hooren boy, heir to the candy-bar empire or whatever it was. He gets kidnapped, parents are frantic, cops are on high alert. Then, out of nowhere, the kidnapper, a guy named Alfie O'Leery — so dim he could be a character in *Li'l Abner* — he shows up at the parents' house, the little boy in tow. When the cops swarm all over him he's totally shocked. Says he was told to bring the boy there, that his boss told him the ransom was paid and he was supposed return the boy. Said his boss was that mobster, "Spats" DeMulder. I bet a lot of cops did a jig hearing that, thinking they finally had DeMulder dead to rights. Except O'Leery's story didn't hold up. Because just at the time O'Leery was supposedly talking to DeMulder, DeMulder was downtown with his lawyer for the third or fourth time being grilled by cops and half the Crown Attorney's office about some actor's death.

Oh, everyone is pretty sure O'Leery was telling the truth about DeMulder ordering the kidnapping in the first place— but the order to let the boy go? O'Leery admitted he hadn't actually seen DeMulder's face that day. He said DeMulder talked to him through the intercom at his apartment— or at least someone who sounded like DeMulder had.

Then there was the story of the nightwatchman. He had finished his rounds and was just settling down to listen to the hockey game on the radio. When — *boom!* — he heard someone screaming bloody murder. He raced outside in time to stop a mugger from sticking a knife in some gal. Only problem? The gal had fainted and when she woke up she swore she hadn't uttered a sound.

Weird, eh?

It's like there's a vigilante out there. But instead of beating punks up, or swinging down in a cape and tights, he tricks people into giving themselves up, or manipulates other people into stopping the crimes. I don't know. Maybe he's only 4'8" and has a club foot or something but has got this amazing voice. It's like he's a super-mimic and a super-ventriloquist all in one.

It's like, not so much that there's a new vigilante in town, so much as there's simply a hint of one— a Rumor.

∞  ☼  ∞

As Mr. DeMulder's attorney I will neither confirm nor deny
any criminal activity or concede my client's connection to anything of an illegal nature. However, I will acknowledge that
Mr. DeMulder had been under increasing stress in the weeks
leading up to the incident in question. His varied business
enterprises — upon which I will not elaborate — had suffered
a number of strange setbacks.

Associates of his had found themselves being arrested in
the course of certain activities— of which Mr. DeMulder main-
tains he had no prior knowledge and disavows any connection.
Apparently anonymous tips to the police were responsible. This
meant that Mr. DeMulder was finding himself somewhat starved
for reliable manpower in his various day-to-day enterprises.

Other incidents just seemed like sophomoric pranks border-
ing on harassment.

An entire liquor order for a bar in which he had an interest
never arrived. And a bar without liquor doesn't keep many
customers. When the supplier was contacted, it was explained
that a man presenting himself as a representative of the bar
had phoned to cancel the order earlier in the day.

Employees of Mr. DeMulder would fail to make arranged
rendezvous, or would arrive at incorrect times— all supposedly because of calls rescheduling those meetings, allegedly
from Mr. DeMulder or other acquaintances whose voices the
tardy employees insisted they recognized.

Aside from the stress and frustration of this pattern of puer-
ile persecution, the impact on Mr. DeMulder's finances was
not inconsiderable, what with ordered supplies not arriving,
employees being redirected from where they were needed—
and, of course, employees being incarcerated by the authorities.

It is fair to say Mr. DeMulder was being pushed to the breaking point.

∞   ☼   ∞

Please understand that I am rather restricted by doctor-patient
confidentiality— even if I am technically employed by the province. But I hardly need explain that to you. However— well, I
suppose it won't make much difference in a few minutes, will it?

I had six sessions with Anthony DeMulder, three prior to
his trial and three after his conviction for homicide. I found
Mr. DeMulder to be a reasonably articulate man, particularly

considering his education and occupation. But he also seemed to be suffering from paranoia and what I might designate shell shock, or at least battle fatigue— if he had been a soldier. But, of course, he wasn't a soldier. But he had experienced a great deal of stress leading up to the incident. Apparently he had endured weeks of orchestrated harassment that affected his business, his life, and ultimately his relationships. I'm not telling you anything that isn't part of the public record or wasn't brought up in court.

Mr. DeMulder had come to believe that someone was deliberately trying to destroy him, to bring down his business empire. All right, yes — why mince words? — his *criminal* empire. Anonymous tips to the police. Misleading messages. One of his warehouses even developed a reputation for being haunted, prone to what were described as "Banshee wails" in the night, and he was unable to get anyone to staff it. He became convinced this was all the work of some unknown adversary. Sheer paranoia, of course, but in his mind it became a floating fact just waiting to hitch itself to a foundation— any foundation.

And it found that foundation when Mr. DeMulder's paranoia settled on one Joey Markinson, a man more commonly known to his friends and associates as The Book.

This was particularly ironic since, according to all prior accounts, The Book was Mr. DeMulder's most trusted employee. Unfortunately, that just made him a prime suspect in Mr. DeMulder's mind as whoever was undermining his enterprises would've needed a great deal of insider knowledge. The Book also had a reputation both for cold-blooded ruthlessness and high intelligence— both characteristics that dovetailed with Mr. DeMulder's notion of a canny traitor in his organization.

Apparently it was a phone call from another employee that finally set Mr. DeMulder on his fatal course— an employee who warned Mr. DeMulder that The Book had been heard asking some men about whether they would be interested in switching loyalties. Given Mr. DeMulder's own experiences with employees accepting unverified phone calls, it is perhaps unfortunate that he did not question the veracity of this call. But, as I said, he was under profound stress and already prone to paranoia.

To prove his suspicions, Mr. DeMulder set up a secret wire recording of his erstwhile trusted right-hand man's weekly poker game. Sure enough, he overheard The Book conspiring with the other players to take over Mr. DeMulder's organization. Not just that, but The Book described how he intended to assassinate Mr. DeMulder the next day when the two met for lunch at Mr. DeMulder's favorite deli on Yonge Street.

In his own mind, and according to the rules of the world in which Mr. DeMulder lived, he had no choice but to act.

When The Book entered the deli, Mr. DeMulder stood up at his table as though to greet him. And then, in cold blood, he gunned down The Book in front of a dozen witnesses— including a rabbi and an off-duty police officer.

He claimed self-defense. But, of course, no gun was found on The Book, as was made clear at the trial. And the men at the poker game Mr. DeMulder had been eavesdropping on swore that no such conversation about killing Mr. DeMulder had taken place, that The Book barely said more than "raise" and "call" the whole evening. The wire recording itself proved unintelligible when played back in court.

Mr. DeMulder was found guilty and sentenced to hang.

Strangely, his attitude changed in the sessions I had with him after his conviction. He was calmer and — apparently — now accepted that The Book had at no point been involved in a conspiracy against him. But that was where Mr. DeMulder's newfound lucidity seemed to falter. Because he had developed another theory— one, I'll admit, I never fully grasped.

He insisted he had been the victim of a vigilante— a mystery man like you read about in the papers these days (I would so dearly love to get one of them on my couch).

Apparently a lady reporter had earlier been asking around about someone she had dubbed The Rumor, and Mr. DeMulder, in his paranoia, had picked up on this. Others in the so-called underworld community had also begun muttering fearfully about a mysterious crimefighter who was never seen, never identified, and who never left any hard evidence— The Rumor.

Mr. DeMulder associated this so-called Rumor fellow with a popular actor named Ken Anton. Except Ken Anton had died under mysterious circumstances months ago.

When I queried this, Mr. DeMulder laughed and said, "There's dead... and then there's *dead*."

He mentioned something about the actor having been electrocuted to death by a radio, and how all the incidents associated with this so-called Rumor seemed to involve some sort of electrical apparatus. Radios were always present in the vicinity when disembodied voices were heard or telephones were used to convey bogus messages. And there was that infamous wire recording of The Book.

"The ghost in the machine," Mr. DeMulder muttered at one point in our sessions.

Look at the time! It's just turned the hour. Assuming the usual efficiency of the Corrections services, I'm guessing Mr. DeMulder has just been hanged.

Gives you pause, doesn't it? A bit of a hollow, sinking feeling? Though I freely acknowledge he wasn't a very nice man, and had no doubt been responsible for many other crimes of which we'll never know.

To be honest, I'm not fully comfortable with this phone call, now that I think about it. Even if you are from the College of Physicians. What did you say your name was again?

Hello? Hello? Is anyone still on the line?

Hello?

∞   ☼   ∞

Based in Kingston, **D. K. LATTA** writes fiction, reviews, and pop-culture commentary.

# THE ISLAND WAY

*Mary Pletsch & Dylan Blacquiere*

BEFORE I TURN off my alarm, I have a few seconds in which I can pretend. For that instant I can let myself believe that my memories of salt spray in my face and the schooner's deck rising beneath my feet and the night wind howling against her sails are nothing more than souvenirs of a particularly vivid dream. Logic murmurs in my thoughts: the days of tall ships ended more than a century ago.

But I still smell of brine and brimstone, and as I slap the snooze button on my clock radio my hand bumps against an article clipped from the *Guardian* newspaper. FISHERMAN SURVIVES CLOSE CALL WHEN BOAT SINKS. A young man with a big smile and a crooked front tooth grins at me from the newsprint. The clock radio flashes 7:00.

I've had maybe four hours of rest. I need a shower and a coffee, in that order, before I can face waitressing the lunch shift at the Sea Star. Last year at this time I was getting up to go to high school; it still feels weird to think of myself as an adult.

I shower, throw on my work shirt and some black dress pants, then walk down to the Arcade for some coffee. The Arcade isn't what mainlanders think of as an arcade, even though there's a decrepit pinball machine and Ms. Pac-Man in the back room. It's more like a grill and snack bar, and it's the closest thing to a coffee shop that my village has. If you want a full breakfast, you go to a restaurant, but if you just want a hot drink you go to the Arcade.

The coffee in the Arcade is weak and always served far too hot. I could save money and drink better coffee if I made the stuff I had at home. I rarely do. I had to explain to my last boyfriend that it wasn't about being too lazy to make my

own coffee, or liking the Arcade's coffee better. It's about supporting local business and keeping my neighbors employed.
That's the Island way of doing things. If we don't help each
other out, who will?

He didn't get it, and our relationship didn't last long. He also
didn't like that I went out at night without telling him where
I was going, and I guess I can't blame him there. I do blame
him for acting like he was better than my friends and family
just because he was from Toronto. He was only in PEI for a
summer job anyway. He went back to Ontario to start college
a couple weeks ago, and I'm surprised at how little I miss him.
That'll teach me to date somebody from away.

I notice the autumn chill in the air as I walk the few blocks from
my basement apartment in Uncle Lennie's house to the Arcade.
The village is quiet. The tourists are long gone. Fisherman's
Quay is closed, not that anyone local ever eats there. There's
better lobster to be had at Andrea's Restaurant. Andrea's is shut
now, too, like the fishing museum and the Albatross's Nest gift
shop. They'll open up again in May for the summer season.

Only the Sea Star Family Diner and the Arcade stay open
year-round, for which I'm grateful. The Arcade gives me my
coffee, and the Sea Star gives me my paycheque. The Sea Star
used to belong to Papa, my dad's father, and then his second
son, my Uncle Lennie, took it over. Now, just like them, I'm in
the family business.

I shove open the front door of the Arcade and Gracie Gallant
behind the front counter greets me. Gracie's run the Arcade
for as long as I can remember. Candy lines the area below the
counter, while bags of chips hang from clips on the wall. In
the corner, cans of pop have been wedged into a cooler originally designed to hold bottles. Old-fashioned white boards
with clip-on letters spell out the menu: coffee, fries, pizza by
the slice, ice cream. Gracie's pouring me a large coffee before
I get the chance to speak.

I pay for my coffee, stir in some cream and sugar from the
containers at the side of the counter, and then I go see who
else is in the Arcade this morning. I walk to the end of the
counter and turn the corner, where tables line a long, narrow
room running the length of the building. The place is packed,
but in the back corner Uncle Lennie raises his arm and waves
to me. He's sitting at a table with Papa, Art, and Preston. Art

is married to Lennie's wife's sister; Preston works for Art on his fishing boat.

"Good morning, Maggie," Art says with a wink. He borrows a chair from the people at the next table so I can sit down.

"Look at this shit," Preston growls by way of greeting, dropping the day's newspaper in front of me.

OTTAWA ASSEMBLES THE CONFEDERATION GUARD, NEW CROSS-CANADA SUPERTEAM, screams the headline, right above the date: September 28, 2018.

I skim the article while my coffee cools to a drinkable temperature. Point of national pride … role models for the youth … blah, blah, blah. I'm not really into superheroes or any other kind of celebrity nonsense, but anyone with an internet connection has heard at least a little about Canada's metahuman defenders. Personally, I think it's a funny coincidence that the provincial and federal governments started promoting our metahuman heroes right after Alberta's economy tanked and dragged the rest of the country down with it. Everyone look up at the flashy superheroes in their colorful suits. Don't look down at the quagmire you're sitting in.

I open up the paper only to discover that most of the front section has been devoted to superhero news, most of it centring on the new team. True North has been selected leader. That's hardly news. True North has been running around Ontario since the 1930s, and Ontario still thinks it's the centre of Canada. Technically, there've been at least five True Norths, more if you count the body doubles, and they long ago gave up the fiction that it's been the same guy all these years. Me, I'll personally punch anyone who says the body double who took a bullet for the Prime Minister last year doesn't count as a true True North. If you make the sacrifice, you deserve the credit.

Québec's contribution, unsurprizingly, is controversial. Jos Montferrand is the popular choice and a genuine hero, credited for pulling a busload of school kids out of the Magog River after a traffic accident— but he's also a vocal separatist. He's publicly dithering about whether or not he can accept the invitation in good conscience, and the government is trying to find a suitable backup, just in case.

Meanwhile, nobody's arguing about Newfoundland's obvious choice: Jane Wreckhouse. How they're going to make her storm winds into something that doesn't ruin every PR opportunity the team gets, I don't know, but Wreckhouse is drop-dead gorgeous in a way I'll never be. She doesn't need to demonstrate her powers. All she needs to do is smile.

Some racist assholes in British Columbia are complaining that Jarminder Arjinpour isn't "Canadian" enough, by which they mean white enough, to represent their province. To which I say, one, their province should probably be represented by an Asian and, two, nobody can tell what race Jarminder is after he transforms. Maybe those buttheads should go out into the wilderness and get bitten by a Sasquatch— then they can have Jarminder's job.

Some of the other provinces are still undecided. Everyone agrees that there should be a Native superhero on the team but everyone also thinks she or he should come from some *other* province, except for the Natives themselves. They'd rather have their own representative, separate from any of the provinces. To resolve the First Nations question, Ottawa suggested giving each of the territories a representative, principally to get Nirliq the Snow Goose on the team. But Nunavut's greatest hero declined, stating that Inuit are not First Nations people, and First Nations people deserve their own team member.

I sip my coffee and flip a few more pages. New Brunswick's currently debating whether they have to choose a bilingual hero or if they can push for two, one Anglo and one Acadian. Nova Scotia has a list of hopefuls, as do Manitoba and Saskatchewan. All we get is a listing at the bottom of the page: "Prince Edward Island is still compiling a list of potential candidates." I snort. I don't think PEI has many candidates in the running.

"We don't need none of them folks in long underwear runnin' around here," Preston declares. "We need *jobs*."

I lift my eyes and look meaningfully at Papa and Uncle Lennie. Lennie lifts his coffee to his lips, almost in time to hide his scowl. Papa blinks innocently back at me.

"Whole paper's full of that nonsense," Art spits. "Where they gonna get a hero round here? We don't have weird power plants or fancy science labs or mutated animals running about biting people. Not unless they want a super drinker, then they can go look down at the Legion on a Friday night."

Art's pretty much right. PEI is lucky to pump out a famous author every few centuries, an Olympic athlete once or twice per generation, and the occasional NHL player. We've got a small population. We're lucky to have any metahumans at all. Somehow, though, I don't think Tignish Tommy's ability to turn seawater into wine is going to get him onto the Confederation Guard. It's all Tommy can do to dodge bootlegging charges.

Lennie changes the topic to a catfight between two local women that happened at the Legion the other night. Preston and Art immediately take sides, Preston with one lady, Art with the other. They debate heatedly while I peruse three pages of essays and editorials.

Pride in traditional Canadian heritage vs. the perpetuation of stereotypes. The opportunities for new immigrants, minority Canadians, and people with problematic powers to find a place on the team. *Ugly people with problematic powers*, I correct, thinking of Jane Wreckhouse. The Québec question. The Native question. The Northern question. I turn to the centre page.

There's a centerfold diagram of the prospective super team, including all the members chosen or in the running. True North, whose current incarnation I begrudgingly admit is pretty easy on the eyes. Jos Montferrand, broad-shouldered and barrel-chested. Jane Wreckhouse looks like a friggin' supermodel, as always. A big question mark over the outline marked *Prince Edward Island*.

I try to imagine Papa or Uncle Lennie in one of those costumes. It doesn't work. I love Papa and Uncle Lennie dearly, but they carry the consequences of a few too many beers around their waists, and their mustaches don't make up for the lack of hair on the top of their heads.

I check my reflection in the mirror on the wall and realize that all I've got going for me is my youth. I might not have to worry about going bald, but there's no way I'm ever going to look like Jane Wreckhouse. I've got Papa's big nose and Lennie's hairy brows and, more importantly, I'm an Islander through and through.

"Hey. Maggie. You goin' to university next year?" Art says abruptly, jarring me out of my thoughts.

I give him the answer I've rehearsed more times than I can count. I shrug and say, "I'm not really sure what I want to do with my life. I figured I'd work for Uncle Lennie, save up some money, and think about my options."

Art snorts dismissively. "You're smart, Maggie. Everyone always says so. You deserve better'n what you can get around here."

Preston shoots Art a dirty look across the table. "Y'know, unlike *some people's kids*, Maggie here isn't gonna forget where she came from."

Art's sons all have jobs out in Alberta. It's a sore point between Art and Preston. On the other hand, Preston's kids are chronically in and out of work, and he's usually got one or two of them living with him at any given time. I'm not convinced that's an improvement.

To Art and Preston's eyes, I'm doing the same: living in Uncle Lennie's basement, working in his restaurant during the tourist season, preparing to collect employment insurance in the winter. So many of the jobs here are seasonal.

And my life's calling doesn't pay.

∞   ☼   ∞

In the end, Ottawa "solved" the PEI problem in the typical way. They gave Manitoba's spot to a Native superhero and "suggested" to the other top contender that she purchase a house in PEI and make it her primary residence. In spring 2019, the former Gimli Glider moved to Summerside and became the Avonlea Aviatrix.

Summerside is forty minutes away from the Anne of Green Gables house in Cavendish. The Aviatrix's PR people don't seem to care. All that matters to them is that she has long red hair that looks great with her new green and white costume. She doesn't wear pigtails, thank God, but that isn't stopping the newspaper cartoonists from drawing her as Anne of Green Gables with a cape. She came back to the Island in July for a publicity tour, posing for photos with the tourists, getting filmed at Province House and Gateway Village and Singing Sands and of course, Green Gables House.

I try to be fair. She's not all that bad. As powers go, hers look pretty good on TV: there's just something about a human being who can fly without the aid of wings. She's good with the fans, too, signing autographs and the like, kneeling down to talk to the little kids. She's got charm and charisma and looks great in the costume.

She just isn't from here, and never will be.

∞   ☼   ∞

Now it's almost September again and I'm on shift at the Sea Star, trying not to think about the Avonlea Aviatrix all over the news, or how I've spent the past twelve months trying and failing to find a better-paying job. I love my co-workers and my Uncle Lennie, but I don't want to wait tables all my life.

I'm serving a tableful of tourists their burgers and fries when a buzz starts up behind me. I turn around and there she is, the Avonlea Aviatrix herself, stopping by the Sea Star for lunch. The mother at my table digs in her purse for paper to get an autograph, and I can see my co-workers in the kitchen cracking open the doors to get a peek at the hero herself. I stare at the hostess, willing her to take the Aviatrix to someone else's tables, anyone else's tables, but, no, the Avonlea Aviatrix gets seated in my section.

I hand the Avonlea Aviatrix a lunch menu and introduce myself as plain old Maggie, not Captain Maggie Doucette, the latest in a long line of captains of the Phantom Ship of Fire.

My vessel's best known as a ghost of the Northumberland Strait, though we've lived on the North Shore for five generations. We don't rely on sail and rudder alone to steer her; we can charm the winds and tides to take us where we would. The phantom ship responds to her captain's thoughts, so we have no need for a crew.

I have sailed into the teeth of raging storms and I have lit up the Northumberland Strait with a corona of unearthly fire. I have sent criminals to watery graves and I have pulled unlucky sailors from the gullet of the ocean. This is my Island, and my family has protected its people for centuries.

During the Second World War, Papa singlehandedly destroyed eight Nazi U-boats. Lennie didn't destroy any Soviet subs — it was a *cold* war, after all — but when he's drunk he swears he chased off at least twice that number. When he's sober he admits the number's closer to six.

Me, I took the helm on my thirteenth birthday, in the year of our Lord two thousand and fourteen, and I've never found any enemy submarines in Canadian coastal waters. Most of what I've been left with is drug smugglers making beach drops in the middle of the night and the occasional leaky oil tanker that needs to take its environmental damage somewhere else.

I used to wonder what the hell was the point in a day and age when terrorists come from the sky and any idiot can drive a transfer truck full of dope over the Confederation Bridge. Still. I do what I do because my family's always done it; and sometimes there're rewards for the ability to shape the movements of the sea.

Take Gracie Gallant's ten-year-old son, Calvin. Cal was swimming last month out past the breakwater when he got caught in a riptide. It was his lucky day that I had been off work, his damned lucky day that I'd gone for a swim myself and I don't need my ship to charm the tides. Cal thought it was his good fortune that the current changed and shoved him back to shore, and I let him think it.

The Avonlea Aviatrix asks for a Diet Pepsi. I go get it for her, and when I return to her table she asks me if I know a good mechanic in the area. Her car's brakes aren't working well.

Part of me really wants to ask her why she doesn't simply fly everywhere— why she even bothers with a car. Part of me wants to tell her that if she was from here, or even really *lived* here, she'd already know where to go. Part of me wants to inform her that my job doesn't pay enough for me to get a car, even though I've saved the lives of a lot more Islanders than she has.

I bite my tongue and tell her where Uncle Lennie takes his car.

The Avonlea Aviatrix orders lobster with drawn butter, new PEI potatoes, and side Caesar salad. I take her order to the kitchen and remind myself that, if I'd gone to Ottawa to join the Confederation Guard or, hell, if I'd gone to school out of province, Cal Gallant would be six feet underground in Saint Anne's Cemetery.

∞  ✿  ∞

On my break I walk out back of the restaurant: not to the smokers' table on the north side, where my co-workers gather for cigarettes, but around the corner on the east. I sit with my back against the restaurant and look out to the horizon. In between the trees I can catch a glimmer of the ocean.

"Maggie?"

I look up. Uncle Lennie squats down next to me. "That could've been you, you know."

I run my fingers through red soil. "I know."

"Me and your grandfather… we've wondered a long time. Why you didn't say anything when they were taking nominations?

Pretty girl like you. They'd've loved you in the Confederation Guard. A lot more than that Aviatrix. She's not even a real Islander."

I watch the sunlight sparkle on the distant waves. "She's not here most of the year. They keep her busy with the rest of the Guard doing public appearances across Canada. I hear they spend most of their time in Ottawa."

"Would've been a great opportunity for you."

"Tell that to Calvin Gallant."

Lennie was quiet for a long time. We watch the sea, lost in our own thoughts, until I break the silence.

"We've been here," I murmur, "since… what? 1786? What year did Prospere Doucette first summon the Ship of Fire?"

"1758. When the British began deporting the Acadians from Prince Edward Island. It was called Isle Saint-Jean back then. Papa told me once that Prospere swore the British would never keep him from his home." Lennie glances over at me. "You know. Back when thirteen was plenty old enough for a person to start a career at sea."

"1758," I repeat, fixing the date in my mind. I need to remember my own history. "They didn't know the word *metahuman* back then."

"Doesn't seem to me we are," Lennie replies. "We never had no mutagens or lab accidents or space debris transforming us into something we weren't before. We are what we've always been: a local family with a duty to protect."

Somehow, heading out into a screaming nor'easter aboard a preternatural ship that burns without being consumed seems a bit above and beyond any ordinary call of duty; and then I'm immediately ashamed of the thought. How many desperate sailors have we Doucettes led to safety over the centuries, or plucked from the waves, or rescued from pirates? How many invaders have we driven away? How many hundreds of lives did my ancestor Mathieu save during the Yankee Gale of 1851?

They forget us, once we've brought them to shore. I don't know why. It's a thankless job, and sometimes I feel bitter about that. Yet somehow I feel it's important for it to stay that way.

"I didn't want to be the first Doucette in over 250 years to open her big mouth to the mainlanders." I crack a smile. "Besides, where would I dock a flaming three-masted schooner in Ottawa? I'd probably burn down the city. Can't imagine the ship would like all that freshwater very much, either."

Uncle Lennie chuckles. "Can't imagine she would, at that."

I lean with my back against the restaurant, realizing there's a reason why the Avonlea Aviatrix is what she is, and why I am what I am. "It's not about fame and glory. It's about... it's about supporting the local community and keeping my neighbors safe."

Lennie says quietly, "Sometimes it doesn't seem fair." For the first time I wonder what Uncle Lennie might've done, who he might've become, if he hadn't been captain of the Phantom Ship before me. He's been running the Sea Star for as long as I've been alive. I'd never considered that maybe, when he was younger, he might've wanted to do something else with his life. I look down the street to the front door of the Arcade, where Calvin Gallant and his little sister are eating ice cream cones on the sidewalk, and I realize that I can't imagine being anything other than what I am.

I put my hand on Uncle Lennie's, understanding why he stayed, why I'll stay. "Islanders help each other out. That's just the way we do things here."

Red soil stains my fingertips. Out on the ocean, for just an instant, I catch a glimpse of an old-fashioned three-masted schooner. She waits for me, my Phantom Ship, and I know the Island is where I belong.

∞　✿　∞

**MARY PLETSCH** and **DYLAN BLACQUIERE** live in New Brunswick, where they share their home with books, comics, and four cats.

# BLUNT INSTRUMENTS

*Geoff Hart*

**THE VOICES WHISPER** incessantly in my ears: news of the world, patriotic slogans, occasionally old comedy routines. Sometimes there are the sex dreams. Those hurt; I wish I knew who I was cavorting with, or even whether they were dreams or memories. Whatever drugs they're giving me make it impossible to distinguish the two. I don't know who I am, don't even know my name. I have a strong sense of a life before this, but it's there by inference, like the empty socket left behind after a tooth has been pulled. I have a sense of gratitude to those who feed me through tubes and who keep me here, safe and knowing that someday I'll be useful again. I remember newsreel images of starving Biafrans, napalm strikes on jungle, other horrors. Here, they promise me, I'm useful and a guardian of everything we hold dear against The Forces of Evil. (Yeah, I hear the capital letters.)

∞ ☼ ∞

Then there are the awakenings: my eyes open, my body still damp, and I slowly focus on the circle of flickering fluorescent light, and the voice of my handler, no longer filtered through water.

There follow what could be called "battles." Not pitched fights with dozens of men on each side firing guns at each other, but epic knockdowns between various titans. I hear bits and snatches from the Special Forces troops who sit opposite me in the chopper, casting scared glances my way when they think I'm not looking. Because of my impenetrable hide, they wake me to fight the energy villains: those who've mastered electricity, electromagnetism, sunlight, plasma, dark energy, nuclear power— even photosynthesis. Some are geniuses, some not so much (even by my standards), but it always goes down the same way. They drop me from the chopper, we size each other up, and then we set to whaling on each other until one of us can't take anymore. Usually the perp; it takes a lot less energy for me to stand there and grin and take a beating than it takes them to exert every last scrap energy, hoping they'll blow me away or blast me into tiny bits.

Nobody's blasted me into tiny bits, but I hurt for days afterwards. Maybe it could happen, though. I don't take anything for granted, least of all survival.

Sometimes they give me the killer robots, giant critters, and other things best handled by a good pummelling. I hear hints they have others who specialize in other types of perps. I've seen the wombs they keep us in, but never the residents. Guess they figure it wouldn't be a great idea to let us compare notes. Sometimes I have to fight two or more perps simultaneously. Three or four is worst, particularly when one of them's like me and can take a pounding, while their buds nip at my heels, trying to bring me down so the big guy can step on my throat.

When the smiting's done, I either hand them the cuffs and convince them to do the smart thing, or beat on them again until they stop moving, then snap on the cuffs myself. I don't *think* I've ever killed anyone, but I undoubtedly came close a couple or three times, and my handlers are always quick to reassure me that a loss here and there would be acceptable. We're the good guys, they remind me, and if the bad guys want to share in our rights, they shouldn't be bad guys.

∞    ☼    ∞

My handlers aren't stupid— or at least they've learned from past stupidities. Since the CN Tower fell, they know enough to drive the perps outside urban areas to minimize the collateral damage. Today, they drop me out of the copter onto a stretch of three-lane highway, just uphill of a soaring cloverleaf, and I see her, standing there, fists clenched, lycra straining against an unlikely bosom. She's as scared as I am. She probably knows as much about me as I know about her— basically, nothing; they didn't even give me a sitrep this time, or hint about why I'm supposed to be fighting her.

She gathers balls of energy around her fists and casts them at me, screaming. When they hit, they *hurt*, like the worst sunburn ever. But me and pain are old friends, and my hide keeps the heat from penetrating. My ugly goes skin deep, but it does have its benefits. I ball my own fists and whack the ground, the concussion knocking her off her feet and flinging her back under the overpass, which shakes like a jello sculpture. I pursue, not giving her time to get her feet back under her, and she scuttles backwards like a crab, leaving bloodstains after the first few feet.

"Surrender," I hiss, knowing I'm wasting my breath.

"*Die!*" she screams in return, and fires another energy blast past my head. As I look up to see the source of the rumbling, she lashes out with a kick that takes one leg out from under me, and uses the recoil to push herself into a shoulder roll and back onto her feet. She fights smart. I lose track of her then because I'm on my back watching tons of pre-stressed concrete fall toward my face in slow-motion. I have enough time to cover my eyes with my arms before the weight of the world lands on me, crushing the breath from my lungs.

Lucky for me, I've been here before; it's an old supervillain gimmick, and something of a cliché— for the good reason that it works so well. All those sessions pumping iron pay off; I squirm onto my stomach, gather my knees beneath me, arch my back, and shed all that weight with one mighty heave. Then I wipe the grit from my eyes and look around for my foe.

I said she's smart; she hasn't waited around to see if she finished me off. She's not flying, but she's skipping so high with each jump, energy glowing around her feet, that she makes an easy target. I pick up a chunk of rubble the size of my fist, judge the apex of her leap, and fling it. It catches her in mid-skip, and she goes down in a tangle of arms and legs that doesn't bode well for her future spinal health. I lope up to her, and it's only then I notice the cameramen in black body armor, assault rifles slung over their shoulders. I ignore them, and when I get to her, she's lying with one leg beneath her at an angle that makes me wince. Bone sits at an unnatural angle in one forearm, but it's not protruding. "Just" a nasty compound fracture. Sometimes I don't know my own strength.

I kneel beside her. "Surrender. *Please*! I don't want to hurt you anymore."

*"Fascist!"* she spits at me, and the spittle runs down my face. But there are tears in her eyes, leaving tracks through the blood smears on her face, and there's pain and humiliation in her eyes, and she gathers what remains of her strength, and energy begins forming around the fist of her remaining usable hand...

One of the camera men shouts something.

"What did you say?" I ask, disbelieving.

"Pound her to hamburger, you fucking monster!"

I look back at her and something changes in her eyes. Presumably she sees what's writ large across my face. When I'm done strewing the two men across the landscape and the stench of cordite is drifting away on a light breeze, I turn back to her. "This is going to hurt," I warn her. She grits her teeth and closes her eyes, and I carefully grip her arm, not wanting to do any more damage with these fingers, thick as her wrist. I pull gently until the bone pops back in place, and splint it there with the still-hot barrel from one of the dismembered rifles and strips of cloth torn from a uniform. Though blood runs from her bitten lip, she makes no sound. She'll need a doctor, but she won't lose the arm.

"The leg is going to hurt worse, I'm afraid." She nods, eyes still closed, and when I pull it out into the correct alignment, feel it click back into place, she sobs. I bind her legs together with a belt from one of the cameramen.

Then her eyes open as we both hear the sound of the chopper. I pick her up in my arms. "We've got to get out of here," I say.

"In a moment," she replies, and with her good arm gathers one of those energy balls around her fist, and flings it weakly at the chopper.

Then I turn and walk away with her in my arms, greasy smoke rising into the sky behind us.

∞   ✿   ∞

**GEOFF HART** is a scientific editor, technical writer, and translator from Montréal.

# BLOODHOUND

*Marcelle Dubé*

**THE SMELL INSINUATED** itself into Luke Corrigan's dreams; he turned away from the open window of his bedroom, trying to escape the acrid stink.

Finally he woke up and swung his feet out of bed and sat on the edge, naked and sweating, his heart beating fast. In the war, he'd wake up just like this, convinced that something was in the trench with him. Only once had it been a German. Usually it was just rats.

He reached for the filter on his bedside table, then paused. He needed to figure out what the smell was before putting on the filter.

It was still dark, and the only sound was the loud ticking of the alarm clock by his bedside. Moonlight streamed through the window of the barn loft that was his bedroom, gilding the barrel stove against one wall, washing the rough pine planks of the floor in pale light, and bouncing off the old, warped mirror above the chest of drawers, where he kept the flowered porcelain pitcher and bowl for shaving.

The smell teased him, first appearing, then disappearing, leaving only the ancient smells of hay, manure, and horses filtering up through the floorboards of the loft, along with the more recent smells of gasoline and grease from the little repair shop he had set up in the far corner of the barn.

He wrinkled his nose and took a deep breath. Some smells grew bright and sharp when he did that. Not this time. Whatever it was, it wasn't near. Still, something about it was familiar enough to raise his hackles.

He pushed the tangled sheet away and stood up to pad over to the window. The hot Manitoba night filled his room.

Filled the valley with dust and parched crops and small dead things lying by dried-up waterholes. Even the crickets didn't have the heart to chirp. His back was damp from the sheets, and he could smell the sweat on his scalp.

Harriet MacNeil's farm stood middle-of-the-night quiet, with a half-moon and a wash of diamond stars beaming down on the seared fields beyond her farmhouse. Nothing moved.

Breathing shallowly, he turned his head one way, then the other, trying to make sense of what he was smelling. Dry earth thirsty for rain. Boulders gradually releasing their warmed stone smell. The faint whiff of a coyote that had passed by a few hours ago.

Other smells were so prevalent that he only noticed them by their absence: Rex, the MacNeils's dog, whose smell was as much a part of the scent landscape as the smell of the maple trees in the farmyard; the faint, gagging smell of Jamison's pig farm three miles upwind; the ever-present perfume of a wild grass that he had yet to identify but had come to call "sweet hay," which was what Allie, Missus MacNeil's granddaughter, called it. He had moved into the loft above the empty barn in February, where he near froze to death before he figured out the wood stove, and even then the smell of sweet hay had lingered.

And now, underneath them all, the ghost stink of death riding the wind.

He stuck his head out the window and looked in the direction of the pig farm. There, on the horizon, was a long, glowing snake that seemed to leap toward him even as he watched.

∞　☼　∞

Harriet MacNeil woke from a deep sleep to the sound of her name. Allie? Then the voice penetrated her sleep-befuddled awareness. Luke. Her strange tenant.

She sat up suddenly, clutching the threadbare cotton sheet to her chest, and the old iron bed that had belonged to her parents squeaked beneath her bulk. What was Luke Corrigan doing in her bedroom?

He was a dark figure standing by her bedside. Rex stood next to him, whining a little.

"What is it?" she asked, automatically looking to the window, but there was no glow of fire, her ever-present fear, especially now, in this drought. The farmhouse had been built in 1912, after the original one burned down, but the barn was even older.

"Fire," said Luke. "You have to take your granddaughter and get away from the farm."

"What?" She pushed the sheet off and climbed out of bed, despite the fact that she wore only her cotton nightgown. At sixty-three, after bearing six children and losing two husbands, one to a horse's hooves and one to influenza, not to mention struggling to keep herself and Allie afloat, she had outgrown any idea of modesty. Luke stepped back, giving her room to go to the window. Rex followed her, and leaned against her when she stopped. The Lab was getting on in years, too.

Even the linoleum beneath her feet felt hot and sticky. After a moment, she turned back to her tenant.

"Have you been drinking?" She wouldn't have thought it of him, but a lot of the men who came back from the front had taken to drink. Not that she blamed them. Buchenwald and Dachau... who could live with the things these young men had seen?

Luke Corrigan had been lucky, in a way. A piece of shrapnel had injured him, sending him home months before the war's end, and leaving him with an ugly pink scar peeking through his short brown hair, just above his left temple. But at least he had his life, and all his limbs.

"No, ma'am," said Luke calmly. "I saw it from the window in the loft. You need to take Allie and Rex, and head for Souris. You need to get across the river."

"I'm not leaving," said Harriet, running her hands through her white hair. She automatically began twisting it into the thick braid she customarily wore.

"Ma'am," said Luke, and she could hear the frustration in his voice, "it's bad. Jamison's pig farm was taken by the fire. You need to get the little girl and warn everyone on your way into Souris."

She finally got tired of squinting in the darkness and turned on her bedside lamp. For a fleeting moment, she wondered what her neighbors would say if they could see her in her nightgown, in her bedroom, alone with a man. A young, good-looking one, at that.

Her lips twitched. The women would be jealous, she figured.

Then she got her first good look at her young tenant and the twitching stopped. There was a grim look on his face. He was completely serious.

"Luke, how do you *know*?"

His nostrils flared and his nose wrinkled, like Rex's when he was sniffing something particularly odious.

"Ma'am…" he hesitated, then took a step toward her. It was a measure of her trust in the young man that she allowed him to take her by the elbow and lead her firmly out of her bedroom, past Allie's room, and down the hall to the far bedroom, the one where the window faced south. The moment he opened the door, she saw the glow past the corner of the barn and her breath caught in her throat.

Despite her instincts urging her to *go*, go *now*, she stumbled to the window and looked. Fire burned from one end of the horizon to the other. She didn't see how Jamison's farm could have survived.

"Oh, damnation," she said, then whirled and ran out. Rex barked sharply and ran after her.

∞   ☼   ∞

He'd lost his sense of smell in Antwerp, when a piece of exploding shell glanced his skull and laid him out for three weeks. It took him a while to figure out what was wrong, and even longer to get over the grief of it. Every time one of his buddies exclaimed over how good a woman smelled, or someone covered their nose against a foul odor, fresh loss slammed into him.

He tried to hide it from the docs, but they found out and told the army. He was sent back to Toronto on a disability pension and had to watch the end of the war from the newspaper headlines.

A few months later he caught the fever that was going around. He was so sick with it that he was hospitalized for a few days. When he finally regained consciousness he realized that he had also regained his sense of smell.

After the initial rush of joy, he began to realize that he could smell things now that he'd never smelled before. He left the hospital as soon as he could, because he couldn't bear the stink of death that hung over it.

He couldn't stay in the city. The smells… There were so *many* of them. Layers of them, some good but most overpoweringly bad. Garbage day was almost his undoing.

Then he heard about some research on smell taking place in Winnipeg. He packed his tattered army rucksack and hopped a freight train, sharing an empty car with three other returned soldiers, one missing an eye and a hand.

The Winnipeg doc seemed to think it was wonderful until Luke explained the reality of the situation. That was when the doc came up with the nose filter. Luke didn't know what it was made of, but it sat in a soft rubber cup that fit over his nose and strapped to the back of his head. It looked like a pared down gas mask and made him look like he had a muzzle, but it allowed air to flow through while filtering out most of the smells.

It helped. That, and moving into the countryside.

He picked a home where he would live away from regular folk, especially womenfolk. Especially *young* womenfolk. He could tell when it was their time of the month and when they were fertile. It was unnerving.

Missus MacNeil was well past those years and little Allie wasn't yet there. It made for a more comfortable living arrangement. He paid Missus MacNeil a small rent for the loft above the barn, and she fed him. In return, he kept her old Chevy JC Master pickup running and did a few odd jobs around the place. She no longer farmed but leased the fields out to neighboring farmers.

Now, as he drove his Harley-Davidson scouting bike down the bumpy dirt road, heading for the Jensen place, Harriet's nearest neighbors, he wondered if it wasn't time to move on again. Missus MacNeil had looked at him strangely when she realized he was right about the fire. A few times lately she had commented on his excellent sense of smell. It was bad enough being a freak. He didn't need the whole world knowing he was one.

Even through the filter, the odor of burning prairie was overwhelming. Above the stink of the burning grasslands and scorched earth, he could smell, faintly, the burned pork stench of Jamison's pigs.

He wanted to gag, but didn't dare open his mouth against the wind buffeting him. The goggles protected his eyes and a leather helmet protected his ears but nothing protected his mouth.

The dust of his passage caught up to him as he turned onto the Jensen road. The farmhouse was only two hundred yards away, dark with sleep. A Plymouth was parked against the side of the house, either painted grey or grey with dust. A barn stood beyond, empty by the smell of it. He took a deep breath and caught the unmistakable smell of cattle. They were probably in a paddock behind the house. Jensen was lucky. Most farmers in the area had sold off their stock when it became clear they wouldn't be able to feed them.

He'd hoped the sound of his engine would wake someone up, but no lights went on. He braked hard by the porch steps and kicked his stand on before swinging his leg over and running up the steps. He banged on the door, yelling "Jensen!" before trying the handle.

The door swung open. Luke stood on the braided rag rug in the entrance, yelling for Jensen. A light went on upstairs and a moment later a figure stood at the top of the stairs, dark and threatening, a shotgun in hand.

"Who's there?" growled Jensen. "What the hell do you—"

"Fire!" said Luke, cutting through the man's anger. "Get your family out, man! You have to get over the river. Head for Souris."

Even as Luke spoke, Jensen ran down the steps, shirtless and barefooted, wearing only a pair of dungarees half done up. He still held the shotgun, but it was pointed toward the floor. He pushed past Luke and stepped out onto the porch.

"Dear?" came a woman's voice from upstairs.

Jensen swore, then rushed back inside.

"Marie!" he called. "Get the kids up! Fire's coming!" He headed back outside only to stop and turn toward the stairs. "Grab only what you can carry," he called up to the woman who had come to stand at the top of the stairs. She had a shawl wrapped around her narrow shoulders, and her pale, thin nightgown only went down to her calves. "We have to get out now!"

∞   ☼   ∞

*Last one*, Luke promised himself. He had tied a kerchief over his filter and behind his head so that it covered his mouth. He was now bathed in sweat, but at least he could breathe through his mouth without fear of swallowing a bug or worse, debris from the fire floating on the wind that ran from the fire. It was still a half-mile away, as near as he could tell, but already the heat of it beat against him.

From the main road he could see a truck parked in front of the house. These folks might not know about the fire, although that was hard to believe. Its roar overwhelmed every other sound, even the sound of the Harley.

There were no lights in the house, but that didn't mean anything. The fire had eaten through the power lines some time back.

He turned down the road and headed for the house. He had driven past it often. It was painted white, like most other homes in the area, but now it glowed eerily in the night, caught halfway between the pale moonlight and the ruddy light of the fire creeping nearer.

He came to a stop next to the pickup and got off, his legs wobbly from the beating his body was taking on the motorbike. A horse whinnied nearby, and his concern grew. No farmer would leave his horses trapped in a barn with a fire coming. These folks clearly didn't know about the fire.

A faint smell wormed its way through his filter, something familiar and unpleasant, but he didn't have time to investigate. Shaking his head, he ran up the unpainted wooden steps and banged on the door. He got one knock in before the unlatched door opened.

He took a step back even as the smell registered. He had smelled this before, too often, on the battlefield.

Blood. And shit.

Dear Christ Almighty. What had happened in this house?

Breathing shallowly through his mouth, he stepped forward and gingerly crossed the threshold. It was dark and quiet in the house, under the ever-present grumble of the advancing fire. He thought he could hear a clock ticking from the room to his right.

He should call out, but battle instincts took over. He crept along the wall until he reached the doorway. In the gloom, he made out a chesterfield and a pair of stuffed chairs, a table by the window, a fireplace. Nothing else.

Moving silently, he found a formal dining room, a kitchen and off the kitchen, a laundry room where the sharp smell of bleach caused him to quickly close the door.

At last he stood at the foot of the stairs, looking up. He'd known the slaughterhouse smell came from the bedrooms, but he still had to check the downstairs first. The fire slowly gained on him, and still he hesitated, reluctant. He knew he would find something he had hoped to leave behind on the battlefield.

He could leave. Could pretend he had turned back before reaching the farmhouse. Let the fire take this house and cleanse it from its nightmare.

Even as he thought it, he climbed the first step.

Then the next.

At the top of the stairs, he headed away from the smell to check the two far bedrooms first. They were unused, the bedspread neatly tucked over the pillows. Whoever used to sleep there hadn't been around in a while.

Then he turned toward the other end of the hallway. There were two bedrooms there, too, although he already knew that one would be empty. But not the other.

He didn't pause. Didn't dare, or he would turn around and leave. He followed the smell that now filled his nose and his mouth, filter be damned, to the far bedroom on the south side of the house, facing front. The door was half open and the room beyond flickered ruddily.

Luke pushed open the door gently; it moved without sound. He glanced over his shoulder nervously, but there was no one behind him. Finally he stepped into the room, and into something wet.

Between the moon and the glow of the fire, he saw an old man, his bare chest and one arm covered in blood from the wide gash at his neck, lying tangled in a pale sheet, eyes open, as if he had been struggling to get up when the attack occurred.

He found the wife on the other side of the bed, crumpled on the hardwood floor. She had been stabbed three times. Her hands were still up; he could see deep slashes across her palms. He knew it was futile, but he crouched by her side and felt her neck for a pulse. He was unsurprised to find none. He had seen death often enough to recognize it.

He stood up and looked around. The closet door was open, the clothes shoved to one side. Hat boxes and protective cloth bags had fallen from the shelf, along with loose papers. The drawers to the bureau had been pulled open and some socks and women's underpants had tumbled out. A small box that looked like it might have contained jewellery stood open on top of the bureau.

He stood for a moment, looking around, fixing the scene in his memory. Had the looter been surprised to find them still here? Or hadn't he cared?

Luke closed his eyes. After witnessing so much death and dying, he was surprised at how the death of these two filled him with frustrated rage.

Finally he shook himself. He couldn't do anything for these folks. They were dead; if he didn't get a move on, he would die here, too.

Before leaving, he pulled the kerchief off his nose, pulling the filter down with it. The air in the bedroom felt blessedly cool on his sweaty face. He breathed in the stink of death. There was blood. And shit and piss. And below it the old skin smell of the old man and the faint talcum powder and coffee smell of the old woman.

And beyond that, a stink of bitter, nervous sweat, overlaid by beer and pickled eggs.

∞   ☼   ∞

Harriet rattled the old Chevy to a stop in front of the house and slid out of the driver's seat onto the hard-packed earth of the drive. The skirt of her cotton dress billowed around her legs as she moved around the truck. To the south, the horizon was a wall of orange and red and yellow. It was still at least half a mile away, she judged, but she could smell the smoke now, a little. And the wind had picked up.

She was being foolish to return to the farm, but she couldn't bear the thought of letting the fire get the quilt her mother had made for Harriet and John's wedding, or the needlepoint sampler her daughter had made when she was Allie's age. She had to rescue the baby book Charlotte had made for Allie, and the rest of the photo albums.

She had left Allie and Rex with the Fredericksons, who were heading into Souris, for their son's place. The river was wide— it would stop the fire. Jacob Frederickson had argued that she should come with them, but Sheila had looked at Harriet with understanding, and told her to hurry and be careful.

She ran to the front room, not bothering to turn on lights. She knew where everything was. Halfway there, she veered off toward the washing room and grabbed the wooden-slat laundry basket. She dumped the clean clothes awaiting ironing on the narrow counter next to the wringer washer then ran back into the front room, her leather shoes slapping against the worn linoleum.

The sampler hung above the ancient claw-footed horsehair chesterfield. She unhooked it from the wall and dropped it with a clunk into the basket, then grabbed the doilies resting on the back of the chesterfield and on its arms. Grandma Myrtle had made them.

The wedding photos — hers and John's, and later hers and Michael's — were packed away in the cedar chest at the foot of her bed. She ran up the stairs, her shoes thumping on the runner.

It was the middle of the night and already sweat ran down her back. The July heat had been brutal this year and they had all heard the stories of the prairie fires sweeping through communities to the south of them. She could hear the fire now, a dull roar filling the world with threat.

Swallowing, she turned away and hurried.

Five minutes later, the laundry basket was full and she struggled with its unwieldy bulk toward the front door. Breathing hard, she was just setting the basket down in order to open the door when she heard the kitchen door open. She was about to call out when something made her close her mouth and take a step back.

Who would be coming into her house at a time like this? In the middle of the night? It wasn't Luke— she would have heard his motorcycle, even over the fire.

A few tendrils of hair had escaped her loose braid and now clung to her damp face and neck. She pushed them away from her eyes.

She could slip out the front door and into the truck, and be heading down the road before whoever was in her kitchen realized she was here.

But that would mean abandoning her home, the home she had lived in all her life. She could — and would — abandon the house to a grass fire. But she was *damned* if she was going to abandon it to a looter.

∞  ☼  ∞

Luke followed the stink of scared horse past the barn and across the road to a field filled with stunted, brittle ears of corn. Even when the wind shifted, snatching the scent away from him, he was able to follow the dark passage of horse and rider through the trampled corn.

He had expected the bastard to head for the next farmhouse, but he seemed to be cutting across the fields to avoid the homes along the road. Maybe the fire had spooked him.

The corn gleamed palely in the moonlight while the ever-advancing fire cast its glow against the few clouds scuttling before the wind.

The fire looked no closer but he found himself gunning the engine to riskier speeds. Between the dusty goggles and the night, he could barely see the horse's path through the field. One hole in the ground, and he would go flying.

He didn't know whose field this was, but he spared the farmer a little sympathy. The corn rustled thirstily at his passage. If the fire didn't take it, the drought would.

He was glad of the leather jacket, despite the heat. Even through the leather, he could feel the sting of the stalks whipping against his arms and shoulders as he raced recklessly between the rows.

Where was the man going? The bridge to Souris was to the south, but the horse's path was taking Luke southwest. The ground rose slightly, hiding whatever was on the other side, and for a dizzying moment, he felt as if he were going to launch into the starry sky.

The kerchief whipped against his chin and neck and the sweat poured down his back and down his forehead, kept at bay by his goggles. He should go into Souris and report what he'd found, but his jaw clenched on the idea.

Too much chance of the bastard getting away.

Then he topped the slight rise and saw a familiar roof line. There, just below the rise, was Missus MacNeil's house, and just beyond it the barn that had been his home.

He paused, both feet on the ground, to survey the scene. Something moved in the darkness by the house and he blinked furiously, trying to focus. Then the shadow whinnied. Tied to the porch railing by the back door was a horse.

It was pure chance that Missus MacNeil and little Allie were away, and not still sleeping in their beds, like the old couple had been. If not for his damned nose, they'd *all* still be asleep, vulnerable to this murdering thief.

His hand gunned the engine without him consciously decid-
ing to. He hung on to the handles as the wheel hit a bump and
his bottom left the saddle only to land again with a jar he felt
all the way up his spine.

The horse was nothing but a darker shadow against the
moon-bleached wooden porch. The animal panicked at his
approach and jerked away from the porch, trapped there by
its reins looped around the railing. It whinnied in terror as he
approached, unnerved by the high whine of the Harley's engine,
until with a sharp tug it pulled the old railing out of its socket
in the post. Suddenly freed, the animal began to run toward
the road, the post bumping against the horse's shoulder. A bag
that looked suspiciously like a pillowcase hung from the horn
of the saddle and bumped against the saddle with every stride,
urging the horse on to greater speed.

The bastard was now on foot.

Luke slid the bike to a dusty stop by the back stairs and got
off. He ran up the creaky back stairs, not even bothering with
stealth, and pushed through the open kitchen door. There was
no hope of surprising the intruder, not with the noisy machine
he'd just been riding, but the kitchen was dark and empty.

He took a deep breath through the filter and kerchief and was
rewarded with the faint stink of old beer and pickled eggs. The
bastard was somewhere in the house, rifling through Missus
MacNeil's possessions.

His nostrils flared as he stepped further into the kitchen.
His head turned to the left, and he realized that the murdering
son of a bitch was somewhere on this floor. As his eyes finally
adjusted to the darkness, he heard scuffling coming from the
front room, and then a decidedly unfeminine oath burst forth
from a feminine throat.

Missus MacNeil.

All the blood left his head to surge to his limbs; he found
himself sprinting through the kitchen and down the hallway
to the front room. With its curtains drawn, it was even darker
than the kitchen had been but even so he caught the movement
of two figures struggling by the settee. Then he saw the larger
figure raise an arm and Luke's imagination supplied a knife
at the end of that arm.

With a roar, he launched himself at the figure. His momentum carried them both into the rocking chair by the cold wood

stove. The thief lost his footing, falling backward against the heavy stove.

Luke scrambled to his feet, but the man had stopped moving. He dropped to one knee and felt the man's neck. The bastard still lived. He'd only been knocked out.

"Missus MacNeil?" he asked, feeling around on the rug for the knife.

"Luke?" said Missus MacNeil in the dark. There was a wobble in her voice.

"Yes, ma'am," he said. "Are you hurt?"

He heard her take a deep breath and wished he could go to her to check her out for himself, but he didn't dare leave the man.

"No," said Mrs. MacNeil finally. Then, more firmly, "I'm fine. What about him?"

"Knocked out but alive," said Luke with regret. "We need to tie him up."

"Right," said his landlady. "I'll be right back."

He heard her leave through the back door and presumed she was heading for the barn to find some rope. At last he pulled the damned kerchief and filter off his face and took a deep breath of the relatively cooler air.

The immediacy of Missus MacNeil's fear stink caught at his nose, immediately followed by the stench of an unwashed male body, a smell he had last caught at the old couple's house. The smell of blood and death clung to the man like a ghost.

Then Missus MacNeil came back, carrying a lit lantern in one hand and a coil of rope in the other. She was breathing fast. She set the lantern on the wood stove; they both got their first look at the looter.

He was a big man, but they already knew that. A week's growth of salt-and-pepper beard added to the general scruffiness of his appearance. Drying blood caked on his worn denim shirt and pants confirmed his crime, even if Luke hadn't smelled the old couple on him.

"He was going to kill me," said Missus MacNeil quietly, looking down at the unconscious man.

Luke nodded and stood up. He'd left the man's feet free for now, until they could put him in the back of the truck. He scouted around the debris of the rocking chair and finally spotted the knife. It was a big knife, the kind Missus MacNeil used for chopping vegetables.

"He killed the old folks living in the white house three farms down," he said. He'd searched the man's pockets and now held up two gold rings, one set with tiny diamonds.

Missus MacNeil's eyes filled with tears. "Elsa Rhysling," she said softly. "That's her engagement ring and her wedding band."

Luke swallowed his rage and handed the rings to his land-lady. "Maybe you could give this to her next of kin," he said.

Missus MacNeil nodded jerkily. "Yes." She looked down at the man. "Do you know who he is? A returning soldier, maybe?"

Every fibre of his being wanted to deny it, but the bastard might well be. He knew a lot of soldiers had found it hard to return to civilian life after the war. But to turn to looting and murder?

He sighed. "We need to get out of here," he said firmly. "We'll tie this bas— we'll tie him up in the back of the truck. You can take him to the police station in Souris."

Missus MacNeil looked at him sharply. "What about you?"

He shrugged. "I won't be far behind."

∞   ☼   ∞

Harriet drove the Chevy as fast as she dared to Souris, not caring if she hit every pothole on the way. The murderer tied in the back of her truck could stand a bit a bruising.

She kept an eye on her rear-view mirror and saw when Luke Corrigan peeled away from the road just before the bridge. She wasn't surprised. He was a strange boy. Nice enough, but he didn't do well around other people.

She considered the get-up he'd been wearing when he got on his motorcycle. Whatever that thing was he wore under the kerchief, it gave him a strangely bulbous profile. And with his goggles and his wind-ruffled and ash-dusted hair, he looked like something out of one of those magazines Allie loved to read.

By the time she saw the lights of Souris, she realized that the fire had changed direction along with the wind. It was now heading further west. Her house would be spared.

She never made it to the police station. A crowd had gath-ered on the far side of the river to watch the fire's progress, including three fire trucks. A policeman waved her to a stop as she got to the other side of the bridge; he climbed up on her running board to talk to her. Behind him, the crowd pressed in closer to hear. She recognized a couple of her neighbors and nodded at them. She didn't see Sheila Frederickson anywhere. They must have taken Allie to their boy's place.

"Everybody get out of your house?" asked the police officer, scanning the interior of the cab.

He was an older man but still fit and hard edged. He'd taken his uniform jacket and cap off, and sweat stained his pale shirt in half-moons beneath his arms. His grey hair gleamed in the light of the street lamp. Scully, she finally remembered. His name was Scully.

"My granddaughter's already here," said Harriet, suddenly realizing that Allie could have been left to fend for herself, all because Harriet had wanted to go back for a few *things*. Her hands began to shake. "I have a man tied up in the back," she added. "He murdered Elsa Rhysling and her husband, Tom."

Scully's eyebrows rose, wrinkling his forehead, and he craned his neck past her cab to look into the bed of the truck. He studied the sorry figure lying there for a moment, then his lips tightened and Harriet figured he'd gotten a good look at the blood on the man's clothes.

"Right," he said, hopping down from the running board. "You two," he said, pointing at two younger men in the crowd, "help me get this man out."

"Who've you got there, Harriet?" called a voice from the crowd. She couldn't make out who. She opened the door and slid down off the seat. Her knees buckled as she landed and she would have fallen if not for Officer Scully's steadying hand on her elbow.

"A murderer," she said out loud. "A looter. He killed Elsa and Tom Rhysling and was set to murder me. I don't know if he hurt anyone else."

Those nearest to her relayed her words and soon the crowd was buzzing and pressing closer to see who the man was.

Officer Scully looked down at her, frowning. "You managed to knock him out, tie him up, and put him in the back of your truck? All by yourself?"

Harriet shook her head tiredly. "No," she said. Then she hesitated. Luke would hate to be the centre of this kind of attention. And she owed him her life.

"There was a man," she said finally. "A masked man. He saved my life."

Officer Scully looked back at the bridge. "Masked? Where is he now?"

Harriet shrugged. "I don't know." But she hoped she'd see him again.

∞   ☼   ∞

Based in the Yukon, **MARCELLE DUBÉ** writes fantasy and crime novels for Carina Press and Falcon Ridge Publishing.

# THE JAM:
# A SECRET BOWMAN

*Bernard E. Mireault*

GORDON SAT WITH his arms wrapped around his knees near the wall of the ramshackle shed. It housed the roof access stairwell of the ancient apartment building that he now called home. The building was one of a group of five in a tight cluster, but his was the tallest at twelve storeys. The view was good; a million things to look at, some illegal.

His dog, Harvey, a Labrador-sized mixed breed, was asleep beside him with his black nose on his paws. His business had been done an hour ago but the dog knew the routine and seemed happy with it. Harvey didn't seem to need much exercise to stay fit; he had the physical trimness and reflexes of a ninja. Gordon wished that he could claim half as much.

He scratched the top of the dog's head for a minute and then slowly stood up and had a good stretch. He wore a loose-fitting costume: dark green jogging suit with an inverted orange triangle sewn onto the chest and a hood that had been modified into a mask. There were other little bits of orange sewn onto the forehead and cheeks and the clumsy hand stitching showed plainly. The hood covered the back, top and sides of his head and face, with large square holes for the eyes. It split at the bridge of his nose and fell to either side of his head where it eventually attached to the shoulders of his outfit, leaving the lower half of his face visible and creating a dark cave on either side of his neck. His gloves and boots were dirty white, as was the jury-rigged tool belt that he wore around his waist, with four small tubes on either side of a large rectangular interlocking buckle. Most of the costume's components were regular athletic wear. The boots and gloves bore large cuffs, custom-made by his sister.

Gordon had a final look around before he returned back to his tiny apartment four floors below. Eastward, downtown Montréal sparkled and blinked like some weird jewel in the autumn night. He loved the older neon signs, they had so much style. When he was younger he used to find himself walking those streets several nights a week, going for some live music and beer at one of a handful of dive bars. These days money was such an issue that it just didn't make sense to spend it at a bar; when he felt the need he just did his drinking at home. As for music, he wrote songs and played them on his own guitar. That was good, too.

A weird scream. A strange, quavering cry. His dog leapt up and pointed in the direction where the sound had come from. The costumed man crossed the roof and, with care informed by late-onset vertigo, knelt down about three feet from the edge and braced himself, looking cautiously over. Below him was the top of the neighboring apartment, an eight-storey building with a roof garden; assorted plants growing in a multitude of large white buckets arranged in rows. A young man dressed in grey and beige military camouflage came out from behind the roof access shed holding a bow and quiver in one hand and an acoustic guitar case in the other. Moving quickly he laid the case at his feet, took the string off the bow, and broke it down into three pieces. He turned his attention back to the guitar case, undoing the fasteners quickly and flipping the lid open. He placed his weapon and quiver inside, then shrugged off his jacket and pants to reveal a white T-shirt and faded blue jeans. He stuffed the camouflage outfit into the guitar case and snapped the fasteners shut. All this had taken place in roughly thirty seconds and all to the tune of the strange wail coming from street level.

From the higher roof Gordon concluded he was witnessing the aftermath of a terrible crime. Shooting arrows at pedestrians? Could this be for real? He was stunned.

The young man stood up, guitar case in hand, and was about to pull open the roof-access door when suddenly he stopped. His took a phone from the back pocket of his jeans. He stared at the little screen for a moment then put the guitar case down and typed on his device furiously with both thumbs.

What was there to be done here? Gordon's mind raced. The two buildings were very close, separated only by a narrow alley. Moving closer to the edge and looking down he saw that the fire-escape stairs of both structures were exactly opposite each other and their landings were level and separated only by a small gap that could be crossed safely. If he got down there quickly then maybe he could get across and back up in time to follow the guy. But here were problems with that plan. Until he got below the level of the neighboring roof he would be exposed to his target. And he always felt intense vertigo going down metal fire-escape stairs because you could see right through them to the ground below.

*This is more important than your damn vertigo,* he admonished himself. *Get over it and get over there!*

The young man with the guitar case continued texting, moving away from the light by the entrance to the stairwell and turning his back to Gordon. He had earphones on.

Emboldened, Gordon said a couple of words to his dog and, gritting his teeth, set off down the fire escape stairs as quietly/ quickly as he could go. He made too much noise, but his quarry was wrapped up in whatever he was texting and whatever he was listening to. He never looked in Gordon's direction. In under a minute Gordon was where he wanted to be.

So far, so good.

His tongue poked out of the corner of his mouth in concentration as he carefully crossed between the fire escape landings on the seventh floor. Sprinting back up to the roof level of the lower building, he climbed a small metal ladder to the rim of the roof and slowly brought his eyes over the edge, just in time to see the stairwell door swing shut.

Gordon pulled himself quickly up and ran to where arrow guy had been standing moments ago, and he heard the sound of footsteps on stairs come to an abrupt halt. He stepped into the shadows on the side of the shed, in case his quarry came back. When nothing happened after a couple of minutes, he risked a quick peek into the small window set into the access door. He glimpsed his target standing halfway down the first flight of stairs, still absorbed in typing on his phone with one thumb. Gordon eased back around the side of the small structure and into the shadows, lost in thought. He could still hear the odd keening, but it was fainter now. He went low and quiet to the street side of the roof, slowly getting into position for a peek over the edge. He took off his mask and let it flop down his neck like the hoodie it actually was. If he was spotted he'd prefer to be less memorable. His long blond hair was tied back in a ponytail, and he was overdue for a shave.

Cautiously he looked over the edge and then backed away after a few seconds, digesting what he had seen.

Lying on the sidewalk below was an old man in a three-piece suit with an arrow through his shoulder, surrounded by a small crowd of passersby. There was bright red blood pooling beside him but there wasn't that much yet, and hopefully help was on the way.

Gordon winced, imaging the pain of a broadhead arrow passing through his body. Who could do that to another human?

A young woman was kneeling by the victim and supporting his head while talking into her phone. Everyone had a phone out. No doubt police and ambulance would be there soon and the whole thing was already livestreaming on YouTube.

Returning to the door, Gordon cautiously had another fast look through the small window. The psychotic asshole hadn't moved at all and was still thumb-typing, without a care in the world

Gordon moved around to the shadowed side of the shed again. The walls were so thin that he could hear the guy breathing and faint hints of the electropop that was being pumped into his earphones. When the bowman started moving again, Gordon would be ready to follow. He put his mask back on.

Scanning the rooftops, Gordon spotted his dog's head. He was looking in his direction. Gordon gave Harvey a single wave and received a sharp bark in return. He was just beginning to hear distant sirens when the footsteps he was waiting for abruptly resumed; after his quarry turned the first corner, Gordon hurried to follow.

He knew he didn't need to worry too much about noise, but he tried to be silent anyhow, easing the door open as gently as possible. His boots had crepe soles and made almost no sound as he rapidly tiptoed his way down the stairs, leaning heavily on the banisters. He listened for the sound of the footfalls he was following and tried to match them as closely as he could. His problem was not keeping up with the guy while staying out of sight; it was not running into him from behind. He had stopped abruptly to send another text.

The stairwell was deserted but for the two men. Locked in step but always separated by two flights of stairs, they went down three floors before the man with the guitar case exited the stairwell on the fifth floor. The door was similar to the one back on the roof, heavy wood with a small square window cut through it at eye level. Through it, Gordon could see the dark-haired man with the guitar case standing in front of the third door from the end of the hallway, fishing in his pocket, presumably for his keys.

Gordon waited for the sound of the door opening and closing, and a good long minute besides, before easing the stairwell door open and tiptoeing down the hallway. He went just far enough to get a fast look at the apartment number and quickly retreated the way he had come. This was why the guy wasn't too worried about making a quick getaway; he was already home.

Gordon knew what to do next.

When he got back to the roof, he paused, flipped open one of the tubes on his belt, and extracted a pencil wrapped in a small square of paper. Holding the paper up against the side the shed he scribbled down the apartment number while it was fresh in his mind.

Back on his own rooftop Harvey greeted him joyously. Good ol' dog! It helped to roll back his anger and sadness a bit. Harvey was good. Some things were good. "It's a hell of a thing, Harv."

He opened the access door into his own building and raced down the four floors to his apartment, Harvey always ahead of him, waiting only when a door had to be negotiated. Pulling a key out of his right glove, Gordon unlocked #8-4 and let them both inside. He checked the time on his clock-radio: 10:45 pm.

He pulled off the costume and put on his regular clothes: jeans, T-shirt, sneakers, and his ancient and much-loved jean jacket. Not unlike the guy he was looking to see in handcuffs. He picked his tool-belt off the floor and found the note with the bowman's address . He put it in his wallet. He slowly looked around his apartment, took a few deep breaths, and then gathered up all the parts of his costume that were strewn around the cramped space. He threw them all into a cardboard box and shoved it into a closet.

Gordon washed out and filled the dog's water and food bowls to the brim,. He left the large bag of dry food on the floor against the wall of his kitchenette. Harvey could be relied upon not to gorge, taking only as he needed. He was a great dog— uncanny, really. Gordon took an extra minute and gave Harvey a good back rub. Whatever it might've done for the dog, it certainly helped Gordon calm down. He stood up and gave his dog a peace sign. "I'll be back soon, buddy." At least, he hoped he would; dealing with the police was always tricky.

He closed his apartment door and locked it. Now he moved quickly again and, eschewing the dilapidated old elevator, he went straight down the stairs, which exited from the side of his building into the same alley that he had crossed earlier and higher up. He hit the broken pavement and started to jog toward the throbbing glow of the crime scene.

∞   ☼   ∞

"Sir, the man claims to be a witness and to know the current location of the shooter."

"Bring him here."

As senior officer on the scene, Pierre-Luc was calling the shots, which was always fun. He didn't mind civilian onlookers taking video; he knew he looked good on camera and welcomed it. He had noticed the blond guy running up to the line and seen him talking to the perimeter guys about something. He wanted to know very much what that was. The boys let the guy through and in a moment they were face to face. The guy had strong body odor, the kind produced by fear and stress. Like a burned battery. The inspector took two steps back.

"I saw the one who put the arrow in that old guy. I followed him home and got his address. It's on the fifth floor of the building right in front of us! He has a collapsible bow that he hides in an acoustic guitar case." The guy with the blond ponytail held out a small piece of paper with the apartment number written on it. The policeman took it, glanced at it briefly and then back to the face of his informant.

"May I see some identification?"

The ponytailed guy took out his wallet and found his Québec Medicare card. He handed it to the policeman.

"My name's Gordon Kirby and I live in the next building over…"

∞   ☼   ∞

At 11:42 pm, a small military-grade battering ram propelled by four large, heavily armed men smashed in the door of the apartment Gordon had identified. A small SWAT team flowed in professionally and quickly secured an amazed twenty-something male.

A quick search turned up the acoustic guitar case and much, *much* more.

∞　✪　∞

Once again Pierre-Luc was senior officer on the scene, but he knew that it would be short-lived. Some bigger fish would move in and take over once he had filed his initial report. He'd been putting it off for too long already as he racked his brain trying to think of some way to profit from all this.

The SWAT team was long gone, high-fiving each other as they streamed out of the apartment, jabbering adrenaline-fast about where they were going to party later. Pierre-Luc took note. A few of them were pretty hot.

All he could think of for now was to clear the place while they waited for the CSI team and couple of young computer forensics to show up. The guy had three seriously overpowered computers with security software up the wazoo.

As soon as he was alone, Pierre-Luc took out his phone and shot video of the guy's apartment; the armory of automatic weapons, the huge supply of ammunition. A sword collection that covered two walls. The mirrors on the ceiling in the bedroom. The crazy, obscene black-light posters in the bathroom. Maybe he could sell it later. This was going to be a big case.

∞　✪　∞

Gordon Kirby sat in a jail cell at Station 13, not far from where he lived. There had been no handcuffs but after giving his information to the policeman at the crime scene, he was packed into a squad car and dumped here. It had been three hours since he had seen or heard anyone. They had taken his belt, his wallet, and his shoelaces and then demanded his mobile phone. When he denied having one, they strip-searched him, and then locked him in a cell about the same size as his apartment. He had been escorted on the journey by four different police officers, each one handing him off to the next like a baton in a relay race. Nobody answered any of his questions about why he was being held. Nobody even looked at him, though there had been quite a bit of unnecessary shoving. It appeared that he had once again slipped between the cracks — more like shoved into the abyss — of local police procedure. Not a first and no surprise there. They had a hard job and he sympathized with them up to a point, but he couldn't help but feel that they were merely lazy and callous That they enjoyed locking up a stranger in a cage.

His mother had always said that no good deed goes unpunished, and his experience backed that up one hundred percent. He was happy that he had at least thought to water and feed Harvey, but he felt foolish for not eating when he'd had the chance. He was hungry now.

The holding area seemed deserted, though he imagined that everyone was hanging out by a water cooler somewhere, and if he wanted attention he'd just have to shout. Slow night. A late September Monday was about to turn into a Tuesday and his freedom was off the air temporarily due to technical difficulties. Sorry, folks!

The cell he occupied had a bare toilet stripped of niceties such as toilet paper. There was a water fountain and a molded concrete bench with rounded edges sticking out of a concrete wall. Through the stout steel bars he could see the wall across the hallway and if he pressed himself close to the bars he could see up and down the hallway and into the three neighboring cells, all of which were empty.

He couldn't believe how rancid he smelled, even to himself. The sour acid smell of spent adrenaline and stress, of fear, assaulted him every time he inhaled. It was embarrassing, and on that score he was glad to be alone.

He had been lost in his thoughts for quite some time when he heard the metal clang of a door opening and the sound of hard-soled shoes approaching. The same officer who had locked him in now unlocked the cell door and motioned for him to follow. As Gordon left the cell, out of the corner of his eye he saw the policeman prepare to give him another shove and he danced out of the way. The officer almost lost his balance when he pushed his hand through thin air, and Gordon turned around to face him. He was shocked to see the squat policeman's hand on his weapon, his eyes squinting in rage and his teeth bared like those of a fat, pissed-off wild animal. It was an unlovely sight.

Gordon held up his hands in submission. "Sorry, sorry."

It took a moment for the policeman to master his temper, and then he impatiently beckoned Gordon to continue down the hallway. Apparently, all the policemen employed here were mute. They went through two security doors and down another hallway, this one painted light blue, and Gordon was herded into an empty interview room. The door was slammed behind him and then ostentatiously locked.

He took one of the two seats available and wondered how long it would be before whoever wanted to question him showed up. What questions could they ask? And what could he answer that they hadn't already found out? He knew that the police often kept people waiting in rooms like this for hours to "soften them up." Gordon catalogued his surroundings; four walls, light blue. Unpainted concrete floor. Ceiling with a single light bulb in a wire cage and a smoke alarm (no doubt housing a concealed video camera). At least three different kinds of insects were flying around. He wished that there was something he could read to pass the time.

Two hours dragged slowly by. By his reckoning it was about three in the morning. He repeatedly went through his memory of the events that had led to this. Yes, he was going through an inconvenience here (though far less of one than having a barbed arrow through the shoulder) but maybe, just *maybe*, he had helped nail an insane predator to the wall.

Finally, footsteps approached, the door was unlocked and in walked the police officer he had spoken to at the crime scene. He slammed the door shut, and it took him two tries to get centered on his chair. *Holy shit, he's drunk!* thought Gordon.

Once he was settled in his chair, he looked up at Gordon and wrinkled his nose.

"Fuck! You stink!"

"Thank you."

The policeman frowned and took a phone out of the inside pocket of his jacket and spent the next fifteen minutes thumb-typing text messages. Gordon looked on, silent.

The man in front of him was neatly turned out; slick suit (a different one than he'd been wearing earlier), short hair gelled, and face cleanly shaven. Classically handsome with a tall, trim body. A young prince.

An over-the-top cologne clogged up the small, vent-less room's breathable air. The insects that Gordon had been tracking earlier seemed to have all disappeared; he wondered if the cloying smell affected them as it did him. He felt slightly nauseous. It seemed ironic that his rank body odor, while unpleasant, didn't make him feel half as bad as the perfume did.

Eventually the policeman put away his phone and looked up at his captive.

"You're going to keep quiet about this. You're not going to tell the media, you're not going to blog it, you're not going to say a word to anybody."

"No problem. I have no internet. I have no mobile phone, and I have no interest in contacting 'the media.' Is that why I'm being held, so that you can control that? Don't worry. I'm just hungry, and I want to go home. I was only trying to help."

The policeman looked at him suspiciously. From inside his suit his phone began playing some electropop tune; he pulled it out and squinted at the small screen before rolling his eyes, shutting it off, and putting it away again.

"Gee, that's rough, eh? Sucks to be you, huh?" The sneer on the policeman's mug reminded Gordon of a llama that he had once seen face-to-face while visiting the Winnipeg zoo as a child. He had approached it in wonder, but the instant he was within range it had spit in his face so hard that it *hurt*.

"I'm okay. Just wondering why you chose to lock me in a cell as if *I* were the one who tried to kill an old man with a bow and arrow. I was trying to *help* you."

The policeman didn't respond. His eyes were unfocused as he stared blankly. Minutes went by.

"Did you get him?" Gordon finally asked.

"That's none of your business. Your business is to shut up and be quiet."

"What's your name?"

The policeman looked up at Gordon with wide, disbelieving eyes. "I said to *shut up* and *be quiet*."

"I'm going to find out who you are and I'm going to give your name to René Marble."

The policeman's eyes opened wider. René Marble was a name all dishonest cops were frightened of. The cop's mouth opened, but no words came out.

"I tried to *help* you and in return you've got me locked up, obviously trying to run some sort of stupid scam. If you don't release me *immediately*, I promise you that I *will* be in touch with the media and that internal affairs will come down on you like an old brick wall. I swear."

"What's your relationship with Marble?"

Now it was Gordon's turn to not answer a direct question.

∞ ☼ ∞

Pierre-Luc was angry and nervous. Who the fuck was this punk who threw out the one name he was most worried about? The policeman who policed the police. Maybe he should tone it down until he knew better about what was what here.

∞ ☼ ∞

Gordie walked out of Station 13 at 5:32 in the morning. His stomach was burning and his mouth was full of digestive juices as he tromped the five blocks home. He was also very angry. What a world! What a poor, shitty, screwed-up world.

He unlocked the door to his apartment and met Harvey's joyous greeting with his own. He immediately felt better. He squeezed into the tiny kitchenette and began to prepare his long-delayed meal: a can of brown beans dumped into a thin pot, the smallest stovetop burner set to 4. Bread removed from the freezer and six slices liberated, leaving four. Toaster loaded and firing away with margarine on standby. He sat on his favorite chair and waited for the first set of toast to pop as he relived his most recent ordeal. He wished he had some beer. He could use a drink.

∞ ☼ ∞

Gordon clawed his way out of sleep, and looked at his bedside clock. It was 3:30 pm. His doorbell was buzzing. His doorbell almost never buzzed. He guessed that it was probably the police. He was right, though pleasantly so.

A few minutes later, René Marble sat in his living room sipping a cup of instant coffee. The head of internal affairs at the Service de Police de la Ville de Montréal surveyed his surroundings with amusement.

"You're living in a doghouse."

Gordon smiled. "Thank you."

"You had a busy night last night."

"Yeah. Do you know what happened?"

"Sure. We have a fairly thick file on you, Mr. Gordon 'The Jam' Kirby, and whenever something comes up with your name on it, I get notified. I'm sorry I wasn't around last night to straighten things out. It was my wife's birthday, and we were out of town."

"No problem. Did they get the guy with the bow?"

René pulled a briefcase onto his lap and undid the fasteners. Opening it, he withdrew a copy of the local English-language newspaper and passed it to Gordon, who unfolded it and read:

## BOW AND ARROW ATTACK IN N. D. G.

*Lauren Recaule*
Fast Media News

(Montréal) A 24-year-old resident of Notre-Dame-de-Grace was arrested and charged yesterday with the attempted murder of Christopher Enos, a 67-year-old pensioner. The attack was allegedly carried out with a bow and arrow from a rooftop in the west-end borough of Montréal.

The alleged attacker, whose name is being withheld by police, had no apparent connection to the victim. At approximately 8:00 PM Monday evening Mr. Enos, a librarian, was pierced through the shoulder by a barbed hunting arrow while walking home. Bystanders quickly called 911, and police and paramedics arrived on the scene soon enough to save the man's life. Mr. Enos is currently in stable condition at the McGill University Health Centre and is expected to recover. Lt. Pierre-Luc Goddard of the SPVM has been credited with discovering the identity of the attacker. At a press conference earlier today he stated that a search of the assailant's apartment had turned up "many startling things" and that there would be "many revelations to come" with regards to this case.

See **Arrow** on **A3**

Gordie put the newspaper down. "'Many startling things'? René, what's the deal here?"

"Gordon, your information has led to the apprehension of a homemade terrorist who was ready to make a much, *much* bigger mess. In his apartment they found three military-grade fully automatic weapons and thousands of rounds of ammunition. Plus grenades. Explosives. Swords. They got into his computer and found a diary where he mentions staging an attack at a rock concert at the Bell Centre, eight days from now. We also recovered email indicating that he was part of a larger group. This is going to be big.

My question for you is: how were you involved? Why did Lieutenant Goddard detain you for over six hours? He pretends that you don't exist."

"I guess he wants the credit for himself. I don't care. Actually, I prefer it that way! I just happened to be in the right place at the right time and witnessed this asshole making his getaway. I followed him but didn't have to go far; he lived in the building right next to mine. I got down to the crime scene and gave them my story, and then they put me in a squad car and stuck me in a cell down at Station 13."

René winced. "They are not famous for their humanity."

"Yeah, I got that. Nobody even spoke to me when I asked why I was there. I was cooped up for hours before Goddard came to see me. And he was drunk as a skunk. He threatened me with jail if I told anyone I was involved in the bowman thing. Sketchy, all very sketchy."

"That sounds like our Lieutenant Goddard. He is indeed poorly drawn. We have a rather large file on him in my department. His time will come, but not the way he thinks." René smiled grimly.

Harvey sauntered in from the kitchenette and, after a mandatory sniff of the policeman's shoes, lay down between them and closed his eyes.

Gordon asked the policeman, "So, I did good?"

"Yes, you did good."

∞   ☼   ∞

A mainstay of the Montréal comics scene, **BERNARD E. MIREAULT** is the creator *Mackenzie Queen*, *Dr. Robot*, and *The Jam*.

# IN THE NAME OF FREE WILL

*A. C. Wise*

HER BONES ACHE with the promise of rain. That's what comes of having them shattered, sawed through, pieces of her pinned like doll parts to the wall of the Freedom Tower. That's what comes of being a message for Captain Freedom, showing him his vulnerability and his inability to protect those he loves. Giving him a reason to suffer. To seek vengeance. To grow into a stronger man.

Bullshit. Utter fucking bullshit.

She flexes stiff fingers. She's been waiting just over an hour, in the park's pre-dawn gloom, outside the glow of lampposts lining the path. Her skin, greyish now, blends with the shadows between trees. Her bones may ache, but death has taught her patience.

When the predator finally passes, he doesn't notice her. These are his hunting grounds— six women so far, their bodies left for hapless joggers to find. Always this park. He's a local, choosing convenience over discretion. So much for don't shit where you eat.

She steps out smoothly behind him, uses his shirt to haul him off balance. Once he's down, she settles her weight over his midsection, knees pinning his arms so he can't reach for any weapons.

She looks him in the eye. Panic turns to a sneer and back again; seeing her, then really seeing her.

She could do it quick and quiet — a knife between the ribs — but she owes him this: looking him in the eye as she chokes the life from him. Because she knows what it feels like to die.

She's strong, another thing death gave her. Force of will, the ability to make a decision and stick to it. The will it takes to come back from the grave, to put yourself back together after you've been cut into pieces and pinned to a wall.

Her cold hands squeeze his throat. He thrashes, fighting to live. She's right there, looking him in the eye as he goes slack.

She stands and wipes her hands on her pant legs. There's only time to step into the shelter of the trees again before the shaking starts, her whole body wracked with violent tremors. She remembers how it felt as her blood left her body, the terror as the world narrowed, then winked out. She knows exactly what she did to the man lying on the pathway behind her, what she took away from him.

Her stomach heaves, bile between chattering teeth. She doubles over, making herself small, fetal. Her vision narrows, tunnelling. She lets it, closes her eyes, breathes shallow and waits. Eventually, the shaking stops.

Good. The sun will be up soon, and she wants to change into clean clothes before the Freedom Squad comes for her.

∞   ☼   ∞

Will is the first into the abandoned warehouse, the silver-white of his suit generating its own luminescence and casting a soft glow around him. Perched on an empty shipping crate, she watches them approach— Captain Freedom, Star Sire, and Fury.

She's surprised it took them this long. She's left three bodies in as many months, and made little attempt to cover her tracks. On the other hand, one body might be a random act of violence, two a coincidence. Three is a pattern, a sign of a deranged mind requiring superheroic intervention. Anything less is beneath the Freedom Squad's notice. Unless a villain makes it personal.

When they draw close enough to see her, but haven't yet, she bangs her heel against the corrugated metal, drawing their attention. Will — Captain Freedom — is the first to look up, the catch in his breath audible.

Even wearing shapeless sweatpants and an oversize grey hoodie, even with the new pallor of her skin and the shadows in the warehouse, she knows she doesn't look that different. He can't fail to recognize her.

"Jenny." Even shocked he says her name the way he always did. Never Jennifer, or even Jen. Always Jenny. "Is it really you?"

"Impossible." Fury speaks almost before Captain Freedom finishes. A moment later, Star Sire's sonorous voice reverberates through the space.

"I sense no deception. She is who she appears to be, though there is…"

"Stop." She cuts them off.

She has no interest in letting them define her; she will tell them what she is, explain her existence on her own terms. Three pairs of eyes shine in the light of Captain Freedom's suit as she drops lightly to the floor.

Fury tenses, hand going to the baton holstered at her hip. Outwardly serene, but eyes watchful behind his domino mask, Star Sire hovers just above the floor, arms crossed. Captain Freedom raises his hand, commanding them to wait.

"I came back," she says, the words plain and unadorned.

She's shorter than any of them, not even counting Star Sire's hovering. But their lithe perfection no longer intimidates her. In death, she has come to accept her body, growing so intimately acquainted with it after putting it back together. Her height, the slight roundness of her hips and waist, her once-glossy hair, her skin, her bones. She fought for every single one of these details; they are precious.

"But how?" Captain Freedom's expression softens. Through the eyeholes of his mask, something almost human shows, a splinter of light she could mistake for genuine pain.

"It's impossible, Jenny. I… held you. I buried you." He falters.

A sudden image intrudes: Will dressed in jeans and a T-shirt, Captain Freedom's persona shed. Icy bare feet tucked under a blanket pressed against her thigh, trying to steal her warmth. She remembers yelping, almost spilling popcorn, before swatting at him them pulling him in for a kiss, bathed in the TV's glow.

The memory— it happened just before she died. How could she have forgotten? Shaken, she steps back, keenly aware of Captain Freedom and the others watching her. She closes her eyes, probing at the fresh sense of loss. What else has been stolen?

She searches, and… There. The edges of the memory, sudden and sharp, snap her eyes wide. The memory isn't hers. It's a jagged shard, inserted into Captain Freedom's life to make her loss more poignant. The moment, if it ever occurred, has no lead-up, and no aftermath but her death. It is one of a series of images, broken free of context and strung together in an arc designed to increase not her pain but Will's. As though her life — that life — had no meaning except where it touched his.

She shakes herself, a faint buzzing haunting the periphery of her hearing. When it fades, the understanding remains, a harsh clarity banishing guilt. She straightens, pulling aside the neck of her sweatshirt to reveal a scar. Captain Freedom gapes; she tugs the sweatshirt back into place.

"I put myself back together," she says. "I changed the story."

"Those men..." Fury says, shattering the tension, finally giving Captain Freedom an excuse to look away.

"I killed them." The words are cold, unflinching in the dark space.

She turns her full attention on Fury, and Fury is the one to look away. Only Star Sire meets her gaze when she shifts to him. There is something unexpected there; perhaps he is acquainted with death, too.

"You have committed a crime." Star Sire's voice echoes, low and deep, only the faintest note betraying him as other than human. Even if he understands her better than the others — perhaps because of it — he has the least sympathy.

"Then you should take me to Freedom Tower." She holds out her wrists.

She turns her attention to Will, challenging. His perfect definition softens toward defeat. Looking away, he touches her arm. His voice is barely a murmur as he guides her into the rain.

"Okay. Let's go."

∞ ☼ ∞

"I brought you chicken pot pie. I know it's... I mean, it was your favorite." Will tries on a smile as he sets a tray on the low table in front of the couch. "I'm sorry that took so long."

"It's okay. Wooster has been keeping me company, catching me up on your exploits." She holds up a tablet, displaying the home screen of the Freedom Squad's customized computer interface.

She's holding herself rigid, perched on the edge of the couch. How did she used to sit? She leans on one elbow, tucking her feet up beside her. Will takes the other end of the couch, keeping a wary distance.

Rather than thinking too hard about whether she's wearing a neutral expression, whether she's remembering to breathe at the right times to set him at ease, she thinks about the other members of the Freedom Squad and the meeting Will's just come from, where they likely discussed her fate. Star Sire doesn't trust her; Fury doesn't either. She occupies the liminal space between prisoner and guest— confined to a comfortable common room with the doors locked, but not actively restrained.

Only Will trusts her unconditionally. Of course he does. She broke his heart by dying, and he wants to believe time has turned backward. He's still looking for some trick, some deception to explain her presence and why she claims to have murdered three men and left their bodies for the Freedom Squad to find.

"You should try it. It's good." Will gestures to the pie.

She pierces the crust releasing steam, and the creamy smell of butter and herbs.

"My mother used to make this for me." She frowns at the memory, sluggish and slow. "She made it the first time I brought you home. You asked for the recipe."

Pictures come with the memory— Will, Captain Freedom, the man who didn't blink when he single-handedly faced down the League of Seven's death squad, brought low by meeting her mother. Palms sweating, nervous, unsure what to do with his hands. And her mother, teasing him, a smile crinkling the corners of her eyes, asking about secret identities and form-fitting costumes.

When he'd finally calmed down enough to appreciate her mother's humour, they'd had a lovely meal. It was the moment she'd known she was in love with Will, wanted to spend the rest of her life with him.

The memories belong to someone else.

She reaches for them, these phantom memories. They are hers, but they aren't. There are gaps. Her life is a book; the page she's on is here and now but preceding pages are nonexistent until she riffles backward through them. And every single page she reads intersects with Will. There is no her without him.

The crackling flaky pastry is dull and tasteless in her mouth. Two conflicting truths exist in her head: she has never tasted this chicken pot pie until now; she remembers her mother pulling it fresh from the oven on a cold winter day. She remembers cheeks chapped red from the cold and oversize mittens. She remembers her aunt's farm on the border of Québec and Ontario, the racket of cats and cousins and noise, and her, an only child.

She remembers the maple tree in her backyard and the swing, the ropes holding it up cutting into the bark. She remembers...

But that version of her — *Jenny* — doesn't exist. Never did. She wants that life. She longs for the bliss of oblivion, for a giant reset button putting everything back the way it used to be.

Knowledge tickles the back of her mind. She could bring it back, that life. She doesn't know how she bent the rules to cheat death, how she understands these things about herself, or Will, and the story that contains them. She simply *knows*, the way the memory of Will in front of the TV, or Will meeting her mother, came to her.

It's tempting to let it go. But then her memories subsume her, the her she is now. The real her. The tiny concerns of Jenny's life — grocery lists, work, evenings with Will, Sunday dinner with her mother — grind against dying, being ripped apart and putting herself back together. This is her story now; she won't let the old narrative catch her up, sweep her along. Even if it could heal her wounds. Even if it could make her fall in love with Will again.

"Thank you, Will." She sets the plate aside.

It's the first time she's spoken his name aloud since coming back. It tastes strange in her mouth— sharper and more immediate than the food.

Questions crowd his eyes. He's taken off the domino mask. The faint glow remains, even out of his costume. He looks like a regular man— maybe a bit handsomer, more defined, but human nonetheless.

"I killed those men, Will." She straightens, meets his eye. "No one forced me to do it. I'm not being mind-controlled. I'm not my own evil clone." ˙

She allows a slight smile at the last. Will flinches as the words hit close to home, but she brushes them away.

"Your methods weren't working. Your methods *don't* work."

She retrieves the tablet and calls up a video from the local news showing the Freedom Squad's takedown of an attempted robbery.

Will is a streak of light in the foreground; Fury a blur of motion pummelling a crook. Star Sire rips out a section of the bank's counter and smashes it across the door to prevent a criminal's escape. Glass shatters, and beyond the window three other members of the Freedom Squad can be seen inadvertently causing a multi-car collision.

"Or this." She flips to video of Zephyr smashing the Red Death through two successive buildings, chunks of concrete raining down, dust filling the air, panicked screams everywhere.

"Or this."

She turns the tablet to show a still photograph of the first victim of the man she executed in the park. The woman's arms are wrapped around a Golden Retriever. She grins at the camera; her cheek is not shattered, bruises don't ring her neck, her body is not lacerated, left to rot beneath a pile of leaves.

The death, the damage, she doesn't show him is her own— her body pinned to the wall of the Freedom Tower. Proto Star, Captain Freedom's nemesis, his opposite, his twin, used endurium bands to hold her in place. A metal only Captain Freedom, or Proto Star himself, could break.

"I don't understand." Will's expression is tight, pained.

She flips back to the second video. "How many people were saved in this fight?"

"Red Death was holding seven hostages, but if we hadn't reached him in time he could have killed dozens."

"And where is he now?"

"In High Gate, maximum-security ward."

"How many times has he been there before?"

Will frowns, forehead creasing. She flips back to the photograph of the smiling woman with the Golden Retriever.

"If you'd caught the man who killed her, would he stand trial?"

Will's frown deepens, but he has an answer this time. "Of course."

She sighs, setting the tablet aside. "Before I killed him, Jackson Penton murdered six women. People like that don't get better. They don't stop unless they're stopped, and prison doesn't cure them. The Red Death has been in and out of High Gate at least thirty-seven times. That's only counting since he became a supervillain and they started putting him in a supposedly inescapable institution."

"If this is about what happened to you…" Will reaches for her hand.

His touch is an electric shock. She can't stop herself from flinching back, doesn't want to. She stares at Will. Can he really not see the larger picture?

His expression is guileless, his eyes wide. Then she sees it — a flash, a spark of color, or the lack of it — something looking out from behind Will's eyes. It's not possession, not mind control, not any of the other supervillain tricks. It's something worse, something much more insidious; the narrative, holding him tight.

But he is oblivious. Beyond the edges of her vision, at the back of her mind, outside the frame, something wants her to give in, to let go.

She wants to shove back, hard, but there's nothing to shove against. She laughs, a low, broken sound made raw and harsh by death. The spark in Will's eyes is gone, replaced by something else. Concern?

She doubles over. She can't breathe. But of course she doesn't breathe anymore. Dirt, six feet of it to be precise, and the worms crawling through it, the rot of leaves, the damp of rain— all of it is inside her, trying to force its way out of her throat with the laugh. It hurts, not like the pain of dying or putting herself back together, but it's the first genuine sensation she's felt since returning. The first thing that's really hers.

"Oh, God. Don't you get it? Even your name is a joke. Captain Freedom. Will? Free Will?"

"Jenny..." He touches her arm, and the sound of his name for her snaps her back. She pulls her arm away, anger returning and cutting off the laughter abruptly.

"Don't call me that. It's not my name. It never was, but especially now."

"What are you talking about?"

She's shaking, the absence of breath a force in itself. Her stiff muscles want to cramp, to lock up. Rigor mortis setting in for good.

"Tell me one thing about me," she says, jaw tight enough to make her teeth ache.

"What?"

"One thing. Go on."

"I..." He falters.

"You can't. I was a prop, meant to bring you pain. I died so you could grow, but have you? Has anything really changed?"

"I don't understand." He reaches for her, stops short.

At the fear in his eyes, she softens, realizing her fingers are curled into fists, her arm trembling with a held-back blow. She forces her muscles to relax, and they answer with a cold ache.

"I killed those men to stop them from hurting other people." She says it as calmly and as evenly as she can; she holds Will's gaze. "I killed them to stop you and the rest of the Freedom Squad from going after them, because it would only make things worse."

Will opens his mouth, but she holds up her hand.

"The car crash outside the bank. No one was killed, but four people were severely injured. One woman may never walk again. Another man owned a small flower shop. The car he was driving that day was his sole means of delivering his product. That man and that woman were the primary sources of income for their families. That's two lives, plus the five lives dependant on them. Just two examples from one single day in the life of the Freedom Squad."

"I didn't know." Will shakes his head, voice hitching.

"No. Of course you didn't." Now it's her turn to touch his hand, cold flesh on warm. "Because it all happens on the edges of your story, and you're the main event."

He looks up sharply, the pain back and real. She feels the twinge again, the regret at the hurt her words are causing. She felt something for him once and called it love. Or some version of her did. Not the one sitting beside him now, but another her without scars and knowledge. Jenny. And just because that isn't her now doesn't mean Jenny's life wasn't real, wasn't valid. If there's time someday, she'll mourn.

She shakes her head. "I'm sorry."

Will looks at her as if he were a wounded animal, not understanding its own pain. If there was some way she could break through, make him see what she sees. The edges. The frame. The narrative driving them, and that the narrative can be subverted, the natural order upset. But she had to die to see it, and Captain Freedom is practically immortal.

"Can we go up on the roof?" she says. "I could use some fresh air."

"I suppose there's no harm." He shrugs, then his shoulders slump. Not just his voice, but his whole body, is weary.

He puts his hands in his pockets; she's both relieved and saddened he doesn't try to take her hand.

There's a breeze coming off the distant river. Up here, above everything, it feels fresh and cool. The sun is starting to set, turning the city fiery gold.

"What will happen to me?" she asks without turning from the view.

Will keeps his gaze on the distant river, winking in the sun. His hands remain in his pockets.

"There'll be a trial. I'll stand as a character witness, do everything I can to get your sentence reduced. If we're very lucky, there's a chance you'll be remanded to my custody for rehabilitation and avoid jail."

She watches him out of the corner of her eye. There is no enthusiasm in his tone. He's broken.

A dull ache settles beneath her breastbone. If there was another way... But there isn't. She knew downstairs in the common room— there is no way to crack through the armor that is Captain Freedom to the humanity underneath. Will's answer now will always be his answer. It's written into the very fabric of his being.

She almost reaches for his hand; she imagines twining her fingers with his inside the depth of his pocket. It's something Jenny would have done. Something she wishes she could do. He turns to face her, surprising her.

"If I could have stopped what happened to you, I would have."

The words strike a blow, steal breath she doesn't have. He believes them, utterly and completely. They are truth for him, irrefutable.

"I know," she says. "And I'm sorry, because that's the point. There is nothing you could have done."

Before she can change her mind, she vaults the railing separating the rooftop from the open sky.

The wind of her falling snatches Will's howl, his shock, trailing in her wake and shredding like ribbons. He can't fly; if he could, he'd save her. His powerlessness, his frustration, is all there. The echo of his cry is a dull ache beneath her skin. There's no wanting great enough, no act of heroism or sacrifice that could keep her from suffering, then or now. It hurts. She was disposable, but not to Will.

Even this knowledge doesn't make it easier to strike the ground.

∞   ☼   ∞

Putting herself back together the second time isn't as bad. Or, rather, it's worse in a different way. Her bones grind wetly inside her skin. She doesn't have the same rage, the endless well of pain to draw upon. Her strength is leeched, wrung out, but she forces herself to keep going, to ignore the threads that slip and tug and whisper at the corner of her mind, telling her to lie down. Rest. Give up.

She has work to do.

Among the news stories Wooster shared with her while she waited for the Freedom Squad to decide what to do with her was a report of another escape from High Gate. Proto Star is on the loose.

∞   ☼   ∞

The man grunts, hot fingers pawing cold flesh. She lies perfectly still, keeping her end of the bargain. As requested, she fixes her gaze on the ceiling, unseeing, maintaining the illusion. It's easier than she imagined, not blinking. His face is a blur at the edge of her vision, her neck canted at an angle as if freshly snapped.

It should bother her, the sick need, the shining fever in the Undertaker's eyes. Instead, she pities him. There's a loneliness beneath his stench of formaldehyde, his funereal clothes. He insisted on telling her his story as they worked out their agreement. The tragedy of his life, the loss of someone he loved, turning him into what he is today. He even looks the part— dark circles beneath his eyes, long, bony hands, nails yellowed.

She only half-listened, focused on the Undertaker's particular fetish: his desire for dead flesh and his need for consent.

A drop hits her cheek, hot for an instant and cooling. She doesn't flinch. The Undertaker weeps, soundless, his body shuddering as his hips jerk in desperate motion. He's seeking something, something he'll never find.

She lets her mind roam, distraction from the pale man and the horror of their deal. After she died, did Will seek comfort, superimposing her memory over Fury's or Zephyr's face? Or maybe he sought out a shapechanging member of the team, an illusion almost good enough to take away the pain.

The thought should bother her, but it doesn't. Even the hurt of Proto Star's continued existence has cooled, becoming something dense and still, buried at her core. He ripped her apart, and Will let him live. He pinned her to a wall, and Will took him to High Gate prison, a facility he'd escaped countless times before.

Where there should be rage, there's only practicality, cutting diamond sharp. If Will couldn't break his code even for her, he'll never change.

So it has to end. It's not about revenge; it's a simple matter of numbers. She will destroy Proto Star to prevent more deaths like hers, more lives existing at the edges of the Freedom Squad's sphere of influence needlessly torn apart. And after she kills Proto Star, she will track down the Red Death, the Task Master. Maybe she will even come back for the Undertaker some day. She will find every member of the Freedom Squad's rogue's gallery and kill them one by one.

The Undertaker grunts, body spasming before going slack. The expression on his face is not ecstasy, but pain. He pulls out of her quickly, turning away to clean himself up. She blinks, finally, and sits up.

While she straightens her clothes, the Undertaker undoes a complicated series of locks on a small case. Molded padding cradles a gun, sleek and black, reflecting the lights. She lifts it, a solid weight fitting comfortably in her hand.

"You're certain this will kill Proto Star?"

The Undertaker flicks a glance at her before looking away, ducking his head under her gaze.

"The bullets are anti-endurium. The only substance that can kill him. If you can get the shot off, it'll do the trick."

"Good."

She fits the gun back into the case and snaps it closed. Her hand is on the door when the Undertaker calls after her.

"Can I see you again?" His voice breaks. She glances over her shoulder; his eyes shine in the dim light, full of need. She lets the door falling shut behind her answer him.

∞    ☼    ∞

Her bones grind and creak as she pulls herself onto a roof from the fire escape. She huffs a deliberate breath, just to feel it. The breath steams, curling visibly. The streets were too close; she surveys the city from above.

Wisps of cloud drag against the moon, pale gold or sick ivory, depending on the angle of view. The city is wide awake, despite the hour— horns blaring, sirens screaming. Girls in needle-thin heels and too-short skirts spill out of a club. Across the street, women wearing everything they own pass a bottle between them.

A jagged landscape of rooftops stretch away from her. She scans the space above them, searching for signs of Proto Star. The main difference between him and Captain Freedom is that Proto Star can still fly. It's a darkness in Will's past, something he was never able to tell her. Terrible as it is, she almost envies him that— a past, a secret. If she wants those, she'll have to make her own. Maybe the Undertaker was her start.

A sound and a voice jolt her from her thoughts. Even if Captain Freedom can't fly, he can still climb.

"Jenny!" Will vaults the wall, landing with a sandpaper scrape.

His glow fills the space around him, blocking out the city lights. His muscles are taut, body poised for action. She should have known he'd follow; truth and justice and all that bullshit. Or love.

"No," she says, and only that.

No more speeches, no more trying to convince Will of anything. It isn't about justice. She isn't a vigilante; she isn't even a villain. It's a simple numbers game. Too many people on the margins get hurt waiting for the Freedom Squad to act.

She pivots, runs for the far side of the roof, pushing stiff muscles as fast as they'll go. There's no fear of the jump. If she falls, she'll put herself back together again. But she doesn't even make it that far. Dead tissue is no match for living matter fuelled by blood and breath and a sense of right.

Will tackles her. They go down hard. He's quick, but she's strong, and her strength is unexpected. She pushes away, catching him off guard long enough to stand. He grabs her arm, gripping hard.

"I don't want to hurt you, Jenny." Will's eyes are bright, the line of his mouth beneath the mask grim.

She yanks free, considers taking a swing. Could she, now, bruise even Captain Freedom's perfect jaw? Does she want to? He's been nothing but kind to her. He deserves better— better than her, better than this world.

She takes a step, and the ground drops out from beneath her. Disoriented, she falls upward. Hands grip her shoulders;

her feet kick free over the rooftops and streetscape below. She twists, looking up. Proto Star is carrying her as easily as a doll. Will shouts behind her.

"Bring her back, you fiend! Let her go!"

"My pleasure." And Proto Star lets her slip a few inches, before catching her again. She doesn't gratify him with a scream.

Instead, she's thinking how Will's language has shifted him farther away from humanity. The raw pain, the confusion, her chances of reaching him have spooled back inside him, tucked within his armor, and not a crack shows. He's playing out his role now, and so is Proto Star.

She swings her dead weight, building momentum with the movement of her legs. Confused, Proto Star's flight dips erratically. That she is actually trying to fall is unexpected enough that he lets her go. She hits one of the flat rooftops, remembers to tuck and roll. She comes up, ready to fire when Proto Star lands.

But somehow, impossibly, Will is there too. He jerks her arm and the shot goes wide. A bolt of light that is every color and no color at once sizzles into the building behind Proto Star. Another scar for the city.

The three of them stand in a perfect tableau as the gun whines, recharging.

"Jenny, don't," Will says.

"Jenny." Proto Star narrows his eyes, recognition dawning and turning his expression to gloating delight. "Welcome back."

He is the dark mirror of Captain Freedom, his aura shadow, but still managing to shine. His costume even mimics Will's— form-fitting and all of a piece, but a sullen gunmetal shade. And he wears a cape. Otherwise, they are identical in almost every way.

"How did it feel?" Proto Star cocks his head, voice silky.

She shrugs, bones shifting, bringing a dull throb to give lie to her words. "I've felt worse."

And then it comes for her, the thing that is worse.

The tendrils of the narrative bury themselves in her brain, breaking her, making her small, stripping away the dead shell that nothing can penetrate. Knowledge spirals up— a black thread like smoke, tasting of bile.

"A baby. Oh God, Will, there was going to be a baby." The words slip out as she crashes to her knees.

She doesn't want a baby, but Jenny did.

Fractured images come hard and fast, slices of her life sharp enough to cut. Not her life, someone's life— laid out between frames. The warmth of Will's body, slotted against hers, arm around her waist as they look down into a crib. Milky warmth as her lips brush the child's downy head.

Everything unravels from her— the child's first step, first day at school, first kiss, first love, graduation, starting a family, all going on forever. But not. Cut short. The thread snapped with her death, with her body ripped apart and her bones shattered.

The loss tears at her, a hole going all the way through, like her entire being is the absence left in the wake of a pulled tooth. She cannot sob, has no tears, and the pain is all the worse for it.

The gun almost drops as her arms go slack, her body slumping and trying to melt into the rooftop. Will calls her name from far away. She sees her loss echoed, confusion and betrayal. Something raw and primal rips out of Will. He tears his mask off, scrubs at his eyes.

Proto Star watches, a slight smile playing at his lips, enjoying his enemy's pain.

She blocks him out. Will reaches for her, hand trembling. He is nearly broken, and through the cracks there's hope. It would be so easy to take his hand, let him pull her into his arms, share his warmth, share their pain, lessening and doubling it by half. They could grieve together.

His grip is firm against hers. Her legs wobble as she stands. He reaches his other hand for the gun, palm up.

"We'll fix this. We'll find a way. I swear."

She wants to believe him. The flickering play of emotions across her strong features seems almost human. And yet, and yet.

The threads of the narrative are hungry at the edges of her vision. The baby that never was, never will be, is one more piece of collateral damage. In the images forced into her mind lie a myriad of other possibilities. Tarnished, dull, but still reflective— other realities, other ways the story could have gone.

If it wasn't her standing beside Will, it would be someone else, some other shard of pain driven jaggedly into Captain Freedom's heart. That's the way the story goes, the way it always goes. Wounds scar. They heal. Memory remains, a ghost beneath the surface as a new future opens up before him. Then the wounds reopen, a fresh trauma made worse by the burden of the past. Over and over, Captain Freedom is hollowed out, broken and remade.

But the debris, like her, is left to remake itself. Or it is swept under the rug, forgotten.

She pulls her hand out of Will's, glances at Proto Star, who leers at her, waiting. The calculation is simple. She looks back to Will, meets his eyes. Her regret is genuine.

"I'm sorry, Will," she says, and pulls the trigger.

∞  ✿  ∞

The prolific short-fiction writer and editor **A. C. WISE** is a Montréal expat currently living in the USA.

# NUCLEAR NIKKI VERSUS THE MAGIC EVIL

*Jennifer Rahn*

**NUCLEAR NIKKI STRUTTED** her stuff across the Dead End Causeway and into Magic Eddie's 8-Ball Bistro and Magnetic Disco Pub. Her orange, six-inch stilettos clacked loudly against the tile, guaranteeing she'd be turning the heads of many a punter. She struck a pose just inside the door, one knee bent outward to ensure her silhouette showed off her legs and the fact she was wearing a ridiculously short skirt along with a cape that did nothing for warmth, and a few other things that didn't go far in the realm of practicality. Her current reality had degraded from superhero to superwhore— one little mistake in her battle with Monstrous Maxie five years ago had wiped out her superpowers.

Her eyes adjusted quickly to the dimness: six or seven men were hunched over tables. A few of them glanced up before returning to their beers and card games. The muted thud of a disco beat wafted from the back, not disturbing the dull inertia of the room. Nikki pushed down a wave of panic and sauntered over to the bar, flipping back her curly wig to make sure it didn't cover her breasts.

Mango Joe didn't bother serving her a drink, which enraged her because she hated being ignored, and was a relief since she didn't have much credit. Only three more chits remained on her colony card. Once those were gone, she'd have to get off this hellhole whether she wanted to or not.

She glanced around the room and saw Savage Bill staring at her with that trademark hint of smugness playing around his lips. He had a cowboy name but dressed nothing like one.

If anything, "Disco Bob" might have suited him better: white tux, no shirt, gold chains, tacky tats and blond hair slicked straight up. He leaned back as if he were all that, and slowly reached into his shirt pocket to draw out a card with five chits on it, which he loosely dangled from finger and thumb, letting it swing so that Nikki's eyes followed it. She didn't like Bill, no one did, because he didn't ever play fair, not even by supervillain standards, and the last time she'd taken him on, he'd left bruises that had hurt her business for over a week. But in three days those five chits would pretty much be a stay of execution. She slid off the bar stool and clacked over to where he sat.

"Where'd you get so many?" she asked, jutting her chin toward the card.

"What do you care, hon? I got 'em, you need 'em, and that's that. You'll do whatever I want, Sugarpie."

Couldn't argue with him. Nikki wasn't able to wipe the dislike off her face as she let him lead her out of the bar, but then Bill already knew the score and it wasn't like she was trying to win over a patron who'd keep her on for a while.

Bill dumped her in a back alley when he was finished, her hosiery ruined, wig gone, one of her shoes broken — but none of her bones this time — leaving her to wipe the blood from her mouth with the back of her hand that tightly clutched the card of chits. Normally she'd charge a month's worth for that kind of service, but paying clients were pretty slim pickings these days. She got up from her knees and stumbled along with her broken heel until she slipped in the muck draining through the alley and whacked her head against a dumpster. Before she blacked out, she had just enough awareness to hope the pavement wouldn't further wreck her face.

∞     ☼     ∞

Nikki woke up in a plasticast basement with weak daylight trickling through the slit of a window near the low ceiling. Father Mike was busy by his little camp stove, boiling something he was probably going to make her drink. He wore a heavy apron, gloves, and goggles; the leftovers of his former supervillain costume. He'd once terrorized the universe with his psionic superpowers; now he was trying to make amends by bringing salvation to the fallen supers in this backwater outpost.

"My chits!" She ran her hands over where her pockets should have been and felt around on the sheets covering the couch.

"What? These?" Father Mike shoved his goggles up on his head and held out the clear plastic card that now had a bloody smear across it. "They're fake. They're just breath mints glued onto an empty card. Honestly, Nikki, you know better than to trust Savage Bill. Why did you go with him?"

She wanted to say something tough, but instead burst into tears. Father Mike brought over the tea and sat down next to her. "Maybe now you're ready to take that pet rescue job I lined up for you?" he asked.

Nikki shook her head. "They only pay two chits per week. What's the point?"

"Well, it's part-time work. You'd have to also take other positions." He wouldn't let her push the cup away. "Drink it. There are painkillers in it."

She took a few sips, then gingerly stood, wanting to spend her last futile days of misery in private.

"Thanks, Mike," was all she could manage. His face fell and he hovered around her helplessly as she shrugged back into her cape and picked up her things.

"I wish there was more I could do to help." He fingered his own card of chits thoughtfully.

"Keep 'em," she said. "There's no point. And thanks for all you were able to do."

She trudged back to street level, holding her useless shoes by the straps and walking barefoot along the deserted promenade. The morning bells chimed, signifying the start of another workday. Right on cue, thousands of TinHead drones shot into the sky, monitoring the weather, checking stability of infrastructure, and scanning for garbage, both the regular and the human kind. One of the TinHeads skimmed toward her on its hover jets. She held out her card to let the inquisitive robot pluck a chit from its surface, and got her stay permit updated for another day. She wandered aimlessly, feeling too empty to head back to her scruffy flat and get cleaned up so she could find some new clients.

Caught up in her misery, she didn't notice the tail until she was halfway across the skywalk, too far away from anywhere she could run and hide. Resigned, she turned to face her stalker, probably a villain intent on stealing her last two chits.

She'd attracted the only supervillain in the colony who was full-goose crazy. Rodeo Rick had wandering yellow eyes, which matched his pants and gawdawful neckerchief, but not his stupid purple boots or lasso. He had a rep in the villainous circles as being into the demonic stuff. She hoped he wasn't in the mood to beat her up as well as rob her. He hung onto the railing as he shuffled toward her, his stringy hair and manic grin a complete mess.

"Nuclear Nikki?" he asked as he came near.

"Yeah?" she answered.

He giggled annoyingly. "Have I a job for *you*."

"You're contracting *me*?" she asked skeptically. "Right."

"No, no. Really. I'll even pay you."

She tiredly raised an eyebrow. "How much?"

"A year's worth."

"You don't have that much, and I don't do villains." That was a lie, but Rodeo Rick creeped her out even more than Savage Bill did. She turned to leave.

"Oh, but I do have that much." He jogged around in front of her, panting like an idiot. "Here, I'll even pay you half in advance." He pushed six cards into her hand. She held them close to her face and squinted at them carefully. They were real.

"What do you want?"

"Turn a trick on a supervillain."

She sighed. "Where? Here?"

He almost seemed normal for a few seconds as he threw back his head and laughed. "Oh, not *me*. Never, ever *me*."

"You want me to do someone else?"

"*Yesssss.*"

He pulled something out of each pant pocket, presenting the item in his right hand first. Nikki plucked the translucent yellow stone from his palm and looked at it curiously. "Swallow it," he instructed. When she hesitated, he added, "I've *paid* you."

She put the hard object in her mouth, feeling it soften and slide past her tongue easily. Warm as it went down, it wriggled in her esophagus, then stuck somewhere in her chest, as if it had slid around her heart. "What is this?" she asked.

"Look! Look!" Rodeo Rick hopped as he pointed at her knees.

Nikki glanced down, looked back at him, then at her knees again. Were they healing? She rubbed her fingers against the broken skin, finding the torn edges were disappearing and seeing the bruises lighten as she probed the holes in her stockings. The stone was giving her a real superpower.

"Where'd you get this?"

He ignored the question and crept back toward her, holding out an old-fashioned perfume bottle. Made of pink crystal, it was topped by a gold spray atomiser with a little pink tube connected to a little pink bulb with a perfect pink tassel. When she took it, he jerked his hands back and wiped them on his jacket.

"Be careful," he advised. "It's perfume."

"I can see that."

"Okay, here is your job. You go see him," he handed her a card with an address on it— Hawthorne Mansion, "and make sure, make ssssuuuurrrre, you have the perfume sprayed on your shoulders. Especially the neck area. He likes to kiss there, okay?" He had been pointing at her neck and shoulders as he spoke, but now wiped his hands on his jacket again. "Just dust it on lightly, not too much, or it will kick in too fast. And then that's it."

"And then you give me another six months," Nikki reminded him.

"Yes, of course I will."

He ran off, but since she now had six months of time, she relaxed. She could take one day for herself, indulge in some new clothes, maybe even a facial. Father Mike would definitely be getting one of these cards, especially if she had six more coming.

∞     ☼     ∞

Six o'clock. Nikki presented herself at Hawthorne Mansion, which unlike the other colony-side places with pretentious names, actually was a mansion. She wondered who would have enough money and political influence to land such an extravagant home, or for that matter why the villains always got the nice places. The steel gate opened onto a cobblestone pathway that led through a real garden. She sauntered up to the front door, feeling confident in her new blue silk bodysuit and stiletto boots, not to mention the blond hair extensions she'd had put in just that morning. Little makeup had been required, seeing as how the yellow stone had taken care of most of the damage. She didn't much care for the scent of the perfume she'd been given, but what the customer wants, the customer gets, and after a while it kind of made her lightheaded, in a good way.

She rang the bell, letting her finger press the button a little longer than necessary, before striking her customary pose as the security cameras swivelled toward her. After several moments, the door opened. Nikki's heart flipped as she recognized Rodeo Rick's buddy as DethKode, the top dog in supervillainy these days. She was surprised he'd live out in the open, but now it made sense why double R wanted to buy him a treat— getting on his good side would definitely have advantages. DethKode looked like some kind of demonic nerd, staring at her from his half-hidden position behind the half-opened door. He was wearing the obligatory paraphernalia, from crushed red velvet suit to the upside-down gothic cross around his neck. He was starvation-skinny, his dark hair hung limply around his pale face and his beard was shaved into one of those styles that made the chin look extra pointy. Very retro. Scrolling numbers glowed from the computer screens lining the walls behind him.

Nikki inspected him slowly, smiling at how much it discomfited him. "Hi. Your friend sent me over." She handed him the address card she'd been given.

He took it with impossibly thin fingers and examined it closely before staring at her again. "Who was it?" he asked.

Nikki might have been reduced to turning tricks, but she wasn't in the mood for doing villains any extra favours. Since Rodeo Rick hadn't said to name him as benefactor, she decided to leave that detail out. "He never gave me his name. You know how it is in this business, Sugar. But guess what? He paid half your bill, so this is only going to cost you half a month of chits." She pulled down the zipper on the front of her bodysuit and stepped toward him, still smiling, actually enjoying herself. He let her in. He probably hadn't had any in a long while, because he got into it as soon as the door was closed; as promised, he really seemed to like her neck and shoulders.

He may have bitten her a few times, Nikki couldn't quite remember. Maybe she bit him back. She was flying high by that time, even though she couldn't remember what they'd been smoking, or if they'd shot something up along the way to a couch somewhere in the third, computer-stuffed living room. Everything was black, red, or silver, but that just made her laugh. She thought DethKode was having a good time too, since he didn't slow down all evening.

She had no idea how she got home. But there was a full card of chits stuffed in her pocket when she checked. Dethy had given her a tip. He'd probably also called her a cab.

She wasn't feeling any of the euphoria from yesterday. Her head hurt and her back and neck were stiff. At some point, her new blond hair extensions had been pulled out. She fed a chit into the autoslot to prevent the TinHeads from bashing down her door, then pulled off her clothes with her eyes shut and stepped into the shower.

The hot water stung her skin. Swearing, Nikki shut it off and peeled open her eyes to stare at the mirrored interior of the shower. Patches of her skin had turned black; darkness had spread around her neck and under her chin, where she had sprayed the perfume. Nauseated, she rubbed at her chest to get the lump in her throat to settle. She felt a rush of warmth flow from the stone at her heart through the area of her blackened skin. The dark spots didn't fade, but suddenly they hurt a little less. She quickly finished her morning routine and sprayed over the spots with makeup.

She got a few offers on her way to see Father Mike, which she politely declined with waves and kisses, hoping she wouldn't regret it five months from now. Having a choice felt good. Mike wasn't home, so she headed for the downtown soup kitchens, wanting to pass along the chit card she'd mentally promised him, and to thank him for standing by her for so very long, even when she hardly ever followed his advice.

Downtown was closed off by numerous police transports, which forced small vehicles and pedestrians to take the skyroute. Nikki jostled along with the crowd and was shoved aside by an excited group of teenagers headed in the opposite direction. She turned her head as they passed, amused that they seemed to buy their clothes at the same place as DethKode. They were talking loudly.

"They said he was with a superhooker. They're looking for her now."

"Who said?"

"The cops."

"Are they sure he's dead?"

"Not just dead, decimated."

"Lies. He can't be dead. His defenses wouldn't let some chick kill him."

Nikki tried to stop, but the press of the crowd wouldn't let her. She finally managed to push her way to the edge of the sky-route and looked out toward Hawthorne Mansion. Ambulances surrounded the doorway, but she could see the paramedics dragging something out the front door. She stepped back into the flow of people and pushed her way into the nearest coffee shop. The media feed showed DethKode looking like he'd been dead for fifty years. He was a crumbly, brown skeleton, recognizable only by his hair, clothes, and the silver gothic cross sunken into his chest. The feed flipped to a view of the destroyed interior of the mansion, which looked like someone had taken a quantum hull shredder to it. The police handout of the suspect showed a blurry security still of Nikki in her blond extensions and blue bodysuit, describing her as an ubervillain who'd taken out the biggest supervillain in the colony.

Nikki swallowed hard, glad she was no longer a blonde or even long-haired and that she'd chosen to wear red today. No longer daring to go to the soup kitchens, she paid for a trans-port home and texted Father Mike that she needed to talk to him when he got in. She sat for a long while with her head in her hands, unable to make sense of what had happened. She probably wouldn't have moved from that position if someone hadn't decided to break into her apartment.

"Alice, get lost!" She picked up one of her shoes and threw it at the intruder who'd picked her lock. Awesome Alice — another fallen superhero junkie superwhore — ducked and came in anyway.

"You've got some. Why don't you share? Bitch!"

"I have not." She wasn't about to give *any* chits to Alice.

"How'd you afford this, then?" she held up the bottle of perfume.

"When did you take that? Did you break in before?"

"Of course I did. I have to because you never share."

"Neither do you." Nikki sat back down on the bed, feeling too exhausted to chase Alice out. She'd leave when she was done being annoying. Tomorrow, Nikki was changing the locks.

"So where'd you get it?" Awesome Alice moved over to the mirror and threw her hair back over her shoulder in preparation to spray her neck with the perfume.

"None of your damn business."

Alice sprayed her neck liberally with the bottle, then set to primping herself in the mirror.

"Oh wow," she said after a few moments.

"You're not that hot," Nikki replied.

"No, I mean, what's in that bottle? Did you spike it with something? I feel ... so ... like I'm high or something."

"Good for you."

"It's burning! It's itching!"

"I didn't tell you to put it on. You're probably allergic"

"You bitch! You deliberately planted that because you knew I'd steal it! Why didn't you just leave me some chits?" Awesome Alice ran out of the door, not stopping to slam it shut behind her.

Nikki thought, *And why would I leave you chits?* She got up and had almost closed the door when a terrified scream echoed from the hallway. *It's just Alice raising a fuss*, she thought, but more voices started up, and someone shouted to call the cops— a useless gesture; in this colony they existed solely to protect and serve the supervillains in charge. Nikki cautiously stepped into the hallway.

She could see what was left of Alice. Her neck had withered to a brown, brittle stump, and her head had snapped off and rolled into the far corner until it rested by the mailboxes, leaving behind a gooey dark streak.

Nikki backed away, stumbling into her apartment; she quietly closed and locked the door. On her dresser sat the bottle of perfume. Moving over to the mirror, she pulled the scarf from her neck and rubbed off the makeup. Only dull red patches remained and they were shrinking. She picked up the perfume, smelled it, then tasted it. Numbness spread across her tongue, but it wasn't like any narcotic she'd ever done before. Why hadn't it killed her? As if in answer, warmth flowed from the yellow stone in her chest.

The euphoria kicked in quickly this time, shooting through her brain like electric heroin. All she could think about was the bottle of perfume, all her hands would reach for even as she tried to resist. *Damn*, but she wanted more of it. Staring at her reflection in the mirror, she pointed the atomizer at her throat and squeezed the bulb. The fine mist dampened her skin, feeling cold for a few seconds, the euphoria escalating as she breathed it in.

Things eventually got really cold— and painful. Nikki opened her eyes and found herself on the bed, shivering. The light from her small window had changed from sunlight to streetlamps and she felt simultaneously ravenous and nauseated.

Father Mike must have gotten her message, because he was here now, a freaked-out expression on his face. Nikki lost it then, her shivering becoming full-body convulsions. Her hands were grey claw things that lashed out at Father Mike. Terrifying growling noises erupted from somewhere. Her throat? Father Mike pushed her down and wound rope around something — maybe her — as he kept repeating the same thing: "Anima Christi, sanctifica me. Corpus Christi, salve me. Sanguis Christi, inebria me. Aqua lateris Christi, lava me. Passio Christi, conforta me. O bone Iesu, exaudi me."

The words triggered a deep, throbbing pain in chest, close to her heart. No, it wasn't the words. Father Mike was using the incantation to channel his superpowers— the powers he'd vowed never to use again. The pain writhed around inside her like a snake until it finally erupted through her chest. The shivering subsided and her body felt like it was shrinking, or deflating.

"Dear God! Finally!" Father Mike left her for a moment to fetch some washcloths. Nikki rolled over and tried to sit up, but found it hurt too much. One of her wrists really was tied to the bed. She looked down, shocked to see that her skin had been lacerated. Her chest hurt, and something hard was rolling around in her shirt. She pressed a hand against it, seeing the yellow stone she had swallowed drop from her bodice. It landed in her palm, covered in blood. Nikki peeked down her shirt and saw the thing had forced its way right through her skin. She quickly closed her fingers over it as Father Mike returned with the cloths and gently began to wipe the mess off her face and clean her wounds.

"What happened?" she rasped at him, although she already knew; the stone and perfume had given her superpowers.

Mike looked shaken, pale, and weepy. He wouldn't make eye contact as he carefully cut through the rope around her wrist.

"You were saying *things*, Nikki. It was not your voice. I don't know exactly... what..." He started crying. Nikki stared at him in amazement, forgetting her pain long enough to sit up and put an arm around him. She looked around the room, dismayed to see that it looked as if someone had taken a laser cutter to the walls— just like at Hawthorne Mansion. Father Mike shuddered in her arms.

"Hey..." she said to him softly.

"You were doing things ... I don't know ... what..."

She looked down at herself again. "I did this?"

Father Mike nodded, trying to get his sobs under control.

"Ugh, I'm so sorry, Mike. I took some really bad drugs. It was stupid of me. I just— I need to not make such bad choices."

Father Mike peered at her through his tear-stained goggles, clearly struggling to accept a rational explanation, as it now seemed to Nikki that he'd been trying to exorcise her. He was teetering, wanting to believe it was just a really bad trip.

"I got some money, you know? I wanted to celebrate. I just shouldn't have. Here, look. These are for you." She dug the cards out of her pockets and pressed one into his hand. He stared at it like it was some disgusting dead thing and held it out to her, shaking his head.

"It's okay, Mike, I won't do it again. I promise. I only had one dose, and it's gone now, really, it's okay. Thank you so much for taking care of me. I don't know what I'd do without you."

She hugged him close, and he let her, finally relaxing with a heavy sigh.

"Please, *never* do that again."

"I won't. I promise."

After a while he pulled away from her seeming embarrassed at having been less than fatherly.

"Well, I'm glad you're all right. I guess I'll be going. I'm a bit tired." He fiddled with the card of chits she'd given him. "I don't want to take these..."

"But you need them," Nikki said gently. "It's okay to take them. If it's okay for you to keep giving to everyone else, why isn't it okay for someone to give something to you?"

"Right. Thank you." He smiled weakly. "You rest, then. I'll let myself out."

Nikki lay back with the yellow stone clutched in her fist, staring at the ceiling as she listened to Father Mike's footsteps fade. She unbuttoned her shirt and looked at the hole in her chest. It looked like a gunshot wound but only oozed feebly. The stone must have still been healing her, even on its way out.

She dozed fitfully for days, only getting up to feed chits into the autoslot, or take a few bites of supplibars. The yellow stone and perfume bottle sat on her dresser. Throwing them away would probably not be safe. She put the bottle in the shower, thinking if she diluted it enough, maybe it couldn't hurt anyone— or she might end up poisoning the entire colony.

A slow knocking sounded at her door, sending chills up Nikki's spine. Opening the door a crack, she saw Rodeo Rick leering at her, but now he wore all dark blue, and seemed much more in control of himself. He stood calmly with his hands behind his back, and none of his idiotic laughter. He had combed his hair and slicked it back, corporate-style. She pulled the door open a bit farther and leaned against it.

"Hello," she said.

"I see the stone's come out on its own. I'm sorry about your face. If the stone had stayed where it was supposed to, it would have protected you."

"It's all right," she replied, not wanting to mention Father Mike.

"Here's the rest of what I promised you." He held out to her six more cards of chits.

"Thank you." She took the cards and started to close the door, but he put out a hand to stop her. He was a lot stronger than Nikki expected. He looked completely different— still crazy but much more dangerous.

"I'll have my stone and perfume back," he said and pushed his way inside. Nikki backed up, trying to think if she had anything she could use as a weapon hidden in her apartment. *Only the metal pipe, hidden under the bed.* She mourned her long-lost superpowers.

"Hey, what was that stuff, anyway?" she asked.

"Exactly what you needed to get the job done. And it was nicely done, I must say." Rodeo Rick picked up the stone from her dresser, contemplating it as he rubbed it with his fingers. He pursed his lips with a hint of a smile and turned toward her. "Father Mike? Is he your friend who removed this from you?"

"What are you talking about? It came out of my chest and was sitting there when I woke up."

"Oh, I very much doubt that. You see, this stone is subject to control. *My* control. I'm the only one who gets to decide where this goes, and where it stays. Or doesn't stay. You understand? And *I* control the person who swallows it." He tapped the air with the stone as he spoke. "I *paid* you," he reminded her. "But *Father Mike* removed my control over you, and that interfered with my *business*. So it seems I now have a problem with your friend Father Mike."

Nikki shook her head. "He didn't do anything!"

"Sure he did. He made you get hurt. All of that would have healed," he gestured toward Nikki's body with the hand that held the stone, "if he'd left this where it was supposed to be."

She tried to shut down her fear and turn on the charm. Whether as a superhero or as a hooker, she'd faced men who'd terrified her a hundred times before. *This wasn't any different,* she told herself.

"Hey, that doesn't matter," she said, trying to smile. "We don't need to worry about that."

In a flash he was across the room and next to her, catching her by the neck with a hand that seemed too large, with fingernails that were too sharp. "You should worry. Now tell me, girl, where is the perfume?"

"Alice stole it."

"And you think you can lie to me. I don't need to ask you verbally."

Nikki struggled against the pressure he was applying to her throat. As her vision dimmed, she could feel his thoughts forcing their way into her mind. She tried not to think about Father Mike, but of course that's what she did, picturing his home, his face, his funny offworlder clothes. Rodeo Rick immediately rifled through her thoughts, trying to see if she had given Mike the perfume bottle. Nikki was blacking out and couldn't think straight. No, she hadn't given Mike any perfume. She had given him something...

Trying to remember, she pictured Mike the last time she'd seen him, but mostly remembered his voice. *Anima Christi, sanctifica me. Corpus Christi, salve me. Sanguis Christi, inebria me. Aqua lateris Christi, lava me. Passio Christi, conforta me. O bone Iesu, exaudi me.*

Rodeo Rick faltered. A kernel of Father Mike's influence lingered inside Nuclear Nikki. The path he'd created to force out the perfume-induced demon had left an open portal to the power he'd used. She concentrated on the words, hope flaring inside her as she became a channel for Father Mike's universe-altering superpowers. *Anima Christi, sanctifica me. Corpus Christi, salve me. Sanguis Christi, inebria me. Aqua lateris Christi, lava me. Passio Christi, conforta me. O bone Iesu, exaudi me.*

"No!" He recoiled from the words, letting go of Nikki's neck and shoving her away. She fell next to the bed.

with you?" She elegantly stepped over Rodeo Rick as he feebly clutched at her, twisted her ankle from his grasp and picked up the yellow stone and bottle of perfume from where she'd hidden it in the shower.

She went for a walk. She smiled graciously at any potential clients, but for some reason, after seeing the bleeding guy shambling along behind her, they all backed away, scurrying into the shadows. She tossed him a glance over her shoulder. He was going to *try* to get the stone back from her, and probably knew how. Something would have to be done about that.

Nuclear Nikki strutted her stuff across the Dead End Causeway and into Magic Eddie's 8-Ball Bistro and Magnetic Disco Pub. There sat Savage Bill, all smiles, and too full of himself to realize that she had changed. She was all powered up. He still had his stupid white tux and stupid little card of fake chits dangling between his fingers, thinking he was tempting some stupid whore who was desperate to get them. Thinking he could get Nikki to fall for that twice.

"Hey baby, I got 'em and you need 'em," he actually said.

Nikki smiled and sauntered over to where he sat.

"Sure, baby. I've got something for you, too."

"What's that?" he said, his tone clearly saying anything she could possibly have would be completely uninteresting.

"Just a little bit of candy. Try it. Tastes like honey-lemon-liquid-love."

Nikki took the magic yellow stone from her purse and pushed it into his mouth. He pawed at his throat as it slid down to his heart, then took a deep breath and looked up at her as she sprayed him in the face with the perfume. She gave him a strong dose of it so that the transformation would occur quickly. He tried to speak, but his voice devolved into growls. Nikki knew he wanted to ask what was going to happen, so she answered him.

"You're gonna do whatever I want, Sugarpie. And you can start by ridding me of him." She stepped aside so that Savage Bill could see Rodeo Rick coming up behind her with his broken face and Nikki's metal pipe in his hand. Rodeo Rick saw Bill and suddenly didn't look so sure about getting his stone back.

A few of the punters looked up, leaving their cards at the tables and shrinking into the dull inertia of the room. Super

*Move, Nikki!* She grabbed the pipe from under her be[d]
ran at Rodeo Rick, swinging wildly. She felt it connect[ed]
enough force to jar her elbow, making her drop the pip[e]
stumble away. She blinked several times before she wa[s]
to make out his slumped form on the floor, his face sm[ashed]
up and blood pooling under his head.

She laughed, although none of this was funny. [Father]
Mike's words still ran through her head like some backg[round]
soundtrack. She spoke the incantation out loud, amaze[d]
she could remember the words when they had no mean[ing to]
her, then said it again, and again, holding on to the rem[nant]
traces of Father Mike's powers.

On the floor, Rodeo Rick twitched and shudder[ed.] [His]
body flipped over; something worked its way out of hi[s]
Nikki said the incantation again, until a black stone, [pulsing]
with energy as the yellow one had, forced its way out, [up]
through his skin and the cloth of his shirt. She edged [to]
cautiously pick it up. Rodeo Rick came to, blearily turn[ing his]
head from side to side as he tried to make out where [he was.]
His eyes focused on the stone held by Nikki's finge[rs and fear]
instantly crossed his face. He made a grab for the sto[ne and]
for Nikki's ankles when she scrambled away. She trip[ped and]
fell, her chin painfully scraping the plasticast floor.

"Give it back!" he yelled, clawing his way up her c[lothing.]

By reflex, she popped the stone in her mouth. As sh[e did]
she thought about what had happened when she'd sw[allowed]
the yellow stone.

This one was much more powerful. Rodeo Rick gave [a]
little moan as his strength left him, funnelling into Nik[ki. "I]
have that stone *back*," he gurgled through his broken [mouth. He]
reared up on his knees, momentarily frozen, and then c[ollapsed.]

Yesterday, Nikki would have been afraid. She wo[uld have]
huddled in a corner, stuffing pantyhose into her mou[th so]
she wouldn't scream.

Today, Nuclear Nikki breathed in deeply, tasting t[he power]
that ran giddily through her veins, laughing like an idi[ot at how]
easy it would be to do whatever she wanted, to whom[ever she]
wanted, and whenever she wanted. It was a rush.

"Oh, my, my, my." Nikki took her time, dressin[g in her]
favorite bits of clothing, wiping on heaps of lip gl[oss, lus-]
ciously pulling on red, thigh-high boots. "Whatever [

Savage Bill was ultra-charged with violence and smiling his evil grin wider than usual as he stood to greet his new prey.

Nikki smiled at her reflection in the mirror behind the bar. Ubervillain indeed. Moving into Hawthorne Manor would suit her *nicely*.

∞   ☼   ∞

Calgary writer **JENNIFER RAHN** is the author of two novels published by Dragon Moon Press.

# SPIRIT IN THE CLAY

*Bevan Thomas*

AS THE GUNS *rat-a-tat-tat*-ed and the bombs fell, I was over the hill with the rest of my unit, racing toward the enemy. My sergeant yelled something and close-by someone else screamed, but I kept on going, firing my submachine gun again and again. I don't know if I hit anyone, I didn't know who was alive or who was dead. I just kept firing as the ground exploded around me, as the whole world seemed to break in half.

With my last breath, I tried to recite the Shema: "*Shema Yisrael, Adonai Eloheinu, Adonai Ech*—" And then silence. Darkness.

A light! It was bright like the sun yet I could stare at it without hurting my eyes. The more I stared at the light, the more relaxed I felt. It was getting bigger and bigger— no, I was getting closer. I was going into the light. I was going… home.

Suddenly there was a crash like a giant window shattering, and the light blinked out. I was falling! Falling through the darkness as if I were inside some inescapable tornado! Swirling and swirling in the darkness! Swirling and swirling and swirling and—

"Do I have the honour of addressing Corporal Daniel Druker of the Royal Hamilton Light Infantry?" The voice penetrated the silence, clear as a bell, and the darkness dissolved.

I seemed to be floating in the middle of a room, above a large round table. The room was dark, though I could make out five human silhouettes seated around the table, linking hands so that their arms formed a sort of five-pointed star. A single candle was in the middle of the table; I hovered above its flame.

"Do I have the honour of addressing Corporal Daniel Druker of the Royal Hamilton Light Infantry?" It was one of the five at the table who repeated these words. Unlike the others, he was now glowing, which enabled me to see him.

He was a balding old man with grey hair and a black suit. The sort of man one sees every day. He could have been a lawyer or a banker approaching retirement, except for his glowing aura and the energy I could sense crackling behind his eyes. And except that I recognized that face, that voice— from the radio, the newspapers, the newsreels.

"I am William Lyon Mackenzie King, Prime Minister of Canada," the figure said. "And I will ask again, oh wandering spirit: do I have the honour of addressing Corporal Daniel Druker of the Royal Hamilton Light Infantry?"

"Yes," I said.

"Excellent!" The Prime Minister beamed. "Doubtless you are wondering what has happened."

"I remember the sound of guns and bombs. I was— I think I was in France."

"Yes, you were."

"And then I was in darkness, heading toward a light."

"Yes, you were."

"Was I— did I die?" I asked.

"Yes, you did," the Prime Minister replied. "I apologize sincerely for drawing you back to the material plane, away from your eternal rest. But your country still needs you."

"What?"

"You are confused. I will try to explain. I am a spiritualist; that is not something I share with most people. I can commune with the spirits of the departed, 'ghosts' if you will, and with other spirits besides. This has proven of pivotal importance in our current crisis— this world war is being fought on far more fronts than most people realize. The artificial monstrosities grown by Josef Mengele's mad scientists, the diabolic sorcery invoked by Heinrich Himmler's warlocks in the Thule SS, and even darker villains... We keep the existence of these abominations hidden from the Allied public; can you imagine the mass panic if people knew the Nazis can reanimate the dead and conjure demons from Hell? We fight a secret war underneath, above, and around the public one; the Nazis have their weapons, and we have ours." The Prime Minister sighed and rubbed his eyes before continuing. "We recently acquired something, something that could give us a chance of winning this wretched conflict."

"What is it?" I asked.

"I think it would be better if I showed you."

King rose to his feet and walked out the door, followed by the four hazy silhouettes of his companions. We walked down a dark hall filled with various indistinct shapes, large rectangles that might have been shelves, squares that might have been windows, the occasionally vague blob that might have been a person, though they were even less distinct than the figures that King had worked with to summon me. Perhaps it wasn't that the hall itself was dark but simply that what I had become could not view things as I once could.

As the Prime Minister walked, occasionally beings of shining light hovered around him, and then disappeared. These I could see clearly: sometimes they were heroic men, sometimes beautiful women, sometimes barking spectral Irish Terriers that scampered at King's heels.

"Yes, I walk with many spirits," the Prime Minister said. "They give me guidance, strength, and hope." He unlocked a door and opened it. "Follow me."

The room was empty except for a large chair in the middle: on the chair was seated a large man. This man was not an indistinct silhouette; I could see him perfectly, sitting naked with his eyes closed. He was a tall figure, muscular — even brutish — with grey skin and no hair at all, not even eyebrows. A sense of power radiated from him, a strength far greater than even his brawny body would suggest.

"This is the Golem of Prague." Prime Minister King gestured at the figure. "We don't have the time to elucidate all the risks we took, all the sacrifices we made to acquire this mighty artifact. It was formed from clay and given life hundreds of years ago by the famous Rabbi Loew to protect the Jews of Prague from persecution and mob violence. The creature has slumbered ever since, waiting for its vast strength to be needed again." King sighed. "The strength which is needed *now*."

"Then why haven't you awakened it?" I asked.

"We tried. We had someone with knowledge of Kabbalistic lore: Rabbi Shmuel Agron of Utena, one of the last true 'Masters of the Name,' but he was torn apart by a pack of baying hellhounds."

"Hellhounds?"

"Demons summoned by warlocks of the Thule SS. We have been unable to find anyone else with a sufficient mastery of Kabbalah for the job; most of the other possibilities have already been captured or murdered by the enemy. The Nazis fear the Golem like nothing else, you see. Which means we've had to improvise."

"Improvise?"

"If we can't awaken the Golem's spirit, perhaps we can place another spirit inside its body, drive it like a car."

"Place another spirit in— you want *me* to do that?"

"That's right, Corporal Druker. We will bind you to the Golem so that you can make it move, make it fight."

"But—"

"Do you know that Nazi soldiers are already on Canadian soil? They came over the North Pole with a coven of warlocks, searching beneath the ice for some primeval weapon. Our agents tell us they're close to awakening something very potent and when they do... So much occult power has been gathered there, far more power than my own forces can repel. If they are to be stopped, we need the Golem. We need *you*."

"Couldn't you have summoned your rabbi's ghost, have him deliver the rites that way?"

"No," King sighed. "His spirit could not be reached; it went too quickly into the Light."

"But why choose me?" I asked. "What makes me so special?"

"You died fighting for your country. You showed courage, loyalty, and self-discipline in battle." The Prime Minister smiled. "Also, you're Jewish. We're not certain if that would make a difference to the Golem but we conjecture that it's a safer bet. So that's it, Corporal Druker. This is what your country is asking of you. Will you answer the call?"

∞   ☼   ∞

A boat dropped me off on the Arctic island where the Nazis were located, though we were on the opposite shore, hidden by some hills. Around my neck I wore a little wooden amulet carved into the shape of an eye sewn shut. The Prime Minister had assured me that it would keep me hidden from both psychic and mechanical detection, so the enemy would have no warning before I struck.

I moved fast for a man made of clay, fast without ever tiring. I was in the Arctic, dressed only in a simple white shirt and pants, and I didn't feel cold at all. I didn't feel anything except excited anticipation.

The Prime Minister and his associates had chanted some stuff back at HQ— I hadn't been able to make out what they were saying but with each word I had been drawn closer and closer to the Golem until I was inside it. For a moment everything had been black, and then King had put one hand against the Golem's forehead and another against its chest while continuing to chant, and suddenly— I was seeing through the Golem's eyes. I could see everything clearly like I had when I was alive. Then I had made the Golem's arms lift and its legs rise up from their chair. I was inside the Golem! I was the Golem! The Golem was me!

I loved adventure comics and their costumed heroes. I'd joined the army because I wanted to fight the bad guys, and Hitler was the biggest bad guy of them all, especially to a Jewish boy from Hamilton like me. I'd dreamed of having superpowers. And now I did.

I saw the first Nazis as I skirted the hills, just regular soldiers with regular guns. I wanted to say something as I ran toward them, some quip to show who I was and that I wasn't scared of them. But the Golem cannot speak.

I nevertheless made a big impression. My first blow sent one of the Nazis flying like a football, my next smashed two of them into the ground. The surviving soldiers were screaming and I knew enough German to understand the words: "God in Heaven, it's the Golem! Golem!"

More and more guns fired, a whole unit of soldiers stormed toward me. But they couldn't do anything except shred my clothes. I was invulnerable, unstoppable— the soldiers' bullets were like raindrops, their bodies as breakable as bone china in my hands. I was a one-man battalion— no, a one-man *army*.

Another group stood on the ice at the island's edge. They wore sky-blue fur-lined cloaks with black hoods that kept their faces in shadow. Big leather pouches hung from their belts and their necks were festooned with amulets of feathers, bones, and coloured stones. Each warlock also wore a heavy swastika of bronze on a chain, hanging directly over his heart. In their hands they gripped stone knives and gnarled staves, all pointed at me.

The language of the warlocks' chant sounded similar to the soldiers' shouts, but older, rougher... more primitive. I'd run almost naked across the Canadian Arctic and through a hail of bullets and I'd felt nothing, but those sorcerous words made this clay man shiver.

A howling wind rose up, a wind that caused the snow around me to swirl, that made the ice under my feet shake and crack. The swirling snow formed into the shapes of huge beasts that howled, growled, and barked. "Hellhounds" the Prime Minister had called them, the hellhounds that had murdered Rabbi Agron. I had imagined that such fiends would be scorching hot, like an inferno, like little fiery dragons in canine form. Not these creatures, though. They were monstrous wolves formed from frost and snow and frigid wind, a ravenous pack that swarmed over me and tried to rend me with claws and teeth of jagged ice.

I pounded the hellhounds with my fists of clay. Though they were spectral, I could still hurt them as if they were of flesh and bone. In a few moments the demon wolves were nothing but shattered ice. I strode from the wreckage toward the warlocks, and they took a few steps back in horror. They spit guttural words at one another, and then, as one, they all reached into their leather bags, threw handfuls of blue dust onto the ice, and resumed chanting.

The ice cracked, shifted, bubbled, and then rose up, higher and higher. A huge figure towered over me, a giant of ice taller than a church steeple, its face devoid of features save for a wide toothless mouth and two burning red eyes.

The ice giant stared down, strangely curious about what I was. Then the warlocks pointed their weapons at me and spoke a command in unison. The giant bellowed and stamped its feet like a child having a tantrum, seeking to crush me underfoot.

I dodged the first stamp, then the second and the third! The giant was fast but I was faster!

Then I tripped! I fell backward into the snow as the giant's foot once again descended. But the Golem's body reacted faster than I could think, leaping upright, grabbing the ice giant's foot and pushing back with irresistible mystic strength!

The giant roared all the way down as it toppled onto the screaming warlocks. When the warlocks died, their spell died with them. Only their mangled bodies remained, crushed under scattered blocks of ice.

But one warlock was still alive, standing at the edge of the ice, right beside the frigid waters of the Arctic Ocean. He was different from his companions— his swastika was gold and his staff ended in a curved steel hook, like a giant fishhook. In his other hand he gripped a stone dagger dripping with blood. Germanic runes were carved in the ice at his feet, and around them were little piles of ash, bloodstains, scattered fish bones, and the eviscerated, headless corpse of a large black bull.

"Golem, hear my words," the warlock said in German. "I know a wandering spirit makes your Jew clay move; your Prime Minister put your spirit into it. Clever. I speak now to that spirit in the clay. You scattered my men. You destroyed my *seidrmen* and their spirits. But they accomplished their task— their task was not to destroy you but to give me time. Time to awaken the Great One. The ritual is done, the offering is cast. I have caught the Great One on a hook just as the god Donar did long ago. The Great One is hooked! The Great One awakes! It will swallow Canada! Swallow America! Swallow the Jews and all the enemies of the Reich! The Reich will last a thousand years! The Great One awakens through me!" His voice rose to a shriek as he thrust his hook into the water.

While the warlock had been screaming, I'd been running, running toward him as fast as my clay legs could propel me. Whatever he was trying to summon, this must have been why the Nazis were here. *This* was what I'd come to stop!

As I got close to my enemy, I reached for him— to grab him, break him, *anything* to stop him from completing his ritual. Just before my fingers touched him, he shrieked "The Great One is here!" and then something grabbed the warlock's hook. He was yanked off the ice and pulled into the ocean depths!

The water began to churn, the waves rose, the ice split. A huge *something* —a giant undulating hill of shining greenish-black — thrust itself out of the ocean. Then another hill and another! I stared at them in horrified confusion— what was I seeing?

I made out a huge reptilian head larger than a tank, covered in greenish-black scales and with blazing yellow eyes. The head rose higher and higher on what at first I took to be the creature's neck, until I realized it was not merely a neck but an impossibly long body. A sea serpent had been awakened, a sea serpent unimaginably vast, unimaginably old, unimaginably malevolent. Those furious, monstrous hills were its *coils*! Coils large enough to crush the entire Canadian Navy in one destructive embrace!

The monster roared, a roar far louder than the ice giant's, an endless roar that reverberated all around me. Perhaps a roar loud enough for Prime Minister King to hear back in Ottawa. I'd failed! This Nazi-summoned god-creature was going to devour Canada, the United States, and make the Nazis the masters of the world. The monster was beyond gigantic, beyond evil. It was vaster, stronger, and more malevolent than anything I could have ever imagined. How could I, a mere thing of clay, fight it, let alone defeat it?

But I had to try. How could I not? If I was going to die — if the dead *could* die for a second time — then I was going to go down fighting!

The serpent exhaled, enveloping me in a huge cloud of greenish mist. The fumes were almost certainly poisonous, enough poison to kill an entire platoon of soldiers, but the Golem didn't breathe, couldn't be poisoned, perhaps couldn't be killed.

I smashed my fists hard against the monster's side, the fists that had already smashed through soldiers and hellhounds. I pounded again and again, but couldn't make so much as a dent in those impervious scales!

The sea serpent seemed to sense that its poison couldn't hurt me and I was much too small to entwine in its coils. So it opened its mouth wide, each fang longer than my body, and it struck!

I leaped out of the way. Once. Twice. The serpent howled in frustration and struck again. I tried to punch it in the eye as the ghastly head rushed by, but my enemy blinked and my fist clanged harmlessly against its eyelid. Even the eyelid was invulnerable! How could I fight this monster? The whole world was depending on me, but I had no idea what I should do.

Then I knew. I trembled a little as I realized what I had to do, a course of action alarming enough to make even a ghost afraid. I stood on the ice and held up my hands. The serpent opened its jaws wide and I leaped into its mouth!

In darkness I tumbled down that terrible, never-ending throat. I tumbled for a long time, but eventually I grabbed hold and dug deep into the serpent's soft interior flesh. I pounded, I ripped, I tore again and again. I couldn't see; I didn't know exactly where in its body I was. Was I destroying the lining of the neck or some vital organ? All I knew was that I wouldn't stop, couldn't stop until my enemy was destroyed!

Even inside its body, I heard the serpent's scream, its desperate cry of agony. I didn't stop! I kept on pounding! Again and again and again! Never stop! Never surrender!

∞  ☼  ∞

I awoke to find myself lying on my back. Above me were shifting patterns of light and shadow. Where was I? What had happened to the sea serpent? Was I dead again? Had I won?

I could feel my body rising toward the light, the light bright like the sun yet I could stare at it without hurting my eyes. In fact, the more I stared at the light, the more at peace I felt. It was getting bigger and bigger— no, I was getting closer. I was going into the light. I was going... home— wait! It wasn't time for me to go! It wasn't time! If I crossed over now, who would protect Canada from the next occult attack? From the next monster? I had to stay!

The light faded. I was in darkness.

Three seals swam over my head, dancing together as I lay below them. No, I had not died again; I was at the bottom of the Arctic Ocean. I slowly pushed myself to my feet. It was weird to be underwater and yet not worry about holding my breath. Then again, was this any weirder than anything else that had happened to me that day?

I tried to swim up but I couldn't. Couldn't swim at all. That was something else the Golem couldn't do. But even if I couldn't swim, I could walk. Hopefully I'd be able to climb back to the island, pull myself to the surface, get picked up by the boat once it returned.

Somehow, in my heart (did I still have a heart?), I knew that the sea monster had been defeated. Had it dissolved? Had it vomited me up? I wasn't sure, but I knew it was gone, at least for now. The Nazis would still have more monsters in reserve, maybe ones much mightier than this serpent, ones that would love to swallow Canada whole and the world soon after, but I was not afraid. I would stand against them. Thanks to Prime Minister King, I was no longer merely Daniel Druker.

I was the Golem.

∞   ☼   ∞

**BEVAN THOMAS**, a driving force of the Cloudscape Comics Society, writes and edits comics and fiction in Vancouver.

# BLACK FALCON SAVES CITY, WORLD

*Sacha A. Howells*

THERE SHOULD BE noise when he comes down from the sky, like a jet or one of those Apache helicopters. It's that awesome. But there's nothing, maybe his cape flapping if it's windy. He's like god. Blue Titan doesn't float— he stands in the air like gravity does not exist.

"Near disaster today when the Prince Edward Viaduct almost collapsed," the man head said on TV.

"But Toronto's own Blue Titan was there to save the day," the woman head said. "*Again*." What's with the pink stripes in her hair? She's a news anchor. It's all over the place, checkout girls at the market with utility belts and teenagers on the bus wearing capes.

The Channel 2 Eye in the Sky showed Blue Titan holding up the bridge like it was balsa. "Someone calling himself Mantarr the Invincible has claimed responsibility," she said. "Be sure to vote in our online poll: supervillain or crank?"

"*Mantarr*," man head said. "Let's hope it's not too late to go back to the drawing board on that one."

"Phil, you are *terrible*."

They don't get it, this life. It's not about names and costumes and perfect physiques. It's about work. And our sacred duty, and accomplishing something in life, and helping humanity.

Maria's fat lazy ass came in the room about three feet after her fat lazy front. "Jesus, Manny. Where's the remote? I'm not watching the stupid news."

I tucked it under my back. "Like I'm suddenly chief of remotes?"

She stood there with her hand on her waist and looked at the TV. "Always with this. Electroman, Dog Girl. Pigeon Lady. Gimme, my show is on." The couch groaned when she sat.

"I'm watching," I said. The people were safe off the bridge, and you could see red beams of heat from Blue Titan's eyes, welding the girders back together.

"Blue Freak they should call him. Electrofreak for sure. The *Comet* says there's like three Kid Sparks a year."

"Ha ha ha. They save people every day when you're doing whatever, answering phones at the dentist."

"Oh, the bad stupid dentist that pays for the rent and the food and the cable and your dumb karate."

I stood up and threw the remote across the room. "It's *jujitsu!*"

"Maybe if you had a better job than at a pet store, you could get out of my apartment."

"It's not a *pet store*. Birds, exotic birds. And maybe it's my apartment and I let *you* live here."

She snorted. "Yeah, and maybe you pay less than a third of the rent. You think you're all set, the creepy little brother I'm going to float for life. Guess what? *It ain't happening.*"

"I'm putting fifty dollars more to the rent starting next month. A hundred." I had some money saved up, but I wanted to save it for equipment. Maybe a scuba tank, I was thinking I probably needed an underwater suit. Just in case.

I went into my room and slammed the door, hard. I'd taped headlines from the *Star* on the wall, floor to ceiling: BLUE TITAN SAVES GRADE SCHOOL. SOLON GIVEN KEY TO CITY. LEAGUE OF RECTITUDE FOILS MOLEMEN. When it was me, I'd buy the whole stack of papers.

"Almost twenty-one years old," she yelled through the door. "Twenty-one years old, living off your sister and working at the pet store."

Living with a secret identity is a special hell. But those closest to you, the people you love, even when they're being a bitch and won't let you watch a major operation on the national news, they can never know. For their protection.

"Exotic birds."

∞ ✿ ∞

Valkyrie, the Red Veil, I don't know what they do. Los Fantomas. Mostly, when I'm in the field I carry my equipment in a backpack, go by a dumpster to change and just hide my clothes and hope they're there when I get back. I carried a little bag for my street clothes for a while, but you could tell it wasn't part of the suit, it just looked stupid.

I've lost a couple pairs of jeans.

I walked fast down 46th Street. I was late for my class at Ken's Academy of Jujitsu, my dojo. Ken wasn't somebody who waited, and I was supposed to practice katas for my blue belt.

A roar ripped the air overhead. I cupped my hands over my eyes. A yellow slash of light snapped through the sky, maybe a hundred feet up, and the sonic boom rolled down the corridor of buildings and shook in my lungs.

A woman in a business suit jumped and spilled coffee down her blouse. "Well shit," she said, and threw the paper cup on the sidewalk.

"The Bolt," I said. I tapped her on the shoulder. "That's the Bolt." I took off running. The trail hung in the air like vapor, the smell of burning hair and electricity, and I followed it for four, six blocks. In the wake people ducked into doorways and hid under bus benches. An old lady was crying with a magazine held over her head, like she was keeping out of the rain.

The trail broke ninety degrees right, but I kept on running, the boots in my pack kicking my lower back. I wanted to see him, feel the power.

The trail finally faded, and I stopped at a newsstand. I bent over with my hands on my knees and sucked air. The old man behind the stacks of magazines squinted up into the air and shook his head. "Fucking monsters," he said. "Murderers, it's what they are. And nobody can stop them. Not even human, half of them."

I shook my head, tried to talk. There had been incidents where civilians got hurt. That school bus in Buffalo, the mall in Vancouver. Can't be helped. But they were heroes. They were heroes. My legs ticked and shook.

"I hear the Black Rider eats homeless," an old woman whispered. "The curfew's so we can't see what they do."

"Not for nothing lady, but you are cray-zee," said a teenage girl in a domino mask and a Silk Serpent tank top. "If you've got some reason to be out at night you can get a *permit*."

"You can take every last one of the bastards," the old man said. He was wearing an old Expos cap, from back when they still had sports.

"Easy, Pop." The other man behind the counter had the same busted nose and thick neck. "They hear."

My wind came back and I started walking back the way I came. That close to the power, you could still feel it crackle in the air. I reached out, tried to close it in my hand, keep the feeling forever. The hair on my arms stood up. I looked at a street sign. I was miles from the dojo. No way I was making my workout.

Maybe I should buy a gun.

∞   ☼   ∞

Maria was snoring on the couch with the light from the TV flashing on her face. She'd left a plate on the table under tinfoil, and I peeled it back to look. Enchiladas with the can sauce I like. It was October and cold. I knew she didn't like to run the heat, so I draped Mom's old afghan over her. Her mouth was open and she looked twelve years old.

Our door was right next to the stairwell, and I climbed the eleven stories to the roof. An alarm was supposed to ring, but I'd disabled it. This was the Falcon's Nest. Gravel crunched under my feet as I tiptoed to the old-fashioned air vent. Behind the rusty grate, I pulled out a duffel bag.

Bodysuit, check. Cowl, check. Combat boots, check. Utility belt, gauntlets, cape, check. Dang, it really was cold. Maybe I should build a little shelter out here. Nobody else ever came up. The outfit was all black, with a gold beak at the front of my cowl— menacing, but you could still tell what I was. When they saw me, the criminals, they'd know to run. I balled up my street clothes and stuffed them in the vent. Maybe a space heater.

With a foot on the ledge of the roof and my fists on my waist I felt strong, perfect. My city lay out there below me, millions of people sleeping and eating and watching TV, knowing that *we* were up here watching over them. It felt good.

I slid a leg down onto the old fire escape and shinned down to the first landing. Fourteen more floors to go.

No, Falcon's *Perch*.

My rounds were still pretty simple, I hadn't found my turf. I mostly stuck to the alleys around my building, making sure there was a pair of eyes. Vigilance, that's one of Black Falcon's watchwords.

The streets have stayed pretty quiet since the curfews, and after a couple hours of nothing I decided to finish my patrol and head home. Last thing every night I headed down to my grade school, Church Street Junior. People tossed their filth over the fence, needles and condoms and half-pint bottles of liquor where the kids had to walk in the morning. I pulled a supermarket bag out of my utility belt and bent over, stuck my hand through the gate to pick it all up. The gloves protected me.

Good night's work.

∞   ☼   ∞

I loved CloudCuckooLand right when I opened, before the customers and my stupid coworkers. Just me and the birds.

I wandered between the cages, stopping to fill empty water droppers from a plastic pitcher. Green-cheek conures, cockatiels, a scarlet macaw, a pair of black-headed caiques. In a big cage by the register was Captain Mike, a beautiful African grey I was teaching to say his name.

I could tell they felt the bond, knew that I was one with them. I whistled and cawed to them sometimes, even flapped my arms and bobbed while they swivelled their heads to watch.

The bells over the door jingled and the birds squawked at them. Gary walked in, shambling and scrawny and picking at his nose. "Hey Manny," he said. "So'd you buy it?"

"Shut up," I said. It was Gary's friend, the guy he bought pot from, who sold me the gun. A stringy, jumpy guy with too many teeth in his mouth and a fishhook-shaped scar on his cheek. Observance. That's another watchword.

He took four hundred of the dollars from the shoebox in my closet, the Falcon's War Chest. Not the kind of citizen a hero should consort with, but sometimes we have to get our hands dirty. Can't be helped.

I stacked 25-pound bags of seed, hoped Gary would leave me alone. I could hear him coming up behind me, smelled his breath. He ate a lot of cheese, too much. I could turn right now and flip him into the rack of flax and palm oil, snap his neck as he flew over my shoulder. But I didn't. Even though anyone with the tiniest bit of information about Black Falcon and his connection to mild-mannered Manny Hinojosa was dangerous. With great power comes great responsibility.

"I didn't even buy it," I said. "Too expensive." It was in my pack, rolled up in a towel like a heavy, happy prize, like a secret bar of gold.

"I already know you did," he said. "I knew you'd fucking lie."

"It's for hunting," I said.

"A pistol. What do you know how to hunt?"

"I could hunt stuff. Elk."

"Right." He laughed like a donkey. "Thin the herds in Queen's Park."

"Look, I just need it, okay?"

"I know what you're doing," Gary said. "I know your secret."

I didn't say anything, kept moving bags of Goldenfeast Australian Blend, but I was sweating. What would I do if Black Falcon was revealed this early in his career? I'd barely even started, no one would remember me at all. I didn't strike fear in the hearts of men or anything.

"You're going to rip off Drakos." The owner, an old Greek who checked our pockets for thievery whenever he came in, which wasn't a lot. "Come back on your off day, mask, gun, you know where the safe is, you're home before the nighttime curfew." He nodded. "I see you casing the place." He arched his eyebrow and looked at me weird, and said, "*The Living Eye sees.*"

Gary from work thought he was a super, this pig-faced jerk who I knew for a fact kept skin magazines under the passenger seat of his hatchback?

The bells on the door jangled again and the birds all made their squawk and a man came in, tall with dirty red hair and arms that seemed to jump around by themselves. "Fly free above huddled masses!" he said. "Ark of the covenant, ark of the covenant!"

"Oh great," Gary said.

The guy ran from cage to cage, fumbling with the gates and opening the ones he could figure out. "Ask the birds of the air, and they will tell you!" he shouted, and tripped over a box, knocking over a stack of empty cages and spilling a basket of cuttlebones.

Crazy Gene came in every couple of weeks to liberate the birds.

"Fly with the wings you are given!" He was almost done, stuck on the big macaw's gate. He gave up and ran for the door, missed the handle, banged his head, and stumbled out holding his eye. "Take your freedom, share it with me!" he shouted.

The door banged closed and the bells jangled again. Me and Gary started cleaning up, and the birds stared from their cages. A cockatiel that had hopped out to peck at a ball on a string flew back to his cage when he saw me coming, and Captain Mike clacked at him and said "Captain Mike."

"Come on," Gary said. "Let me see it. Don't be a dick."

I let him hang. Secrecy's one of my watchwords, too.

∞  ☼  ∞

It was the first of the month and I was going to give Maria her extra rent in cash, brand-new bills counted out right into her fat hand, so I walked to the bank on my way home from work. It was right after five, the bank machine was out of service, and the line was long. The janitor already had his big floor polisher drifting over the tiles and the security guard was hanging over the counter talking to one of the tellers, flirting and smiling and touching her hair.

I wasn't getting out of there soon, so I went down the hall to the bathroom and clicked open the big handicapped stall, took off my backpack, slid down my pants, and sat. A magazine was folded over the handrail, the gossip rag Maria read. LADY MAGPIE LOVE NEST, the cover teaser said, and I lifted the corner to see.

Then I heard a shout, or a bang, or a clap. I listened, but it was quiet. Then something high pitched— a scream, a baby crying? I pulled up my pants and grabbed my pack and peeked out into the hall. It was empty, quieter than it should be. I crept along the hall until I could see out into the bank lobby, where people were stretched out on the floor, hands on their heads. The only ones standing were two guys I hadn't even noticed. Normal clothes I guess, but in masks now, like Mexican wrestlers. And one had a pistol and the other had a shotgun.

"We don't *want* to hurt you," said the one in the red mask, a devil with a black sequin beard and little gold horns. "But we don't really give that much of a shit."

The security guard was unconscious with a fat swollen eye, handcuffed to a desk.

"Phones in the bag," the other one said, a black cat with pipe-cleaner whiskers and a dirty green sweater. "Anybody's pants starts ringing, you're shot in the face." He held out a pillowcase and walked down the line.

It was really happening, and I was ready. I was ready. In the hallway I opened my pack and pulled out my cowl. One of the women on the floor could see me, and her face was like *what*? I turned around, no time to worry about my secret identity. No time for my boots, all those laces, why didn't I ever think of that?

I strapped on my utility belt and when the buckle clicked in, everything went kind of quiet behind me. Shit, they didn't hear that, they couldn't, I oiled the clip with WD-40 twice a week just for exactly that thing.

I turned around and the one with the red mask was right there in front of me. I dug for the gun, all tangled up in the towel, then thought no: crescent kick into Indian Death Lock. Then the stock of his shotgun cracked my face in two. My feet slipped on the floor and I fell and the shined-up tile whacked my head. The pain was like. It was like. There was a new mind in my same head that could only scream but did not have a mouth.

"The fuck are you supposed to be?" he said. The barrels of his gun looked at me like two more eyes.

The windows blew out, not in — the panes left their frames and shattered, the shards sucked out into the street — and they were there.

Blue Titan glided into the room, six inches off the ground. I'd never seen him in person. His skin really was blue like it looked on TV, but clear, like glass. His black hair looked like glass too. Volcano glass.

"No, no," cat-mask said. "Robbie, you said they only show up for shit like alien invasions." A wet stain lagooned down the front of his jeans, and we all pretended not to notice.

Valkyrie was behind him. Taller than me and glowing, with wings on her helm and a braided horsetail of straw-blond hair. She wore a polished iron breastplate and carried a four-foot sword strapped to her back. The muscles in her bare legs stood out like metal cables. Devil-mask started shooting and Blue Titan was at him before you could feel the air move, held him up by the neck and squeezed until he passed out. A foot from me Valkyrie trussed cat-mask up with rope and dumped him on the floor, dazed and submissive. I reached out to touch her boot and she kicked my hand.

Blue Titan dropped devil-mask like an empty sleeping bag and walked over, bent down to look at me. "That's yours?" he said and pointed to where my pack had spit out the gun, snub-nosed and silly on the floor. I nodded and held up my cowl. The beak was torn and I'd bled on it. His breath didn't smell like anything, and I realized that he didn't have to eat.

He picked up the pistol, dumped the bullets into his palm, and crumpled the gun like newspaper. Then he held his fist at my ear and squeezed. The little explosions in his hand banged my head against the floor again, my ear went zero. He dropped the hot slugs on my chest and glided back out to the street.

Valkyrie nodded her chin at me. Her eyes were white as sheet ice. "People like you," she said, "get people like her," she pointed at the girl lying by me, "dead." She turned and dragged the two bodies behind her like sacks.

"We shouldn't have to live with gods," I said with my broken mouth. I was a dying seal barking on a rock. The girl next to me, still with her hands on her head, began to cry.

My ear roared back alive, horrible and loud.

"I'm going to be sick," I said. She couldn't understand me.

∞   ☼   ∞

Fredericton expat **SACHA A. HOWELLS** was a 2014 National Endowment for the Arts Distinguished Fellow at the Hambidge Center.

# BLUEFIELDS REHARMONY NEST

*Kim Goldberg*

DR. AURELIO ANNOUNCED, "We are about to get started, Opul, if you would care to join us now." On her lounge chair atop the cliff, Opul sat facing the shimmering orange sea.

Dr. Aurielio called Opul's name again, but she remained impassive. "Very well," he said as he gathered the rest of them: Ixcel the Ice Child, Leap, Dark Blade, KwaKwa, Doonah the Maker. They all dragged their chairs into a circle behind Opul. All patients at Bluefields must participate in daily group. It was written into the admissions contract, there were no exceptions. A patient needn't share, but sitting in the circle for one hour each morning while others spoke was mandatory. "If the moon won't come to the river, then the river must come to the moon."

∞  ☼  ∞

Even with her bioelectric flux at low ebb, Opul recognized the reference immediately. It was from an ancient Breitenbas legend on Kellar IV about the Moon-Bride who sought to be united with her new husband, the Black River, on the planet's surface. But the Moon-Bride did not know how to climb down from the sky, so her husband ascended to meet her, creating night with his blackness.

Opul saw little connection between the myth and her current situation. The only thing she knew for certain was that there was no escaping Dr. Aurelio's group session— not unless she planned to hurl herself off the cliff and into sea. She considered it for a moment, but she doubted she had the energy or the motor control to choreograph so grand an exit. So she continued to lie on her lounger while the rest of the menagerie of dysfunctional superheroes joined Dr. Aurelio and brought the circle to Opul.

"Who has something to share this morning?" Dr. Aurelio asked after the patients had settled themselves. He had strategically seated himself directly across from Opul, she looked away.

"Anyone…? KwaKwa, how is your world today? Still having those headaches?"

KwaKwa could usually be counted on to share. He was not bashful about his emotional processes, and he had a surprising degree of insight. KwaKwa's monumental physical strength had manifested by age four; already, he'd been able to lift and toss large boulders, which he did to save members of his tribe, the Seetles, from being enslaved or eaten by the other intelligent species of his homeworld, the Ramorgs. However, the arrival of offworld colonists had pushed KwaKwa beyond the limits of his powers. With their mechanical grapple-maws they were more effective hunters than the Ramorgs, and more relentless by far. He became wracked with night terrors and excruciating headaches, necessitating his stay at Bluefields.

"The headaches are better now," KwaKwa replied. "But I awoke from a dream this morning that I don't understand. It was quite unsettling."

"Tell us about it," Dr. Aurelio urged.

"I was walking through the forest," KwaKwa began, "when I found a ravine filled with hundreds of dead jimbos caked in—"

"The Mother will be saved!" Leap blurted.

All heads swivelled. "The Mother must be saved because The Mother is sacred!"

"Leap… What have we said about interrupting?" Dr. Aurelio asked.

"If Leap would prefer to share first, that's fine with me," KwaKwa offered.

"No, that is not fine," Dr. Aurelio cut in. "Leap, you'll just have to—"

"The Mother must be saved! All hail The Mother!"

"Leap! That's enough!" Dr. Aurelio didn't use his stern voice often, and never on anyone other than Leap. But poor Leap had impulse-control issues, not to mention attention-divergence issues and mother issues.

"Sorry," Leap replied.

"You will have a chance to share after KwaKwa has finished," Dr. Aurelio instructed. "All right?"

"Yes, of course. Sorry. The Mother will be saved! So sorry."

Leap fidgeted for a few more seconds and then grew still as KwaKwa resumed recounting his dream.

Opul returned her absent gaze and sense-mind to the ocean. She missed the entirety of KwaKwa's disjointed tale of dead jimbos and hurtling spears, which somehow became forests of snapping tortas that swallowed a shuttle pod of blood-red gemstones as it orbited a woman's furry neck.

∞   ☼   ∞

Dr. Aurelio listened in a distracted way to the dream saga. He was far more intrigued by the subtle interplay he had just witnessed between Opul and Leap. This was not the first time such an exchange had manifested between the two of them. Leap was the most volatile patient here, and also the most dangerous— or at least had been initially. He was the only current resident whose admission had not been voluntary. When a superhero goes rogue and starts committing mayhem, the Interplanetary Corps of Superheroes has little choice but to round him up and ship him off for treatment. And if treatment fails, his powers must be disabled. Permanently.

Dr. Aurelio did not want that outcome for any of his patients, and recently, it had started looking like Leap might escape it. The once-explosive lagomorph had become subdued in recent weeks. Calming him was no longer the chore it had been in the beginning, and the soft chamber was no longer necessary. Dr. Aurelio would have liked to credit Leap's turnaround to his own therapeutic skills and proven track record as the pioneer of superhero psycho-reharmonization therapy. But he was honest enough to admit that, in this case, the truth lay elsewhere. Specifically, it lay somewhere deep within the badly frayed sense-mind of Opul the Mender.

Opul was by far Dr. Aurelio's toughest nut to crack. While her outward symptoms appeared to be psychological — despondency, abysmalism, alienation — her fundamental malady was in fact physiological and bioelectric. So deep was her wound that it touched her bioenergetic core and its architecture of neural webs. Opul needed more than group validation and gentle guidance from a trained professional. Much more. And the only one she could get it from was herself. At best, Dr. Aurelio was nothing more than a passive conduit for her powers of autonomous neural repair, if such repair was even possible in so extreme a case.

Normally, patients were barred from using their superpowers while at Bluefields. There was simply too much risk of them injuring themselves or others while in recovery. But in Opul's case Dr. Aurelio had decided to make an exception. Once he had fully assessed the neurological basis of her condition and her special aptitude, he realized that the only likelihood of her ever regaining the full use of her sense-hairs and her mending power (really more of an energy-streaming ability) was if she actually began to *do* it again, to mend something or someone close at hand. It was indeed a "use it or lose it" situation. Neurons that fire together, wire together.

"The Mother must be saved! The Mother..." Leap erupted again but quickly trailed off once Opul's gaze fell upon him.

Opul's effects on Leap told Dr. Aurelio that she was already starting to regain her powers. Although, to see her immobile in her lounge chair, with her long sense-hairs limp against her head and shoulders, one would never guess she was engaged in mending.

Dr. Aurelio had reviewed vid images of Opul at work: in full-out mending mode, she stood erect while sweeping her elongate arms rapidly in front of her and bringing them back to her torso in broad gathering motions; her lustrous mane of sense-hairs lifting from her scalp, defying gravity, each strand twisting and turning every which way. But he had never observed her mend firsthand. It was rumored that she could even mend wounded planets ravaged by war, natural disaster, or cosmic accident, could stream and heal all of a planet's broken or tangled geoenergy threads. Amazing! How he longed to see her in action.

On Earth, for as long as she'd lasted there, she mended from a concrete highway underpass in a small coastal town in Canada. Yet the primary geowound she was sent to heal was thousands of bounders inland, where a vast swath of forest had been sheared off and the land was now mired in an upwell of black tar that had lain buried for millennia. From all accounts, Opul would have completed her mission, even from that distance. But her sense-hairs and neural webs were severely damaged by the unanticipated levels of radio-frequency radiation on the planet. The concrete underpass provided the only shelter she could readily find from the toxic radiation. So she lived there during her sojourn on Earth. In order to do her mending each day, she'd had to stand at the mouth of the underpass. Anything that shielded her sense-hairs from the withering radiation also shielded them from the planetary energies she was there to reweave.

Now, Opul was beginning to mend Leap's tangled energy threads. Perhaps not just because he was close at hand; all the patients were. But Leap was the only one who had been born on Earth. And come into his powers on Earth. And ultimately wreaked his great havoc on Earth before being captured by the Corps and sent for reharmonization. It was as though, at some subliminal level, Opul's bioenergetic core knew that the key to her own autonomous repair would be found in reconnecting with the source of her damage: Earth. Perhaps the key also lay in Opul completing the mission she had been forced to abort. Namely, the healing of Earth. Or, in this case, a proxy for Earth in the form of Leap.

"...I knew they weren't really gemstones," KwaKwa sobbed. "The red was dripping off them and landing on my face. I knew they were the slaughtered jimbos from the ravine. And it was my own neck that was being circled until I couldn't breathe!" KwaKwa broke off his tale and wept.

Ixcel the Ice Child (who was really three hundred years old but looked twelve) slipped her tiny pale hand into KwaKwa's big mitt and gave it a squeeze.

"I have scary dreams too sometimes," she said.

"Do you?" KwaKwa stopped bawling long enough to speak. Ixcel nodded.

"Sure. We all do," Dark Blade said.

Doonah the Maker patted KwaKwa's shoulder. "We got yer back, buddy."

"But what does it mean?" KwaKwa asked Dr. Aurelio.

"What do *you* think it means?" Dr. Aurelio replied.

"I think the blood that landed on my face was really my own tears. And the strangulation by that shuttle pod was my powerlessness against the offworlders. And the ravine of dead jimbos is the loss of our fertility. And..." KwaKwa dissolved into tears again.

"You've done significant work today, KwaKwa," Dr. Aurelio said. "This is a lot of progress."

Then he turned to Leap and braced himself for an incoherent litany of Mother worship.

∞  ✿  ∞

That night, as Dr. Aurelio sat at his desk in the glass conservatory writing up his daily notes, his thoughts turned to the woolenwood forest to the rear of the compound. The patients at Bluefields were free to wander the trails, observe the wildlife, or simply meditate and restore themselves beneath the soft protective shield of the forest canopy.

The cornerstone of his doctoral thesis decades earlier involved cross-mapping the psychological profile of a superhero to the vital impulse of a tree. Each is driven by one need only: to fulfill itself according to its own laws, to represent itself in the world at large. Superheroes do not choose to be superheroes, do not choose to act when called upon to do so. They cannot *not* act. It is as hardwired into their genes as the tree's impulse to build up its own form. When superheroes are unable to access their powers, unable to represent themselves, to fulfill their mandate, the damage to their psyche is profound and potentially irreversible. It is as mortally damaging as a tree's inability to represent itself would be for the tree.

Opul visited the woolenwood forest more than any other patient in the current batch. But never at night. Nights were reserved for something else.

Dr. Aurelio glanced up from his desk and, as expected, saw Opul's dark silhouette standing at the cliff edge, illuminated under the triple moons. The first night he had observed her there, he wondered if he needed to worry that she might jump. Indeed, what he saw floating on the ocean when he raced across the moss after her silhouette disappeared from the clifftop made his heart do several backflips. But after he understood her nightly ritual he determined he had no cause for concern.

∞  ✿  ∞

Opul stood at the cliff edge along the east side of the compound. A wooden staircase led down to Lullo Cove. She was waiting for the steam to start rising from the sea. That was the best thing about this place. Thermal vents on the sea bottom opened at night, and the ocean warmed considerably.

When the first wisps of vapor appeared, escaping the sea like departing spirits to join the triple moons above, she began her nightly trek down the 118 steps. At the bottom, she disrobed and walked into the steaming sea. The salinity was high, contributing to great buoyancy. By the time she was waist-deep, her bare feet could no longer stay in contact with the sandy bottom. She let her body recline until she was floating on her back, arms and legs splayed wide. Her sense-hairs spread themselves on the surface like a halo around her head— like they used to when she was mending. She lay like this for as long as she could, before the ocean became too hot to bear. Sometimes that was one hour, sometimes two. It depended on the ambient air temperature and the degree of thermal venting on any given night.

She lay like this in the hope that her sense-hairs would remember their shape and resume their function. She lay like this to drink in the milky energy of the triple moons. She lay like this to ground her bioenergetic core to an infinite pool of negative ions. She lay like this to absorb the restorative minerals of the sea. She lay like this.

∞   ☼   ∞

It was easy to see why Dr. Aurelio's first observation of Opul's nightly practice had triggered his arrhythmia. When he discovered her nude and motionless body adrift in the ocean below, his heart jackhammered until she righted herself and walked ashore. It had been weeks since he had witnessed that (and only once— to repeat it would have been voyeuristic and an invasion of patient privacy). Now the image of Opul's magnificent mane of sense-hairs, spread wide like a halo on the moonlit sea, was forever seared into his memory. How like the dendrites on a neuron. How like the roots of a mighty tree!

Dr. Aurelio's dissertation had not only earned him his doctorate in Xenopsychology, it ultimately launched the entire discipline of psycho-reharmonization for superheroes. To this day, Dr. Aurelio is still considered the leading authority in the field. Tonight in his office, dwarfed by the dark expanse outside and the ethereal mysteries of a fractured sense-mind floating in the sea, he felt more humbled than exalted. It seemed he was powerless to help either Leap or Opul.

Opul was the only one who could reach and repair Leap. And she was certainly the only one who could repair herself. Did he have anything to offer these scarred souls? All he could do was listen.

Yes, Dr. Aurelio could do that. He could listen.

∞ ✿ ∞

**KIM GOLDBERG** — the author of six books of poetry and nonfiction and a winner of the Rannu Fund Poetry Prize for Speculative Literature — lives and speculates in Nanaimo, BC.

# LOST AND FOUND

*Luke Murphy*

**DAYS LATER, AND** I was still finding his things. I'd spot a razor blade under the bathroom sink or one of his books jumbled among mine, and I'd pick it up like it had thorns and put it in the box in the closet. He said he'd call when he was ready to collect his stuff. I didn't even know where he was. Had he moved in with that other girl? Were they coiled together on knotty sheets while I stared at the ceiling?

I tried not to do it. Three days I walked in circles around the apartment telling myself not to do it. I tried to distract myself: web surfing, cheap wine, bouts of self-pity. It didn't work. I needed it. My skin fizzed like cheap pop. I scratched my arms and bit my lips. *My boss called. Why wasn't I at the office processing forms? I told him I'd quit.*

At four in the morning I watched a web video that promised me I Wouldn't Believe What Happened Next (spoiler alert: I did, without much trouble) and realized I'd worn out the distraction capacity of the internet.

I walked to my bedroom. I lay down with my clothes on, shut my eyes, took a few deep breaths. My weight of flesh and bone and blood sank into the mattress.

I felt the shape and outline of my body, sensed its boundaries, and floated out of it.

I drifted up to the ceiling, turned and looked down at the fleshbody lying on the bed below me. Its eyes were closed, mouth slack. Greasy hair and grubby sweatshirt. When had I last showered? Physical me looked wretched.

But ethereal me felt glad to be weightless again. No pinched nerves or lower back pain. I held up the hands of my lightbody in front of my face, saw a vague form made of ghost-colored mist. Perfect. I floated to the wall and pressed myself into it. A chalky sensation in my lightflesh as I passed through it. I pushed deeper into sudden darkness, moved through sour-tasting concrete and rasping brick and burst into the night air. Streetlights glared seven stories below. I flitted above the luminous streets of Toronto and flew.

∞   ☼   ∞

We've all got two bodies. Our other body's where our conscious-ness lives, and it's made of thinner stuff than the flesh. Quantum particles, maybe. Lots of people slip out of their skin at one time or another, mostly when they're in shock or asleep or on the operating table. And everyone does it one final time. But I had the good or bad fortune to have learned how to control the process when I spent a week in hospital with appendicitis at the age of six. The incense-and-crystals crowd calls it astral projection, and I've been doing it for almost as long as I've known I shouldn't talk about it.

∞   ☼   ∞

I soared into a layer of thin clouds far above the city and rested in the air. Below, the sprawl glittered between the two black-nesses of lake and forest. I pictured his face— making a lop-sided smile after he'd said something funny, the way I always thought of him.

"Where is he?" I asked. A light tug pulled me northeast.

Just like last time, a week ago.

For the third evening in a row he'd texted me to say he'd be working late at the ad agency; I thought, *let's find out for sure so I can stop wondering.* I lay down and left the flesh behind, came outside and felt that pull to the northeast. His office wasn't that way. I let the pull direct me over streets and parks to a row of townhouses. A window drew me toward it. The curtains were closed, but the light was on. I remembered the rule I'd made when I first learned the knack: no spying. Yes, but this was different, wasn't it? I didn't wait for an answer, just ghosted through the wall and into a bedroom and saw.

They couldn't see me, of course — I'm invisible in this state — but her eyes were squeezed shut anyway. And he never looked up from what he was doing.

He came home later that night; I tried to keep it casual —
"How was your day, hon?" "Oh, you know, the usual" — but
it jumped out of my mouth. Then came the denials and the
shouting and the weeping and he progressed quickly to *how
did I know?* Was I following him around? No, of course I wasn't.
Well, how did I know then? I just suspected. Bullshit. What kind
of woman stalks her own boyfriend? Make that *ex*-boyfriend.

Somewhere below, a helicopter clattered toward a hospital, a
red light vanishing in the night. The northeast was tugging me
again to where my answer lay. I could find out what I already
knew: yes, he was with her. And then?

"You know my secret now," he'd said while standing in the
doorway. "You can keep yours, whatever it is. I don't care."

I stared northeast at the glowing grid of streets and pictured his face again. I felt hollow. I had no boyfriend, no job,
no money. Above, the dark was a chasm my ghostbody could
plummet into. I could float up and keep going. Feel the air
become thin, see the horizon curve and the stars brighten in
clear space. Could I survive up there? I didn't know. I flitted
up into the colder dark.

A gust of wind propelled a cloud of frozen ice crystals through
me. Each one twinkled inside me like the taste of a wind chime.
My ghost mouth tugged itself into the shape of a smile.

"I need a new life," I said to the empty sky. "Where do I
find that?"

No response, of course. Not a gentle tug nor a flash of insight.
There was no new life. Upward was the chasm. How far could
I go?

A lonely note sounded in the night; it held and faded and
sounded again. Far below a freight train crept, its whistle calling to the world, wheels beating steadily on steel. Enough self-
pity. The rest of the world was getting on with things, and I
was alive, healthy, and doing something most people couldn't.

I flitted down to skyscraper height and followed the train
westward through downtown. A streetcar dinged on Spadina
Avenue and clattered through an intersection. Something was
drawing me. I sank lower, followed the streetcar north. It passed
College Street; I broke away from it, dropped to rooftop level,
and flew west above the silent street. I felt the tug more strongly
now: it was like a child pulling at my sleeve, begging me to
come and see, come and see.

A few blocks further and I was in Little Italy, passing over the dense rows of shuttered bars and restaurants and patios, and still the voice whispered, *come*. The pull on my sleeve grew to a gentle hand wrapping my wrist, taking me past a comics shop, a clothing store, a barber, and there I stopped. Not the barber. Above it. The second floor was offices, venetian blinds closed behind the stencilled name of an accounting firm. Up again. The windows on the third floor had shabbier blinds and no name on the glass. Something was stuck to the corner of one pane. I went closer. A postcard taped to the glass and two words handwritten on it: "Help Wanted."

A sign where nobody could possibly see it.

Except me.

I flew home, plunged back into my skin and bones, and fell into the first proper sleep I'd had since, you know.

∞   ☼   ∞

By nine I was awake. One load of laundry later I put on a clean shirt and skirt and biked over to Little Italy.

I found the barbershop but had to cross the street to verify that there really was a tiny patch of white on the third-floor window. The door to the upstairs offices led into a stairwell where the lino predated the moon landings. Two scratched mailboxes hung at the foot of the stairs. One for the accountants on the second floor, the other unmarked. The stairs smelt of no cleaning. I stopped on the middle landing. My heart punched my ribs like a piston. Why was I so tense? What was I supposed to find here?

The door on the third floor was closed and had no name on it. I knocked on chipped cream paint, heard nothing, pushed the door open.

"Yeah, I know, I'll be able to pay—" The old man behind the desk fluttered an anxious hand. The voice on the other end of his phone was a tinny squawk. He looked up, managed a warm smile, and gestured to a collapsing armchair. "I'll have it by the end of the month. *Si. Grazie.*"

He put the phone down and turned to me. I was still standing. The seat of the armchair was covered in a Greenland-shaped stain, hopefully coffee. "Welcome," he said. "What can I do for you?"

I said, "I'm here because…" Seconds of silence ticked by. Partly because I had nothing prepared, partly because I was occupied with looking at him. He was short, in his sixties or

older, in an ancient brown shirt and with the haircut of a man
who tells the barber to do whatever's easiest. He could be one
of the Mediterranean men watching soccer in the neighbor-
hood's pre-gentrification bars. Except his eyes, old and wise
and gentle, didn't belong: not in this office, not in this city, not
in this century.

He gave me the kind of encouraging smile one uses to coax
sense out of the addled.

"Sorry," I said. "I'm here because of the help wanted sign
in the window."

His face changed like the sun coming out. "Fantastic! Glad
to meet you. I'm Tony."

"My name's Lilya." His handshake was muscular for a small
man. He'd worked hard in his life.

"Lilya?" He turned his head at an angle and looked me over.
"You're Zoroastrian? Parsi?"

"My family is. How did you know?"

"You're of an ancient people," he said. "I am Catholic, a
newcomer. Coffee? Anything?"

On the carpet, a dusty jar of instant coffee rested next to an
ancient steel kettle.

"No thanks. What does the job involve?"

"We find stuff. Things or people that go missing."

"We?"

"Just me now."

"So you're like a detective?"

He made a waggling gesture. "Sometimes. I'll give you an
example." From his back pocket he took a spiral notepad, pages
fat with writing, and tore the top page off. "Now, you want
to come in the back here? If you work for me, you can have
this office."

I followed him down the corridor. Two doors faced each
other; he pushed open the one on the left and ushered me in.

Against one wall lay a single bed, covered only with a bottom
sheet. No desk, no chair.

Sensible me wanted to flee. Instinctive me knew better. The
room was full of dusty emptiness. Nobody had been in here
for a long time. Tony had a hopeful but embarrassed air. He
casually positioned himself between me and the water-damage
stain on the wall.

"I had a co-worker, but he retired," he said. "Been doing everything myself. Hard to find good help."

"Tony," I said, "how do you find stuff?"

He handed me the piece of paper. "Why don't you show me how you'd do it?"

"Ana Costa," it read in a curious hand, like a medieval manuscript written with a cheap ballpoint. "Benaulim, Goa, India. Lost purse."

"Can you do it with me here?" he said.

"You mean…" My mouth was dry. I'd never talked to anyone about my knack, not since a crushing conversation with my parents after I'd recovered from appendicitis.

"Can you leave your body?" he said.

This was how Robinson Crusoe must have felt after he found that footprint. I wasn't alone. Tony knew. Tony would understand.

I just had to trust him.

I took a deep breath. "Yes. But…" But I'm not ready to leave my unoccupied body in a room with a man I just met.

"You don't know how to get to India? I'll teach you to go anywhere, like" — a dramatic gesture — "that."

I studied his face and the thousand years behind his eyes.

"And then?" I said. "I know how to find things, or people. But I can't pick up this woman's purse and leave it on the kitchen table."

"You don't touch anything. I'll show you how to whisper to them. They can't hear but they will know."

"And you'll come with me?"

He nodded. "I'll keep you safe, teach you the rules. We stay out of places we're not wanted, don't see anything we shouldn't."

His hands were open. Join me, his whole body begged.

With some effort I looked away from him, toward the door. The lost-and-found business could be just a cover. Imagine what he could do for an intelligence service or a criminal organization. His charming front could be a scheme to recruit me for my skills. Why should I trust someone I knew nothing about?

"I'll need to think about this."

He made a tiny nod. His shoulders sagged and for that moment I saw the great boulder of loneliness he carried. Then he smiled, and the moment was gone.

"I'll walk you downstairs," he said, in a voice that knew I'd never come back.

∞   ☼   ∞

The phone was ringing at the reception desk as we walked past. He ignored it. "Landlord again. I'm always late because my paycheque's always late."

"People pay you for what you do?"

"Not directly. I have a source of money. It's not much."

"Oh."

"You're wondering," he said. "How I can afford to take on help."

"I wasn't." I was actually wondering what this mysterious source was.

"The cheque comes in every month. I find more things, I get more money. Only I don't find so many things because I'm doing everything else. I write down the requests and I manage the office and I pay the bills and in between, if I have some time, I do some finding."

"Do people phone you? Or email?"

"Not usually."

I waited for him to explain further. He hummed an odd-sounding tune and continued downstairs. "So where are you from?" I finally asked.

"Lisbon, originally. Italy for a while. Came here a few years back." He halted on the stairs. His face was suddenly blank. He took out the notebook and wrote something rapidly with the page turned away from me. "Sorry. Busy day."

We had reached the hallway. He found a key in his pocket, opened the mailbox.

"*Mirabile dictu*," he said, and took out a brown envelope.

"The cheque's arrived?"

It went straight into his pocket. I caught a flash of an X-shaped logo. It looked vaguely familiar.

"Lilya," he said, pumping my hand, "it has been a great pleasure meeting you. If I could do anything to change your mind…"

*You could tell me who you're working for. Who you really are and why you do this.* But I didn't say it out loud; I thanked him for his time and left.

I spent the day distilling my résumé into its least pathetic form (that's right, employers: I'm *highly motivated* and *people-focused*), reading help-wanted postings online, and researching whether lying on a job application could get you arrested for fraud.

Around midnight I realized that there was only one job I wanted. I pushed out of the boundaries of my skin.

The bars and terraces on College Street were bursting with light and music, but I flew over them and found the third-floor window, with the postcard still there. Passing through glass always makes me shiver. The office was dark, the reception desk empty but for a scrap of paper: "Jean-Philippe Delacroix — Bamako, Mali — lost dog."

I glided down the corridor. I'd start looking for information in the other room, the one I hadn't seen inside. I eased myself through drywall and wooden studs. In the dark I made out a small sparsely filled bookshelf, a battered suitcase on the floor, a little table, a narrow bed— and a figure in it. Tony was asleep. Good. That envelope, torn open, lay on the table. In the dark I couldn't read the writing.

"You came back, Lilya."

He sat up in bed, looking at me. I panicked. I was supposed to be invisible.

"You really want to know?" he said. "I'll help you."

He stood and clicked the light on. He was wearing the kind of old linen nightshirt that you only see in period films, his thin legs and bony feet showing below the hem. Embarrassment flooded me. This was where Tony lived: in a bare room in his office with an iron bed and no decorations but for a wooden cross on the wall. His few books were tattered. I was certain that all his clothes fitted in that little suitcase.

Tony tapped the envelope. "You see?"

The logo printed on it was a pair of crossed keys. He pulled from inside it a cheque stub. I couldn't read much of the Italian on it, but I saw the name of the payee: Antonio di Padova.

He reached toward me and touched my mistformed hand. A burst of warmth ran through me, a taste of mint and sunshine.

"Go home now," he said. "Sleep. We talk tomorrow."

∞　✿　∞

"Good morning, Tony," I said, and settled into the sagging armchair. "Here, I brought you a proper coffee."

He sipped slowly, eyes closed, a smile easing onto his face. "Such luxury. Did you find out what you needed to know?"

"I did my research. You're older than you look."

"And I look like an old man." He laughed, eyes shining within a thousand creases. "So many people want my help. It keeps me young."

"Do I need to convert to your faith?"

"You need to be who you are."

"What would the money be like for me?"

"If you're good at finding, the Vatican will pay you well enough."

"But you're a monk. You don't need much."

"I'm a friar," he said. "Same vows of poverty and celibacy, but I live among the people. You're not bound to poverty, so you'll get paid better."

"So you don't sell your services to anyone? And you won't come on to me?"

He looked at me and said quietly, "I'll die before I break my vows."

"Okay, Tony." I cleared my throat. I wanted to make this sound official. "I mean, Anthony of Padua. I want a job where I can fly around the world helping people. I hereby apply for the position of sidekick to the patron saint of lost things."

∞   ☼   ∞

Born in Europe and based in Toronto, **LUKE MURPHY** is a writer, animator, designer, and film and video editor.

# CRUSHER AND TYPHOON

*Brent Nichols*

**THE RAILROAD LAY** sprawled across the mountain valley like a discarded toy. Dan Carter sat on the tiny porch on the back of his personal train car, gazing at where the tracks ended, and thought about the dreams that had died when Sir John A. Macdonald abandoned the National Dream.

"Bloody airships," he muttered. You couldn't see the country you were passing through in an airship, not like from a train. People said train travel took away the intimacy of riding and walking, but airships were much worse.

It had been ten years since polio had withered Dan's legs, three years since the National Dream had lifted him from the depths of self-pity. It had set his very blood on fire, carving a nation out of a wilderness, driving his way west until he challenged the granite walls of the Rocky Mountains themselves. He used to lie awake dreaming of the day he'd roll triumphantly into Gastown.

Now he never would. Now he was a scavenger, not a builder of nations and dreams. His job was to salvage rails and spikes from the road bed, load them onto flatcars, and ship them back east to be melted down for scrap. When he was finished the CPR would be no more, and even the role of scavenger would be taken away.

In the distance a dozen white men were pulling spikes and lifting rails while a couple of dozen Chinese watched. The Chinese were more victims of the airship infestation. The CPR had brought them to Canada in large numbers, put them to work building half a railroad, and discarded them like the rails.

Most of them were beyond salvage, Dan knew. They spoke little English, and the gulfs of race and culture would keep them unemployed. Unable to return to China and unable to move on, they had gathered in a makeshift village beside the tracks. Now the tracks were coming up and they were being left behind, in an inhospitable cleft between mountains, with winter coming on.

"At least they're able-bodied," Dan muttered.

"What's that, Mr. Carter?"

Dan glanced at Phil Jones, his assistant. "Nothing, Phil." He thought for a moment. "On second thought, I'd like to take a look at the work site."

"Really?" Phil no longer bothered to hide his annoyance at Dan's requests.

Forcing a wheelchair over rough ground was a hell of a chore, Dan was willing to concede, but it was, after all, the man's job. "Yes, really," he said curtly.

Phil sighed, got up, and went to grab the wheelchair ramp.

∞   ☼   ∞

Lee Wu sat on a low hill of broken rock, watching men lift rails that he'd worked damned hard to put in place. He was drunk, his head spinning from the rotgut whiskey he'd been sipping for most of the day. It was vile stuff, but it reduced the knot of frustrated rage in his belly, diffused and dispersed it until it was a warm glow that was almost pleasant.

A shout drew his attention to the shantytown near the tracks. He could see four young white men swaggering into the rude collection of shacks. They weren't workers from the rail salvage project. These were men of a different sort, two of them with pistols on their hips. One man shoved old Yi Ah out of his way. She reeled to the side and toppled, her brown limbs sticking up like twigs, and the white man kicked her foot out of his path.

Wu was halfway to the shantytown before he knew he'd decided to act. The ground seemed far away, and he cursed the alcohol he'd drunk. There was a time, long ago, when he'd been a warrior. That was in China, a world and a lifetime away, and he was all too aware of how far he'd fallen.

Still, he remembered a thing or two.

A handful of Chinese men stood in an uncertain cluster, looking to each other for courage, and the four strangers strutted toward them. The confrontation was about to reach its peak, and Wu could only hope that no one would draw a gun.

He could see other white men leaving their work at the rails and sauntering over to watch. Bitter experience told Wu that they would be no help at all. This was a problem for the Chinese, and the Chinese would have to handle it.

The four white men reached the cluster of Chinese and shouldered their way through, grinning, clearly hoping someone would object. A brawny hand hit Zhao Bo in the chest, knocking him onto his rear end. Bo's face turned red, a man laughed, and Wu picked up his pace, knowing the fight was about to start.

∞  ☼  ∞

"Faster," said Dan, and Phil made a disparaging sound behind him. He did pick up the pace, though, nearly spilling Dan from the seat as the chair bounced on rocks and bits of scrap lumber. They reached the long line of gawking workmen, and Phil slid the chair between two men, allowing Dan to see.

Dan was just in time to see a thin young man in a white Stetson draw a six-gun from the holster on his hip. The gun swung up, the sun glittered on the cylinder, and there was a blur of motion too fast for Dan to follow. The gun went spinning through the air, landing in the weeds thirty or more feet from the site of the brawl.

Almost a dozen men were pushing and shoving, sometimes throwing a punch. Directly in front of Dan, though, two men were facing off. The skinny man in the Stetson was holding his wrist and facing a slim Chinese man in a blue shirt. The skinny cowboy let go of his wrist and advanced, throwing punches left and right. He was good, too, snapping out crisp jabs and crosses, never telegraphing, never slowing down.

And every punch missed.

The Chinese man stood in front of him, bobbing and weaving, ducking, seeming to flow out of the way each time a fist came lashing at his face. There was a confident smirk on his face as he dodged one blow after another, until the cowboy lowered his arms, red-faced and panting.

His companions, though, were faring better. Two of the Chinese men were down, and another man staggered back from the fight, hands pressed to his face, blood pouring down his chin. The remaining two Chinese looked at each other, then broke and ran.

One cowboy stepped forward, coming up behind the Chinese in the blue shirt, and slammed a punch into the back of the man's neck. The Chinese man stumbled forward, crashed into the skinny man's chest, and collapsed.

After that, things turned ugly. A Chinese boy on the ground, he couldn't have been more than sixteen, rose to his hands and knees, and the nearest cowboy drove a boot into his ribs. The boy collapsed with a grunt, curling into a ball. Two more kicks landed, then a third, and a girl in a long grey dress burst between the watching cowboys. She was shouting in Chinese as she dropped to her knees beside the boy, covering him with her body.

The cowboy kept kicking. She cried out as his boots hit her, and Dan echoed her cry, a wordless bellow of outrage. At first he had watched the fight with an instinctive sympathy for his fellow white men, but this was unconscionable.

The cowboy lost his patience and stooped, grabbed her by the hair, and hauled her to her feet. He punched her in the face and threw her to one side.

The men to Dan's left and right watched, and did nothing.

"Don't just stand there, you miserable cowards," Dan shouted. One man gave him an uncomfortable glance before looking away. The rest ignored him.

"Fine," he said. "If I'm the only man here…" And he put his hands on the arms of his chair. The chair started to roll as he pushed himself upward, but Phil, useful for once, caught the handles. With a final heave Dan made it onto his feet and stood swaying, gathering himself. When he was rested he could make it across a room. Here on rough ground he knew he wouldn't get far. Still, he could not watch a woman being beaten and not do something about it.

He took a step. Then another. His legs shook, he had to wave his arms for balance, but he managed a third step, and a fourth. He was six or eight feet from the cowboy in the white Stetson, and the man turned to gape at him. Dan took another step, clenching his fists, and the cowboy laughed.

The laugh trailed off as the man looked past Dan's shoulder. The workers, shamed at last into action, started passing Dan on both sides, and the cowboys quickly closed into a tight, defensive group. One man drew a pistol, and the two groups froze, several paces apart.

"Maybe it's time you men cleared on out of here," Phil said. There was some muttering and threatening on both sides, but the four cowboys edged back, trying to look as if retreat was their own idea.

A few feet from Dan, the Chinese man in the blue shirt sat up, then rose to his feet. He took a step, clapped a hand to the back of his neck, staggered sideways, and bumped into Dan. The two of them collapsed together in an undignified heap.

∞   ☼   ∞

Wu woke up with a blinding headache. This happened often since Bo had finished his still, but this time was worse. He groaned and opened an eye.

"How do you feel?"

Wu blinked. There was a white man looking down at him, smiling. Wu was on his back in a small, elegant room. The light stabbed into his eyes, so he closed them.

"Do you speak any English? Hello? English?" The man jostled Wu's shoulder.

"Go away."

"Ah! You *do* speak English. It's my train car, so I must decline your request."

Most of that speech went over Wu's head. He forced an eyelid open, then another. Windows beside him let in a stream of sunlight, and he turned his head away while his eyes adjusted. The urge to groan again was strong, but he suppressed it. There was a time when he had endured much worse, without so much as a grimace. *Have I really fallen so far?*

"Are you all right? You took quite a punch."

Memory came flooding in, and with it a wave of humiliation. Four clumsy, slow-moving amateurs, three of them preoccupied with Wu's friends, and they had managed to best him. He brought his hands up in front of his face. His knuckles, grown soft in the long years he'd been out of training, were smooth, unblemished. He hadn't even landed a punch.

He sat up, gritting his teeth against the pain. He wanted to hold his neck, to explore the knot on the back of his head, but he wouldn't do it with this smirking white man watching. He glared. The chair with its enormous wheels just deepened his shame. Wu, mighty warrior of the Granite Palm Brotherhood, had been rescued by a cripple!

"Easy," the man said. "You've taken quite a—"

Wu lurched to his feet with a snarl. The train car spun around him, his vision faded, and he stumbled toward the door. The world went black before he reached it, and he groped blindly for the doorknob. He got the door open, stumbled down a short staircase, and was a half-dozen steps from the railcar before his vision came back.

He made his way to the shack he shared with several other young men and sat with his back against the wall. He had the shack to himself, so he gave in to weakness, cradling his head in his hands. At first he was alarmed by the way his dizziness persisted. At last he figured out that he was still drunk. He'd been unconscious for no more than a few minutes.

For more than an hour he sat there, steeped in pain, feeling sorry for himself. He couldn't sustain the self-indulgent mood, though. Old habits, old training were reasserting themselves, and he found himself thinking strategically, tactically. Violence, once a mainstay of his life, had returned, and dormant skills were stirring in Wu's mind.

Those four men had lost much face. They would return, when the salvage team had moved on and the Chinese were alone. They would not be so careless next time. They would be cautious. They would be armed. And they would be look-ing for revenge.

The others had no experience with mayhem. Only Wu had faced violent conflict before, and he was a wreck, a shadow of his former self.

He stood, rolled his neck from side to side, and let the pain wash over him. Pain was irrelevant. When he had mastered the pain, pushed it into a box in the recesses of his mind, he lowered himself into a cat stance.

He felt ridiculous, like a little boy playing at kung fu.

"Power flows from within," he murmured. It was the lesson at the heart of all his training. Water could not flow from a bucket of stones. An arrow would not fly straight from a crooked bow.

A disgraced drunkard with a heart full of shame could not master kung fu.

∞   ☼   ∞

Dan looked up at the sound of a knock, surprised that Phil had remembered a simple courtesy. "Come in."

The slim Chinese man entered, closing the door behind him. He had washed and shaved, and though he still smelled of alcohol, it was much less than before. He stood in front of Dan, his pose humble, and said, "Excuse. Did not close door when I left."

"That's all right," Dan said, perplexed.

"Did not say thank you," the man said. "Thank you."

"You're welcome," Dan said. "I'm sorry I couldn't do anything sooner. Are the others all right? That girl?"

The man looked up, surprised. "Big..." He gestured with his fingers around his eye. "Marks."

"Bruises?"

"Yes. Bruises," he said. "Will get better."

"Oh, good." They lapsed into silence. "My name is Dan."

"Hello, Mr. Dan. I am Lee Wu."

Dan grinned. "Just Dan. I'm pleased to meet you, Mr. Wu."

Wu shook his head. "It is Mr. Lee."

"Wu Lee?"

"No, Lee Wu. Mr. Lee. Or Wu. You call me Wu."

Dan shook his head, baffled. "All right. I'm pleased to meet you, Wu."

The silence stretched out. Finally Dan said, "Would you like something to eat?"

Wu scowled, then smoothed his features. "No."

*He can't be eating much,* Dan thought. *But he's proud. I've just insulted him.* "How about tea?" he said. "You're a guest in my home. I have to offer you tea."

Wu stared at him, then inclined his head. "I would like tea."

Dan wheeled his chair to the tiny stove in the corner. Phil, the oaf, had left the tea canister on a high shelf, and Dan braced an arm on the counter, straining upward.

"I help?" Wu said.

"I can do it," Dan said testily. The chair started to roll, then stopped. Wu had to be holding it, but at least he didn't reach for the tea canister. Dan strained and stretched, and at last brought the canister tumbling into his lap. He glanced back at Wu, checking for signs of amusement. Wu just stared at him, face impassive.

*Christ. I'm as touchy as he is.* The thought made him laugh, and the tea canister fell to the floor as his legs shook. He could have reached it with only a little trouble, but he made himself sit still. "Do you mind?" he said, gesturing, and Wu picked up the tea. "Thank you."

Dan brewed the tea, but he let Wu carry the cups to the little fold-down table. After that he asked Wu to get a box of biscuits from a cupboard. That must have been an adequate sop to the man's pride, because he sat across from Dan and devoured half of the biscuits in a minute or two.

"I want you to be my new valet," Dan blurted suddenly. He hadn't known he was going to say it until the words were out of his mouth, and he saw Wu's eyes narrow. The man was suspicious of charity.

"The pay's not very good, I'm afraid," Dan said. "I have this lout working for me now. I need someone better." He lowered his eyes. "There's too many things I can't do on my own." The fact might have been perfectly obvious, but it still shamed him to admit it.

"Yes," said Wu.

∞    ✿    ∞

Two days later the train rolled out of the valley and over the crest of Kicking Horse Pass. They were only a few miles from Golden City, a fast-fading town that wouldn't long survive the death of the railway.

Most of the workers trekked into town each night, choosing the comforts of hotels and boarding houses over the canvas tents that the train carried. For Dan the hotels with their staircases were no comfort at all, and he stayed in his train car. Wu was an alert presence at his side, attentive and cheerful. He was a tremendous improvement over Phil.

In the evenings Dan would read or go over blueprints, and Wu would go outside and launch punches and kicks into the night air. He called his fighting style "kung fu," and he was very good at it. Dan realized he'd hired himself a bodyguard as well as a valet.

He was going over the designs of his walking suit one evening when Wu tapped on the door. "Come in," he called, beginning to roll up the blueprints.

He bumped the inkwell on the corner of the desk, grabbed for it, and barely caught it in time. He was putting a cap on the inkwell when Wu said, "What's that?"

"It's nothing," Dan snapped, and started rolling the blue-prints. He could feel a flush rising on his neck. Then he caught sight of the hurt look on Wu's face, and he paused. Finally he sighed and unrolled the papers.

"It's a steam-powered walking machine," he said. "I designed it. I doubt anyone will ever build it, though."

Wu's brow furrowed. His English had improved considerably in the three weeks he'd been in Dan's employ, but this had to be stretching his linguistic abilities. He reached down, tracing the lines on the top sheet without ever quite touching the paper.

"It's a dream, that's all," Dan said gruffly. "That's my life. Ideas. You're a hands-on man. You don't know what it's like to be trapped in your head." He thumped the arm of the wheelchair. "Trapped in a chair. Nothing but ideas and no follow-through." He rolled up the blueprints, ignoring the fact that Wu was still trying to decipher them, and shoved the roll irritably into a cubbyhole in his desk. "Forget about it."

∞　✿　∞

The next day the salvage train stopped beside an abandoned shed. Wu rolled Dan outside to take a look.

A brass and iron machine filled one end of the building. Long wooden bins held chunks of rock, detritus from the end-less blasting. Along the opposite wall there were small trays, each filled with gravel. Dan got Wu to lift a tray down. It held crushed stone, a mix of gravel and sand, most of it granite with some quartz mixed in.

"Wheel me closer to that machine," he said. He stared at the valves and gears for a time. "It's a rock crusher," he said at last. "Someone was prospecting."

"Pros..." Wu said.

"Prospecting." Dan repeated the word slowly. "Looking for gold. There was quartz in the granite, so someone started breaking it down, looking for traces of gold." He handed the tray to Wu. "I guess he didn't find anything." He looked at the crusher for a bit. "Take me back to the car," he said. "Then I have a different sort of job for you. That machine is salvage-able. It's not worth much, but we might as well take it apart and bring it along."

∞　✿　∞

The crushing machine was remarkably compact for the power it was able to exert. There was a boiler, a condenser, a complex gearing mechanism, and a steel hammer and strike plate. Wu took his time, examining everything before he tried to take anything apart. He checked the boiler, started a fire, then scrounged some blank paper from Dan's desk and made careful sketches. By the time he was sure someone would be able to put the machine back together, the needle on the pressure gauge had moved halfway across the dial. He pulled the lever on the side and the machine shuddered into motion.

Everything moved as he had predicted, and he smiled, pleased with himself. He extinguished the fire and returned to his sketches.

As he worked, though, part of his mind wandered. Every piece of the rock crusher fit exactly in its spot. Wu had fit nicely in his place in a complex machine, once. Things had gone badly, he had fled to Canada, and he had never quite fit again.

He had found a dreary place in the CPR for a time. But now the CPR, like this rock crusher, was a machine without a purpose, the parts about to become scrap and waste, rusting forgotten underfoot.

The crusher was still too hot to touch. He returned to the train. Dan was on the little porch, engrossed in a ledger, so Wu moved past him and stood in front of Dan's desk.

Ideas were Dan's department, not Wu's. But Dan had taken action during the fight at the shantytown. If Dan could act, maybe Wu could have an idea. He took the blueprints for the walking machine from their cubbyhole, covered them with his drawings of the crusher, and returned to the shed.

That afternoon, Wu jogged to the shantytown. He spoke to his friends, outlining parts of his plan. Wu wasn't offering much, but the men were idle and hungry. He would buy a sack of rice and a sack of sugar with his meager salary, and in exchange his team would go to work.

∞   ☼   ∞

A week later the salvage train was three miles further down the track. Dan was seated in a grassy meadow, sketching Kicking Horse Pass, trying to capture the majesty of what he saw in humble charcoal. It was Sunday, and he and Wu had the train to themselves. He was growing frustrated with the sketch when Wu cleared his throat somewhere behind Dan.

Dan turned the chair around. Wu stood there, hands clasped behind him, looking strangely diffident. "I... show you something," he said.

"All right." Dan set aside his paper and charcoal. "What is it?"

In response Wu circled behind him, took the handles of the chair, and wheeled him across the grass. They reached the rail bed, bumped over the tracks, and descended to the meadow on the other side. The chair stopped, and Dan blinked in surprise.

Standing beside the private car was a... contraption. That was the only word for it. The thing had a vaguely manlike shape, with legs and arms of steel and copper. He could see pieces taken from the crushing machine and pieces he didn't recognize. Wu must have pillaged every bit of machinery in the shantytown, from sewing machines to scraps of corrugated iron. The result was a monstrosity, but Wu beamed with pride as he pointed at it.

"Your design," he said. "Some changes. But it works. It walks." He gestured at Dan. "You go in. You walk."

Dan looked again at the monstrosity, and his perception shifted. In a flash he recognized what he was seeing. It really was his design for a walking machine, with nearly every part substituted for something else, something scrounged or cobbled together. It was a parody of his dream, a mockery, and he felt heat fill his face. "You bloody heathen!" He was as angry as he could ever remember being. "Get that piece of garbage out of my sight!"

He twisted the chair around, turned his back on the travesty of engineering, and wheeled himself, one painful foot at a time, across the grass. He had no idea where he was going. He just needed to be away from Wu, away from the machine, away from it all.

He might have travelled fifty feet, with exhaustion blunting the edge of his rage, when he saw the riders. There were six of them, staying well back from the train as they curved toward the pass. It was hard to make out details, but he thought they were wearing masks.

The lead rider was a skinny man with a white Stetson. Dan didn't need to see his face to know who that was, and what it meant.

It meant trouble.

He could see Golden City less than two miles away. It might as well have been on the moon. By the time he got halfway to town it would all be over.

He spun the chair around, grimacing at the effort it required in the tall grass. The salvage train stood alone, the metal contraption beside it. Wu was nowhere in sight.

The manlike machine seemed to stare at him, mocking him in his helplessness, and he squeezed the arms of the chair until the tendons stood out under his skin. If Wu had just stuck around, maybe they could have gone for help. But no, Wu, the man of action, was no doubt trying to save his people.

He was busy getting himself killed.

*He's not entirely a man of action. He had at least one idea.* Dan sneered at the thought that was tickling the back of his mind. A man of action could become a man of ideas, but it didn't work quite the same way in reverse. A man trapped in a chair could not simply decide to be a man of action. Maybe if the walking suit had been constructed properly, in a real workshop, with suitable supplies. The metal travesty in front of him didn't look as if it could even move.

And yet here it was. In the open meadow, two miles or more from the shed where Wu must have built it.

He sat there, staring at the machine. He dropped his hands to the wheels of the chair and started himself rolling.

∞    ☼    ∞

Wu was in his element, and he gloried in it. The battle was hopeless, but he felt more fully alive, more fully himself, than he had since fleeing China. He had broken men's guns. He had broken men's bones. One of the gang was dead, lying face-down in the street beside his horse. The man in the white Stetson was with him, both legs broken, his gun gone, sobbing quietly.

The remaining four cowboys, though, were armed, unhurt, and angry. They were working their way from building to building, covering each other, shooting at anything that moved. Wu was one building ahead, slowly retreating. He let them catch occasional glimpses of him, and encouraged them to waste their ammunition. He kept them afraid, and gave the others time to flee the town.

Wu was going to die. He accepted it. The Canadian West, so different from Shanghai, gave a man so few places to hide, so few directions to retreat. And if he escaped they would return and take their revenge on any Chinese they could find.

So he would let them kill him. The survivors would ride away satisfied. But he would hurt them first. He would leave them with no appetite for this sort of fun.

He slid out a window on the east side of Ping Yan's shack, once a makeshift saloon for railroad workers. The Chinese hadn't been allowed inside, back then. He could hear the cowboys call to each other as they reached the west wall of the shack, and he measured the distance to the next building. For three buildings in a row he had retreated. They were hurrying now, growing impatient, growing careless.

They were ripe for an ambush.

He flattened himself against the wall at the north corner. The man to the north had shorter legs than the man to the south, yet he moved faster. He had the more aggressive nature, and it was going to cost him.

In the last moment before he was about to move, Wu heard a strange sound. It was a grinding metallic noise, and he heard the cowboys call to each other, their voices rising in puzzlement. That meant distraction, so Wu stepped around the corner. The nearest fool was staring back over his shoulder, so Wu plucked the pistol from the man's hand and dropped him with a palm strike.

That caught the attention of the others, and Wu had to scramble back as bullets scorched the air around him. He sprang and pulled himself onto the roof of the saloon.

That was when he saw Dan.

The walking machine was lumbering across the meadow, arms and legs swinging, steam puffing out at the hip joints. *We'll have to tweak that,* Wu thought absently. *Or he'll have to carry more water, and he'll be even heavier.*

That the machine was heavy was unmistakable. Dan left a trail of crushed grass and dented earth behind him as he bore down on the shantytown. Wu couldn't see the cowboys, but he heard them asking each other what the Hell that was, coming across the grass toward them.

A bullet tore through the roof several feet away, and Wu tensed, then made himself keep still. The roof would creak if he moved. Two more shots came through, one uncomfortably close, and the shooting stopped. Wu glanced left, toward the doorway. The man would go outside, stand well back from the building, and shoot him from there. He ought to be coming through the doorway right about...

Wu sprang, twisted in midair, grabbed the edge of the roof above the doorway, and swung down feet-first. The door was just starting to move, and he drove one foot into the boards just above the doorknob. The door slammed shut, his foot burst through, and he felt his sole strike flesh. A man grunted, Wu landed on his back, and he spent a bad moment getting his foot free.

Luckily neither of the remaining cowboys looked back. They were walking slowly toward Dan, guns levelled.

Dan would need help shortly. Wu rolled to his feet and sprang through a window, landing hands-first on the floor and rolling. He crashed into a stool, knocked it over, and came to his feet in time to see the cowboy, one hand pressed to his side, drawing a bead with his pistol.

In a single fluid motion Wu dropped backward and lashed out with his foot. He caught the leg of the stool with his instep and flipped it up an instant before he landed on his back on the floor.

The stool sailed up, a bullet clipped the seat, and the stool crashed into the man at knee height. He cried out and doubled over, and by the time he straightened up Wu was in mid-air. A foot took the man in the middle of the chest, and he crashed backward into the wall.

Wu stepped to the doorway, ignoring the fallen man. It was a solid kick. That man was out of the fight.

Outside, the two cowboys were shooting at Dan. The walking suit had a steel chest plate, and Dan had his arms up to protect his face. Bullets bounced and ricocheted, and the man on Wu's left swore as a near miss kicked up dust beside his boot. His gun clicked empty and he fumbled cartridges from his belt.

Wu saw his chance and sprang through the doorway, lunging for the man on the right. The man spun just in time to take a kick to the stomach. Wu followed with an elbow strike, then turned.

The last man was backpedalling frantically across the grass, dropping cartridges as he went, dodging Dan's thrashing metal arms. Dan's blueprints had crude hands on the ends of the arms, but the machine he wore had blunt steel bars without even elbows. The steam-powered shoulder joints let Dan thrash the arms left and right, and that was more than enough to keep the cowboy retreating. At last he dropped his pistol, turned, and ran toward the shantytown, perhaps thinking he could hide. Wu heard Zhao Bo let out a cry like a hunting wolf. Several men echoed the cry, and Wu smiled as he heard fists striking flesh.

The attack on the shantytown was over.

∞    ☼    ∞

"I'm not sure I really did anything," Dan said later that evening.

"You save me," Wu told him. "But suit needs weapons."

Dan nodded. "That thought did cross my mind. I have a few ideas." He chuckled at the absurdity of the conversation. Still, you never knew what the future might hold. "Maybe we'll start by rebuilding the suit. From scratch, in a proper workshop." He gestured at the window behind him, beyond which stood the bulk of the walking suit. "You've done a brilliant job working out the basics. Now we've got something to build from."

Wu reddened and smiled.

"The reward money should get your friends through the winter," Dan said. At least two of the cowboys had prices on their heads, and a third man might have been a notorious American bank robber known as the Montana Kid. A squad of North-West Mounted Police was on its way to collect the prisoners and distribute reward monies.

Life wouldn't be easy for the Chinese, but the world was in the biggest state of flux it had ever known, and change meant opportunities. They would find a place in the new world that was emerging.

"What about us?" Dan mused aloud. "What will our place be in this new world?" He shook his head. "I was so focused for so long on building this railroad. Making my way all the way west to Gastown. You too, I guess."

Wu nodded.

"Well," said Dan, "we could press on to Gastown anyway." He leaned back in his chair. "It won't be easy. I'll have to leave this nice comfortable railcar behind." He looked at Wu. "It won't be easy for you, either. You'll have to help me into and out of a lot of wagons and steamboats and stagecoaches. But we'll get there."

Wu nodded again, looking undaunted by the challenge.

Dan smiled. He'd get to the coast, not by rail like he'd imagined, but overland, seeing every inch of the country. Let other travellers drift over the Rockies in airships. Dan was going to see Canada the way a man should. From the ground.

As for when he reached Gastown... well, the acts of greedy and evil men weren't restricted to the wilderness. He might find a role to play in the big city for a steam-powered walking machine and a kung fu warrior.

∞   ☼   ∞

**BRENT NICHOLS** is a writer based in Calgary.

# BLACK SHEEP

*Jason Sharp*

AS ESCAPE PLANS go, it was pretty disgusting.

Before I'd even been sent to the Special Handling Unit of the Joliette Institution for Women, the Feds had known they'd need to keep me away from water. They'd gone to the trouble of building a new wing all for me. It had climate control to keep the interior humidity low. The toilet was a composter with a long drain pipe. I got damp cloth for sponge baths and hand-cleaning rather than a sink or trips to a bathroom. There wasn't even a sprinkler system for fire suppression— something I'd had my lawyer tackle, but the government had cited some special anti-terrorist law that let them get away with it.

Even my drinking water was rationed out. Every two hours during waking hours, a plastic bottle with a quarter-litre of water was pushed through the slot in my cell door. If I drank it and pushed the bottle back through, it'd arrive again, refilled, in two hours. If I didn't... they'd wait until I *did*.

So it took a while to work out how I was going to do it.

Timing was another issue. I had minimal contact with the outside world— TV, newspapers, books from the prison library. My lawyer dropped by every few weeks. Rarely — very, very rarely — I received snail mail from my thirteen-year-old cousin; the envelopes were always pre-opened and, I had found on one occasion, actively censored. But Lucie had, nonetheless, told me — quite accidently, I'm sure — when to break out.

It was the last Saturday of July: the tail end of Québec's construction holiday, when projects across the province shut down for two weeks and all the workers go on vacation. I had uncles and cousins on jobsites doing electrical work, plumbing, and brickwork, so this was one of three weekends when they could all get together. Lucie had written that Aunt Hélène and Uncle Serge would be hosting a family reunion at their place in Montréal.

Thus, on the last Friday of July, I made point of not using the composting toilet before lights-out. It didn't make for a comfortable sleep; by the time the lights came back on at six in the morning, the pressure in my bladder was something fierce. I thought dry thoughts and took a stab at the crossword in the previous day's *Gazette*, watching the clock.

At 6:57, I finally shuffled over to the composting toilet.

At 6:59, I heard the faint footsteps of the guard bringing my breakfast. I pulled up my jumper and scurried over to my bunk.

At 7:00, the footsteps stopped. "Stand clear of the door," the guard's muffled voice barked, and then, "What—" and *then* came the simultaneous sounds of vomiting and urination. I reached out and called the liquid through the door slot— then combined it with the urine I'd kept clinging to the bowl of the toilet. Darted forward to pop the top off the water bottle and added its contents. Flash-dehydrated my breakfast. Wicked the moisture off the skin and clothes of the heaving guard.

I now had a pool of about 1.8 liters of bile, urine, and water on the floor of my cell. I pulled the solution up in a thin column and fired a narrow high-velocity stream into the narrow gap between the door and the wall. The liquid cut through the locks in a matter of seconds, and I slammed myself against the door.

It jammed against the guard's spasming body, but there was enough of a gap for me to squeeze through. Another door opened, and I propelled my captive liquid across the room; the guard coming through the door slipped and fell, and then he puked and pissed himself as well.

In a matter of minutes, I'd incapacitated eight guards and had close to ten liters at hand. Once I was outside, I sucked the humidity out of the air and formed a fog cloud to conceal me from snipers as I cut through the outer fence and fled into the stand of trees beyond.

∞   ✿   ∞

I'd shed my orange jumper, so I emerged from the forest lining the back fence of a townhouse lot wearing nothing but a grey cotton bra and matching panties. I clambered over the chain link, poking myself in a few places, and fell down into the yard of an end unit. A quick sprint across freshly mowed grass brought me to a side gate. I continued out, across a street, through a narrow line of bush, and into the back lot of a big box store.

I spied a middle-aged woman in the parking lot loading groceries into the trunk of a little silver Toyota and jogged up to her. "Good morning!"

"Good morning!" she replied, her expression turning quizzical as she took in my near-nudity.

"Any chance you could help me out?" I asked.

Sweat was already beading on her skin. "Um… Maybe… Is there a problem?"

"Well, I've lost my purse, and so I don't have my phone or keys," I explained as the woman's T-shirt and jeans darkened with moisture and her face grew pale. "I was wondering if… hey, are you okay?"

Her head wobbled. "I'm… I'm feeling…"

"Dizzy? Here, let's sit you down before you fall." I eased her down to the asphalt, leaning her against the metallic green SUV parked next to her car.

"What's going on?" she mumbled. "I was fine until just a… just a minute ago…"

"I think you're dehydrated, dear," I said with a sympathetic smile.

∞   ☼   ∞

The Sûreté du Québec cruiser followed me onto the shoulder of the road.

I put the Toyota in park and flipped the lid off the travel mug sitting in the cup holder.

I watched through the driver's mirror as the cop approached with one hand on a holster. I lowered the window, placed both hands on the wheel, and waited.

"Good morning, Madame," he said, taking in my state of undress and standing about two metres away from the door.

"Morning, officer," I replied. "What's wrong? I thought I was doing the speed limit."

"Is this your car, Madame?" he asked.

"Yes," I said. "Well, mine and my husband's."

"Can I see your licence and registration, please?"

"Yes, of course," I replied, reaching for the glove compartment. I fished around for something that looked official. "Okay, here's the registration," I said, transferring the piece of paper to my left hand.

The cop stepped forward to take the paper. A jet of luke-warm coffee shot from the travel mug, past my face, through the open window, and directly into his nostrils. He doubled over, hacking and choking, and I put the car in drive again.

∞ ☼ ∞

Perhaps the three fishermen in the rowboat didn't see a lot of half-naked women out on the river. Or perhaps they did but didn't care that I was middle-aged and out of shape. Either way, they waved and whistled as I cruised past, so I smiled and waved back.

At some point, one of them would probably comment on how quiet my outboard was and the other two would tell him to shut up and fish. Truth be told, I hadn't used the outboard since I'd stolen the boat from a backyard dock in Lavaltrie. I simply parted the water around the bow, pushed it in around the stern, and moved forward.

This trip up the St. Lawrence was blissful. The kind of zen I couldn't find in Joliette. The heat of the sun was glorious on my skin. The presence of all the water around me was reas-suring. The sound of the boat cutting through the water and the calling of gulls was soothing.

As I was cruising past Île Marie, a Sûreté du Québec power-boat passed in the other direction. I waved, one of the occupants waved back. I wasn't surprised to see a police presence on the water, nor was I particularly surprised when the powerboat made a 180-degree turn. Lights came on, and a garbled voice shouted something about killing the motor.

I chuckled at the irony and pulled the water out from under them. The powerboat fell into the bowl-shaped trough until the gunwales were below the level of the river, and then I released the water looming around the boat.

∞ ☼ ∞

It took the rest of the morning and the early part of the morn-ing to finish what had to be done: Get to Montréal, ditch the boat, dehydrate the creepy dude watching me come ashore and steal his pants, liberate some cash from a bank machine, buy an outfit, and hail a cab.

It dropped me off at Aunt Hélène's house at quarter to two.

Muffled music, voices, and splashing were audible from the backyard, but the front was deserted. Nobody out smoking on the porch, no kids playing hockey on the hot asphalt driveway. The nearest visible person was a woman kneeling at a flower garden four houses down.

I exhaled sharply, jabbed the doorbell, and waited.

The door opened to reveal a pudgy woman with short, curly black hair not unlike my own. She stared blankly for several seconds before finally saying, "Martine..."

"Hi, Auntie," I said.

"We ... I didn't know you were coming."

I shrugged. "Not watching the news, I take it?"

"No..." Aunt Hélène hesitated. "I suppose... I suppose I should let you in."

She stepped back to admit me into the old house. It was cold inside, the air-conditioning sucking a small fortune in hydroelectricity off the grid. "Thanks," I said. "Shoes on or off?"

"Leave them on," she said, turning away before bellowing, "Louise!"

My mother's voice came from out back. "What?"

"It's for you!" Auntie answered. "Just wait here," she said to me before disappearing into the kitchen.

Mom appeared momentarily, wearing a sundress and flip-flops. Her sunburned face shifted from curiosity to shock, and then she marched forward until she was practically nose to nose with me. "What are you doing here?" she growled.

"I'm here for the party," I said.

"You know what I mean," she said.

"I got out."

"Got out, or got let out?" she demanded, folding her arms in front of her chest.

"Does it matter?" I asked.

She nodded.

"I got let out," I said.

"You're lying."

"Yes, I am."

She sighed, her head kind of wobbled about, and then she threw her hands up. "What do I do with you? Do I call the police?"

"They'll be here soon enough," I said. "There won't be a scene, I promise." Well, more accurately, I'd try not to create one.

Couldn't really speak for the law on that one. I'd embarrassed and inconvenienced a fair number of their buddies already today.

"At least you're not wearing prison clothes. Where'd you get those?" she asked, pointing at my T-shirt and blue jeans. "Did you steal them?"

"I bought them. Although the money was stolen," I answered. "Look, I haven't got a lot of time. Are we gonna spend it all on the usual crap, or can I see my family?"

Her glare would've melted a weaker person. "Behave," she said in a voice colder than the air-conditioning.

I nodded, and she let me slip around her. I pushed the screen door open and stepped onto the deck.

The party deflated as my presence registered. Uncle Serge, flipping burgers on the barbeque to my left, let a patty fall to the deck; beside him, my brother Maurice glared at me. Aunts, uncles, and cousins sitting in deckchairs or standing around the pool turned and stared. A few unfamiliar faces — the older ones perhaps neighbors, the younger ones perhaps new boyfriends or girlfriends — followed suit, confused. Even the kids in the pool seemed to notice something was amiss, though it didn't stop their murderball game.

My brother darted forward and hissed, "You've got a lotta nerve."

"Nice to see you too, Mo," I said.

"Do you have any idea how humiliating it is for Mom just having you here?"

"For her or for you?"

"For both of us, then," he said.

"No," I said. "You guys had nothing to do with it. Anybody who wants to blame you is stupid. Now, where's Nana?"

"Sleeping." I pivoted on my left heel, but Maurice quick-stepped around me to block the way inside. "She needs the rest," he said. "She'll be up again soon enough."

"Sooner I see her, the sooner I leave," I said.

"She won't even recognize you. She's that bad," he said.

"Doesn't matter," I said. "I want to see her."

"Then I'll talk to Mom and Hélène. See if we can rouse her for a bit. But if you push your luck, superpowers or not, I will kick your ass. Got it?"

He was practically nose to nose, just like Mom had been minutes earlier. I stared back at him for a bit, then said, "I understand what you're saying. Lucie here? I don't see her either."

"No, I heard she's got food poisoning or something."

"Damn," I said.

"She told you, I take it," he sighed. "Makes sense. She seems convinced that you're innocent of everything."

"You gonna tell her parents?"

"They should know," Mo said. "Go grab some lunch or something— but stay the fuck away from my kids."

He withdrew to the barbeque as I ambled toward a picnic table draped in a checkered vinyl cloth and covered with bowls and dishes of various sizes. My cousin Jocelyne and her husband Sammy noticed my approach as they were filling their paper plates and shied away.

Pursing my lips, I picked up a plate of my own. Pickles, cheese, coleslaw, a bit of Mom's pasta salad. Some cold cuts and pork and beans I hoped hadn't been sitting out too long. A bun with specks of rosemary and some real salted butter— not the margarine I always ended up with in Joliette. A can of Labatt Blue, my first beer in three years.

Not a soul showed any interest in me when I looked up from the cooler, so I found a vacant patch of lawn by the back fence and watched everybody as I picked at my meal. I spotted Mo's wife Sylvie by the pool, keeping an eye on their two little boys as they splashed about. She had a bit of a belly that might've been middle-aged weight or a third kid on the way, it was hard to tell.

Mom had come out and was speaking with Mo. Now that I wasn't arguing with her at close range, I noted that she'd lost weight. The bulge of her elbows and knees contrasted with the narrowness of her forearms and lower legs. It didn't look healthy.

My cousin Jacques and a good-looking black boy were drinking beers and throwing plastic horseshoes at one of two bright pink posts along the west side of the fence. I didn't know the other guy, but when he looked over and caught my eye he smiled.

I pushed away from the fence and joined them as Jacques took aim and skipped a horseshoe just past his target. "Merde," he muttered.

"You should've made that," I said.

"Yeah," he said. "I was wondering if you were going to show up. Martine, this is Alain. Alain, this is my cousin Martine."

"Nice to meet you," I said as we shook hands.

"Likewise," Alain said as he prepared to throw his first horse-shoe. He had a Caribbean accent of some sort, probably Haitian.

"So are you in construction too?" I asked Alain as his first horseshoe fell neatly beside the post.

"Yes, we met on site," he said. "How about you?"

Jacques said, "She's a hydrogeologist."

"Hardly," I snorted. "I'm a supervillain. The obvious names were already taken, so they call me Mojili."

"Are you serious?" Alain asked.

"Yes," Jacques and I replied, and Jacques added, "Yes, she's a supervillain. Lead story on the radio earlier, remember?"

Alain peered at me. "That was you?"

A little stream of amber shot out of his can and splashed his chin. He looked down at the can and then at me.

"Sorry for the waste," I said.

"The news said a lot of people had been hurt," Alain noted.

"That's true," I said. "Couldn't be avoided."

"Holy shit." He turned to Jacques. "Why didn't you say anything?"

He chugged some beer, belched, and finally answered, "Why would I want to broadcast that *she's* my cousin?"

"I can't believe I'm having this conversation," Alain said. He had a look on his face that said he was thinking about excusing himself to go make a call.

"Look, Alain, I get it," I said hastily. "I've done a lot of terrible things. I ought to be in prison for them. I will be going *back* to prison for them. But today matters to me. Our grandmother's got Alzheimer's. Late-stage. I have no idea how long she has, no idea where she's living these days. But the single member of this fucking family who still voluntarily communicates with me told me about this party, and I knew that it was my single best chance to see Nana again before she dies. Are you going to deny me that?"

"You've killed people," Alain said. "Stolen millions. Caused immense destruction. Why should I do anything for you?"

I said, "The cops will find me soon enough. You calling them won't change that. It'll just accelerate things and piss me off."

"I'm not afraid of you," Alain said.

"Sweety, everybody else at this party is scared of her," Jacques interjected. "As a kid, she came close to killing a few of us for various reasons. Almost drowned me with a bottle of soda."

Alain stared at him.

Jacques said, "Here comes your brother."

I turned to see Mo approaching. "Auntie's waking Nana," he said. "She doesn't want to bring her outside in this heat, so I'll show you to her room. Then you can have your time and leave, okay?"

"Okay," I agreed.

I followed him back into the house, closing the patio door behind me. We returned to the front hall and stopped in front of a closed door.

"She's in Serge's office?" I muttered. "Jeez, Mom and I were arguing, like, right there, and she didn't tell me."

Mo frowned. "Easier to get a bed down here than to get her upstairs." He tapped softly on the door.

It cracked open and Aunt Hélène slipped out. Looking to Mo and then me, she whispered, "She's awake, but she wears out quickly. Try to be brief for her sake."

I pursed my lips. "Does she... is she going to know who I am?"

"Probably not," Hélène said. "She doesn't speak much and she can't do much. If she indicates she needs something, call for me."

"Okay," I said.

She stepped out and waited. I took a breath and entered the office.

One of them closed the door as I froze in place at the foot of the bed.

Nana was covered up to her chest with a floral cotton sheet. Soft, warm arms that had once hugged me tight lay limp and gaunt on top of the sheet. The smooth cheeks I'd once kissed were wrinkled and hollow. Her once-sharp eyes now narrow and faded in color.

"Hi," I managed to say.

She blinked.

"It's Martine," I said, finally bringing myself to move again.

"Martine," she wheezed.

"Yes, Nana, that's right. Do you remember me?"

She blinked but didn't answer.

"Okay," I lied, "That's okay." I slipped into the single chair sitting beside the bed. "I know you're not doing well. That's why I'm here. I'm sorry it's been so long."

"Martine," she murmured.

I leaned forward, placing a hand on her arm. She didn't react.

I stared at her, barely aware of the distant sounds of the party beyond the walls.

"I never wanted this to happen, Nana," I said. "It's been eight years since your diagnosis. That was the last time Mom voluntarily spoke to me. She said you took it in stride. That you figured your heart would go long before you ever got really bad."

Nana blinked.

"It killed me to hear it, though," I continued. "You had so much patience with me. Tried so hard to help me turn out right. I know I should feel more guilt that I didn't, but I guess that's part of my problem."

"Water," she said.

I smiled. "That's the rest of it, yes. The water."

The tip of her tongue appeared between her lips.

"Oh," I said. "Sorry." There was a white plastic pitcher on Serge's desk, but no cup or glass. I sighed.

I took control of the water and lifted it out of the pitcher. It drifted slowly over the bed, a shimmering sphere hovering over Nana's chest. A string of clear drops floated down toward her lips, and she opened her mouth to receive the first. She swallowed slowly and opened her mouth again.

"Take them at your own pace," I said, lowering the second drop to her lips. "I know you hoped this would go away and I'd be normal again," I said. "It didn't happen. I didn't go to school, didn't get married, didn't give you more great-grandkids."

She took a third drop. I sent a fourth down and twisted the arrangement of the remainder so they now descended in a slow spiral.

A hint of a smile tugged at her lips.

"I got into a fair bit of trouble with this," I confessed. "There's a lot of ways to hurt people when you control the main ingredient of their body. Get creative enough and you can cause landslides, floods, and bad weather. I took advantage of it. Took a lot of money that wasn't mine. I lived like royalty and I loved it."

Nana's lips puckered up as she kissed the next droplet.

My sight began to blur. "Figures that I can't control my own waterworks, eh?" I sniffled. "I want you to know something,

Nana. Something I can't tell anybody else— even the rest of the family, because, if I did that, somebody would tell the cops."

She stuck her tongue out, and I brought the next droplet down on its pink tip.

"It took a while for me to figure it out," I said, "But I realized I had enough money on my hands that I could maybe try to help somebody find a cure for this. Couldn't use it all, of course. Wouldn't have. I was enjoying my life too much for that and I had to keep up appearances. Also had to be sure that, if the cops took me down, they'd assume I'd spent the difference between what I'd stolen and what I had left. I knew a person who was able to set up a trust fund without obvious links back to me.

"Then I started making inquiries, looking for the right kind of researcher— somebody dedicated enough to their work to ask no questions about their funding, yet competent enough to make effective use of it. Took a while, but the money started flowing in that direction about four years ago."

Her right hand twitched, as if reaching for the spiral of water droplets, and so I brought them down to surround her wrist like a wide pearl bracelet.

"Sitting here now, I wonder if I wasted that money or if I should've spent more," I added.

Her eyes were fixed on her hand; she didn't comment.

I'd have to answer that myself.

She blinked again and set her hand down, crushing some of the droplets into the sheet. I wicked the moisture back into the air.

"Done?" I asked.

She blinked again, closed her eyes.

I directed the water back into the pitcher.

∞  ☼  ∞

Mo was waiting for me as I closed the door to Nana's improvised room. We stood in silence for a few moments, and then he asked, "You okay?"

"I don't know," I said.

"Fair enough."

"Is she staying here until…?"

"Auntie and Uncle are going to try," he confirmed. "They're getting pretty tired, though. If she holds out for more than a few weeks, I'm not sure what we're going to do."

I nodded.

"I can hear sirens," he said.

"Let me get one last look at my nephews, and I'll be out of here."

He exhaled loudly. "All right... come on."

We walked back to the patio door and looked out at the pool. The kids were still playing murderball or volleyball or something, laughing and splashing. "Philippe's doing well in grade 2," Mo said.

"Good," I said.

"Luc starts kindergarten in September," he added.

"That's him?" I asked, pointing to an excited youngster with orange water-wings.

"Yeah," he said.

I observed the boy reach up for one ball, then slip out of the way of another. The water surface around him moved up and down with him, and the waves generated by the other kids dampened as they approached him. While the rest of the kids were immersed to their shoulders, Luc floated higher in the water, his arms essentially resting on the surface.

"Mar?" Mo prodded. "They're here."

"I'm going," I said. "You can take away the water wings, Mo. Luc's in his element."

I turned away and started for the front door. A Sûreté cruiser, lights flashing and driver's side door open, was framed by the living room window. Other flashing lights were visible through the frosted glass pane to the left of the door.

"Hang on," Mo said. "You're saying..."

I paused with a hand on the doorknob. "You'll need help with him, Mo... but I can't provide it from Joliette."

"You said you'd surrender without making a scene," Mo said.

"Yeah, well, give my apologies to Mom," I said, opening the door. Cops ducked behind cars, a shrill voice yelling through a megaphone, and I reached out to the thousands of ton of water suspended in the hot July air.

∞  ✪  ∞

**JASON SHARP** is a writer based in Ontario.

# MIDNIGHT MAN VERSUS DOCTOR DEATH

*Chadwick Ginther*

**DOCTOR DEATH WAS** back in town.

Fossils were missing from the local museum. Those fossils were followed by three summer students. Their paleontologist teacher was hot on their heels. No bodies had been found but given the blood at the scene foul play was suspected. The cops were baffled, but I recognized the signs of my nemesis.

Every city is haunted by villains. And eventually every city raises its own champion. It's almost a competition. Bragging rights. I fought a smile. Bragging *rites*. Mort Cheval was no different. What was once two large Prairie towns, was now a small city. New developments consumed farmers' fields like a cancer. Things got disturbed. Things woke up. But when a city actually has death built right into its name, things get a little special, and it takes a special sort of hero to stem the tide. That's me. It's my job to put the bad guys back to sleep. I'm the Midnight Man.

Not a lot of people with my skill set are on the side of the angels. For many the Fight is a religious calling. I was wary of anything smacking of religion, but I did have a calling. It was a mad thing, dressing up in a costume to fight evil. But there are villains who raise the dead and murder the living, all without receiving justice.

I took the tools of my first defeated foe, and used them against the next. And again. Mister Murder, Sister Slaughter, Mademoiselle Mortuary, Uncle Anesthesia. They hated the handles I gave them, but they never had to put up with them for long, because I put 'em all in the ground for good. Only one of the blackguards I couldn't keep there: Doctor Death.

Since Doc was into fossils now, he'd need cheap labour to help with the digging.

∞   ☼   ∞

I waited at the bottom of an open grave. Some would say I'm absorbing death. Stretching my thanatomancy— my death magic. Truth is, I like to make an entrance.

This graveyard was supposed to be a place for the dead to rest, but because of Doc three were walking tonight. I fastened my black leather Hades cap emblazoned with a skull and crossbones, and slid on my grave-sight goggles. I popped up to take a look, and Doc's walkers flared red in my goggles against the grey penumbric haze. Thin lines, like veins and arteries, spiderwebbed over their bodies, gathering in thicker power clusters that glowed like fireflies where Doc had injected them full up with evil. They were easy to spot. Easier to see I was outnumbered.

I grinned. A slow pop of the holster flaps, and I was ready to draw my two Colt Model 1911s. Each pistol was loaded with lucky sevens of tombstone bullets. I was often outnumbered, but never outgunned.

As I jumped into the fray, I turned on my emblem. The white double Ms on my jacket flared briefly, blinding Doc's goons and spotlighting my targets. I drew my pistols midair, firing before my feet touched grass. The Colts' muzzle flashes were lightning bright, their reports thunder loud.

The first walker I hit turned grey, reclaiming the waxy pallor of death as its embalmed body fell. Its spirit oozed out before the body hit the ground.

I ran toward the walkers as if the Devil were chasing me. Another shot. Another flunky trying to get back to Doc so he could reload it in some other dead meat. I holstered my right hand Colt and tossed a ball-and-chain bomb. The eggshell thin casing shattered against a tombstone behind the walker. A puff of silver dust glittered in the moonlight, enveloping the body and the trailing end of the spirit.

It was sucked back into its body and locked in. Dead meat. Dead spirit. Another bomb sorted the first goon.

The last one wouldn't fall. He kept coming until I was out of ammo. Whatever spirit Doc had stuffed inside, it wasn't coming out till Doomsday. I still had one ball-and-chain bomb, but if tombstone bullets couldn't drop the meat it would be useless.

His arms stretched toward me. The tips of his fingers had been gnawed to the bone, leaving him with grisly talons, and his forearms were armored with some sort of reptile skull. He walked hunched over, arms grasping for me. I slid on my knuck-ledusters. Hand-to-hand it was.

My big silver rings glowed softly. Story was, these rings had been blessed by the Pope, the one time he'd visited Mort Cheval. Why and how I don't know. But they worked.

The big guy came at me with no form or technique, his mouth gaping open in a mute scream. I ducked under one of his clumsy slashes, landing a double body blow with my dusters. For all the damage I did, I might as well have been punching stone.

Something whipped out, too fast to see, and caught me in the ribs with a sharp lancing pain. I rolled with the blow, but he'd still tagged me good. I switched on my emblem, hoping to blind him, but he nailed me again and knocked me flat. That whip of his, whatever it was, coiled around me like a snake. It felt like stone and looked like bone. The fossils! Some kind of wire ran through the entire length of the weapon, like a tail or a spine. But it moved as if it were still alive. It gave me a squeeze, and I screamed.

The pressure eased, and I gulped a breath. I raised my dust-ers to strike. Too late. Stone ricocheted off the back of my head and I saw double. I felt myself fly through the air and I landed, hard. He'd knocked me back into the open grave. If I didn't clear my head, it would be mine in truth, regardless of whose name ended up on the stone. *Here lies the Midnight Man,* it wouldn't say. *He fought the good fight in a bad war.*

My whole body ached. My head swam. But I wasn't done fighting yet. The goon loomed over my grave, and at last I real-ized that he wasn't wielding a whip, the whip was part of him. A skeletal tail that writhed, waiting to strike.

All at once there was a burst of sun-bright light from the edge of the grave, followed by a reptilian shriek. The sounds of the fight were brief. There was only one person that glow could belong to: Daystar. My on-again, off-again ally and adversary.

"I didn't think you'd show," I called up.

Daystar knelt over me, beaming. Her red hair was wild and sweat-damp. Her brown leathers shone like burnished bronze. "Normally I'm chasing you, not saving you."

Daystar is a paragon. A shining knight. In times gone by, she'd have been a saint, or a prophet. She was a golden goddess, virtue incarnate, and she'd vowed to bring me in the last time we'd crossed paths. I might let her, if I could convince her to help me tonight. I knew how to *use* power, but Daystar *was* power.

She tilted her head as I rubbed some blood from my lip with a gloved knuckle.

"You really have no shame or decency. No—"

"Respect for the dead?"

She didn't answer. We'd danced this dance before.

"I respect the dead fine. I just prefer them to stay that way."

Daystar extended her hand to me, and I took it. She might think she could trap me, but where there was shadow I could make myself unfound. Benefits of a Hades cap. We'd never touched, other than to trade punches and kicks, and it felt as if I were shaking the hand of God. She blazed as bright as her namesake, but even with all that light there were still shadows at the bottom of the grave.

There was no sign of Doc's goons. She must've caught me looking, because she said, "Ashes to ashes." The fossils had been stacked in a pile. "I'll return them when I'm certain they're safe."

The look she gave me said that they'd be "safe" *after* she'd taken me in.

"I can help you bring down Doctor Death."

"I don't need your help."

"Daystar—"

She sighed. "My name is Susan."

"We need to team up."

"You still insist on this lunacy? Your delusions are going to get people killed."

"What's going to get people killed is you refusing my help. Maybe you can take down Doc on your own, but can you keep his hostages alive too?"

Her eyes narrowed. "How do I know I can trust you?"

"You know I hate them," I said. "For all the times we've fought, I never once sided with the darkness over you."

I could see her considering. Time to sweeten the pot. I held out my hands, wrists touching as if I were going to let her handcuff me.

If Daystar waited any longer, it would be morning, and we'd be too late. "Agreed."

"Come into my parlour," I said, gesturing at the columbarium across the graveyard.

She arched an eyebrow but gathered up the fossils and followed me without speaking. I paused when we reached the structure. The only folks I'd ever shown the place had already been dead at the time, so I felt a little self-conscious having Daystar in the Bunker.

Revealing my hideout to Daystar might not be the best plan, but I needed her. I touched the names of my parents, and a door slid open, stone grating on cement. I entered, Daystar followed. The lights came on as the door closed, illuminating the wrought-iron spiral staircase that led us down into the earth.

A composite man was on the slab, awaiting autopsy so I could figure out what made the creature so damned deadly. Daystar set the fossils down next to the body with barely a passing glance and moved on to my oaken workbench. She looked around the Bunker, taking in my outfits draped on dummies, the walls of weapons, the trophies.

She asked, "Is this all the Fight is to you? Some sort of child's game?"

"I was never a child. Doctor Death saw to that."

"He killed your parents."

I nodded. "Old story. One I'm sure you've heard before. First things guys like the Doc do when they blow into town is take over a mortuary. Gives them peace and quiet, and lots of raw materials." I squeezed my eyes shut, but that couldn't hide the vision of what Doc had done to my family after they were no longer useful.

"They used to own this funeral home, didn't they?"

My silence was her answer.

Softly, she said, "They buried my grandmother."

I hoped for her sake that had been before Doc had enlisted them.

"I never realized you grew up here," I said. "Always seemed like you were too good for a place like this."

"This *is* a good place," she said. "When it's not full of monsters."

She laughed at that last bit, and I joined her.

"Mort Cheval is always full of monsters."

"And that's why you went into the family business?"

"Let them take a run at me instead of someone else. I've taken on all comers — living, dead, or undead — and buried them. Where they belong."

Daystar nodded. The dim aura that always surrounded her brightened as if it was stretching out to comfort me, to fill me with warmth. I pushed my chair back from the table. There'd be time enough for a warm walk in the sun when Doc was in the ground— where *he* belonged.

She took a seat at the workbench. "You intrigue me. A bone-dancer who thinks he's a hero."

"I'm not one of them," I said, hotter than I intended. "I kill them. I use their gear— harm's already been done there. But I'm not one of them. I'll *never* be one of them."

Daystar watched me, her eyes searching for subterfuge. "Go on."

"Doctor Death is back in town," I said. Her face showed no recognition. "You might know him by a different name, Marcus O'Reilly." She nodded. "He's responsible for the fossil thefts and the disappearances."

Daystar grimaced. "Why?"

"The museum dug up something remarkable. Something rare."

"And?"

"And Doc is going to wake it up."

Daystar got my meaning immediately. "He'll be the head of a cult of one," she said.

I nodded. "Even the ancient reptiles had gods. Gods of eat, gods of fuck, gods of kill... the gods of eat and kill are pretty hard to distinguish. And when the god of kill is sated, and the world is meat, guess who's going to control what's left of a dead world?"

She shuddered. "Where are they now?"

I gestured toward my car, a customized Lincoln Continental Mark III. It looked badass and had a big trunk. Perfect for my kind of work.

"I thought you'd never ask."

Daystar rode shotgun and the hydraulic lift took us up to the funeral home's garage. I hit the door opener and turned over the engine. The Lincoln growled like it had been built in Hell instead of Detroit, and we roared out into the night.

∞    ☼    ∞

I cut the lights and drove by my grave-sight. The red glow in the distance told me exactly where Doc was. Good thing the heavy tint on my windows kept Daystar's light from giving us away.

I parked the Lincoln by a hill covered in long prairie grasses and peppered with trees shrouded in half-spent leaves. Down a gulley I could see Doc's goons scuttling all over the dig. Doc had assembled some kind of dual-purpose work bench/altar out of slabs of bentonite shale. There were some lumpy shapes huddled in front of the altar; maybe the shapes were still hostages, maybe they were just raw materials now.

LED camping lanterns flickered on the walls of the gully, casting monstrous shadows. But the real monsters were very clear. I could see the fossil that had been the pride of the museum's discoveries, a hitherto unclassified species of marine reptile. Something far larger, and older, than the mosasaurs and plesiosaurs that usually turned up in these parts. I looked around at the trees and grass, rubbed a bit of dirt between my gloved fingers. Hard to believe this prairie had all been under water once.

Normally, grave-sight doesn't turn up much outside of a city. For a wild place to show this much death... I shuddered. It was blazing bright in the gulley, like I was staring at a raging forest fire. I could see the power clusters that had allowed its malevolence to survive through the epochs, waiting for someone like Doc, even as the flesh rotted off its bones and those bones became stone.

I heard a sharp snap. Shale breaking. The fossil shifted. Even from this distance, I could hear the soft patter of pebbles and dirt falling as the fossil moved.

*It moved.*

The press of aeons no longer held its bones. The skeleton ran the entire length of the gulley. Bones rose up from the ground, ribs looking like they belonged to some great ship under construction, not a living creature. The great jaw creaked and groaned, opening and closing like someone trying to get the feeling back into a numb hand.

I whispered to Daystar, "We're too late. It's awake."

"No," she said, pointing toward the far end of the gulley. The shapes by the altar shifted. "The door is open, but it has not stepped through. We've arrived just in time."

I wrinkled my brow. For all my earlier talk, it was very long odds that we'd be able to stop Doc, bury his monster, and get those prisoners out alive.

Daystar must've suspected what I was thinking. She turned to me, her eyes two suns burning in the night. "You will not kill the hostages to stop the ceremony."

"We have to be realistic—"

She shook her head. "Lost causes are the most worthy."

I tried to protest, but Daystar cut me off again.

"The living *must* take precedence over the dead."

From the tone of her voice, there was going to be no arguing with her. So I didn't bother.

"If I don't make it out of this," I said, "I've always respected you. You're the closest thing I have to a friend."

Daystar's smile was sad. Either at my admission, or at the thought that we were both likely to die in that gulley.

"If you die, I will ensure your spirit is never disturbed."

That was something, at least. "And if you die?"

"Leave me in the ground. I could use the rest."

I reached into one of the pouches on my belt and pulled out a vial with a human eye floating in gel. I popped the cork and let the orb plop into my hand. I bounced it on my palm. The thousand-year-old eye was still as round and plump as a freshly picked grape. Sister Slaughter claimed the deadeye had come from the greatest marksman who ever lived. I don't know about that, but she sure could shoot while she had it under her tongue. What I did know, was that the eye was dangerous: once focused, it would imbue me with a desire to kill that equaled its accuracy.

I took off my goggles, tilted my head back and squeezed the deadeye till it burst, the jelly dripping into my eyes. Daystar looked away, grimacing. I couldn't blame her, but tonight was my night. Disgusting as my preparations might be, I couldn't afford to miss.

Standing straight, I flicked the holster flaps open, and drew my Colts. "Let's give Doc his apple for the day."

"Remember there are more important things than your revenge."

I nodded. "Gods are your specialty. Pissing off Doc is mine."

"How do you think you'll manage that?"

"Remember how annoying I can be? The nicknames. The insults."

She fought back a smile. "You *do* like the sound of your own voice."

Doc hated anything with a whiff of humour about it. He was the coolest cool, the blackest black. An asshole.

"When I've got them distracted, you burn those bones straight down to Hell."

Daystar nodded. I touched the barrel of my Colt to my cap in salute and leapt over the edge of the hill, sliding down the shale and into the belly of the beast. The gulley was too steep to sneak around Doc's side and ambush him. Probably why he'd set up his altar that way, he had to suspect I'd show. Which meant I'd had have to run the gauntlet to get to him.

His goons were all kitted out like the big chomper who rang my bell back at the graveyard. Teeth that bite and tails that smite. One of them wore the jaws of some kind of giant shark as a headdress. The jaws creaked open and closed in time with the dead bugger's chants. The ground shuddered and the goons danced to the tremors.

I wove around Doc's goons. They were strong, but not fast. Now that I knew some of them had tails, they wouldn't be able to surprise me again. Tombstone bullets flew. Doc's minions roared in anger and stopped their chants to chase me. I didn't bother with the ball-and-chain bombs, if Daystar and I did our jobs, those angry spirits wouldn't have anywhere to go but the Kingdom.

"*You!*" Doc roared.

"What's up, Doc?"

Doc had shaved his head and white paint turned his face into a reptilian skull. Otherwise, he was dressed all in black, although the crow feathers hanging off his jacket like tassels were a new touch. With the god on the threshold, I couldn't let any more blood touch the altar; and if I shot Doc, I'd make a very big, very messy hole. I aimed high and he threw himself behind his altar. Granite bullets rang off shale. Doc cried out. Must've hit him with a splinter or a ricochet.

I fired at the minions to keep them from resuming the chant. They screamed in anger and pain. I kept my back to the gulley, one pistol trained in Doc's direction, the other plinking his goons.

I singsonged, "Come out, come out, Doc."

He left the altar. I turned to face him and flashed my emblem again. He threw a hand in front of his face, and I fired. He cried out and fell. This was it. I had him. After all these years. I *had* him.

I ran towards him, but something caught my foot and I fell. My jaw slammed against the shale, and my Colts clattered out of my hand. Then one of Doc's super goons hoisted me into the air.

"You deluded scavenger," Doc cried. "You will be the first to be fed to the god. But you will not be alone!"

I smiled.

His brows scrunched together, cracking his facepaint. "I have you. Why are you smiling?"

"I'm not alone."

The sun rose a few hours early as Daystar made her presence known.

Doc shielded his eyes with his hands, and the goon holding me squirmed as if Daystar was holding a blowtorch to his back. I slipped free and rolled toward Doc. When he saw me coming, I was already swinging. My fist caught him in the jaw and spun him around. Not gonna lie. It felt good. Damned good. Too good. I followed up with an elbow to the back.

Not sure if Doc bit his tongue on the way down or broke his nose when his face impacted the stone, but a great gush of blood splattered on the altar. That wasn't good

The entire gulley shuddered. Slabs of shale tumbled down the walls, cracking against the stone on the bottom. Wind howled over the rocky terrain. Dirt and dust filled the air, and I had to spit the grit from my mouth.

Behind me, I heard Daystar cry out. Doc pushed himself back to his feet and turned to look at me. He had a wild look in his eye. Blood streamed down his face. He smiled.

Not good at all.

I had never witnessed the level of thanatomancy Doc was pulling here. It was off the scale, death to even approach him. I picked up my Colts and ran. I hoped Daystar kept the god off me. Even if the hostages hadn't yet been sacrificed, being that close to Doc's death magic would probably give them all cancer. As far away as I was, I could still feel blood trickling from my nose.

I chanced a look over my shoulder. Doc's fossilized gateway to power was scuttling around. It was almost comical to see that motley assortment of bones moving, but it zipped around on those ribs like a millipede. It had Daystar trapped inside its ribcage, its neck curved round trying to bite her. Her hands held open the beast's great jaws. For now.

Help her or get to Doc. Daystar made my decision. A single shaft of light cut through the night, blazing a path straight to the hostages.

"Go," she yelled. "Get them out!"

Caught up in the warmth of that light, I knew I had a safe run. It felt strange: Midnight Man, running with the light.

I reached the hostages and kicked over the altar. Didn't know if it would help. Couldn't hurt. *And* it made me feel good. But that feeling had cost me my shot at Doc.

He'd reached the top of the gulley. Damned crow jacket. Rats always leave a sinking ship, even if they need feathers to do it. By the time I'd raised my Colts, he'd disappeared. If I used my deadeye, I might be able to get him. Make an impossible shot. Magic bullet time.

Daystar cried, "The hostages!"

The Colt quivered at the end of my outstretched arm. An extension of my body. An extension of me. Death personified. I focused my deadeye. The red hate burned. There was no shot I couldn't make. I could feel Doc running. His heart pounded opposite the measured beat of my vengeance. Take him out for everything he'd done to me. To my family. Avenge everything he'd made us do to each other.

Daystar's words echoed somewhere deep within me: *the living* must *take precedence over the dead.* It would be so easy. *No.* I owed Doc more death than I could easily count, but, if I turned my back on Daystar and left Doc's hostages to die, I'd be no better than Doc.

I'd get another shot to bury Doctor Death. And I'd take it. I holstered one of my guns and stretched out a hand to the hostages. The eldest of them, the paleontologist, I assumed, took it first. Her trust seemed contagious, her students stood up wobbly-kneed.

"Stay in the light," I warned.

They ran, slower than I'd have liked, but they ran, and I fol-lowed. I shot at Doc's remaining goons, trying to drive them away from our exit zone. When we were safely clear of the altar and Doc's dead zone, I stopped, and turned my deadeye on the god. Its body had weakened, its ancient bones were starting to crumble and flake in Daystar's light. She could finish it, eventually. But I didn't think she had the time. The god's ribs scratched and scrabbled against Daystar's protective aura. Her glow started to fade.

I had my shot. I took it.

Tombstone bullets threaded the nostril holes of the beast's skull into where its brain had been. Daystar ripped the jaws apart, and the god shrieked in denial. Its body disarticulated, and its bones were paper in a fire, and then ash, blowing away on the wind.

Mingled with the god's scream as it fell was something... *human* wasn't quite the correct word, but whatever that scream was, it had come from Doc's mouth. He may have gotten away, but I killed his god, and that pained him. I smiled.

Small victories.

I hauled Daystar to her feet.

She didn't let go of my wrist.

It was her turn to smile. "I promised I would take you in."

"You did."

"Will you come along quietly?"

A shadow passed over the moon, shrouding me. In that moment I was gone. She'd never find me with my Hades cap on, not unless I wanted her to. Maybe another time. I laughed the entire way to my Lincoln. I have *never* gone quietly.

Daystar glowed furiously bright in my rearview mirror as I roared toward the highway and into the rising sun.

I also like to make an exit.

∞   ☼   ∞

Winnipeg writer **CHADWICK GINTHER**'s novels *Thunder Road* and *Tombstone Blues* were nominated for the Prix Aurora Award.

# SÜPER

*Corey Redekop*

GOOD MORNING. Good morning. Calm down now. Please, remain in your seats. Thank you. Can everyone hear me?

What a bright and eager group! At the risk of sounding giddy, this is always my favorite time of year. So full of promise. New recruits, new ideas, new breakthroughs.

Before we commence training proper, allow me to fill in a few blanks. Each and every person in this room was approached by recruiters from an organization known as LNF Incorporated. You were informed that LNF specialized in experimental medical procedures. After a lengthy process of interviews and examinations and background checks, offers of employment were tendered, confidentiality agreements were accepted and signed (perhaps some of you even read them, ha ha), and you were informed that LNF would be in contact very soon regarding an employment start date.

Consider today day one.

A vigorous selection process pared the number of applicants to the thirty men and women currently sitting in this auditorium. Congratulations! Your presence here serves as ample proof that each of you ranks among Canada's finest medical minds. I know you all have many questions; indeed, your innate and relentless curiosity is a main component in how you came to arrive in this hall under such... unorthodox circumstances. Rest assured, most of your questions will be answered this morning. Any unanswered questions will be dealt with at the appropriate time.

Before I proceed any further, I must ask that you consider the gravity of this undertaking. I cannot stress this enough. Right now you are befuddled, perhaps even terrified, but I promise that those who stay will be presented with challenges that may change the course of human evolution. I do beg your indulgence for remaining so vague, but a sense of fairness compels me to offer one final chance to anyone who wishes to return to life as you knew it. If you back out, there will be absolutely no recriminations. Simply raise your hand and you will be escorted from this room, anaesthetized, and returned to your city of origin. Stay, and be assured a place among the greats of medical science. Stay, and join the likes of Salk, Bethune, Hippocrates, and Banting. Leave, and prepare for a monotonous existence devoid of meaning.

So I leave it to you. Stay or go? Yea or nay?

Lovely. I'm proud of you. That minor detail out of the way, welcome to the greatest challenge any of you will ever face. I am Doctor Haddon Nickle, and—

I'm sorry, as I said, please hold your questions; we have a great deal of ground to cover today. Figurative and literal. But as you're all so keen; yes, I am he. I, along with Professor Carlyle Lalumière, am co-discoverer of the Lalumière-Nickle Flux, *the* most important event in *Homo sapiens* history. I don't mean to toot my own horn, but, if elementary school textbooks label it as such, who am I to argue? Ha ha.

Did you know, the names Lalumière and Nickle, separately and together, were in the top ten choices for baby names for almost a decade after the discovery? Both boys and girls? Fascinating. And flattering.

I digress. Each and every one of you has been recruited as ideal candidates for what you will discover is one of, if not *the* most compelling, unique, and challenging opportunities in medical science. There isn't one person here, with the exception of Colonel Tidhar — he's that rather intimidating fellow standing at attention at the back of the room — who hasn't graduated at the top of their respective classes. You are all world-class doctors with genius-level intellects.

You all are also, to a one, completely alone in this world. Not one of you has a single living relative. Few have friends. None are in relationships, or in any event, relationships that will be missed. Your profiles indicate a high degree of borderline personality disorders combined with near-crippling social phobias that would, in individuals not as innately driven as yourselves, result in lives of silent paranoid misery. You are each a perfect storm of intellectual and introvert.

Simply put, despite your brilliance, not one of you will ever be missed. In the slightest. I can attest with absolute certainty that your social impacts on the world thus far have been, at best, negligible.

Ooh, I see some frowny faces out there. You're thinking this is not what you signed up for. I sympathize, truly. But you are, of course, wrong. This is exactly what you signed up for.

You just didn't know it at the time.

Lest you forget, I *did* provide one last chance to leave. You've been allowed many opportunities to change your mind, but your insatiable inquisitiveness drove you on, past the onerous paperwork, past the byzantine confidentiality agreements, past the heavily armed guards who knocked you unconscious and transported you here in the dead of night.

Where *here* is, exactly, will remain my little secret. For now.

From this point on, no one shall be allowed to leave the base until training is complete. Anyone attempting to leave will be met with the harshest penalties permitted under the secret codicils to the Charter of Rights and Freedoms. That means you will find yourself terminated before you set foot off the base. And by *terminated*, I do not mean you'll be on the unemployment line the next day. Nosirreebob.

This is another reason why you are all, to be blunt, loners. Because should any of you leave, or whisper a word of what goes on within these walls, not only will you be executed, but every single person we even *think* you have a connection to will be eliminated as well.

Settle down, please. Settle! Sit down, please! Oh dear, every time… Colonel Tidhar, if you would be so kind?

Ah, now I have your attention. Now who was that exactly, let me just check the chart… yes, Dr. Dowhy of Fort McMurray. I always pad the numbers for exactly this eventuality, but I do keep hoping we'll one day not have to make such provisions.

Dr. Dowhy will be missed.

Or, rather, he won't. My point.

Please remain calm; the Colonel will have the remains taken care of when we are done. For now, let the doctor's smoky corpse serve as a friendly reminder.

As I was saying, the time for misgivings ended five minutes ago. As we speak, teams are being dispatched to close up all loose ends. Tomorrow, media outlets across the country will be reporting on the death of A from a house fire, or the deadly hit-and-run of B, or the accidental corso-oscillated disintegration of C.

From this point on, it's either remain and learn, or cremation.

Now, that nasty business out of the way...

Welcome to the Canadian government's Sanatorium for Überhuman Palliative, Emergency, and Restorative care, or SÜPER. And no, I was not on the committee that came up with that acronym. LNF is merely a front to keep the public from discovering our true role, although we do have a nifty side business in product testing.

My discovery of the Flux in the late 1970s was a turning point in human development. I don't mind admitting I accidentally stumbled upon its existence during my attempts to fully decode the human genetic structure. The previous year, Professor Lalumière had invented what we now call the Lalumière Orb, a portable device capable of generating a sphere of self-renewing, self-sustaining nuclear fusion. It is not an overstatement to say that this device transformed the world, solving the energy crisis in one blow. We have a tiny orb onsite, powering our facilities. They say it will continue to function well into the thirtieth century.

I had theorized that selective exposure of DNA to Orb radiation could trigger controlled mutations. As you see, I am a prime example of my research. Perhaps it's the humanitarian in me, but I would never expose any test subject to a procedure I would not willingly undergo myself.

I've always believed that scientists may strive to better our world, but it's only the *mad* scientists who get anything done.

However, due to an undetected instability in the prototype Orb, spontaneous precipitation of genetic mutations occurred on a global scale, a process of forced evolution that will continue until that particular sphere runs itself dry. Which, by Lalumière's estimation, does not appear likely in this millennium.

Zero point zero zero one percent of the world's population was immediately affected. Most, happily, suffer only the most trivial of abnormalities. I include myself among that number, although I'm sure most wouldn't classify the extemporaneous growth of a third leg and an extra pair of arms to be trivial. Well, it *has* cost a fair amount of money to have all my clothes tailored appropriately. But my surgical skills have improved dramatically, and there doesn't exist a three-legged race I can't win. Ha!

Oh, at first I was chagrined, but I've learned to take the entire incident as an instructive lesson in safety checks. I always say, forewarned is four-armed. Ha ha!

Some, of course, were affected to a degree beyond mere extra appendages or kaleidoscopic hair. They are why we are here today. These quote unquote *superheroes* are now the civilized world's first, best, and only defense against the evils that beset us, primarily those generated by so-called supervillains.

Seems like every day there's another one, doesn't it? Today a Havoconda or Machismollusk, tomorrow a Doctor Destruction or Doctor Damage or Doc Dojo. (And do *not* get me started on supervillain abuse of the word "doctor"; only a bare handful have *any* medical or scientific training at all, and Doctor Damage has a doctorate in *Medieval English*— bah!)

All this is why we need superheroes, or, as we here call them, *supercapables*, on our side. It is of critical importance that these beings be in tip-top shape at all times. Until now, you have been aware only of the *public* face of supercapables. The reality behind their heroism is where you come into play.

I'm sensing confusion. I think, at this stage, it would be best to start our tour. If you'll all please follow me to the elevator…

Everyone in! Don't worry, room enough for all. This is an industrial elevator, reinforced several times over. Considering the size of some of our patients, a load of thirty doctors will not strain it in the slightest. We'll be descending some one hundred and fifty metres, and it's quite a… Whoa! Apologies; I neglected to warn you of the sudden acceleration. Not to mention the deceleration. You'd do best to hold onto the handrails for the zero-gravity portion of our descent.

Ah, Level One, Hero Triage. The outpatient level, where our, how shall I phrase it, *less complicated* warriors fly in for a tune-up. Your Fantasias, your 'Lastic Lads, your Apexes. Run-of-the-mill supertypes, but they get the job done. Consider this an emergency ward for superhero boo-boos.

You see, supercapables, for all their gifts, do require medical care from time to time, and there isn't a hospital on Earth that

can effectively handle their unique needs. And when you factor
in a hero's need for anonymity, well, you begin to understand
why facilities like this are so vital. We cater exclusively to the
curative, remedial, therapeutic, and restorative needs of the
überbeing. We tend to their aches and pains, and they make
themselves available to world governments when their services
are required. Most of your more prosaic heroes will go their
whole lives without receiving a single phone call requesting
their aid, but they are still granted access to all the medical
knowledge, technologies, and care at our command. In the
long run, the cost of running this facility, and its equivalents
in other countries, is negligible compared to the savings in
global infrastructure expenditures.

You'll be spending a great deal of time here, the rotation
schedule will be posted in the morning. I believe the best training to be hands-on, so you will all work in every department
at one time or another. Specific assignments will come later; if
you are drawn to a particular area of practice, do not hesitate to
let your supervisor know. But Level One furnishes the greatest
opportunity to practice on the widest variety of genetic anoma-
lies. One day you'll be ministering to The Burgundy Barnacle's
crustacean arthritis, the next you'll be slopping irradiated salve
on the self-inflicted wounds of DeathPriest. Oh yes, there's
quite the story there. Someday I'll write a book.

Kidding, Colonel Tidhar! Kidding! The Colonel knows I
would never write such a book. The scandals would cripple the
superhero sector. How do you think the world would react if The
Obviator's bipolar disorder was revealed? Or The Groundhog's
intestinal insertion fetish?

Enough preamble! Behold, behind Curtain Number One we
discover… I'm sorry, I don't know who you are. Please forgive
my theatricality, everyone, but I cannot resist making a little
show of revealing your first authentic wounded superhero.

So you are… Thundra, Mistress of Climate? Superhero
nomenclature has become a veritable cottage industry, hasn't
it? Are you a newcomer to the game, Miss Thundra? Ah, that
explains it. Doctors, before you is a textbook example of how
the onset of puberty is decisively linked to the evolution of
superabilities.

My, that is quite the burn. How did it come about? Well, I
am certainly glad you managed to save all those orphans, well

done there, but superpowers do not always arrive conveniently bundled, do they? Just because you can harness lightning does not mean you're necessarily fireproof. Let's be a tad more careful next time, shall we? When you've been tended to, have the nurse direct you to the armory topside. They'll set you up with a fire-retardant catsuit. Yes, a variety of colors are available, but I'd lose the cape. So last year.

Curtain Two? Ah, now *here* is a gentleman whom I'm sure needs no introduction. Doctors, meet The Reckoning, one of your A-plus certified top-tier heroes. An honour, sir, it's not often we see someone of your stature on Level One. I caught your work last month in Rome, congratulations on saving the Vatican from Gorgon Zola. What's Pope Deus Ex Machina like? Oh, that's a shame, I rather hoped he was more open-minded.

Now, pray tell, what brings you to our doorstep today, Reckoning? Hmm? I do apologize. What's troubling you, *The* Reckoning? Well, let's just hunker down and take a looksee. If you could please remove your tights?

My, my, that *does* look inflamed. I'd like to throw this to my group here, do you mind? Doctors, close your mouths and place your thinking helmets on. We have on our hands a Grade One Flux Mutation suffering what looks to be a rash of cold sores about his extremities, swollen testicles and… Oh, I'm sorry, yes, of course, they always look like that. Moving on, we have additional sores beneath the scrotal sac and a degree of deep bruising, along with what the patient describes as a painful electrical discharge and nuclear piles. Diagnosis?

Interesting idea. Why don't you ask him that yourself, Doctor Dayton? Go on.

Ouch. Please let the doctor's suffering serve as a teachable moment. A degree of *tact* is of vital importance when treating the supercapable. Doctor Dayton, I suggest you trot off to the Level Four burn ward. Yes, just follow the signs. Off you go now! Hurry, and they may be able to save that arm.

Don't concern yourselves, he'll be fine. If we can patch up wounds inflicted by Dark Squid or Trajectory the Human Bullet, we can surely handle a simple third-degree scorching.

Now I do *hate* to be indelicate, *The* Reckoning but I *must* ask if you've at all been in contact with any of the Contagion Quints. *All* of them? I see. Well, this shouldn't be a problem; we are very familiar with the Quints' unique viral signature.

Doctors Fuller and Berki, I don't see why you can't start your rotation immediately. You are now in charge of *The* Reckoning's wellbeing. Head to the dispensary at the end of the hall, they'll whip up an ointment that will clear up this trifling infection. And please stop your sputtering, it's demeaning to your profession. Hurry, before that erythema goes septic. If that happens we'll have to quarantine the entire level. Move!

The rest of you, onward to Level Two!

Now that we're alone again, I can confide that The Reckoning's sexual appetite is the subject of water-cooler scuttlebutt, but that's where such talk must remain. For all our sakes. But let me ask, is anyone here surprised that a dalliance with *all five* of the Contagion Quints has led to a rather volcanic STD eruption? We reap what we sow, doctors, no matter how many battleships we can vaporize with our atomic vision.

Frankly, most of your name-brand heroes are, for lack of a better term, utter assholes, and The Reckoning is an A-Number-One poopchute. Few of you may have interest in proctology, but you had all better get used to having your heads lodged firmly up your patients' asses, and yes that includes The Globule. When you are on duty, these beings are your gods incarnate. When you consider the vital international security work they do and, more importantly, how dangerous even the most mediocre supercapable is compared to humdrum normals like yourselves, well, it behooves you to suck up as much as possible.

By way of example; do you all recall the death of Major Proton? In truth, he was *not* slain in mortal combat with Terminatrobot, that was only a cover story. Some years back, one of our residents removed one of PorcuPinenut's quills from the Major's thigh and called him a... what was it again, Colonel? Yes, "big baby," when he cried. Major Proton transmuted the doctor into a sentient rod of fissionable uranium-235 and stormed out in a huff. That was quite the day.

Anyhow, the Major is now known as Professor Nuke, the happy gent who destroyed most of Saskatchewan during last year's Meltdown War. The doctor? Quadborg packaged her up and sent her hurtling toward a black hole in the Sagittarius Dwarf Galaxy. Uranium-235 has a half-life of 704 million years, so I imagine the doctor will have plenty of time to consider her lack of bedside manner.

Ah, Level Two. We are now three kilometers down. This is where we delve into the nitty-gritty of supercapable physiology. I'll ask you all to get used to checking the radiation detectors on your ID cards. Should that bar turn *any* color other than blue, do *not* proceed from this point. It's only changed to red once in the history of this facility, when X-Raygun had a bout of indigestion. We lost a lot of good people that day.

Levels Two through Five are primarily the SÜPER surgical wards, and—

Leaving us already, Miss Tycal? Are you sure you can't stay and visit the… no, of course, you're busy. I understand. I do hope you'll visit from time to time?

That was obviously Miss Tycal, checking out after a week-long recuperation from her defeat by BlunderGus. She's known for her rapid healing abilities; we're rather superfluous when it comes to her. What is *not* well-known is that any part of her, if severed, grows, starfish-like, into an identical Miss Tycal in a matter of months. In the past we've managed to halt the maturation through reattachment or incineration, but this time her arms and left leg got away from us. Literally. It took days to find them. By that time they were completely sentient, and I simply didn't have the heart to cremate the misshapen little tykes. Miss Tycal, as you saw, does not care to take her new charges with her, not when she's on a mission of vengeance. I do hate it when it's personal.

So now our children's ward on Level Seven has three very odd-looking new residents. Eventually, we plan to reunite them with their hostmother to form a new superteam.

Ah, Surgical Theatre Seven is in use. Let's peek in, shall we? Ooh, a good one. Last night, a squadron of organic zeppelins besieged the headquarters of The Excellent Eight. The blimps were thwarted, but Flexgirl suffered internal injuries. Normally not a problem, but *normal* is not what this facility is about. Flexgirl was in full elongation when she was knocked unconscious and has not retracted to her normal size and shape. We're very wary of reviving her while her body is elongated to thirty-two feet and thin as ribbon candy. The surgeons are now trying to suture an abdominal wound, but it's like trying to knit silly putty.

Looking at the schedule, I see we have a procedure on deck for tomorrow. Doctor Maxfield, you've some practice with thoracic malignancies, yes? Good, you'll be assisting Doctor Pearce with a lobectomy. Yes, well, it doesn't sound *too* bad, but your patient will be Third Degree. As his skin is an unquenchable inferno, you'll have your work cut out for you. I'm sure there's some irony in a man of living flame suffering from lung cancer

We've repurposed a hydrotherapy tank to keep Third Degree fully submerged during the operation, and we're all very anxious to see if it works. I'm rather jealous; good luck to you!

Oh dear, the Colonel is tapping his watch. I do tend to go on, but can you blame me? Back to the elevator! I think we'll have to cut the tour short and bypass gynaecology, occupational therapy, psychology, and the morgue and skip to Level Ten, our convalescent ward. A shame, our psychology department is second to none. You'd be surprised by how often near-omnipotence leads directly to erectile dysfunction.

Level Ten, rehab and long-term care, where we help those heroes who cannot help themselves. Down this hall is an assortment of the *differently* capable. Here you will learn that the überlife is not necessarily all fun and games.

Room 1001. Ladies, gentlemen, please gather around. Don't worry, he's quite unconscious. May I present Mr. Tim Tibbetts. Sad, sad case. Timothy, as you can plainly see, is suffering from a marked excess of dermis. In other words, too much skin. His internal organs are similarly affected; heart, liver, lungs, intestines, what have you, all stretched to near-bursting. This accounts for the marked bulging of his torso. We keep Timothy in a constant state of complete sedation and hooked up to a heart-lung machine. It's the only way his body can continue to operate in its present form.

I see you don't recognize poor Timothy, but you've no doubt heard of his exploits under his *nom de superplume*, the musclebound, nine-foot tall fuchsia force of nature known as The Humongous. In pre-Flux days, Mr. Tibbetts was a mild-mannered accountant with suppressed anger issues. Ordinarily this would have presented no real worry, but the Flux physically externalized his rage, expanding his body mass into the indestructible grunting horrorhero we all love. The thing is, when the rage ultimately subsides and escapes his body like air from a deflating balloon, what is left is a distorted, enlarged mass of muscle tissue and skin draped over a skeletal structure far too puny and frail to handle it.

Timothy *has* begged for death several times now, but our government considers The Humongous a critical weapon in the War on Superterror. Frankly, his care and feeding are among the easier tasks you'll have. The tubes do most of the work, and the bed automatically turns him every twelve hours to prevent bedsores. The real work lies in reigniting his fury. Once it was a simple matter of transporting him to the site of the villainy, waking him, and making various unimaginative allusions to his mother's sexual preferences. But endless repetition has inured him, and even the cattle prods aren't working so well anymore. I fear we may have to resort to torturing his loved ones— if we can get legal on board.

Omelettes, broken eggs, etc. You know the idiom.

Let's head to Room 1010, a much nicer space. Barbara, I've brought the new residents, may we come in? Are you decent? Just a joke, she never wears anything but Lycra undergarments anyway. Doctors, may I introduce to you Barbara Bainbridge, better known as Boulder, a woman fluxwarped into a being of living metal and rock. How are you today, Barb? I see you've crushed another sofa, I'll ring the custodial staff to fetch you a new one. Not a problem; we get a discount on bulk orders.

I see. Well, that's why we're here, isn't it? Doctors, if you've seen footage of her many battles with The Alterdimensionals during Parallel World War II, you'll know that Boulder is the closest thing you'll ever see to a human tank. Particularly when she's equipped with a plasma bolt-cannon. Barbara's outer dermis is a compound mixture of lead and molten lava (don't think we haven't exhausted ourselves trying to figure out how it all works), rendering her nigh-invulnerable.

But it's her inner composition that has forced Boulder to become our longest-term resident. Skin of molten stone and metal is one thing, but her inner organs run the gamut of the periodic table. Barbara's blood is pure liquid mercury, her liver is made of copper, and her colon is titanium. She has eardrums made of cobalt, and her heart is, no, not gold, tungsten. She subsists mainly on rhenium and magnesium alloys, they seem to be what least upsets her zinc stomach. Part of your job will be refining her diet to allow for some variety. One cannot live on beryllium alone, eh, Barb?

Also, Boulder routinely suffers from rather serious kidney stones. Doctor Maxfield! What did I say about tact? You try passing a four-pound renal calculus through your ureter, see how much you giggle then! Just for that, you're now in charge of sifting through Boulder's excretions for rare metals. Until I say so, that's how long! Honestly! Head to the nurse's station, tell them you're the new bowel boy. Doctor Ginther will be more than happy to let you take over his duties. And tell them to prep Barbara for a session with the sonic jackhammer. Go!

Apologies for the intrusion, Barbara. You have yourself a wonderful day.

As you saw, Barbara is fairly content here. She was a freelance writer before Flux, so in her downtime she keeps herself occupied writing nonfiction pieces under a number of pseudonyms. If you get the chance, take a gander at the titanium-reinforced, extra-large keyboard our engineers cobbled together for her. Considering each of her fingers weighs ten kilograms and her hands are the size of frying pans, it's remarkable she only goes through one a week.

We're very lucky with Barb; her natural reticence keeps her amenable. Not all our long-termers have such resilience of spirit. Which brings us to our last door, or rather, aquarium.

Meet one of our less-celebrated residents, Jellied Eel. Wave hello, doctors. Oh, Jelly, naughty naughty. It's difficult to tell, what with the excess of boneless limbs and overall translucence, but he just made a rather vulgar gesture. Yes, that's his genitalia he's fondling there, under that flap. You are incorrigible, Jelly! Ha! You have to yell to be heard through the Plexiglas. Not that he ever listens.

Jelly may not be entirely media-friendly, but when it comes to naval warfare he has no peers. If it weren't for him and his electracles, the entire Atlantic seabed would now be overrun with the spawn of Octopustule.

Doctor Shonaman, Jellied Eel is a patient, not a sideshow! Tap the glass again, and I'll make sure you spend six months on dietetics duty with Regurgitator!

As I was saying, Jelly here is rather *unwilling* to remain in our care. He's a good soul, but unstable. He was an environmental activist at one time, and he'd much rather be causing havoc to fishing fleets and offshore drilling rigs. That's how we caught him, actually; he became ensnared in the nets of an illegal bottom trawler he was set on sinking. We can depend on him to fight when the cause is just, such as when the Fishmongers tried to poison the world's drinking water. But when the job is done he invariably flees, and we have a devil of a time capturing him again.

No, Jellied Eel is not a *prisoner*. We don't use that term here. Jellied Eel is a conscripted volunteer. Also, he's particularly susceptible to waterborne fungal infections, anchor worms, gill flukes, sea lice, and the like, and the only place he can receive treatment is here. Right now he's recovering from a nasty battle with an army of nematodes that annexed his colon. I'll hazard none of you expected to work as an ichthyologist, eh?

And thus concludes our tour. I realize that this is a lot to take in, which is why the rest of you won't begin your residencies until tomorrow. For the rest of the day I want you to rest and acclimate. If need be, please take advantage of one of our on-site counselors to help you through this transition. They're excellent listeners, and psychic empaths as well, so don't bother holding anything back.

Sorry to leave you now, but I have a rather full slate of patients to examine and only four arms. Colonel Tidhar will now lead you to the barracks you'll be calling home for the next several years. After you've freshened up and had a bite at the commissary, you'll be briefed on your various assignments over the next few months. Just to whet your appetite: The Gruesome arrives in the morning for a bowel resection; Madame Carbon is due for her monthly graphene finger- and toenail trimming; Chlorophyllis has come down with her annual bout of early blight; and Captain Awesome once again seared his eyelids when he blinked while using his laservision.

I won't lie to you: I don't expect all of you to survive your residency. Those who do can consider themselves employed for life, either here or, if you show an aptitude, at one of our government überhuman research facilities. Those who don't, well… nice try.

I'll be seeing you around the wards. Keep your heads on straight and you'll do fine.

And remember: sometimes, the only difference between a superhero and a supervillain is a malpractice suit. Ha ha.

∞   ✿   ∞

Based in New Brunswick, **COREY REDEKOP** is the author of the novels *Shelf Monkey* and *Husk*.

# BEDTIME FOR SUPERHEROES

*Leigh Wallace*

MARIE HAD MADE a full pot of tea even though she was alone in the little house. She added a perfect dribble of milk to her mug and took a slow sip. It was late, and everything was tidy. She was an old lady, she reminded herself. She should sit down, take a load off. Instead she pulled three more mugs from the drying rack and lined them up before her on the counter.

Into the ugly cartoon mug she dropped two absurdly large blobs of honey. Into the sparkly unicorn mug she poured some of that artificial hazelnut stuff. Next to the yellow mug with a chip in it she placed a container with a perfectly sliced lemon wedge— not too thick. She made the tasks take up as much time as possible.

Tea in hand, she turned from the counter toward the living room, the living room being the far corner of her unspacious kitchen-living-dining room area, where the soft old furniture was crowded. And there, on the sofa, suddenly and silently, was a ninja. So Marie went back to the counter and poured a second mug of tea. The tacky supervillain mug — with an image of a punching masked woman and the word *Shwoooom!* — half full with two oversized spoonfuls of honey. It was for the ninja, who liked her tea sweet and evil and who was all tuckered out.

Marie shuffled her old feet to the couch, a mug in each hand. She kissed Lacy, her ninja, on the forehead before closing the living room window, which Lacy had suddenly and silently left wide open to the chilly night before collapsing onto the sofa. The ninja hugged her mug like a friend, like she didn't even think it was ugly, because she didn't.

Before Marie could sit down with her own tea there was ninja paraphernalia littering the floor. She put her mug down on the coffee table and gathered up the mask and the gloves with the little black buttons that she had sewn onto them. Lacy had asked her to sew them on. Had begged her to. Even though nobody's ever heard of a ninja with buttons.

"You're wearing the housecoat we got you," said Lacy, cracking open a drowsy eye.

"It's lovely, dear," said Marie.

"Is it warm?" asked Lacy.

"Yes, just lovely." The housecoat was a leopard print, but it was nubbly and thick and Marie loved it.

Marie nudged the ninja's boots with her toe. No shoes in the living room. No. Not even ninja boots. Not even after a long day of fighting crime. The boots blurred off Lacy's feet and onto her lap.

Marie, with her usual unhurried step, put the mask and gloves away on the hall closet shelf, above her limp old housecoat and the ninja's patched old ninja suit that neither of them had ever thought of throwing away. One of the fingers of the ninja's good gloves, the new ones with the shiny buttons sewn on, was pulling open at the tip and Marie thought she might try and get that sewn up tomorrow before the ninja went back out. Or exchange the pair, since they were new. No, it was easier to just mend it. That's what she would do.

"Oh no!" In the living room Lacy was poking at a wisp of thread hanging loose near the top of one of her boots. "Gram! I lost a button!"

Marie paused in the hall. "Who ever heard of ninjas with buttons?"

Lacy shrugged. "I like buttons."

Marie shrugged back. "So put on another one."

Lacy made a scrunchy, lip-bitey face. "I didn't buy any extras."

"Honestly, Lacy."

Lacy didn't look up. "Well, they were expensive."

Marie didn't sit down to her tea yet. She made her way to the hall closet to fetch her sewing basket. "And may I ask why you came through the window? Again?"

"I forgot my key. What do I do about my button?" Between those two sentences Lacy had gone from a sock-footed ninja to a pyjama-clad young woman who looked like she'd been coiled into that afghan all evening, betrayed only by the current of inside air that eddied back from her bedroom. Her buttonless boot was back in her hand.

Marie finished placing the sewing basket from the hall closet down on the coffee table. "Watch the springs. Don't go so fast." But Lacy never went slow. It wasn't her thing. The sofa had lost the will to moan ages ago, anyway. Lacy dove into the sewing basket and scrounged through all of it before Marie had turned back to her tea, which was now getting lukewarm.

"Guh! They're all pink!" The sewing basket was instantly on the floor, its contents strewn all the way into the kitchen.

"Pick that up," said Marie, but the full sewing basket was already back on the coffee table. Lacy was fast. It was her thing. The sofa sighed an unheeded whisper of protest.

"Gram. Girl superheroes don't. Wear. Pink."

"In my day, ninjas didn't wear buttons, either."

Lacy didn't say anything. At first. Then she said, "I like buttons."

Lacy pushed the sewing basket further away down the coffee table with her toe, grabbed a paperback from the overstuffed living-room bookcase, flipped its pages once, and tossed it onto a growing pile on the floor. Marie, with creaking old bones, put the boots in the closet where they belonged, with the gloves and mask. When Marie re-entered the living room Lacy had curled her feet up under the afghan, forgotten the sewing basket on the coffee table, and was deep into another book, an unauthorized biography of The Housekeeper.

"The Housekeeper's making a comeback," Lacy informed Marie.

"Mmm."

"Gram, she was spotted in Toronto," Lacy went on.

"Mmm."

"She was *in her mask*," Lacy insisted.

"Mmm."

"Gram, you're not listening."

The Housekeeper was the vintage supervillain on Lacy's ugly mug, and one of the only other speedsters out there. Of course, Marie knew perfectly well that Lacy's fascination with an old villain didn't mean Lacy would ever go villain herself. It was silly to even think it. Marie would remind herself of that in the empty evenings, when Lacy's mug sat the counter.

Marie was proud of her granddaughter. Lacy was a true hero. Marie sipped her tea, ignoring how cool it had gotten, and took out her knitting.

"I bet she'll go on Ellen." Lacy mused.

"Mmm. Wait. Wouldn't she be too old? Or dead? Or evil? Wait, is she *Elvis*?"

Lacy rolled her eyes and went on reading. Marie leaned over Lacy to flick on the corner lamp for her. Lacy was always reading in the dark. It wasn't one of her super things; it was one of her young woman things.

As Marie unwound her yarn the front door clicked open and heavy, uneven stomps made their way down the hall toward them. Marie put the knitting and tepid tea aside and hurried back to the kitchen. She filled another mug, the one with the sparkly unicorn handle that still shed unvacuumable glitter everywhere, and handed it to the six-and-a-half-foot-tall pirate who just clomped in.

"Thanks." The pirate tossed eye-patch and bandana onto the small dining table against the side wall and thumped over to the sofa with her mug. Marie noted that one foot had a hesitant quality to it. She wanted to ask about it but managed not to. The pirate was a grownup who could surely look after herself. What could a little old lady do, anyway? She didn't want to be a nag. Even if she had let the pirate move in for free, incidentally, *and* handwashed the sparkly mug every day because it wasn't dishwasher safe.

"Hey, Bea," said Lacy without looking up from her book.

"Hey, Lacy," said Bea, the pirate, stopping in front of the coffee table and leaning on one foot. She unbuckled her heavy pirate belt and looked into the sewing basket. "So. Buttons?" She said.

"Yeah. Pink buttons." Lacy glared at the sewing basket. She didn't make eye contact with Marie. Marie ignored her from the kitchen, where there was still one empty mug left.

"Pink buttons suck," Bea said as she collapsed onto the sofa beside Lacy. She looked all tuckered out, like Lacy. Only twice Lacy's size, and all muscly. Muscles were Bea's thing.

"So you like the housecoat, Marie?" asked Bea.

"Oh yes, dear." Marie picked up Bea's eye-patch and bandana from the table, even though she knew she shouldn't. The girls were going to have to start picking up after themselves. But she hung the eye-patch and bandana over the banister to remind Bea to bring them upstairs when she went to bed.

"My feet hurt." Bea stretched her legs out under the coffee table.

Lacy asked. "That's because of your noob boots." She nodded with all the weight of her substantial three years' experience as a superhero.

Bea wiggled her toes. "I like my boots. They're not noob."

"Bea. Seriously. Only noob superheroes wear heels. Seriously."

"These are my pirate boots." Bea glared at Lacy, but Lacy kept reading as if she hadn't noticed. "The pirate thing was your idea."

Lacy chuckled at being a superhero ninja with a pirate side-kick. Being a superhero ninja with a pirate sidekick made her laugh every time. Marie still didn't get it but she managed to be okay with that.

"Don't forget to take off your noob boots inside," said Marie.

Bea ignored her and took a sip of her tea. It was coffee. "Marie, you gave me coffee."

"Because you didn't do your homework."

"Yes I did. I told you I did."

"I checked. You lied." Marie kissed Bea on the forehead even though Bea hadn't finished her homework and had stayed out fighting crime past curfew. She was doing a little better on her second lap of grade twelve, so Marie reminded herself, again, not to worry. "Also, you still haven't taken the garden tools downstairs." She knew she was nagging this time. But was it so much to ask?

Bea grumbled up to her room with loud, uneven noob boot stomps. She left her eye-patch and bandana on the banister.

Marie hovered in the kitchen next to the counter, not look-ing at the empty yellow mug, now sitting by itself. "I wonder where Celeste is?" she mused innocently.

Lacy's pages paused in their continuous flipping for that one instant. "I'm sure she's fine, Gram."

"Oh, I know." Marie barely sighed. "I know." She shooed Lacy off the couch. That was Marie's spot. Lacy settled sideways into the armchair instead, already too bored to read. She'd read all of these books, like, yesterday. Marie ignored her, picked up her knitting and started the needles going. When Marie knitted she was fast. Bea, in a big T-shirt, came down the stairs and flumped onto the sofa beside Marie with her coffee and chemistry book and wriggled her chilly bare toes under Marie's thigh. Marie had bought or knit Bea five pairs of slippers before giving up. Bea clearly preferred to have chilly toes and to keep them warm under Marie's thigh.

"I want to cut my hair," said Bea.

Marie knitted and didn't remind Bea to study. Bea was a grownup.

"Too bad," said Lacy.

"But I hate it!"

"I told you," said Lacy with a tilt of her head. "Right at the start. If you don't cover your hair completely, then you can't change it. People will know."

"Guh." Bea, currently a part-timer while in training, was still growing into the superhero life. "I'll get a wig."

"That is ridiculous."

"I'll go no-secret-identity."

"Not until you find me a new pirate."

"Or *you* could go back to being Celeste's sidekick instead."

At that moment Celeste wafted into the living room. Marie only realized her fingers were white and sore on her knitting needles once she felt them loosen. She'd been knitting much faster than she had intended.

"We were just talking about you," said Marie, smiling and tucking her knitting under the end table.

"I know. Don't get up, Marie. I'll get my tea." The teapot floated and poured itself.

"You're a dear," said Marie.

"I'm glad you like the housecoat, Marie."

"It's lovely," Marie said, smiling at having all her girls home and at how cute Celeste was when she pretended to know everything. One of Celeste's things was being psychic. More or less.

Celeste lifted a saggy sweater off the back of a dining table chair and threw it on over her long white battle gown, pulling her corn silk hair up out of the back of the neck and getting it all staticky.

"Really, Celeste, you should..." Marie stopped as Celeste smiled at her. Celeste usually knew it, before you said it. No, Celeste wasn't going to tie up her hair when she fought crime, as Marie knew perfectly well by now. Celeste's hair was part of her thing. Her angel thing. And Celeste, too, was a grownup.

Celeste brushed something like dirt, maybe dried blood, from her hair.

Celeste kissed Marie on the forehead and went to get her chipped yellow mug and lemon slice. She turned back to the living room, where Marie knitted at a comfortable pace. Bea tapped on a textbook page. And Lacy idly fiddled a pink button over the backs of her knuckles.

The last mug from the counter joined the others on the coffee table. Marie scooched Bea down to make room on the couch, but before taking a seat Celeste paused dramatically and let her eyes fall picturesquely closed as she brought two fingers to her temple. Even though she didn't need to close her eyes or touch her temple to know things. The others were perfectly aware that she didn't, and she was aware that they were aware. But she did it anyway.

"Gail's coming," she announced. Her eyes flicked to the front door. The lock turned clunkily, without a key. Celeste was very impressive but could also be pretty lazy. She let her picturesque hand drop to her side and sipped her tea with a grateful slurp.

There was a knock at the door.

"Gail, you don't need to knock!" Celeste called out, as usual. Lacy and Bea laughed. Marie smiled, the way you do when something happens over again, and in so doing, becomes good.

Gail let herself in. She was in a pea coat and cute woolly beret. She wasn't super. It wasn't her thing. She was just Gail and liked it fine that way. "Hi, guys. Hi, Marie. Nice housecoat."

"Thank you, dear."

While Gail handed Celeste her coat and hat, Marie considered offering her some tea, but Gail usually declined. She worked at a café so she was usually full of tea. Marie decided not to bother. Then she changed her mind. What if, just this once, Gail had a sudden hankering for some tea? What if Gail liked it when Marie offered, even though she didn't want any? Maybe Marie should buy a new mug, just for Gail. An owl mug? Gail liked owls. You can get something like that on the internet these days, right? Come to think of it, it was about time Gail had her own key. Marie realized with a small start that she enjoyed putting out new mugs on the counter and getting new keys cut.

Meanwhile, Gail kicked off her shoes and asked, as per usual, "So, did anyone have any bitchin' and totally underappreciated-by-society battles today?"

Eye-rolls all around.

"How was your work?" Lacy asked Gail.

Gail shrugged. "You know. Work. Boring."

Lacy sat smiling expectantly at Gail. Bea's textbook was closed on her thumb. Celeste leaned comfortably against the little dining table with her ankles crossed. They all looked at Gail and waited.

Marie smiled and shook her head. Her superheroes. They always did this to Gail, and Gail always let them. Marie couldn't help the satisfied little smile that nipped at the corners of her mouth. If only she had a mug and key for Gail. Then everything would be just right.

Gail tilted her head and grinned crookedly. "Well, okay, I made a leaf on a latté today. Sorta. A special leaf." They smiled. They were interested. They kept looking at her. Practically staring. "And, um, I forgot to pee for, like, four hours."

"Sucky!" cried Lacy.

"Peeing rules," said Bea.

"And her feet hurt," said Celeste. Gail shrugged. Her feet always hurt after work. But you could tell she thought it was sweet that Celeste noticed, even though noticing stuff was Celeste's thing. "Bea's feet hurt, too," Celeste added.

"Because my boots are awesome," said Bea.

"Because they're noob," said Celeste.

Marie smiled a little bit more but hid it behind her mug. Gail looked at the clock over the mantel and rounded on Celeste. "Okay. Business. You are not dressed."

Celeste gasped. "Damn! I forgot about the party!" She put down her yellow mug with a clatter.

Lacy snickered. "How does a psychic even forget things?"

"I knew you were going to say that."

Marie almost snorted but didn't, kind of. Lacy shot her a squinky-eyed look.

Gail grabbed at the neck of Celeste's ugly sweater. "It's not too late yet if we get going. This stays here."

Celeste sighed and slumped her head back. "I never know what to wear."

"Why do you think I stopped by?" Gail pushed Celeste toward the stairs, pulling the ugly sweater off her and tossing it back onto the dining room chair. Celeste loved that sweater, which Marie had knitted for her. But she did not love it enough to bring it to a party, of course, which was fine with Marie. Celeste turned regretfully away from the nearly full yellow mug, abandoned on the table. Gail marched her up the stairs. Celeste didn't complain.

Marie's needles went back to clicking at a comfortable pace. Bea's chemistry pages slowly turned. Lacy sat and sipped her tea and when hers was done she sipped Marie's until hers was done too. Marie got up to put the mugs in the sink. Celeste and Gail hadn't come down yet. Lacy and Bea quietly arched their eyebrows at each other, pointing upstairs.

Marie rolled her eyes at them. "I know what they're doing up there," she said. "Even if I'm old."

Lacy and Bea looked at Marie with wide eyes and mouths kinked shut. It wasn't very likely that Celeste and Gail would make it to their party. Marie laughed. Then Lacy and Bea did, too. Marie thought that, if she gave her an owl mug, maybe Gail would feel more comfortable staying for breakfast. Marie liked the kinds of life problems that could be solved with mugs.

"Well, goodnight, girls." She said as she rinsed out Lacy's ridiculous mug, smiling at the outdated villain looking fiercely back at her and thinking of how very, very proud she was of her girls.

"But, Gram, what about my button?" Lacy asked. No. Whined. From Marie's point of view, whining was still one of Lacy's things.

"Lacy, what is the point?" Marie folded Celeste's ugly sweater over her arm and walked with tired, contented feet toward the stairs. "You go too fast for anyone to see any buttons."

Lacy gave that some thought while Marie gathered up the eye-patch and bandana she'd left on the banister.

"I like buttons," Lacy finally said.

Marie climbed the stairs with swishing steps. "They're a waste of money. Back in my day, all a super needed was a power and a mask."

Bea snorted a bit and said, "So, what, were you a superhero?"

Marie paused up on the landing. "Oh, we should all be so lucky." Marie creaked open her bedroom door, carrying her knitting with her.

"So you like the housecoat, Gram? Really?" Lacy called from her spot in the chair.

"It's just lovely, girls. Really." Before she shut her bedroom door, Marie added, "Love you."

It only took Marie a second to hang up the robe and settle into bed. As she drowsed she thought about getting that mug and key for Gail. Why not? While she was out she would pick up metal knitting needles. She gently pushed from her mind the thoughts that metal would not burn, that the tips of her newest wooden needles were blackening with the friction of her carelessly swift knitting. With Celeste around, it was safest to be cautious about having such thoughts, but Marie had a lot of practice concealing them. Even with the image of The Housekeeper staring back at her from Lacy's mug every night.

∞  ☼  ∞

Ottawa writer **LEIGH WALLACE** is an advisor on the Access to Information and Privacy Acts for Industry Canada.

# A HOLE LOTTA TROUBLE: A TALE IN FIVE VOICES

*David Perlmutter*

## MUSCLE GIRL

It was a hole. There was no question about it. The question was: where did it lead to?

That was the question the five of us — The Brat, Power Bunny, Candy Girl, Cerberus, and myself — were pondering as we looked at the thing. As the highest ranking — and, so far, sole — members of the International League of Girls with Guns (referring to our superpowered muscles, as we are all superheroes — not that we were packing heat, so we're clear on *that*), it was our job to deal with it — and, particularly, whatever might emerge from it.

Well, technically it was *my* job, as it appeared in the ruddy woodlands surrounding Lake Winnipeg, where I live, in both my mild-mannered secret identity Gerda Munsinger and my pink-and-white suited super identity, in which I battle evil in all its forms. However, being as I'm "just" a blond-haired elementary school kid, I sometimes feel as if I need some help from my pals.

I became an ILGWG member early in my still-young life and career, after the girls helped me beat down a particularly vicious gang of superpowered criminals I couldn't deal with myself. Since then, according to our organization protocol, we assemble periodically to deal with things that we judge have the potential to be similar blow-ups. That happens more than you think. A *lot* more.

Fortunately, the five of us are the best of friends, in addition to being "professional" colleagues, and stay that way regardless of what happens to us. This story kind of brings that home, I think, along with what we each bring to the team.

Anyway, I have a tendency to go off on tangents when I narrate, so I better turn this over to one of the others…

THE BRAT

So there we were, the five of us, looking sheepishly at the hole. I was shivering a bit in the Canadian winter cold, seeing that I was only wearing my trademark white skirt, blue sweater, monogrammed white T-shirt, and high-top shoes, looking every inch the blond-haired three-year-old I only *appear* to be, *thank you*. The rest of us were a little better off: Muscle Girl in her usual pink tights, white panties and cape, and short grey boots; Candy Girl her purple coveralls and red mask, belt and boots, with her equally red hair flapping in the breeze; Power Bunny, dressed in her usual blue shirt and skirt over her bright pink fur; and Cerberus, a *seemingly* runty Dalmatian puppy, wore her white T-shirt with a gleaming black "C" on it. The fur on Cerb' and PB gave both of them *mucho* more protection from the cold than me, which made me a little jealous.

Also, the cold is unnatural to me, since I come from a hot planet and am warm-blooded. So I was more short-tempered than usual.

Impatiently, we examined the orifice with our superpowered senses for a few minutes. Then I lost it.

"What are we *waiting* for?" I demanded. "Let's go down and see what's *in* the damn thing already!"

"Hang on," said Candy, who's a (you guessed it— seemingly normal) teenager in her off-time, and a skittish and easily intimidated one, besides. "We don't know what's down there. I mean, there could be—"

"Helllllooooo!" Cerberus drawled, sarcastically. "That's a *given*, Candy! You're not *afraid*, are you?"

"No!" Candy snapped, angrily. "I just meant that if we go in there without a plan, we might not come out, and—"

"We'll come back out," said Power Bunny, tersely. "*That's* our plan."

"Really?" said Candy, unconvinced. "Can't we work something out first?"

Although she's the oldest, Candy was the last of us to get her powers. They come from a ring she received in reward for rescuing a dying alien hero from peril; she didn't inherit them naturally (as with Muscle Girl, Cerberus, and myself) or get them through accidental means (like Power Bunny). Because she is the only one of us whose powers depend on something external — and because she is a total Aspie — she's freakishly obsessed with trying to do things as safely as possible, out of fear of becoming disempowered at the wrong time, or permanently.

"*Planning*," I growled at her, "doesn't solve any of the sort of problems we might face down *there*!"

"Now I know why they call you the Brat!" Candy said. "You gotta have your *way* — all the time!"

I was just about to fly over and bop her in the nose when, thankfully, Muscle Girl spoke up.

"Let's just go in and look around for a minute," she said. "There's probably nothing, but, on the off chance there *is* something going on, we'll deal with it, seal up the hole with rock or something, and then get out. Like always."

That made sense to all of us, and we agreed to do it.

"Besides which, Brat," she said to me, "I know *you* want to get out of this cold, but so do the rest of us. And remember: *I* gotta deal with this *every* winter."

"Sure," I said, chastened. "Sorry, Candy. I didn't mean to..."

"Nah," Candy retorted. "No need, Brat. We all wanna get this done. Hero's curse, huh?"

"Yeah," I answered, knowingly. "Hero's curse."

"Well, I, for one, want to see what makes that thing so *special*," said Cerberus. She raced into the gaping maw with her usual quicksilver speed, and the rest of us followed at the same pace.

With our powers, we did a quick sweep of the hole, in the hope that we could declare the place null and void, seal it up, and leave. That was what appeared to be the case. There was just solid rock, with no traps or hidden passages. We prepared to fly out of the hole and out of there, when...

"Holy...!" PB exclaimed, as she saw it first. "The hole's being CLOSED UP!"

"Then what are we *waiting* for?" asked Muscle Girl, rhetorically.

We rushed to the exit as fast as we could, but we were a hair too late. And, whatever the hell was blocking the hole, not even our combined powers could help us break through it. Instead, we crashed into it and collapsed onto the ground together.

We were trapped. That much we knew. But who — or what
— was responsible?

CANDY GIRL

My first thought when I recovered and discovered our joint
predicament was: *Run away*!

Now, I know that is not your average superhero behavior, but
anyone with Asperger's syndrome, superhero or not, is gonna
panic like hell if they're in a strange and difficult situation
with absolutely no way out (or so it seemed to me at the time).
Especially if they haven't taken their anti-anxiety medication.
Which I hadn't.

So, when I woke up from being knocked out and saw we
were trapped, I got to my feet, screamed, and ran down the
nearest passageway.

Fortunately, Cerberus, with her enhanced dog senses, heard
my screaming and rapidly moving feet. She ran in front of me.
"And just *where* do *you* think you're going?" she demanded.

In my anxiety-induced state, I babbled out some incoherent
stuff about how scared I was and how I needed to get out of
there, and how I needed to get my meds and stuff like that,
until she cut me off with a pre-emptive growl. "GET BACK
THERE!" she ordered. "We all need to be on *guard* to get out
of here— so WOMAN UP!"

"Yes, Ma'am," I said, wilting under her fury, and we returned
to the entrance, where the others had regained their senses.
Thankfully, 'cause mine were nowhere to be seen.

That was when the giant screen came out of the wall in front
of us, out of nowhere...

POWER BUNNY

Candy's only half-right about that screen. It was a screen, all
right, but it wasn't a *giant* one— only about the size of the mono-
liths they use for TV screens nowadays. She's got a tendency to
exaggerate things, but I guess everybody in this business does.

Once the screen revealed itself, a transmission came on
without any of us touching it, so it was obviously something
coming from outside of the cave. Those responsible soon made
themselves known...

Our most vicious and bloodthirsty enemies, who had apparently teamed up to trap and destroy us.

Natch!

What made it even worse was that they were throwing a party to celebrate our imminent demise in the cave— or so I gathered from the images on the screen. A *party*! The *nerve*! Sure, we'd collectively and individually caused them a lot of heartbreak and pain, but we're *supposed* to! No need to turn our potential erasure from the Earth into some sort of *celebration*!

Anyhow…

The first of the crowd to address us were Scylla and Charybdis, the sister-and-brother delinquent-cum-magician duo who attend high school with Candy and have been a major pain in our rears in the past.

"Howdy, *buttfaces*!" said Scylla, diplomatically. "Like that *tomb* we set up for you?"

"You…!" Candy snapped at her. She might have smashed into the screen after her, but we held her back.

"Why don't you save some of that energy for escaping, Candy?" Charybdis sneered at Candy, disdainfully. "That is, if you can get that Aspie mind of yours to *think* straight!"

Candy swore viciously. She made for the screen, and we stopped her again, while they laughed at us from afar. "Let me *go*!" Candy snapped. "I'm gonna kill them…"

"Calm down!" Muscle Girl ordered Candy, who relaxed, and then she turned to the screen. "Okay!" Muscle Girl demanded. "What the hell's going on here?"

"Perhaps *I* can explain!"

To the visible annoyance of Scylla and Charybdis, Petra O'Leum, the villainous supergirl who's Muscle Girl's biggest foe, stepped in front of the camera.

"I should have known that *you* had a hand in this, *Petra*!" Muscle Girl said, softly but angrily.

"Not just a *hand*, MG!" Petra retorted. "This whole thing was *my* idea! I located the site for the hole, and then I recruited S and C over here to blast it into shape with their magic. Had to pay them for it, of course, but a small price to get rid of you all *forever*!"

"*What*!" In outrage, Scylla stood up from the divan she and Charybdis were reclining on. "This wouldn't have happened *at all* if it weren't for *us*!"

With an extreme level of forceful strength, Petra angrily pushed her back onto the divan. As for Charybdis, he stayed where he was, unperturbed as usual.

"CRAM IT!" Petra shouted at Scylla, her face turning nearly as red as her chestnut hair. "I am trying to outline my *plan* to these *idiots* here [meaning us], and I'd appreciate it if..."

"Someone say *idiots*?"

At this point, as if on cue, the other members of the party converged around the camera: Machine Gun Steinberg, the nebbish businessman who's often at odds with the Brat; Dumbell, the second most powerful puppy in the world (and perpetually scheming to take out our gal Cerberus so she can be No. 1— always unsuccessfully), along with her human "master," Bad Dan McGoon; and, most annoying to *me*, the dimwitted boy Rabindranath Jhabvala and his pet snake, Crack, who together create a lot of trouble for me in spite of their lack of brains.

Petra obviously didn't want them there. Her eyes flashed in anger, and she cracked her ever-present whip in the air, driving them away. "BACK, *PEONS*!" she growled. "I can't believe I'm even in the same *profession* as you!"

"Who are you calling A PEON?" shouted a livid Scylla. Furious, she shot a blast of magical energy at Petra, who ducked it. However, it must have damaged the equipment, as the transmission ended as abruptly as it had begun.

We were silent for a few moments, as we tried to burn off some of the shock and rage that had been building up inside of us since our capture. It didn't work, because we turned it on each other.

Candy finally broke the silence, throwing a blast of emerald light from her power ring at the now-blank screen.

"DAMN IT!" she shouted. "I *knew* it! They want to *kill* us! If we hadn't gone down into this damn *hole*, this never would have happened! You guys are always so *impulsive*..."

"We *have* to be impulsive, you big SNOT!" snapped the Brat. "How would we survive otherwise if we were faced by them— or any *other* type of evil, for that matter?"

"I'm just *saying*..." Candy began.

"Well, there's your problem, right there!" The Brat pounced on those words like a cat. "You always *talk* about these things, but you never *do* anything..."

"So I'm a just a *fifth wheel* to you!" Candy shouted back at her. "Well, I'm sorry to disappoint you for being *just* a human being and not an all-mighty DEITY, but that was how I was *born*, okay?"

"Knock it off!" Muscle Girl interjected. "This is getting us nowhere!"

"Who are *you* to decide that?" snapped the Brat. "Were you democratically elected to decide what gets us anywhere and what doesn't?"

"I don't have to be democratically elected to decide when somebody's being a JERK!" Muscle Girl snapped, pointing at the Brat.

"How DARE you!" the Brat snarled back. "I am trying to consider our common welfare here..."

"Even though you don't actually *consult* others when you do it!" I said, feeling a bit sore.

"You stay *out* of this, carrot breath!" the Brat snapped. "I can *take* you!"

"TAKE *THIS!*" I snarled.

I rushed at the Brat and punched her into the wall, to the astonishment of the others. She bounced back right away and swung at me. I swung back— I'm not proud of it, but I was fed up with the Brat and wanted to cut her down to size. Muscle Girl tried to stop the Brat, and Candy did the same to me. This went on for a couple of minutes, until Cerberus, bless her heart, got us back to our senses.

## CERBERUS

"*SILENCE!*"

I shouted with such force that everyone except me dove to the floor, while I stood hind-legged to address them.

"Jesus, Cerb!" Candy said, as she rubbed her ears in pain. "What did we do to...?"

"You *forgot!*" I retorted. "All of you!"

"Forgot *what*?" snapped the Brat.

"That *we*, whether *you* like it or *not*," I snapped back, pointing directly at her with my paw, "are a TEAM! And, if we *ever* want to get *out* of here, we better start *acting* like a team— *instead* of like a bunch of *sissy prima donnas* who each think we're *better* than the others!"

By that time, they had all gotten to their feet, and the Brat seemed chastened by my words. They all did, in fact, but she more than the others.

"I'm sorry, guys," the Brat said. "I got a bit hot under the collar, there. Shouldn't have taken it out on you, but I was pretty damn mad about being duped."

"Don't take it out on yourself, Brat," said Candy. "I'm the one who went nuts, being off my meds and everything. You never would have gotten pissy if I hadn't lost my temper."

"Same with me," said PB, sheepishly. "I got such a short fuse that any little thing can set me off."

"Never mind the apologizing!" I interjected. "That's in the past. What matters now is the future."

"You're right, Cerb!" Muscle Girl said. "We need to bounce ideas off each other and figure out how to get out of here. And we can't be too long about it, either— even *our* bodies are gonna give out soon if we don't get some decent oxygen soon. Huddle up, everybody!"

MUSCLE GIRL

Once we got our heads screwed on again and concentrated on what we needed to do, it was easy. You get five female superheroes inside a hole in the ground, each of them stronger than a whole army of men, and the solution is obvious: *punch* our way out...

CANDY GIRL

Hey, I'm not *that* strong, all right? At best, I can only lift my *own* weight, let alone the kind of numbers you guys can bench-press...

MUSCLE GIRL

We're *getting* to that, Candy.

CANDY GIRL

Sorry.

MUSCLE GIRL

As I was saying, each of us was going to fly on her own and punch out her own personal tunnel...

THE BRAT

We needed some alone time, especially me. The exception was Candy, owing to the fact that she's more earthbound than the rest of us, so she went back to the entrance and tried to cut her way through.

CANDY GIRL
No problem. I focused the laser from my power ring on one spot of the rock wall, and it gave, easy. Duh! Why didn't I think of that *before*?

MUSCLE GIRL
Who's *telling* this story, here? I thought it was *my* turn.

CERBERUS
We each had a turn already, MG. Now we're telling the last part of it together.

MUSCLE GIRL
Okay. Just wanted to be clear...

CERBERUS
Good. So then we emerged from the ground at around the same time, a little battered and bruised, but safe and healthy, like we wanted to be.

POWER BUNNY
Easy for *you* to say. You can move faster than us 'cause you're *smaller*, and you were already out and done when the rest of us—

CERBERUS
No bitching, please, PB. That was what got us in trouble before. *Remember*?

POWER BUNNY
Oh, yeah. Forgot that.

CANDY GIRL
Anyway, when we got out, there was one thing we all had on our mind. *Revenge.*

MUSCLE GIRL
Fortunately, we came out from the hole near the spot where Petra had parked her spaceship for the villains' shindig, almost within walking distance of it. But we didn't walk. We flew.

CANDY GIRL
Again, you're overgeneralizing. I ran. I needed to save my superpowers for the fight ahead. My ring was running low on power.

MUSCLE GIRL
The *point* is, we were able to approach them unobserved. But, as soon as we entered with our fists clenched and our teeth bared, they took notice.

CANDY GIRL
It wasn't a fair fight, by any means. Scylla and Charybdis spotted me and tried to summon up some spells to stop me, but I blasted them into another dimension with the rays from my ring. Won't hear from them for a long time, I hope.

MUSCLE GIRL
Petra blazed some curses at me and tried to wrestle me down, but a left hook and a right cross and one more in the belly from me, and she was out for good.

THE BRAT
All I needed to do was lock eyes at Steinberg, and, if he wasn't out cold before I saw him, he sure was after. I have that kind of effect on my enemies. After the fight, I called the cops and they took him back to jail. Simple as that.

POWER BUNNY
Rabindranath and Crack did the same "You goin' down, bitch!" kung fu schtick they try to use against me every time. Ho hum. I swept in and bound the two of them up in each other so they couldn't do anything else.

CERBERUS
Dumbell ran in front of me as soon as she spotted me, and we locked noses. Her shaggy yellow fur looked like it hadn't

been groomed in quite a while, and her black T-shirt with the white "D" on it (is she a copycat or *what*?) looked like it hadn't been cleaned for the same amount of time. Naturally, we weren't pleased to see each other.

"Get out of here," I ordered, "and take your *servant* with you!"

I pointed to McGoon at this point. Despite his nickname, he isn't "bad" in the least, just easily dominated. He quickly fled before I could do any damage to him.

Dumbell, however, did nothing. I returned my attention to her.

"I *told* you to…"

"I *heard* you!" she snapped, in her deceptively mild working-class Southern accent. "You want me out of your sight 'cause you're afraid I'll *beat* ya! And I *will*!"

"Don't be ridiculous," I retorted, holding my temper in check with a powerful effort. "My strength and speed are *greater* than yours…"

"Not by as much as you *think* they are, *hotshot*!"

"…and, as you know, my intelligence is *considerably* greater!"

She called me a *very* dirty name, but I ignored her.

"Face it, Dumbell," I responded. "You may outweigh me by a few pounds, but that's the only category in which you're better than me. You'll *always* be number two."

"I may be number two," she snarled, "but I TRY HARDER!"

With that, she took a vicious swipe at me, which I ducked. Then she started chasing me around the ship. This continued for a couple of minutes, until she cornered me, and forced me to fight her by encasing my small forepaws in her larger ones. We stood upright, wrestling with such force than the ground shook. I was at a disadvantage, as she was larger than me and had obviously — and lazily — conserved much more of her strength and energy than I had that day. Nevertheless, I pre-vailed. With a Herculean effort, I broke free of her grip, and before she could go any further, I snatched her by her shirt by my right forepaw and held her aloft.

"Let me put you in the *driver's seat*!" I said, as I cocked my left forepaw back.

Then I punched her so hard that she flew out the ship's wall and extremely far away.

Haven't heard from her since.

MUSCLE GIRL
So, that was it.

THE BRAT
No, it wasn't. We went back to seal up the hole, which was a bitch of a job, even for us.

CANDY GIRL
You're exaggerating. You guys just cut up some rocks with your powers and stuffed up the hole with 'em. Typical show-off stuff.

POWER BUNNY
Somebody's *jealous*.

CANDY GIRL
Yeah, I guess I am. I'll admit that. I don't want to seem *useless*.

CERBERUS
Which you are *not*, Candy. We all have things we can't do, and things we can. Doesn't mean you're any less valuable to us.

CANDY GIRL
Thanks.

MUSCLE GIRL
I think we all learned a valuable lesson. Being able to do stuff on your own is all well and good, but sometimes you need to be part of a team to understand how valuable you can be. And who your real friends are when your back is against the wall. Am I right on that, girls?

THE OTHERS
Right!

∞ ☼ ∞

Winnipeg writer **DAVID PERLMUTTER** is the author of *America Toons In: A History of Television Animation* (McFarland and Co.).

# THE RISE AND FALL OF CAPTAIN STUPENDOUS

*P. E. Bolivar*

**GREETINGS, AVID READERS!** This is Myra Moon reporting from her prison cell, in an attempt to set the record straight.

You've heard how I was kidnapped by the villainess Jaguar while on assignment in Brazil, gassed by a mysterious Amazonian plant she'd left in my hotel room, and how Captain Stupendous and his Canadian Super League rescued me, but you haven't heard my side of the story. The story of my life, and how it all came crashing down.

Ever since my first interview with Captain Stupendous, with that accompanying photo of me flying through the air in his muscular arms, I was assumed to be his girlfriend. Love at first sight, it was said, but it was never love. I was dating my photographer, Mikey Bell, and at the time we were happy together.

The roof of my condo complex was freezing cold the night of the interview. For months I'd been writing article after glowing article about the Captain's many exploits in the hopes of catching his attention. How he'd flown in to save those people trapped on the sinking ferry off the coast of Vancouver Island; how he'd foiled the Scandalbug's attempt to blackmail Parliament; how he saved his fellow superhero Sufferjet, prevented her from marrying the villain Pherognome, who'd put a spell on her with his magical perfume.

It was that article that made the Captain finally agree to speak with me. Mikey was the one who captured the famous image that accompanied it. Captain Stupendous in his tights and knee-high boots, his red cape fluttering behind him as he hoisted that ugly little man into the air. Pherognome was outfitted in black tuxedo and top hat and trying to hit the lantern-jawed hero with a cane held in his comically too-short arms.

They called the photograph a classic. It won awards, but I never considered it to be one of Mikey's best. Something always bothered me about the way it captured Pherognome's spellbound fiancée. Sufferjet lay sprawled on the ground, dressed in her shining white armor, hand on her dazed head. A veil crowned her long black locks in place of her usual half-helm, her head almost resting on the Captain's rippling thigh.

To my mind she deserved better than to be portrayed as a damsel-in-distress for him to save. She'd singlehandedly stopped the Venusian Horde from destroying Earth, to name only one of her exploits.

When I suggested not using the photo for the story, Mikey balked. "Come on, it looks great," he said. "They look like they belong together! People are going to eat it up." Turned out he was right, and since it got me my interview I couldn't complain too much.

The Captain agreed to meet me on my rooftop, but only if we were alone. Too bad, I would have liked Mikey's company, and to be honest I was incredibly nervous. He could melt me with his eyes, crush me with one hand. That kind of power instilled an instinctual fear in people. I was no different, even if I did write glowingly of his many adventures.

When he finally arrived, his entrance did not disappoint. The clouds opened up with a flash of light, his laser vision burning a hole in the cumulus layer. He slowly drifted down toward me, giving me time to admire him. His suit was white with red stripes down the sides, a stylized C emblazoned on his chest. No maple leaf adorned the uniform, but it was obvious which country he represented.

He touched down on the roof and walked up to me, offering his hand. Before I knew it he was kissing my knuckles, his deep voice so full of bass that it rattled my ribcage.

"Myra Moon, it is a pleasure. I am Captain Stupendous."

And that's how my adventures began.

After a lengthy interview, which included showing me his Chalet of Secrecy up at Whistler, he flew me home. I was exhausted, the night having lasted much longer than I thought it would. He seemed eager to talk about himself and even more eager to impress me, like a schoolboy showing off for a girl he liked.

To be honest it turned me off a little, but I knew I'd be writing something more positive than that in tomorrow's paper, especially if I wanted another interview.

Once he disappeared back into the clouds in a streak of light I hurried down to my apartment for a hot shower and a bottle of wine. Even though my article later talked about feeling warm and flush while flying in his muscular arms, in truth I'd felt frozen the whole way.

I'd finished drying my hair and was on my first glass of red when the doorbell rang. There stood Mikey, a bottle of champagne in one hand, his camera in the other. "Did you get the shots?" I asked.

"Yep. Perfect view from the apartment across the street, just like you said. Want to see them?"

"Later," I replied, pulling him inside for a kiss while slamming the door with my foot.

∞    ☼    ∞

Captain Stupendous didn't seem surprised by the photos of our rendezvous, but their unintended consequence surprised me. The other news agencies dubbed me his girlfriend, but not with kindness: "that mousy brunette"; "lacking in style"; "too plain and chunky for such a super man." They were jealous of my impending Pulitzer, and all the exclusive interviews with him that followed.

Mikey and I rose to fame on the Captain's back, and for the next few years we travelled the world chronicling his exploits, along with those of his new team, the Canadian Super League. We reported on their peace talks in war zones, their famine relief work, and big bad supervillain attacks.

Those caused me the most problems. Even though I constantly denied being involved with Captain Stupendous, the villains believed whatever they read on TMZ and kept kidnapping me to get his attention.

The Ameriterrorist was the first, strapping me to a bomb on the Skytrain while threatening to detonate it if the city didn't pay him two million dollars. He needed the money to buy his family a house in expensive Vancouver.

Another time the henchmen of the Canadarm took me to the International Space Station, where NASA's robotic arm held me hostage while demanding the governments of the world acknowledge its newfound sentience.

Dr. Vortex tried to turn me into a human black hole that would swallow up Toronto for daring to refer to itself as the Centre of the Universe.

Stupendous saved me every time. Mikey and I made enough money that we were able to buy a fancy condo downtown. We finally got married on a trip to Scotland, while reporting on the battle between Stupendous and the Highland Bullboy. We had to change wedding venues after the Bullboy destroyed our castle hotel with his magic horns.

Finally, there was my kidnapping in Rio de Janeiro. I'd like to say I'd gone down there to cover the Brazil-Canada trade summit, but really I was hoping some supervillain would attack the Canadian Super League, who were providing security at the event, giving me another Stupendous story.

By this time the CSL was almost as famous as the Captain himself. Sufferjet, Grizzlyman, SuperSquirrel, Ice Flow, and Stupendous were now the United Nations' official superhero team, since few countries wanted American heroes on their soil. Don't know why anyone would want their protection though. Trouble always followed the CSL, wherever they went, which was why I followed too. Then trouble found me.

I woke up tied to a chair in a well-furnished cave lined with glowing quartz crystal and furnished with plush couches and Tiffany lamps. I heard the unmistakable sounds of the jungle outside. The humidity was oppressive. When Jaguar grabbed me from my room I'd just removed my makeup and put on some PJs. *Good thing Mikey isn't here*, I thought. *I'd hate for him to get a photo of me looking like this.*

Jaguar was prowling back and forth across the cave entrance, her tail swishing from side to side. A stout figure with thick shoulder muscles and strong legs, the villainess truly lived up to her name. Fur covered her body, which she barely hid under a V-shaped swimsuit. I'd met her before, back when she'd still been a member of the Canadian Super League and one of the good guys. Though short she had a feline beauty about her, with more curves than a Grand Prix raceway, and a fierce intelligence I'd always admired. When she first immigrated to Canada I'd written an article on the little that was known of her origin story, but it never made it to press.

Maria Felinus was a brilliant aviation engineer in Brazil, and one of their best test pilots, when her experimental craft crashed in the Amazon. The government called on Sufferjet to help find her. Weeks later, they finally emerged from the jungle. Maria had been transformed into the Jaguar by some mystical force they'd encountered in a hidden city. Whatever adventures they shared had made her and Sufferjet best friends, causing her to immigrate to Canada.

Then one day Jaguar tried to kill Captain Stupendous. Now here she was kidnapping me, like every other villain in the world.

No point in wasting the moment, I thought. Might as well get an interview.

"So, Jaguar, why did you switch sides?"

She'd gained weight since last I'd seen her, though with her curves it only accentuated her full figure. She looked tired, her fur unkempt and mangy. She held a strange gun, probably one of the many weapons auctioned on eBay as the one thing that could defeat the Captain. Her reply was punctuated with a low growl coming from the back of her throat.

"I am no villain. Your precious Captain, he is the villain."

"He isn't 'my Captain.' Don't believe everything you hear. We aren't dating."

Jaguar bared her fangs. "That does not matter. He will come and save you as he always does, and then we will have the truth."

"What truth is that? What wrong has he done you?"

"He stole something that did not belong to him." She paused her prowling to come up to me. With a long slow sniff she smelt me from knees to head. "I can smell him on you, and something else as well. Just like him you reek of Pherognome. What does that little *diabinho* have to do with all this?"

"What? I don't know what you're talking about."

Before anything else could be said the roof imploded, raining stone and dirt on us. Jaguar raised her weapon, but it was too late. A large figure dropped on top of her, knocking her to the ground. It wasn't Captain Stupendous but Grizzlyman, his bear mantle hiding his face, his deadly claws gleaming in the sunlight, shining down through the new skylight.

Jaguar reached for her gun but it was gone, snatched in a blur by the lightning-quick SuperSquirrel, his tail vibrating happily at the shiny new toy in his tiny hands.

For the first time it wasn't the Captain who saved me. I wish he had, because what Grizzlyman did to Jaguar in their ensuing fight brought tears to my eyes, and still does. Only SuperSquirrel intervening stopped the savage giant from killing her.

They carried her unconscious bloody form to their super-charged Cormorant helicopter, with Ice Flow waiting in the pilot seat. Even her cold heart melted upon seeing Jaguar, her tears turning to icicles as they touched her blue cheeks.

I stayed beside Jaguar for the flight home, I'm not sure why. Maybe it was her adamant belief that she'd been wronged, or the glib way that Grizzlyman joked with SuperSquirrel while a woman he'd beaten half to death lay behind him.

I held her hand, wanting to speak with her more, wanting to understand.

As if she heard my thoughts she opened her swollen eyes. Gripping me tightly she asked, "Is she here? Did she come?"

"Who? Ice Flow?"

"No, no…" And then she passed out.

When I got back to Vancouver I cried in Mikey's arms for hours. He held me tight, whispering over and over how happy he was to have me back, safe and sound.

"You never have to worry again, Mikey. I'm done with super-heroes."

"Good. I'm tired of you getting kidnapped."

I laughed through my tears. "Yeah, gets pretty old, doesn't it? Mikey, what they did to Jaguar, it was awful…"

"Was it? She'd kidnapped you, Ace. As far as I'm concerned she got what she deserved."

"Don't say that, please. You weren't there, you don't know."

And neither was the Captain, I thought to myself. Why hadn't he come?

The story of my rescue was front-page news, but it wasn't written by me. The papers described a scene I don't remember: bold heroics from the heroes and awful villainy from the villainess. The news channels even placed the Captain at the scene, which was a total lie.

Jaguar got what she deserved, they said, reminding me of Mikey's words from the night before.

I can admit it now, with no shame. As an investigative reporter I sucked. The pieces should have fallen into place right then and there, but they didn't. Not until the day of the wedding.

When they announced that Captain Stupendous and Sufferjet were getting married my editor begged me to write one more superhero story. But I refused. I couldn't get what happened to Jaguar out of my head, and Grizzlyman was going to be best man. Nothing "best" about that brute.

Like every other normal person in the world I read about the wedding online the next day. But I merely glanced at the photos of a beaming Captain Stupendous holding Sufferjet in his arms and barely skimmed the article about the lavish party and the who's who in attendance. What caught my attention was a small sidebar attached to Mikey's picture from the day Pherognome had tried to marry Sufferjet.

After undergoing rehabilitation treatments under the watchful eye of Captain Stupendous, Pherognome had been released from prison. Though the reporter who wrote the article wanted a comment from the little villain about the super nuptials, Pherognome had disappeared.

My mind went back to Jaguar sniffing me. She'd smelt Pherognome on me, but I'd never been anywhere near him.

I stared at the old picture for a while before returning to the main page and searching through the wedding photos. One in particular caught my eye, showing the Captain standing with his groomsmen. In the background stood Sufferjet, her head resting in her hand, looking dazed.

Even though I'd sworn to Mikey that I'd never investigate superheroes again, I needed to know the truth.

The so-called "reporter" who wrote the wedding article was primarily a blogger and even worse at investigative journalism than I was. Finding Pherognome was simply a matter of making a few long-distance phone calls. Before his career as a supervillain Pierre Ferrer had been a world-renowned perfumer based in Montréal. Soon I was on the trail of a short man who'd leased a luxury storefront in Old Montréal.

I convinced my editor Tony that I had a great lead on a Captain Stupendous story, and he got me on the next flight to Montréal. I found the shop in a narrow stone building on Rue Saint-Paul. Its entranceway was half the height of a normal door, the only signage the word *Parfum* etched in glass above the frame. The door was locked. I rang the bell and waited, my heart beating rapidly.

The door swung inward, revealing a small man with a face not quite as ugly as the one being choked in that notorious picture. "Ms. Moon, I wondered when I'd be seeing you. Come in, please." Without waiting for my reply he retreated into the darkness.

Crouching low I entered and was immediately greeted by a museum of scents. Lavender, rose, and other hints of spring filled the cool air in the entranceway, even though the city was suffering from a suffocating heat wave. Carefully I ventured down the hallway into his shop, where more scents wafted from the exotic bottles lining the cabinet shelves. Closing my eyes I inhaled deeply. Memories of my trips to Istanbul, Zanzibar, Shanghai, and Bombay engulfed me. I thought I caught the aroma of a wet summer night in Vancouver, a day at a baseball game at Yankee Stadium, even the hint of the time I rafted down white rapids in Austria. Then I caught the musky scent of a certain Brazilian Jaguar. It gave me pause, reminding me of where I was and with whom.

He climbed a small set of stairs to a raised platform behind the shop counter. Wearing a fine blue suit and carrying a shiny wooden cane, Pherognome appeared older than I remembered, his eyes showing dark rings of insomnia. He sat in a chair by the cash register and studied me intently, scrunching his nose with distaste. "Ms. Moon, you reek of passenger jet and the sweat of a humid day," he said, producing a bottle from behind the counter. "Please, have a sample, your pungency offends my sensibilities."

"Is it the same spray you used on Sufferjet, Monsieur Ferrer? If so, I will pass, thanks."

Pherognome made a *Pffft* sound then sprayed the air anyway. It filled the room with the scent of cloves and a trace of chocolate that made my mouth water. "Is that why you have come, to speak of the past? Not talk of the present?"

"Both actually. I had a run-in with Jaguar recently."

"Ah, yes, the buxom feline," he said, his eyes rolling briefly into his head as he recalled her. "What a creature! I managed to capture her musk in our last entanglement, before she went bad, of course. Shame what those so-called heroes did to her. I hear she still lies unconscious in the prison hospital."

"Yes, it is a shame, on that we agree. It's why I'm here, in fact. She had some interesting things to say about you."

He raised an eyebrow. "Oui? And what was that?"

"She said you'd done something to Captain Stupendous, that she could smell you on him."

A pause as his beady eyes watched me closely. "And is that what you believe?"

"No. I think you gave him your love perfume in exchange for your freedom. What I want to know is why he needed it."

"Isn't it obvious? He wanted Sufferjet but she did not want him, so he took her by force. Would you care for some tea and cookies? They are freshly prepared."

"What? Um, okay," I said, nonplussed by the sudden change in topic and the shock of hearing my worst fears confirmed. A part of me had hoped he would deny it, tell me I was a fool to doubt the Captain.

A pot of tea had been steeping, as if waiting for company to arrive. As Pherognome placed a fine bone-china tea set on a tray with some chocolate biscuits I wondered if anyone else had ever ventured inside his shop. The back wall was neatly lined with bottles, shining bright, free of any dust or finger-prints. Each jar was neatly labelled: *Joie, Haine, Passion, Confort, Jalousie,* and more.

"Do those really work?" I asked, nodding my head as he served me a cup. "Can you really make someone jealous with your perfume?"

Pherognome shrugged as he sipped his tea, a pinkie raised in the air. "I can produce emotional triggers with these scents, yes, but the power inside me used to amplify the effect to ter-rible proportions, the curse of an experiment gone wrong in my youth. Biscuit?"

"Yes, thank you," I replied, accepting one from the offered tray. "You said 'used to.'"

"Oui. The Captain took the power from me, using the same genetic splicer that turned that poor man into a twitchy mutant squirrel." He smirked at the look on my face. "Don't you know his origin? The Captain made SuperSquirrel, back when he was trying to create heroes to form his league, before Sufferjet arrived on Earth."

I reached into my purse for my recorder.

Pherognome paled upon seeing it. "You cannot record any-thing we say here, Ms. Moon, I thought you understood that. Captain Stupendous would kill me if he found out I'd been talking to a reporter, especially you."

"The Captain has never killed anyone."

"Not yet, but it is inevitable that he will. To silence me, or Jaguar if she ever wakes. Maybe even you, Ms. Moon, if you insist on learning the truth. Too many will know what he has done."

"But why do it at all?"

"Because he is infatuated, just as I was. Did you know that Sufferjet was designed by her alien people to represent the perfect woman, giving her all the attributes we desire in the female form? He confuses his lust for her with love, and feels he deserves her love back. But she will never love him, for no man can have her."

"Is that some rule of her people? I heard her planet is ruled by a matriarchy."

"No, it's because she's a lesbian."

"Oh." My hand itched to reach for my recorder, but I resisted. "How do you know that?"

He smiled. "I knew even when I tried to marry her, but my lust interfered with my reason. Jaguar is not the only one with a superhuman nose for scents, you know. I could smell the buxom feline all over Sufferjet."

"Jaguar and Sufferjet? But that makes no sense, Jaguar turned evil—" I stopped mid-sentence. Jaguar said the Captain had taken something from her, and asked if *she* had come with the rest of the CSL to rescue me. I'd thought Jaguar had meant Ice Flow, but she meant Sufferjet, the woman she still loved.

"Did you hear what happened when Sufferjet found out about Jaguar's injuries? She ripped off SuperSquirrel's tail and threw Grizzlyman out the window of their penthouse headquarters. I'm sure her anger was only assuaged when the Captain used my pheromones to calm her."

"If this is true then someone has to stop him!"

"I agree," said Pherognome, reaching into a drawer and pulling out a wooden box. He opened the lid, revealing a small nondescript spraybottle. "Unfortunately, Captain Stupendous is nigh indestructible in his superhuman form, immune even to my pheromones, even if I still possessed the power to amplify them."

"It's his alien physiognomy. They were all like him, back on his home planet."

"Ms. Moon, your Captain isn't from an alien planet. That is a cock-and-bull story to impress the world. I believe he was born in Hamilton."

I rolled my eyes. "That's ridiculous."

He regarded me with a mixture of sympathy and disgust. "Oh, you poor thing. I believe he found his powers while travelling through the Middle East. Maybe a genie granted them, or he found some ancient Egyptian amulet, whatever made the old Pharaohs like unto gods. His power is magical. It changes his appearance, makes him look chiselled, strengthens his jaw. When he doesn't feel like being 'super' he simply turns back into his everyday form, and no one can recognize him. Not even you, Ms. Moon."

I felt queasy while listening to him, wondering if he'd put something in my tea. But it wasn't the tea. My face felt wet. When had I started to cry?

"The day before my wedding I foolishly decided to announce my impending nuptials to the world, thinking that if I had witnesses then my marriage wouldn't be such a pathetic sham. I didn't mention who I was marrying so no one attended. Except for him. I think as a lark, nothing more. But when he saw us exit our limo, saw her, he flew into a rage. Transformed into Captain Stupendous right in front of me then attacked while his camera automatically clicked away on its tripod."

"Mikey," I said.

He nodded. "At least he never used my pheromones to get you, right? You've been together for years. A small comfort at least."

∞   ☼   ∞

The newspapers reported that Captain Stupendous and Sufferjet had returned from his home planet, their honeymoon finally over. Since his alien backstory was a lie I wondered where they'd really gone. Not that it mattered anymore.

I told Mikey I was in Stanley Park, sitting at our favorite spot overlooking English Bay. He said he'd meet me there soon. I sat on the bench with Pherognome's wooden box on my lap, my eyes closed as I listened to seagulls cry for food above me.

"Hey, Ace," he said, plopping down on the bench and placing his arm around me. I leaned against him, resting my head on his shoulder, taking in his smell. A hint of fragrance I didn't recognize clung to his clothes, but that could just as easily have been new soap. Aside from that he seemed no different from the man I thought I knew. "Beautiful day, hey?"

"Yeah, it is. Did you bring me back anything from your trip?" I asked, almost adding, *A magic genie in a bottle, perhaps?*, but kept my mouth shut.

He grinned, producing a small box. Inside was a necklace with a single blue stone. "Got this in Cairo," he said as he placed it around my neck.

"I thought you were in Jerusalem?"

"I was, but they sent me to Egypt on the way home. What's that on your lap? Tony said you'd gone to Montréal on an assignment. You never told me you had a new story in the works."

I shrugged, sliding the box over to him. "The lead didn't pan out, but I did find this in Old Montréal. Surprise! It's an early birthday present."

Mikey looked sideways at me as he placed it on his lap. I kept my face blank, hoping Pierre had been right: that the Captain couldn't use his powers to see through the box while in human form. If that was true, then he wouldn't be immune to Pherognome's potion either.

Mikey watched me a little longer before finally relaxing. When he opened the box it triggered the bottle to spray in his face. He leapt up with a curse, wiping the stinging perfume from his eyes. "Myra, what the hell?"

I hit him in the chest repeatedly with my fists, driving him backward across the lawn. "You two-timing bastard! How could you? I loved you! And poor Sufferjet... what you've done to her is monstrous!"

He grabbed my arms but did not transform into the Captain like I'd hoped. He was still scrawny Mikey, with his messy hair and pimples. "What are you talking about?" he asked.

"I want a divorce, you creep! Leave Earth and never come back! Once I tell the world about how you drugged and raped Sufferjet your days of playing hero will be over!"

He looked down at the perfume bottle then back at me. "Of course, Montréal. The Pherognome. Ace, I can explain."

"Can you? Go on, try!"

The tears in my eyes seemed to collapse his will. "I love you, Myra, really! You're all I'd ever need, but the Captain needs more. Sufferjet is the most powerful, most gorgeous woman in the whole galaxy. He deserves her. I'm living two lives, I figured, why not two wives?" The last was said with a shrug, as if that explained it all, made it somehow okay.

I pulled out my recorder, waving it in his face. "Thanks for the quote, Mikey, I think I just found my headline."

He stepped toward me, his expression changing to anger. I thought of what Pierre had said— how the Captain would probably kill to hide his crime. Mikey raised his hands in surrender, though his smile told me he planned on doing anything but. "You can't publish any of this, Myra, it's all lies. You're under the influence of that ugly little maggot. He's driven you crazy, turned you against me. Come home, let me help. You love me."

A pop can hit him in the side of the head, followed by a full bottle of water. A mob of bicyclists, rollerbladers, and pedestrians from the nearby seawall climbed the hill, surrounding us. "Get away from her, you pig!" shouted a woman, throwing her purse at him. People picked up rocks and threw those as well. One hit Mikey in the temple, drawing blood. As he stumbled back he yelled, "Enough!" in a voice louder than anything I'd ever heard from him.

Amid a swirl of golden dust he transformed into Captain Stupendous. He levitated off the ground in a triumphant pose, hands on hips.

A dog-walker slung her bag of gathered poop. It exploded across the C on his chest, and I burst into laughter. The rocks kept coming, and even though they no longer hurt him physically, I could tell that mentally he'd been defeated. Raising an arm into the sky he flew away, leaving the crowd screaming in his wake.

∞   ☼   ∞

He was mistaken if he thought he'd find safety at CSL headquarters. Together, Sufferjet, Grizzlyman, and Ice Flow broke his arm (he was merely *nigh* indestructible), shattered his teeth, and shredded his precious uniform until he flew away half-naked. No one has seen him since. Pierre's spray worked like a charm, reversing the special pheromones coursing through the Captain's body, making him repulsive, in either form, to anyone who came near him instead of loved by all.

Pherognome and I were blamed, once a few weeks had gone by and everyone realized they'd been under a spell. Even with the recording no one believed my accusations against him. He wouldn't do those things, they said, not their precious hero. He too must have been under Pherognome's spell. My spell.

At my trial Sufferjet came to my defense, but since she'd been under Pierre's influence once before it was easy for the prosecution to discredit her testimony. Stupid Stupendous had drugged and raped her yet still they took his side.

What made him want to be a hero? What makes any of them? Most would reply, *It's the powers, stupid*. But I disagree. If you could mend bones with telekinesis, wouldn't you become a doctor? If you were impervious to bullets, wouldn't you be a police officer?

I think I know the answer: fame. What other reason would you have for putting on tights and parading around like a peacock? *It's the ego, stupid*.

Now, villains I understand. They want to rule the world because they think they can do it better than everyone else. Who's never thought that? Or they just want to be rich. Makes sense.

Of course I can't judge, having lost my impartiality, along with my freedom. I'm the greatest villain of all time now, having destroyed the world's greatest hero. Only he wasn't so great. He was just another boy pretending to be a man.

I wonder where he is now— hiding on some desolate island maybe, or out in space, playing hero to a race without an olfactory sense?

You know what? I don't care.

∞  ☼  ∞

Alarms sounded throughout the prison. Guards ran past my cell, their fear obvious. When the wall behind me crumbled, I saw Sufferjet hovering in the air in full battle armor, her war helmet hiding everything but a big grin. Curled like a kitten in her arms was the injured Jaguar, barely conscious. She looked thin and frail but happy to be back in her woman's arms.

"Shall we depart these premises with haste?" asked Sufferjet. "Jaguar has convinced me that life as a wanted vigilante is more fun than following the rules of mortal men."

"Sounds good, but I need to adopt a supervillain name to tie this story together. How about 'the Divorcee'?"

Jaguar smiled weakly. "Needs work. We'll figure it out later. Now let's go."

And so we did.

∞  ☼  ∞

**P. E. BOLIVAR** is an air traffic controller at the Vancouver International Airport.

# FRIDAY NIGHTS AT THE HEMINGWAY

*Arun Jiwa*

FRIDAY NIGHT AT the Hemingway was a quiet affair. The bar's three patrons crowded together at a table toward the back. There was a time when you had to know Dev or someone who knew Dev to get an invite on a Friday evening. But Dev had been notoriously difficult about any publicity since the accident, and eventually business moved away from the Hemingway.

Dev set down a pitcher of lager and slid an appetizer tray across the table. "Last call will be in half an hour," he said, though it was only a casual notice. Maia, Rohit, and Ben were regulars, upholding a tradition from the old days, when The Alliance frequented the Hemingway on Friday evenings.

"The rumor I heard was that Shade's an alien, she came from a planet with no sunlight," Maia said.

"No, my brother went to school with her boyfriend," Ben reached over for the pitcher and filled all three glasses. "He knows for a fact that there was an accident at Faustech Labs. Shade, was an intern there, you know, in her pre-Shade days."

"What about the Probabilist? Supposedly, he was a teenage stock-market genius. Made millions before the Alliance figured out he could predict other events too." Rohit leaned over and gave a thumbs-up to Dev, who nodded. They were quiet for the next few minutes as they ate their appetizers and checked their phones.

"Let's talk about someone who's actually done something in the last decade. Not the ones who show up for publicity stunts once a year," Ben said.

"Like who— Gargoyle? Crimson Falcon? They're all paid retainers to stay out of trouble." Maia quirked an eyebrow. "And rightly so. You don't want them jumping in and saving cats from trees or putting out fires. Can you imagine Gargoyle trying to put out fires?" She mimed the action with her hands and the three of them laughed.

Ben pointed to the bar. "What about them? The Alliance. You don't think that the Earth's five strongest heroes just vanished all of a sudden, do you?"

The picture that hung over the bar showed the five original members of the Alliance, all patrons of the Hemingway. Shade, The Probabilist, The Architect, Tesla, and Dr. Kepler the Puppetmaster. In the picture the five of them stood in front of the bar, with Dev standing off to the side.

Ben set his pint glass down unsteadily and motioned for silence. "You remember the news story about Dr. Hugo Moriarty, from eight years ago? World-famous criminal suddenly disappears?" He waited for confirmation from the other two before continuing. "Well, if you look up news after that incident, the number of hero-related stories drops off sharply."

"So what?" Maia countered. "The tenth time Gargoyle and Captain Neutron worked out their marital problems in public, it stopped being news."

"Not just that, though," Ben said. "What about Shade? Tesla? The Puppetmaster? The Architect?"

Dev had stopped what he was doing to listen to the conversation.

"Do you think that they all just vanished overnight?"

"Like I said, paid to stay out of trouble," Rohit said. "There hasn't been anyone who's threatened the world in a big way since Dr. Moriarty disappeared."

"I find that hard to believe," Ben said. "Dr. Moriarty was rumored to control criminal cells all over the world. He was running a big-time operation. Even if the Alliance took him down, why would they keep quiet about it? Who was his number 2? They could still be at large."

"What do you think, Dev," Maia asked, turning around in her seat.

Dev set down the bottle he was holding and thought for a long moment before answering. "They weren't my friends. I didn't know them as people, just who they were when they wore the mask. One day they simply stopped coming. You can speculate on that in half a dozen ways, but maybe they were tired of all the attention and decided that they could work better if no one knew what they were up to."

"But that still doesn't explain how they've stayed out of the public eye for so long," Ben said.

"Between the five of them, they have almost unlimited resources at their disposal. How hard do you think it would be if they all decided to disappear?" Dev brought the bottle around to the table and poured them a round to cap off the evening.

"All the press conferences, the answering to government agencies, the public media circus. Sure, some superheroes get used to it, but that's not saving the world." He raised a glass to toast. "To those who would protect us."

The others raised their glasses and drank.

∞   ☼   ∞

Maia and Rohit left together shortly after, and Ben waited for his cab. He sat at the same table and took in the photograph.

"Let yourself out when your cab gets here," Dev said to Ben. "I have to organize some inventory in the basement."

"I don't believe it," Ben said.

"What?"

"All of the world's problems are still there. Poverty. Crime. War. Disease. I can't believe that they would put their privacy ahead of the world that they're supposed to be protecting."

Dev leaned against the door leading to the basement. "You assume they had a choice," he said softly.

Ben gestured to the photo again. "It's true that Shade became who she was from the accident at Faustech Labs. What about the Probabilist and Tesla? They were born into it. It's like they were handed a gift that no one else has, and they have a moral obligation to help those who don't have it."

Every gift contains a curse, Dev thought but didn't say. "Go home and sleep it off, Ben," Dev said, and he put a Command into his voice. "And when you wake up in the morning, you'll Forget all of this."

Ben nodded slowly and looked down at his phone. Dev didn't like using a Command on someone if he didn't have to, but it was going to be a long night and he didn't have time to debate morality with a college kid.

∞   ☼   ∞

When Dev returned from the basement, a moment later, the Phantasm was waiting for him. Its hands wrapped around Ben's throat, draining the boy of his life.

Dev grabbed a nearby bottle and flung it at the creature's head.

The Phantasm was forced to be corporeal when he ate, and in this case it worked to Dev's advantage. It moaned and dropped the boy. Its face twisted grotesquely, and it opened its mouth to scream.

Dev lifted Ben and moved him to the back of the bar with a flick of his hand. He picked up a chair with his other hand. He and smashed it into the Phantasm's face, while the creature was stunned and still corporeal. Occasionally, one of Moriarty's minions or henchmen or sidekicks discovered who Dev really was and attacked him.

It was dark enough in the bar that Dev could conjure the Shadow legion. At his orders, formless creatures writhed up from the floor and wrapped tendrils of darkness around the Phantasm, trying to contain it. The hollow-eyed creature shrugged them off and moved toward Dev.

"Stop," Dev said, putting a Command into his voice. The Command usually worked on living beings, but he wasn't sure if the Phantasm fell into that category.

It continued to lurch forward. The Phantasm was both notoriously hard to kill and impressively stupid.

Dev flicked his hand and sent tables and chairs hurtling toward the Phantasm. The onslaught of furniture threw it back, but it began to decohere again, losing corporeality and shifting into its ghost form. From their last fight in the Rockies, Dev remembered that the Phantasm was nearly impossible to see or sense when it ghosted. If it escaped now, Moriarty's remaining cells would know where to find him.

Dev was out of options: there was only one thing left to try. "I bet whoever you're working for will be pleased that you found me," Dev said, stalling the creature while he moved into position. "I have to give you credit for getting past all of the defenses and false trails. I'd ask you how you did it, but the place isn't really clean enough to sit down and chat."

When he was sure that Ben was shielded behind him, Dev instantiated a wormhole and tunnelled it into one of the rooms in the basement. The floor beneath the Phantasm distorted, and colors prismed in glittering constellations as the Phantasm was sucked into the temporary warp.

"You'll keep in there till I can decide what to do with you," Dev said.

"That was unreal," Ben said, from behind him.

∞   ☼   ∞

"I can assure you it was very real," Dev said. He picked up pieces of furniture broken in the fight and stacked them on the bar.

"You're one of them."

"Go Home, Ben," he said, with a Command. "You Won't Remember In The Morning."

"Wait," said Ben. "Hear me out. I can help you with whatever you're doing here. I can be your sidekick. Your Renfield. I can help you with anything you need. I swear your secret's safe with me."

"There's a reason I haven't told anyone," Dev said, unable to keep the anger from his voice. "I'm not like the others. You want to know why you're not reading about me on the news? The moment the world finds out you're different, they paint a target on your back. The media wants a piece of you, the government wants to regulate you, and people like him," he pointed to where the wormhole had been, "want to kill you. I decided a long time ago I didn't want that kind of attention. All I want is to run my bar and be left alone."

Ben backed away slightly. "I mean no disrespect, about what I said before. That's your... choice. I just didn't expect that you would be right here in my backyard. I mean, all that time with the Alliance, did they know?"

Dev pulled out a first-aid kit from under the bar and handed disinfectant and gauze to Ben. "You got a gash across your forehead, better clean that up."

"I didn't ask for this," Dev told him. "The fight between the Alliance and Dr. Moriarty happened right here. Moriarty built a device to steal the Alliance's powers and transfer them to himself. He was so confident that it would work that he walked straight in here and set the thing off. And guess what?"

"What?"

"It blew up in his face. All of them, the Alliance and him, died instantly from the backlash. Except me. All their powers transferred to me." Dev flicked his hand and swept the broken furniture aside. He would deal with it in the morning.

"But something that big would have been on the news," Ben said.

"Would have," said Dev. "There are ways of ensuring that things like that never happen. People can Forget a lot."

∞　✿　∞

"Kingsley, are you awake?"

The track lights lit up the length of the basement, a room far too big for the physical space the bar occupied. When the Alliance was still active, the bar had been more than a convenient space for the five of them to meet. It had been the Architect's idea to hide in plain sight. He built the basement with Tesla's help, outfitting it with sophisticated cloaking devices, one-of-a-kind surveillance technology, and enough protection to withstand an army.

"At you service," Kingsley replied. His avatar appeared on a screen to Dev's left.

"The Phantasm found me tonight. We need to know how it found the place." Kingsley, the AI, was the brainchild of the Probabilist and Shade. He snooped vast swaths of network traffic and surveillance footage, finding the signal hidden in the noise, any threats the Alliance should identify and neutralize. Except now there was only Dev left to do that.

"He's in one of the holding rooms for monitoring," Dev added.

"Already on it, boss," Kingsley said.

"What's on the schedule tonight?" Kingsley updated him on a series of international developments, the foremost being the location and activities of Moriarty's remaining associates. Dev geared up. He pulled on his cowl and said, "Let's save the world."

∞　✿　∞

A graduate of the 2012 Viable Paradise SFF Workshop, **ARUN JIWA** lives in Edmonton.

# APOLLO AND GRETA

*Evelyn Deshane*

## I

WE USED TO go to all-night diners at four o'clock in the morning to see if the world was different then. He told me it was a lot lonelier, but I never agreed. I didn't see how it could be if there was a place that was always open, always willing, and waiting for us to come. The big neon sign, red and yellow, told us its name. The restaurant was a person and his name was Denny. He engulfed us as we ordered our eggs and pancakes with extra maple syrup. How could this warmth, this circulatory system of fluorescent lights, ever be lonely? We were inside of Denny; we were a part of him.

I ate my meal of champions in the middle of the night and told my brother that he was wrong. The world wasn't lonelier now. It had exactly the same amount of gut-wrenching sorrow that always existed. Only now it was far more obvious when it was black outside and we sat right next to the throb and buzz of a diner sign.

He was quiet after I explained and made no attempt to counter the argument. We were staying, lonely or not, in this hum. We were orphans and, having aged out of the foster care system, this was the only place where we belonged. This small type of consistency was the only thing we craved more than pancakes.

## II

Our origins were always unclear. He was named after a Greek God and I was named after an actress, a silent film star. Apollo didn't like it when I dwelled on his power, so we romanticized our unknown ancestors. We tried to figure out our parents' lives from the small facts they left behind. Our blood, our names, and the powers we had to keep secret before they could be taken away.

"They probably went to a classic Garbo movie on their first date," he explained away Greta within seconds.

"And Apollo?"

"Maybe they majored in Greek."

All the stories we spun, the lies we lived off of, were always so idealistic. It took me too many revisions of the same tale to realize that in their minds men were supposed to be treated like gods and could crush anything with their thumbprint but women were supposed to be silent. To shut up and learn to live with loneliness in diners, swallowed by men, in the middle of the night.

"Or maybe they just liked comics," I suggested.

### III

When we turned eighteen, minutes after one another, we left the house where we had been placed for the last six months. Without a goodbye note or explanation, I climbed out the window first and unlocked the door for him. He stole the car after I convinced him to. When we drove down the highway entering the Albertan badlands, I saw his spine finally relax.

"What did you realize?" I asked him. "That we're not getting caught or that it wouldn't matter if we did?"

"No," he told me, voice transparent. He clutched the wheel. "I realize that anyone could have done this."

"But *we* did."

"But we *did*," he nodded. After a while, he smiled.

I rose in the back through the sunroof, grabbed a blanket from the seat, and tied it around myself like a cape.

We should have done this a long time ago. Anytime our foster parents had threatened to split us up, anytime they tried to separate us in different rooms, we should have just crawled out our small windows and left it all behind. The badlands of Alberta, where we had always dreamed of going, passed us by too quickly. In the rear-view mirror, the reflection was like a movie on fast-forward, the film blurred and tight against the screen, the way that VHS tapes used to be. We were too nostalgic that first night of driving; we were still seeing our past in the movies we grew up with. Soon, we worked past Betamax and Tim Burton's Batman franchise to DVDs, Blu-rays, and Christopher Nolan's mouth-breathing Batman. We slowly figured out how to become better than Rogue and sound out our names without the worry of others hearing.

By morning, we were blinded by sunlight and I slumped down into the front seat. As I watched Apollo drive, I realized we could not have escaped when we were younger, because we had no idea how powerful we were yet.

"What should our superpower be?" he asked, tugging on my blanket, my cape. I smiled and continued to play Superwoman, Wonder Woman, and the Birds of Prey in one go.

"Mind reading?" I suggested first. This power would have helped us a lot in foster care, wondering what house we would wake up in next and how we could stay together. We would have been able to figure out whom to trust and who meant what they said.

Apollo shook his head. "Don't live in past anymore. We are out of that house, now."

*But*, I thought but did not say, *the world is still populated with liars*.

"Strength would have helped," Apollo said next. "Something like Thor's hammer."

"Maybe," I allowed. "But the strength would be located in the object, not you or me."

He sighed, but understood. We needed something better than that, so we went through all our options.

"Fire power?"

"Too hard to control. And too much smoke would give us away."

"Flying?"

"We would be too easy to spot."

And then he said, "Invisibility?"

We nodded. It was utterly perfect for the two of us. We both gazed at our side mirrors, and watched as the morning turned to grey skies. The upcoming storm chased us down the highway through our back window. The looming skies reminded me of the story Apollo told me about the Tryon Rat Experiment in psychology. The highways and roads twisted and turned as the storm chased us until the end of a maze. Lightning struck and for a brief moment, I saw the reward enticing us further.

From the way Apollo shifted in his seat, I knew he was thinking the same thing.

"Do you think they ever figured anything out about us?" he asked.

"Only that we already knew what the end of the maze looked like."

## IV

As we drove, I thought of Grant Morrison. When he wrote *The Invisibles*, he used to method act. He shaved his head and turned himself into King Mob as he travelled the world, smoking hash and fucking women. But when King Mob was attacked in *The Invisibles*, suddenly Grant got sick. His appendix almost burst, just as his character doppelganger was being sliced open and shot above his appendix. A new type of sympathetic pain emerged then, like a new and foreign place for a heart. Grant wrote the scene and survived, had the surgery so he didn't die. But he was careful afterward about what he wrote and how he used his own image.

After *The Invisibles* ended, Grant took up chaos magic next and wound up in that My Chemical Romance music video. As Apollo and I drove by the red earth, toward the sun, we cranked MCR's *The True Lives of the Fabulous Killjoys* all the way up. In the first video for "Na Na Na" Grant plays the villain Korse, among the Draculoids who live in Battery City during the year 2019.

I imagined Grant Morrison's evolution from King Mob to Korse, shaved head and white suit. This was how all the new series went, at least, from what Apollo and I saw. You restarted and rebooted, got new writers and artists, and attempted to change everything in an attempt to find a new audience. The Fabulous Killjoys were nothing new, nothing special, in the same way Korse was really just another version of King Mob. But that was why we liked the album and listened to it until we could recite the words to one another as our forms of *I love you* and *hello*. It made us feel as if we knew something and like we weren't alone.

When Apollo and I got completely lost in the Alberta roads, we turned on the album again, and headed down a different way. It was so easy stepping off the pathway, especially if there was no map to guide your way.

## V

Iron Man, as much as he was a billionaire playboy, was also a mechanic. I always forgot that. Batman and Robin were really just detectives, too. I always forgot the side lives of the ordinary characters of comics: the reporter Clark Kent and even the foolish, whiny student Peter Parker. It was more appealing to focus on the mutations of the Fantastic Four, the experiment of Bruce Banner, and the casual accident of Doctor Manhattan. We all wanted an excuse to gawk and stare at someone now that freak shows were relics of the past Apollo and I realized a long time ago that there was nothing separating most people from Batman but thin tights and confidence.

Then there's Stan Lee, who Apollo always considered a later version of Alfred Hitchcock. Both men weaved stories together from discarded newspapers and strange events seen from out an office window. They created their characters as strangers with easy faces and gave them horrible fates. That was why big cities were important to their work; the small towns were too terrifying because there was just nothing there. Everyone lived in their house, alone, and let no one inside. With the big city, there were simply too many stories for these men to tell, but not enough people to find them believable. Stan Lee and Alfred Hitchcock were the authors of modern-day myths, attempting to rewrite what we thought we knew about who we were and what we could expect in our lives.

Lee and Hitchcock both made cameo appearances in their films. They walked on stage to judge a beauty competition, to buy a newspaper, and to get a cup of coffee. Stephen King also tried this, but he was too animated. He gave himself too many lines and drew attention to himself. He did not understand: the director and writer are ghosts. They are invisible and do not matter. They are the secret identity that pulls all the strings. When Lee and Hitchcock walk on, they give a silent nod to the audience. They make sure people are paying attention.

I looked wearily at Apollo. He was driving too fast, but not faster than anyone around us. We were driving a stolen car, but he sat in it like he owned it. When we zoomed past the black unmarked police car with the radar gun on the side, we didn't flinch. We were not caught as we headed into another city.

"We'll switch into a new car when we get there," he told me. He moved his dark brown hair out of his eyes. "You know, just in case."

"Just in case," I said, slightly mocking him. He didn't notice, as if mockery was something that could never touch him. "I think," I added aloud. "I want something new."

"Oh yeah?" he asked me. "Like what?"

A cop, his car blue and white, whirred past us both on the road. We held our breaths, as if not breathing really could make us invisible. The cop was on the other side of traffic, heading back toward where we had come from, back toward the speed traps, toward a crime much larger than ourselves. I wanted more attention. I wanted someone to see us, for real this time around.

"That was close," he said. "What did you want again?"

*The world. Everything,* I thought. *A secret plan.*

"A motorcycle," I said. "I want someone to see us. For real this time."

He gave me a weary gaze. "That's not smart, and you know it."

"But it fits," I argued. "You know, how Penguin used to ride in one, his sidekick in the sidecar."

Apollo grinned. "I think you'd look good on a bike."

"Really?" My eyes were bright.

"Yes. Behind me, with your Greta Garbo eyes, I think you'd steal the show."

Those silent eyes that he admired fell. "But not on the front of the bike?"

"No. Too dangerous, like I said. I'll take that."

He thought he was being admirable. He thought he was being a hero. I swallowed hard, folding my arms over my chest. I didn't want to tell him that villains road motorcycles and danger was still danger even if you were being noble. We had no leather jackets, no way to protect ourselves from the asphalt. A nurse who used to take care of one of the other foster kids told us once that motorcycles were really organ donations on wheels. Skin could burn off, completely deglove itself from the muscle, as soon as a crash happened. Boots were needed. Helmets were good. Protection was always imperative if you wanted to stay alive.

Apollo acted like he was the sun and he could keep the road warm. His name was a God's name, and he thought himself truly immortal. For a second, I imagined a crash on the bike and both of us spilling into the road. I imagined sunlight radiating out of his wounds— and nothing but black and white picture shows coming out of mine.

Another cop car zoomed by. It didn't even bother to slow down.

"We know what direction the police are taking," I said, gaining strength. "So we know where to avoid. I want a bike. Let's go get one."

He smiled again. Sunlight shone in his hair. "Okay. You have a deal."

## VI

During our years in foster homes, apartments, and motel rooms, I collected stories. Like bugs and mites, the stories I found dangled like modifiers of city life. They were writer's prompts, vague and incomplete, that lined the walls and stained the carpets. I could speculate far too much about the movements in the next room, the water dripping from the pipes, and the photos on the frontman's desk as we slipped him our credit card. But while every thought and ending was true to me, hotel clerks always eyed our credit cards skeptically. Our real names had always required a special type of longing to believe.

When we stayed in motel rooms, I stole the soap and toiletries to help myself remember. I counted and added the different pastel shades to my collection in the bottom of a thrift-store suitcase. The soaps always left a white line at the bottom of the bag. Each time we took a trip, I found a different commodity to steal. The first time, it was crackers. Then the peanut-butter packets that were part of the free motel breakfasts (which we spawned out to lunch and dinner). I was daring for a while and started to take the towels. Then I realized they were charging our credit cards for them. The soap was my favorite, though it made my hands feel coarse, like they didn't belong to me.

I dropped the bars in the shower, and the soap wore away into half-moon chips, which I held up to the light at night but always failed to conjure up anyone.

One night, we stopped at a store and Apollo left the motorcycle on the kick stand while I went inside through the window. I left my suitcase and took the cash, thinking it to be a fair trade. But the money we stole was always so transient, so ephemeral. For a collector like myself, there always had to be something else around the corner. Money, which the Joker set on fire in *The Dark Knight*, was never important. I wanted things that I could attach my name to and say were really mine. Even the bike only offered a temporary fantasy and illusion. We hadn't crashed yet, though we had come close. I still didn't know what we were really made of.

We passed by a used bookstore and I pointed out the window desperately. The yellow sign that displayed the name *Dixon's Comics and Cards* made us both yield as we turned a corner. The store was part genre fiction and part comic books. Next to the yellow sign was a smaller red one that informed us that the store also offered trading. One comic book for any issue of *The Amazing Spider-Man*; one old cracked-spine of a Stephen King novel or copy of *The Lord of the Rings*, and you could take your pick from the trade bin. We stepped inside and a bell rang.. Neil Gaiman's *Sandman* peaked out from one of the bins.

"How much do we have?" I asked Apollo.

"Enough money, G—"

"But how much other stuff?"

I wanted the allure of paying for comics with comics. Of trading in the only form of currency that seemed to matter to us and getting something in return. But like our proverbial parents, the ones who had made us orphans, we were broke. The man behind the counter would not want to hear me wax poetic about my old life. I could not trade our stories for stories, not yet.

Apollo pulled out a five, a ten, and then raised his eyes.

"Are you sure you want this, G? There are so many others."

"I've been having trouble sleeping," I explained. I held *Sandman: Preludes and Nocturnes* to my chest. "I need something to read."

## VII

From the back of the bike, I watched Apollo smoke. I got off and joined him. He offered me a cigarette; I declined, and we went into our already established script.

"No, thank you. Haven't you heard? Smoking is bad for you."

"And so is sun, and fighting crime, and yet, here we are."

"Fighting crime and breaking the law are very similar."

"And our lungs are only ours for breathing, like our bodies only for eating. Nothing else. Never for pleasure." Then he smiled and touched his stomach. I could almost hear the ripple of hunger tear through him, like a frost quake after an ice storm. "You hungry, Greta?"

I smiled. "Always."

He smiled again as he tossed away the cigarette. Once he had mounted the bike, he extended his hand to mine and helped me on. I wrapped my arms around his waist, holding a fist in the middle of his stomach. We drove, and I felt the weight of the wind, and Apollo's smell against me like a kiss. We found a diner, went in, and ate until they kicked us out.

When we were kids in foster homes, Apollo would always get up in the middle of the night, pace the room, go to the kitchen, and then back again. His midnight snacks became feasts at four a.m., and he'd find me. Even in the houses that separated us, put him with the boys and me by myself, he'd find me. He'd crack the locks on the fridge door, if they had one, and he'd bring me loaves of bread. Candy, milk, ice cream, and meat. He would always find me.

That night in bed, the rare warm Alberta night made me feel as if I were sweating out everything that had happened to us. It was as if I were in an interrogation room, my skin oily and unrecognizable. My freckles stared up at me and I looked to Apollo, his dark hair matted to his forehead and his body stirring against the sheets. I waited for him to wake up that night, but he was still stuck in a dream.

## VIII

I had always liked the DC Universe. It allowed for so much to happen at once. There were too many possibilities for a single Earth to hold, so they just created another one. Earth II. Added another Krypton, and even more inane planets if they wanted. When you read DC, you checked your reason at the door. And I *liked* that, in a way that we get used to certain tastes and proclivities. I also liked Marvel. They had stolen Asgard from the Vikings. It took real balls to get away with something like that.

I sat up all night and into the morning when Apollo didn't wake up. I thumbed the collected works and comic books we had just bought and categorized my new collection. I reread the stories of Thor and Loki and invested myself in their troubles. They were brothers who had grown up together, with constant strife pulling them apart.

I showered and thought I heard the whir of a time machine opening above me, like the Rainbow Bridge to Asgard, but it was just Apollo. He moved back the glass shower doors, and slipped under the water with me, naked. With his hands steady on my shoulders, he whispered in my ear, like Loki must have said to Thor: "I'm adopted."

Our foster homes always matched us up, always said we were twins, despite the contrast of my ginger hair and freckled skin next to his dark looks. I didn't care which reality was a lie.

Everything eventually changes. Maybe after the shower, I would be the one to drive the motorcycle. Maybe we would rob a bank or mug someone, instead of remaining invisible during our thefts. Maybe we would fall against the road and crack into a thousand pieces and become a thousand stories for someone else to pick up and understand.

As our secret identities washed down the drain, our lips met again and again. Even when it was all over, I knew our superpowers would remain forever.

∞  ☼  ∞

Ontario writer **EVELYN DESHANE** received an MA from Trent University and is pursuing a PhD at Waterloo.

# IN THE KIRBY KRACKLE

*John Bell*

You wanted something
I couldn't, wouldn't
give:

A murderous rampage
against your
enemies

Your very own genocidal
god raging in the Kirby
Krackle!

When all I wanted
was to retreat like
Thoreau

Into the last wild
places beyond your
reach

Your comic-book
fantasies, video-game
mythologies

New scriptures of
unbridled death &
destruction

I am leaving but
don't pretend I'm
dead

I am starbound, relishing
my escape from
you

This is my power & it truly
crackles, pulses with
fire

A beacon of loss in
a dark, forbidding
sea

But this won't kill you—
only break your
hearts.

∞ ✪ ∞

**JOHN BELL** is the author or editor of nearly twenty books, including *Invaders from the North*, a history of Canadian comics.

# A WEEK IN THE SUPERLIFE

*Alex C. Renwick*

*MONDAY*

Monday you wake up and all your bones ache, every single one.

People probably don't realize you ache like this, if they ever think about you. Sure, yes, you can fly and you do have superstrength, but you also take superpummelling, day in, day out. Anybody ever think of that?

You're like any other guy; you put your pants on in the morning one leg at a time— except they're not really pants, but tights. And they're not really tights, but some nanotech self-repairing microfiber developed in some government lab back when you had your regular gig and still punched the clock for the feds. But then you had to go and fall for the Commissioner's only daughter, had to find out she wasn't the type to be happy with a workaholic son-of-a-bitch like you. Had to find out she wanted kids — *kids* for chris'sakes, in a crazy messed-up world like this one! — and *that*, plain and simple, wasn't something you could get on board with.

So you started staying out later and later, calling it work, coming home drunk sometimes, it's true, but never really meaning to, not really. Eventually she stopped crying, though she never stopped caring (she really is a saint and you never did deserve her), until one night she wasn't there when you got home three sheets to the wind with your guts so full of bullet holes from those delusional teenage self-styled gangstas you'd tangled with earlier that evening, you looked like a goddamn slab of Swiss cheese.

Bullets can't kill you, though they sure as hell hurt. But unlike other times your woman wasn't there that night to patch you up, to cry over you or kiss or even yell at you because you scare her half to fucking death and she's afraid one of these nights you won't come home at all, and though this actually all happened what feels like a long time ago you're still glad she finally got the juice that night to leave you for good.

For her sake, you're glad.

*TUESDAY*

You spend Tuesday doing the usual. It's harder and way more boring than people might think to find crimes or accidents or even catastrophes actually in progress. Back when you worked for the government you had some military-developed superphone, tapped you into police channels, rang whenever the Commissioner needed your expertise. These days you look for breaking news on your regular smartphone (smarter than many, not as smart as others), or simply fly around the downtown core, waiting for someone in trouble to flag you down like a goddamn taxi, for chris'sakes. Some days, you figure you may as well start wearing a light on your head, turn it on when you're flying around doing nothing so it announces to the world: *Available.*

But today you're in luck. You spot two guys messing with some poor junkie prostitute near the corner of High Street and 82nd. They chase her into a weed-choked gully out of sight from the roadway and one pulls a knife. All this you see from seventy feet up in the air, so you don't get details or hear what they're saying (it's not like you have superhearing or supersight), but you recognize the unmistakable terror in the prostitute's cower, the heart-wrenching inadequacy of her brittle-twig arms raised to shield her face from the bigger guy's blade. The other guy, the littler one, is unbuttoning the fly of his jeans.

You drop like a raptor, *Bam!*, and those guys go sprawling. The knifer squeals when you rip the stupid metalhead T-shirt off his back in one go and tie his wrists so tight to his ankles, he'd better hope the cops arrive before blood loss forces them to amputate later. The other guy's fumbling with his buttonfly, trying to pull up his pants and run at the same time, gets all tangled and falls.

*Hoist with your own petard, motherfukkah!* you shout as you tie him like his buddy, all yoga-pose on his stomach with wrists lashed to ankles. The woman — a girl really, you can see now she's close up, though the years have not been kind — comes over and kicks him a few times with the scuffed toes of her red pointy flats while you look away, out of politeness. You've already texted Emergency Services, the single word like always, so they know it's you, know you've got criminals waiting and the cops should hurry their asses up if they want to make a bust.

*POW!* is what you texted. Global positioning and fancy Emergency Services equipment can figure out the rest.

The girl thrusts her hands down the pants of first the big guy, then the little one, ignoring the one's tears and the other's threats. She comes over with two wads of cash, rubber-banded rolls of bills as good as any you've ever seen hidden down the pants of a petty street hoodlum playing it big. She hands you one roll and shoves the other up her skirt, and after a grim nod of thanks turns and marches off into the scraggly line of trees behind the fast food dumpster over the rise.

Hearing the whine of sirens, you tuck that wad into the waistband of your microfibre supertights and shoot straight up into the air, a beacon so the cops know exactly where to look before you head home.

Sticking around to fill out paperwork really isn't your job anymore.

## WEDNESDAY

One good thing about Wednesday is, it's karaoke night down at the bar.

You'd think hanging out in a basement dive with a bunch of washed-up single losers would be depressing, but it isn't. Makes you feel maybe it's not all your fault you're looking at middle age like staring down the barrel of a gun, no family, no friends to speak of, no savings, and no prospects. Feels good to peer around the darkened room at other patrons, their skin washed in the same dim green glow as yours from the crappy lighting, and think maybe you don't have it so bad after all.

Your turn comes at the mike and you get up, sing a Billie Holiday song — "Gloomy Sunday" — sing it like her, breathy and lonely and lost. Except you don't sing the final stanza. The music keeps spooling out the "It was all a dream" cop-out verse, words scrolling across that big green screen over the bar, but you only schlump back to your stool, start sucking on your drink, not caring if anybody gives a damn whether you finished the song or not.

Order another drink. And another after that. And then another.

*THURSDAY*

It's unfortunate, but Thursday is a total washout. The day started as one big blinding hangover and got worse from there. You thought a little hair of the dog that bit you might help, so you scrounged around for Bloody Mary fixings. You remember your ex called — the voice of an angel! — and invited you to a barbecue at her place Sunday. Says she has some big news, wants you to be a part of her happiness. She doesn't say what the news is (you know she's been seeing that Random Asshole for about a year now), but she probably didn't really expect you to say you'd come.

But you did, you remember that much. You insisted you wanted more than anything in this world to come to her party on Sunday and congratulate her in person, a goodbye and no-hard-feelings sort of deal. And then you remember stumbling to the corner liquor store and buying another bottle of vodka.

You don't remember anything after that.

*FRIDAY*

Weekends, there's always plenty to do. Large gatherings, too much alcohol, people out swimming and driving and moto-crossing and bungee jumping— every hour there's a dozen fires for you to put out, both figurative and literal. You know you could try to move up in the world, seek out the glory jobs, go where all the action takes place: New York, London, Tokyo; bombings, government coups, giant monsters from space... but this is your home town, man. You grew up here, had your first kiss in that park you can see from the corner of your eye and a hundred feet up. Had your first beer in that same park a year later, your first joint the year after that. Lost your virginity not long after about six blocks away, the backseat of her brother's car, which hadn't run since 1962 though he worked on it every day since he'd dropped out of school and told you not to date his little sister or he'd kick your ass.

You smile, thinking about your childhood, your life before the accident down at the power plant where your dad worked before you and his dad before that. Coal, electricity, nukes: it's all the same to the guys with the blue shirts and the hard hats, whose job is only to shovel, to dig, to press buttons without asking why or how or what.

And then came the accident, you the only survivor, nobody expecting you to live after the levels of exposure you got. What made you the lucky son-of-a-bitch with the weird, mutative DNA? All your buddies died on the line that day, biggest tragedy this town had seen since the Great Mine Collapse of 1897. Some died quick, blown to pieces from the explosion, and some died slow, rotting away from the inside over the next few weeks or months or even year.

Except you. It was like you got the strength of the ten men who died, like it all flowed into you as it drained from them, leaving two bereft girlfriends and one grieving fiancée and seven widows and fifteen half-orphans, all of whom still look at you with accusation written on their faces, if and when they look at you at all. It's not *that* big a city though, so some of them go to quite a bit of trouble not to see you, ever.

Yessir: you are one lucky son-of-a-bitch.

## SATURDAY

Saturday barely deserves separation from Friday. You don't sleep much on weekends; it all rolls together into one long two-day hell of rescuing drowning children at the lake and trussing up would-be muggers in back alleys near the bar district (Emergency Services text *P-O-W-!*) and saving pomeranians and their old ladies from fifth-storey condos on fire. You nap when you can between one emergency and the next, wondering when you'll stop trying to make up for ten deaths you can never undo, that weren't even your fault in the first place.

## SUNDAY

Let yourself sleep in, you poor bastard. That's right. And when you do get up at last, sun slanting harsh and high through the blinds, don't worry about all those empty pizza boxes stacked by the back door, or the unpaid bills stacked on that rickety hall table near the front. Don't worry too much that your savings from the old government gig have truly run out, or that your fancy-fibre suit is starting to go at the seams and you have no way to replace it. Even if you had time for a regular job, which you certainly do *not*, a thing like that suit would be way beyond the finances of an ordinary citizen.

That's you: an ordinary citizen. Dropped out of high school because who were you kidding? You were going to go work at the plant like your dad and your granddad, both heavy chain-smokers and dead from not dissimilar cancers long before your accident. Mom lasted a few years longer, but she was a smoker too. You have a mortgage on a house you don't even like anymore, your back hurts when you wake up each day, and you really should schedule a dental appointment one of these years. You're afraid you're developing one of those prostate problems you've read about, but are too scared to actually see a doctor because what if something really *is* wrong down there? No amount of flying around in the sky or bending steel bars or stopping bullets can make something like *that* go away.

Then it hits you: you promised to go to your ex's barbecue, promised to be happy for her happiness and not punch her new man in the face.

Reaching for your supertights, you realize this might be an occasion better suited to civvies. You fling those things aside (ignore the sparking zap when they hit the far wall— that's probably *not* the nanocircuitry giving up for good, shorting out, leaving a black smoky smudge on the sheetrock) and reach for jeans. One leg at a time, just like everybody else.

It's been forever since you've taken the bus, but you lost your license a couple years back (driving under the influence) and flying is way faster and easier and cheaper anyway. Doesn't feel right to fly around in jeans and a T-shirt, though; what kind of jerkoff does something like that?

So you arrive a little late to a party in full swing (you forgot how long it takes to ride the goddamn bus), hotdogs and hamburgers piled by the grill like a mountain of burnt pulverized flesh (which is exactly what it is; you've been to more than one house fire, so you know what you're talking about). She, as always, is the kind and gracious woman you fell in love with. She murmurs hello and says she's glad you came (though you see in her eyes she wishes you'd decided to give this one a pass), kisses your cheek, and glides off to greet somebody else. Your head spins from her honeysuckle scent and the lingering tingle where her fingers brushed your arm.

Thank goodness your old boss (her father, your ex-father-in-law-to-be) is too busy playing euchre by the pool to notice you're here. You chug the first beer too fast and the second one faster, part of your brain you can never turn off calculating how long it would take to rescue that kid from the pool if he suddenly started drowning, or how many trips it would take to carry everybody to safety if a ring of fire inexplicably erupted around the yard, or how fast you could fly grandma to the hospital if her pacemaker exploded.

The third beer you didn't notice going down. It's after the fourth that you punch the Random Asshole in the face.

Of course between the third and the fourth had come the formal announcement of the forthcoming nuptials, which everybody in attendance pretty much expected. Then the announcement of the baby on the way, which nobody seems surprised by either, other than you. You it hits in the gut like a bullet at close range, except a bullet would've been easier to take, because your body would've worked its magic and pushed that bloody thing back out of your flesh. An hour later you'd have only a bruise where the hole had been, and an hour after that not even a dimple to mark the spot. This, about your ex and her new guy and their baby on the way, will stay with you forever.

Sure, a bitter laugh escaped you — how could it not? — and her father your ex-employer the Commissioner noticed you then, he sure did. And he'd come over, gotten up in your grill, shouting, telling you what a rotten way you'd treated his lovely daughter (as if you didn't already know). And you were taking it! Not objecting or anything (everything he said was true, every goddamn word), but still that idiot new guy comes and asks you to leave. A few more words were said, and some might argue over who threw the first punch, but that's about the time you finished your fourth beer, set the empty carefully on the grass, and socked that Random Asshole in the face.

When you're cursed with superstrength, pulling punches is way harder than reeling them out. You probably hurt the guy slightly more than you'd intended, but nothing to send him to the hospital; she'd never forgive you for that. Just enough to give him the excuse he needed to clock you good (well, as good as an average works-out-at-the-Y kind of guy can). And her dad gets in his couple licks, which is only right. And the guys from down at the bureau who know the family well enough to come to a barbecue, a party at the house of a girl some have known since she was an itty-bitty thing visiting daddy at work— well, they all rush to the rescue. Hell, some are probably friends of guys who died that day at the plant, maybe even distantly related, because it really is that kind of town.

You fight back enough to convince them to pummel the shit out of you as best they can, though the most painful part is the sorrow in her voice as she asks them to stop, begs them to stop, pleads with you and with them, and cries.

They finally wind down. You get up from where you lie curled on the grass. The black-guts smell of charred meat hangs heavy in the air from the unattended grill as you limp away too ashamed to let them see you fly when you're dressed like they are, in jeans and a T-shirt like an ordinary citizen.

Still limping, you walk the long way home to your empty house, ignore the unpaid bills and the pizza boxes, knowing tomorrow you'll wake up and all your bones will ache, every single one.

∞    ☼    ∞

**ALEX C. RENWICK** divides her time between Vancouver, BC, Portland, OR, and Austin, TX. As Camille Alexa, she's the author of *Push of the Sky*.

# CHANGE AS SEEN THROUGH AN ORRERY OF CELESTIAL FIRE

*Michael Matheson*

SHURUI PEELS LONG strips of burnt skin off her shoulders in front of the bathroom mirror. She grits her teeth as they tear away down her back. The days between immolations are always painful; the moments in which she burns down to ash blinding, but nothing compared to the waiting— to the slow build of days before the fire frees. Her body a cage, too-narrow knit with bird-hollow bones.

The rest — the rebirth and what comes after—

—The rest is agony.

Has been since she first rose, broken, garbed in lank, slick flesh. Since she tumbled to Earth in a scatter of pinions, remiges, and retrices; her sun-bright feathers ripped away in the heat of her descent. Since she spotted the first Xifeng bathing in a moonlit lake. And fell.

The whole of it, now and always, Chang'e's fault. A terrible gift she hadn't known better than to accept.

"You all right?" asks Zetian from the doorway. Her lover takes a step into the bathroom to lay a glacial hand on Shurui's burning back. The frost of Zetian's fingers a momentary respite. *Like scorched, shed feathers brushing the surface of a distant, long-ago lake bathed silver.* Zetian's qi strong, but mortal. The ice coating her hand fades in a swift billow of steam. It fills the air between them. Zetian barely draws her hand back in time to avoid burned fingers.

"It's bad this time," she says quietly.

"Too long between burns," grunts Shurui, breathing through her mouth.

It's been a long time since their last trip to Mount Sinai Hospital. Most of those visits not long after they officially got together. After they decided to try living together instead of just falling into Zetian's bed most nights. After Shurui carted her couple of boxes worth of possessions on the TTC up to Zetian's Spadina and Willcocks apartment from her own place in the Market.

Shurui remembers the looks the nurses used to give her. How sure they were that Shurui was abusing Zetian. How sure they were she kept lighting her lover on fire.

Not that they weren't right. They just had the wrong end of it: not on purpose. Never on purpose.

Six years of relearning control after living so long alone later, and those years might as well never have happened if she can't control the furnace raging in her. If she can't quiet her qi.

So many centuries later, and she's still a co-opted version of her own Celestial mythology. A western phoenix burning and beginning again instead of her own radiant fenghuang self.

She knows what happens if she can't quiet it. Knows *exactly* where that leads. She learned the hard way. With the first Xifeng.

"You going to be all right?" asks Zetian— Xifeng Zetian. Always a Xifeng in her life. She's drawn to them like the sun. Always seeking their warmth. She nods. Exhales.

It's that care and that patience that have kept them together. Zetian the only one who doesn't think her condition a burden. Zetian the only one there for her when her body can do nothing but scream for days on end. That sense of unity, of co-operation, served them well in their separate careers working with others, but much better once they struck out together. A life of crime far easier if you have someone to share it with.

Zetian waits until Shurui's breathing quiets before she leaves her to her ablutions. Says "I'm here if you need me," as she leaves the room.

Shurui listens to her lover's footfalls travelling away and around corners as she turns on the tap. She cups her hands under an icy waterfall, and pours the water onto her back. The steam rising from her shoulders makes a sauna of the tiny bathroom.

This form was never meant to house the qi of a fenghuang. She didn't think that far ahead when she descended from the peak of Liushi Shan— when she left behind the Kunlun range and gave up the sky. She can't remember what her plans were then. Beyond Xifeng.

She pours more water across her back. Forces her qi quiet. So she can pass for human.

∞   ☼   ∞

An hour later, Shurui sits in the Starbucks set just back from the southeast corner of Harbord and Spadina, waiting for Xinhua. Outside, amid all the concrete and slate grey, autumn paints the trees gold and the sky in pale drifts of cloud, darker at their edges. Darker still in the distance: rain not far off. The smell of it is in the air. Inside, the café is mostly empty; the decor warm, cast in earthy tones.

Shurui likes the muddy, arboreal feel of the place. It offsets the autumn chill; denies winter in its turn, and welcomes spring with fair familiar hands. This is one of her favorite haunts. It doesn't hurt that it's close to home. Her jacket lies slung over her chair behind her. Soft against her back. It's quiet here; she likes the quiet.

A cup of tea steams between her palms. She bleeds off excess qi by keeping the tea's temperature constant. A trick she picked up from a wuyi, Chen Xifeng, not long after Shurui made her way north to the Colony of Vancouver Island back when the mass migration up from California began, during the second BC gold rush.

She learned a great deal from that Xifeng before the wuyi died: better methods for regulating her qi. How to make herbal medicine. The theory of acupuncture— the proper practice of which has always escaped her. She stopped peddling it shortly before she started working her way east, helping build the Canadian Pacific Railway in the 1880s, disguised as a man.

—Had taken up, instead, the sole practice of making herbal medicines and teas by the time she'd found her way east to then-Muddy York's Ward District, back when Toronto's first Chinatown still lay nestled along York and Elizabeth, bordered by Queen and Dundas. And as the old city's Chinatown moved, as it did frequently, Shurui moved with it.

"Your tea's cold." Shurui startles as Xinhua settles down across from her; she slings her own folded jacket over the back of a chair and sets down her steaming coffee. The waft of it fills the space between them. "I'm sorry, am I late?"

The cup in her hands *has* cooled while her attention was elsewhere: thinking on the city as it was. "Not very much." Shurui sets her tea aside. Smiles at her friend.

Shurui watches her while Xinhua settles in, pays half mind to her friend's talk. This young woman, too, is a fixture in her life. Has been since Xinhua was an undergraduate at U of T in need of a history tutor. And their ties go deeper, though she doesn't have the heart to tell Xinhua the whole of it. Though the full body costume of the Xun Long — the Swift Dragon — conceals her face, it does nothing to hide her voice. Unlike Xinhua, Shurui does not speak when they fight in costume.

It means so much to Xinhua, not being known. And Shurui is so tired of having only enemies; of having only dead lovers in her wake.

It has been easy to stay friends, long though the tutoring has been finished. Shurui will always look to be in her early twenties; something she has made peace with. And Xinhua, like her, is desperately lonely.

Sometimes, too, it's easier to talk with someone who understands so little, instead of Zetian who understands too much.

A sleek sports car and several police cruisers in pursuit hurtle past the window, and Xinhua stops mid-sentence. Both women track the rush of air that follows— the masked woman at its centre that streaks through the air. A visible wake of whirling leaves and air lit with bursts of lightning in her wake.

The rest of the café's patrons crowd toward the windows, trying to get a glimpse of the chase scene. "The Xun Long is out early today," teases Shurui, sipping at her coffee to hide the fear awake in her belly. She knows *exactly* who the flying woman is. Her heart races. Does Zetian know the Leiyu is out of hospital already? Shurui takes out her phone casually. Calls her lover. Tries not to panic as the words "This customer is not available" whisper in her ear.

Across from her, Xinhua, lost in her own thoughts, shakes her head. "No. Costume's similar though. Looked more like the Leiyu. Guess she's out of hospital. And she's changed her look again," grumbles Xinhua into her coffee.

Shurui takes a deep breath. Making mental calculations: three blocks; *less* than three blocks. She could run it. Remembering it's her turn to speak, she asks quietly, her mind elsewhere: "Seems soon for her to have been released." Doesn't add that what Zetian did to her skull should have left her in a coma. That when they brought the building down on top of her, the Leiyu shouldn't have lived.

Does the Leiyu know where they live? Could she?

"You read the interview in the *Star*?" asks Xinhua.

"Yes," lies Shurui. *Interview?* "How awful what happened to her," prods Shurui.

Xinhua nods. "She's lucky there wasn't a concussion. She heals fast, but, after what Nepenthe did to her—"

"Nepenthe?" Not Nepenthe: Adaora in Arizona with Tomiko at the time.

"Yeah," says Xinhua, confused by Shurui's reaction. "The Leiyu says that's why she can't remember what happened. Must have been Nepenthe, because who else could wipe her memory?" Xinhua shakes her head and finishes her coffee.

A gift. *An extraordinary gift.* Unless it's a lie? Is the Leiyu that clever? Vindictive and cold, yes. But she does not lie. Has never lied. As far as Shurui knows.

Shurui rubs at sore eyes. At the heat pounding behind her skull.

"Are you all right?" asks Xinhua.

"Fine," says Shurui. Dons a false smile. Forces herself to remain calm through centuries of long practice. Forces herself to trust that the Leiyu is telling the truth; to keep playing her role a little longer, until she can reasonably excuse herself without giving anything away. Straightens in her chair and says: "Tell me how your mother is doing."

∞    ☼    ∞

"Zetian? I'm home!" Shurui waits for the awful moment where Zetian isn't there. Hoping today is not that day.

"Yes, I can tell," answers Zetian from the kitchen. The sound of bubbling pots and the scent of tofu frying in black bean sauce follow her words, the waft of soy and garlic sesame lung-searing strong. "Dinner's almost ready."

Shurui collapses against the wall of their apartment, limp-boned with relief. She shuts the door behind her and shucks off her outerwear. The Leiyu has not yet come for them. She does not yet know who they are. Or may honestly not know who almost killed her. Zetian is still safe. She slips into the tiny kitchen and leans against the fridge by the doorway so

Zetian can't see her shaking. "You're making dinner before a job? You don't want to order in?"

Zetian raises an eyebrow at her and swishes the wok on the stove. "After what happened last time? How's Xinhua?"

Shurui slips a takeout flyer on the side of the fridge out from under its magnet. "She's okay. Too many hours at work and school. And Lin's still on her back about cutting her hair short again. No, seriously, we could bring food *in*."

Zetian covers the wok and turns down the heat. Sweeps out of her eyes steam-frizzled hairs that have escaped from her ponytail, and gives Shurui her full attention. "What is it?"

"What's what?" Zetian waits, close-lipped, while Shurui fusses with the takeout menu in her hands, burns it to a crisp and lets the ashes fall. "The Leiyu's out of hospital," she whispers.

"She's *alive*?" shouts Zetian.

"She thinks it was Nepenthe. It's fine."

"It is not *fine*." Zetian's hands flex, and the entire kitchen flash freezes as she struggles to regain control of her qi. "Why does she think it's Nepenthe?" she asks when she stops quaking.

"She told the reporters at the hospital she can't remember what happened."

Zetian laughs. Pinches the bridge of her nose where her glasses used to rest before the surgery. "I'm not sure if I should be pleased or upset that I don't get the credit for trying to kill her." She looks at the pot, frozen to the stove, and turns off the element. "You're right. We're eating out."

Shurui crosses the room and folds Zetian into her arms. Breathes in the cool, cassia-bark scent of her lover. "She will not come for us."

"No, the Xun Long will come for us," she mumbles.

"Because the Xun Long *always* comes for us," smiles Shurui, eyes closed, chin resting on Zetian's shoulder. "Xinhua's always been reliable that way."

"I'm not sure how much longer I can keep doing this," Zetian says into Shurui's neck. Shurui can feel the tightness of her lover's jaw against her skin.

"Nothing lasts forever," says Shurui. Brushes her lover's stray hair off her face, and kisses her forehead.

For a time, they are the only two people in the world.

∞   ☼   ∞

Shurui hates the quiet before a heist. The waiting. With Zetian on edge, waiting farther down the Spadina strip, there is only the commotion of Chinatown and the rumble of streetcars to district her.

It is not enough.

This place is too familiar to her. She's lived along the Spadina strip, or near it, since Chinatown migrated here in the 1950s — into what used to be a Jewish quarter of the city. So that this incarnation of the city's largest Chinatown (one of six) borders Kensington Market as Koreatown does to the northwest. This, the Chinatown she still thinks of as home even though she's moved north along Spadina to be with Zetian. This, the Chinatown people talk of when they speak of Toronto's Chinatown, despite the others spread across Toronto's amalgamated sprawl. The *Greater Toronto Area* she reminds herself. Those words still awkward on her tongue the better part of two decades later.

What is a decade to her, but a moment? She who has lived long enough in this too-small body that she sometimes struggles to remember which century she occupies.

A small child in a dress, thick leggings, and a miniature jacket, stops to smile up at her, and pulls her back to the present. The tiny mittens on the sleeves of the girl's coat flap in the autumn wind like wings. Shurui smiles back involuntarily as the girl's mother calls her. The little one waves and is gone, vanished back into the crush.

Shurui watches her disappear among the clutches of residents and late night interlopers wandering the streets looking for a meal or heading deeper into the city's downtown core. The street vendors have hauled their wares in for the night, but Chinatown's restaurants are still open. The smell of them strung down the strip is thick and heady. She and Zetian stopped at Mother's Dumplings before they settled in to wait, but her body burns through fuel at an absurd pace, and she's already hungry again. Her stomach rumbles, and she ignores it to watch the street and the crowds.

Still too many people. She doesn't like working with this large an audience. Once she starts burning she won't be recognizable — the coming agony not something she looks forward to, but necessary. It's Zetian she worries about. In costume as the Hei Jiang her lover's features are covered, but it's now, while Zetian's still in street clothes and mingling, that she might be a memorable face.

Then she catches sight of the Xun Long running along a rooftop across the street— shadowing the armored car they've been waiting for. Her focus narrows in, until it is only her and Zetian and the G4S truck. Waits until the truck stops on its scheduled run at the RBC, National, and Scotiabank trifecta at the intersection of Spadina and Dundas— until the guard and the hopper leave the truck to start their ATM refill runs.

Shurui wades into the crowd, shouting *"Huŏ a!" — Fire —* to clear the street; gets only minimal reaction. Cars swerve around her and horns blare as she steps into traffic. Fire boils off her skin and catches on her flesh as she sets herself alight. As she assumes her role as the Fenghuang. She ignores the pain as the fire eats at her; as she has done for centuries. Lets the flames fan and furl in her hands, and lobs a fireball almost as tall as she is at the armored car.

It rips the vehicle into the air, crumpling its side. And now the crowd runs as the car crashes back down to asphalt. Smoke streams everywhere, onlookers screaming as they scatter. Shurui cannot hear them— the roar of the fire in her ears. Her focus narrows further down to the Xun Long as Xinhua leaps from wall to lamppost to street. Shurui flares hotter, a pillar of fire, aware that she only needs to buy time for Zetian to freeze the security team, grab the money, and run. Sirens doppler in the distance as the Xun Long shouts something at her she can't hear.

Shurui stands her ground as the Xun Long rushes her. Xinhua's own qi crashing on the air like a wave ahead of her. And then there is only the commotion of combat, and restraint as she tries not to burn Xinhua.

All she has to do is hold. Until this body burns down to ash. And wait to resurrect. Zetian her anchor.

Always the Xifeng is her anchor.

Everything becomes this moment.

∞   ☼   ∞

Somewhere in the darkness between bodies, there is a memory of bright wings. Of open sky. Of mountain ranges with a dawn so bright no mortal eye can behold it.

And there, too, is Chang'e, bound to the moon, ever waiting to descend. She speaks words Shurui cannot hear. Words meant only for her. Each time she is closer to hearing.

And then she is being pulled back down to her body.

∞   ☼   ∞

Shurui struggles to keep her qi from overflowing the new self it's building to house her. Tendons burgeon and snap taut around hollow bones, light as air. The pain sends her floating up off the ground. Until the meat of organ and muscle tissue bubbles up out of her bones, coats them in bloody gristle, and her new weight drags her down to the hardwood floor. Presses her down into the grain.

She bites clean through her new-formed lower lip as fresh skin knits itself over raw nerve endings in fits and starts. Her lungs still too new, too weak, to scream with.

Zetian is there beside her. Cool hands steady on her half-finished back, keeping her from setting this new body on fire before it's done forming. Zetian sweats from the heat her lover throws off.

When she is done being born, Shurui gulps down air— peels her bloodied nails back from the long furrows they have made in the floorboards. Her breath forms steaming puddles on the wood. Beside her, Zetian sits down and splays her legs to massage cramped thigh muscles.

In the quiet that follows, broken only by the settling and creaking of their ancient apartment, Shurui wishes things were different. Hates herself for thinking it— for Zetian not being enough to tie her to this place. But still, always, wishes she'd never left Liushi Shan. Wishes Chang'e had never shown her that first, beautiful, unattainable Xifeng.

—That she weren't going to lose Zetian and the rest of the life she has built here. Because she always loses her Xifeng.

When her muscles are strong enough she rolls over on her back, rests one arm on her stomach. Her new chest rises and falls. Sweat plasters her naked skin. Each body identical to the last. She wonders if she'll ever be allowed to truly die.

Zetian brushes soaked, matted strands of hair from Shurui's face. Shurui's mobile rings, and Zetian strokes Shurui's shoulder and levers herself off the floor to go answer it. Shurui hears her "Hello?" as through water; tracks the slap of Zetian's bare feet back across the floorboards. Opens her eyes to find Zetian, hanging upside-down in her vision, leaning down above her. "It's Xinhua."

Shurui nods slowly. The mobile is heavy in her hand as she takes it. She croaks to clear her throat. "Is everything all right?

You don't usually call this early." Her voice is a whisper as her new vocal cords acclimate to speech.

Xinhua's voice is softer still than her own. "I'm sorry. I just really need to talk. I can't talk to Lin right now. I mean, eventually, but, she's not—" Xinhua's voice catches. Her inhale shaky. "I shouldn't have called."

"No, it's all right." Zetian helps Shurui up to a sitting position. And she leans on Zetian's proffered shoulder. "What's wrong?"

Xinhua pauses so long Shurui wonders if she's hung up. "I can't... deal with carrying this secret anymore. Can I just talk to you— do you have time?" And there it is. One more burden to bear. Or is this the one Xinhua has already told her? Will this be the day Xinhua tells her of the mantle she carries— a secret shared that can only divide them if spoken aloud. Or will this be the day Xinhua finally means to tell her mother, Lin, that Xinhua cares for women? Shurui cannot imagine what Lin will make of that knowledge; knowing that her daughter will be the last of the Xun Long. She remembers well the days when Lin's own voice issued from behind the blank mask of the Xun Long's costume. The Fenghuang and the Xun Long have been at odds a long time. But she does not know Lin well enough to know if she can make peace with that legacy's end.

Whereas Shurui already knows all too well that everything ends.

How long will it be before *this* Xifeng at her side, too, is consumed by her fire. Before she has to leave behind Xinhua, and the rest of the life she has built here. How long before the next Xifeng? And the next. And the next...

For now, there is only this moment. This time. *This* Xifeng. It is enough.

Shurui lays her head on Zetian's shoulder. Closes her eyes. And lies. To herself. To Zetian. To Xinhua: "Always."

∞　✿　∞

**MICHAEL MATHESON** is a writer, editor, book reviewer, and anthologist from Toronto.

# AFTERWORD:
# THE DEATH OF THE DEATH
# OF THE SUPERHEROES!

*Mark Shainblum*

**I HAVE BEEN** writing, editing, and publishing superhero stories on and off for over thirty years now: doing this in 2015 is profoundly different from doing it in 1985.

In the late 1970s and early 1980s, it had become fashionable among intellectual comics fans to prophesy the imminent demise of superhero comics. The genre was embarrassing for its silly underwear-on-the-outside conventions, scary because of its dark vigilante (maybe even *fascist*?) heart, and artistically stultifying due its big-fish-in-a-little-pond dominance of the comics medium. Popular only among a dwindling minority of hardcore fans, superheroes were bound to disappear, and we shouldn't even mourn them, because their death would finally allow the comics art form to flourish.

Yet here we are, in the 21st century, and the superhero genre has done anything *but* "go away." It has, in fact moved from the outer spiral-arm fringes of the pop-culture galaxy to the all-devouring black hole at its core.

In previous generations, superheroes had occasionally erupted out of comics and into the mass-consciousness, only to fade away again as the two or three years of the fad ran its course. But that's changed, there no longer seems to be a boom-and-bust cycle. Rather than liberating the comics medium by conveniently dying, the superhero instead *escaped* its single-medium ghetto and became a permanent, mass-culture icon as ubiquitous as the knight, the fairy-tale princess, the cowboy, the secret agent, and the cop. In transcending comics, superheroes also managed to step aside just enough for the whole art form to flourish. But that's another story.

Why is this happening? Superhero fables tap into cross-cultural archetypes and suit a globalized entertainment marketplace particularly well. And our movie-making technology is finally equal to the task of capturing the epic scale and scope of superhero sagas. But it's obviously more than that.

By the standards of 1985 we've all *become* superheroes. We have instant access to almost all of the world's knowledge and virtually limitless, externalized memory. We all now have, thanks to personal technology, something like telescopic vision and super-hearing and are constantly in contact with one another at levels only slightly short of telepathy. There are people alive right now who can control computers with their thoughts or who have silicon chips wired directly into their nervous systems. And we're just at the infancy, at the blastocyst stage, of this process. We haven't even really *begun*.

Superheroes may have a dark vigilante heart that can never fully be trusted, but that's only one side of that infamous double-headed coin. As our own, very real superpowers increase exponentially with every passing day, how can we be surprised that we're becoming more and more fascinated by superhero stories and what we can glean from them?

I'm not.

—Mark Shainblum
Ottawa, Ontario
April 2015

∞   ☼   ∞

**MARK SHAINBLUM** is the co-creator of *Northguard* and *Angloman*. He received an Aurora Award for co-editing *Arrowdreams: An Anthology of Alternate Canadas*.

**Our titles are available at major book stores
and local independent resellers who support
Science Fiction and Fantasy readers like you.**

EDGE Science Fiction
and Fantasy Publishing

www.edgewebsite.com

**Our titles are available at major book stores and local independent resellers who support Science Fiction and Fantasy readers like you.**

*Eclipse* by K. A. Bedford (tp) - ISBN: 978-1-894063-30-2
*Elements* by Suzanne Church (tp) - ISBN: 978-1-77053-042-3
*Europa Journal* by Jack Castle (tp) - ISBN: 978-1-77053-104-8
*Even The Stones* by Marie Jakober (tp) - ISBN: 978-1-894063-18-0
*Evolve: Vampire Stories of the New Undead* edited by Nancy Kilpatrick (tp)
 - ISBN: 978-1-894063-33-3
*Evolve Two: Vampire Stories of the Future Undead* edited by Nancy Kilpatrick (tp)
 -ISBN: 978-1-894063-62-3
*Expiration Date* edited by Nancy Kilpatrick (tp) - ISBN: 978-1-77053-062-1

*Fires of the Kindred* by Robin Skelton (tp) - ISBN: 978-0-88878-271-7
*Forbidden Cargo* by Rebecca Rowe (tp) - ISBN: 978-1-894063-16-6

*Game of Perfection, A* (Part 2 of Tyranaël) by Élisabeth Vonarburg (tp) - ISBN:
 978-1-894063-32-6
*Gaslight Arcanum: Uncanny Tales of Sherlock Holmes* edited by Jeff Campbell &
 Charles Prepolec (tp) - ISBN: 978-1-8964063-60-9
*Gaslight Grimoire: Fantastic Tales of Sherlock Holmes* edited by Jeff Campbell &
 Charles Prepolec (tp) - ISBN: 978-1-8964063-17-3
*Gaslight Grotesque: Nightmare Tales of Sherlock Holmes* edited by Jeff Campbell
 & Charles Prepolec (tp) - ISBN: 978-1-8964063-31-9
*Green Music* by Ursula Pflug (tp) - ISBN: 978-1-895836-75-2
 *Green Music* by Ursula Pflug (hb) - ISBN: 978-1-895836-77-6

*Healer, The* (Children of the Panther Part One) by Amber Hayward (tp)
 - ISBN: 978-1-895836-89-9
 *Healer, The* (Children of the Panther Part One) by Amber Hayward (hb)
 - ISBN: 978-1-895836-91-2
*Hell Can Wait* by Theodore Judson (tp) - ISBN: 978-1-978-1-894063-23-4
*Hounds of Ash and other tales of Fool Wolf, The* by Greg Keyes (tp)
 - ISBN: 978-1-894063-09-8
*Hydrogen Steel* by K. A. Bedford (tp) - ISBN: 978-1-894063-20-3

*i-ROBOT Poetry by Jason Christie* (tp) - ISBN: 978-1-894063-24-1
*Immortal Quest* by Alexandra MacKenzie (tp) - ISBN: 978-1-894063-46-3

*Jackal Bird* by Michael Barley (pb) - ISBN: 978-1-895836-07-3
 *Jackal Bird* by Michael Barley (hb) - ISBN: 978-1-895836-11-0
*JEMMA7729* by Phoebe Wray (tp) - ISBN: 978-1-894063-40-1

*Keaen* by Till Noever (tp) - ISBN: 978-1-894063-08-1
*Keeper's Child* by Leslie Davis (tp) - ISBN: 978-1-894063-01-2

*Land/Space* edited by Candas Jane Dorsey and Judy McCrosky (tp)
 - ISBN: 978-1-895836-90-5
 *Land/Space* edited by Candas Jane Dorsey and Judy McCrosky (hb)
 - ISBN: 978-1-895836-92-9
*Lyskarion: The Song of the Wind* (Part One of The Chronicles of the Karionin) by
 J.A. Cullum (tp) - ISBN: 978-1-894063-02-9

*Machine Sex and other stories* by Candas Jane Dorsey (tp)
 - ISBN: 978-0-88878-278-6
*Maërlande Chronicles, The* by Élisabeth Vonarburg (pb) - ISBN: 978-0-88878-294-6

*Tesseracts* 2 edited by Phyllis Gotlieb & Douglas Barbour (pb)
- ISBN: 978-0-88878-270-0
*Tesseracts* 3 edited by Candas Jane Dorsey & Gerry Truscott (pb)
- ISBN: 978-0-88878-290-8
*Tesseracts* 4 edited by Lorna Toolis & Michael Skeet (pb)
- ISBN: 978-0-88878-322-6
*Tesseracts* 5 edited by Robert Runté & Yves Maynard (pb)
- ISBN: 978-1-895836-25-7
*Tesseracts* 5 edited by Robert Runté & Yves Maynard (hb)
- ISBN: 978-1-895836-26-4
*Tesseracts* 6 edited by Robert J. Sawyer & Carolyn Clink (pb)
- ISBN: 978-1-895836-32-5
*Tesseracts* 6 edited by Robert J. Sawyer & Carolyn Clink (hb)
- ISBN: 978-1-895836-33-2
*Tesseracts* 7 edited by Paula Johanson & Jean-Louis Trudel (tp)
- ISBN: 978-1-895836-58-5
*Tesseracts* 7 edited by Paula Johanson & Jean-Louis Trudel (hb)
- ISBN: 978-1-895836-59-2
*Tesseracts* 8 edited by John Clute & Candas Jane Dorsey (tp)
- ISBN: 978-1-895836-61-5
*Tesseracts* 8 edited by John Clute & Candas Jane Dorsey (hb)
- ISBN: 978-1-895836-62-2
*Tesseracts Nine* edited by Nalo Hopkinson and Geoff Ryman (tp)
- ISBN: 978-1-894063-26-5
*Tesseracts Ten: A Celebration of New Canadian Specuative Fiction*
edited by R.C. Wilson and E. van Belkom (tp)
- ISBN: 978-1-894063-36-4
*Tesseracts Eleven: Amazing Canadian Speulative Fiction*
edited by Cory Doctorow and Holly Phillips (tp)
- ISBN: 978-1-894063-03-6
*Tesseracts Twelve: New Novellas of Canadian Fantastic Fiction*
edited by Claude Lalumière (tp)
- ISBN: 978-1-894063-15-9
*Tesseracts Thirteen: Chilling Tales from the Great White North*
edited by Nancy Kilpatrick and David Morrell (tp)
- ISBN: 978-1-894063-25-8
*Tesseracts 14: Strange Canadian Stories*
edited by John Robert Colombo and Brett Alexander Savory (tp)
- ISBN: 978-1-894063-37-1
*Tesseracts Fifteen: A Case of Quite Curious Tales*
edited by Julie Czerneda and Susan MacGregor (tp)
- ISBN: 978-1-894063-58-6
*Tesseracts Sixteen: Parnassus Unbound* edited by Mark Leslie (tp)
- ISBN: 978-1-894063-92-0
*Tesseracts Seventeen: Speculating Canada from Coast to Coast to Coast*
edited by C. Anderson and S. Vernon (tp)
-ISBN: 978-1-77053-044-7
*Tesseracts Eighteen: Wrestling With Gods*
edited by Liana Kerzner and Jerome Stueart (tp)
- ISBN: 978-1-77053-068-3
*Tesseracts Nineteen: Superhero Universe*
edited by edited by Claude Lalumière & Mark Shainblum (tp)
- ISBN: 978-1-770530-87-4

*Tesseracts Q* edited by Élisabeth Vonarburg and Jane Brierley (pb)
  - ISBN: 978-1-895836-21-9
  *Tesseracts Q* edited by Élisabeth Vonarburg and Jane Brierley (hb)
  - ISBN: 978-1-895836-22-6
*Those Who Fight Monsters: Tales of Occult Detectives*
  edited by Justin Gustainis (pb) - ISBN: 978-1-894063-48-7
*Time Machines Repaired Whie-U-Wait* by K. A. Bedford (tp)
  - ISBN: 978-1-894063-42-5
*Triforium, The (The Haunting of Westminster Abbey)* by Mark Patton (ebk)
  - e-ISBN: 978-1-77053-097-3
*Trillionist, The* by Sagan Jeffries (tp) - ISBN: 978-1-894063-98-2

*Urban Green Man* edited by Adria Laycraft and Janice Blaine (tp)
  - ISBN: 978-1-77053-038-6

*Vampyric Variations* by Nancy Kilpatrick (tp) - ISBN: 978-1-894063-94-4
*Vyrkarion: The Talisman of Anor* (Part Three of The Chronicles of the Karionin)
  by J. A. Cullum (tp) - ISBN: 978-1-77053-028-7

*Warriors* by Barbara Galler-Smith and Josh Langston (tp)
  - ISBN: 978-1-77053-030-0
*Wildcatter* by Dave Duncan (tp) - ISBN: 978-1-894063-90-6